The Sha
of Friends

CW00545277

VINOD SABHARWAL

BlueRose
Publishers

First Published in December 2020

ISBN: 978-93-5427-285-1

BLUEROSE PUBLISHERS
www.bluerosepublishers.com
info@bluerosepublishers.com
+91 8882 898 898

Cover Design:
Mohd. Arif

Typographic Design:
Namrata Saini

Distributed by: BlueRose, Amazon, Flipkart, Shopclues

IN MEMORY OF
MUM AND DAD

ACKNOWLEDGEMENTS:

I am deeply indebted to all those who have read and advised me on the content of this novel.

The novel would however not have been completed without the inspiration from my wife, Usha and our lovely daughters, Sonya and Mala – my gratitude to them is past telling.

Special thanks to Claire Hunter and Shankara Hettiarachchige for pointing out some of my deliberate mistakes.

Finally, sincere thanks to the staff of Bluerose Publishers for their assistance and patience, without whom this novel would not have seen the light of day.

> *"And can it be that in a world*
> *so full and busy,*
> *the loss of one creature*
> *makes a void*
> *so wide and deep that nothing*
> *but the width and depth of eternity*
> *can fill it up!"*

Charles Dickens

PROLOGUE

2005

It is strange and unfortunate that even the most cataclysmic, life-shattering events, which can change the course of lives, befall us without the faintest of warnings. Whereas, even trivial matters and ailments show advanced signs and symptoms, certain events, albeit unwelcome, happen without any of our senses detecting them. There are no alarm bells, no counselling, no impending pain, no gut-feeling, no foreboding. They just happen! Yet life goes on... just as night follows day and just as the sun is sure to rise in the east. Neither Roger nor Ruth had any inkling or premonition of the turmoil awaiting them that Saturday morning.

Roger Bellan worked as a Credit Controller with a small company that specialised in manufacturing door hinges. It was a job with little prospects and no challenges. He had taken the job some months ago after being made redundant from a bank in Rickmansworth, where he had been a Senior Manager for over fourteen years.

As he gazed briefly out of the third-floor window at the fire-fighters playing volleyball in the compound of the fire station next door, he reflected on the telephone call from Peter Wilton, the Group Finance Director. He had waited for this with trepidation - the call which would either announce his redundancy or a promotion.

Peter's voice was gruff and seemed a bit choked. "Roger, can you pop into my office, please?"

His tone was enough to indicate that the news was going to be far from good.

With a shrug and a sigh, he forced himself to deflect from the past. Ruth was always telling him not to harp on what could have been. "Roger, look on the bright side. You have a loving family, a bright daughter, a nice house, and an expensive car; what more can you ask for?"

The redundancy package had been handsome; better than what Roger had anticipated. He was lucky to get a job so quickly; most of his colleagues were still posting CVs when he received confirmation of his current post. It was not ideal, but it was a job. "Take it and keep looking. Something better will turn up soon," Ruth had said.

His eyes rested on a small, framed photograph on his desk. It was a present to him on Father's day. His lips curled slightly, displaying a flicker of a smile as he gazed at Alison's picture taken on her seventeenth birthday only a few months ago. The picture was slightly off focus but her pretty, warm face was eye-catching. What he loved most about her was her readiness to smile and laugh at all times. She was planning to sit her A-Level exams next summer. Already, she was looking forward to studying Business Studies at Manchester University. He knew he was a fortunate man to have a daughter like her and a wife like Ruth.

That evening he had a small beer with Ranjit, who worked in finance and was always keen to discuss sports, especially cricket, something very close to Roger's heart. He had been a good athlete in his school days and later had concentrated on cricket. He still played most Saturdays in summer for a club in Rickmansworth.

As he drove home, he was glad that it was Friday, with two days away from the hassle of work. He wondered low long he would stay with his current job.

Roger parked in the double garage of this four bedrooms' detached house and as he walked towards the front door, Ruth opened the door. "Hi," she said warmly. "Fancy a meal at the Peking Duck?"

"Why?" Roger enquired, coming up to the door.

"Be...cause, I haven't cooked anything. Alison's gone to Sammy's eighteenth and is likely to be late. I fancy Chinese."

"Give me a few minutes; I'll change into casual wear."

"Please wear the blue checked shirt that Alison got you for your birthday. She keeps complaining that you never wear it."

"Okay," he shouted, halfway up the stairs.

Food, especially the starters at *Peking Duck* was always good. Just as Roger was settling the bill, he enquired, "How's Alison coming back?"

"Oh, someone or the other will give her a lift," she replied, placing a comforting hand on his.

He smiled, admiring her lovely, chocolate-brown innocent eyes, perfectly complimenting the wavy brunette hair, falling just short of shoulder length. *Lucky man*, he thought.

As they drove back, he enquired about a good friend of Ruth, "How's Anne doing?"

"So-so...she's probably got another four to five months. The cancer has spread to her bladder now. You know how she is, puts a brave face, but underneath it all, she is in constant pain. She is more worried about how this is all going to affect the children."

They stopped at some traffic lights, both wondering in silence how cruel life could be, especially when tragedies hit the nicest people. Roger drummed his fingers on the steering wheel and after a moment muttered half to himself and half to her, "I hope the children are as brave as her."

"I'll pay her a visit tomorrow," she said quietly. "I wish the hospital was nearer. Charing Cross is so difficult to get to. Why don't you ask Bill over for a drink or coffee sometime?"

He glanced sideways. "Sure, I'll ring him tomorrow," he mumbled.

Saturday morning was clear and sunny with a strong breeze. Roger walked to the parade of shops about four hundred yards away and bought a local paper and *The Guardian*. He walked briskly back, taking long strides and breathing in the early morning fresh air. It was cold and he pulled the collar of his jacket close to his neck. As he approached his drive, Ruth came hurriedly towards him, almost running. "Roger, Alison's not in her room! Seems like she's not been back from the party."

"What! Are you sure? Have you rung Sammy?" He was puzzled. This was most unusual. Alison always rang when plans changed or if she was going to be late.His puzzlement turned to concern and finally into anxiety. They searched the house but got no clues of her recent movements.

Sammy's party had concluded at about 1 A.M, after which, according to Jane, a friend of Alison, they had taken a taxi together. The driver had dropped Jane first, a mile or so from Alison's house. That was at about 1:20. Not wanting to be alone with the driver, Alison had decided to walk. She should have been home ages ago!

Roger had never seen so much worry in Ruth's eyes. A hollow pain began to gnaw in his stomach and with growing trepidation, unease tightened around his throat.

PART 1

CHAPTER 1

1953

A nurse leaned towards the woman and gently shook her by the shoulders. "Congratulations, it's a boy."

She turned her face, slowly, to study the nurse. "I know," she mumbled, half asleep, tired. "Can you please check if he has holes in both earlobes?"

"Pardon?"

"You heard, please check." With that, the woman closed her eyes and breathed out heavily.

The nurse seemed puzzled; the only explanation must be the state of the mother and the long night.

"But..." the voice trailed.

"Please check," repeated the woman, turning her face away.

The nurse bent over to check the new arrival. Gently she turned the baby's face with her forefinger. Narrowing her eyes, she zoomed in at the ear-lobe. *Yes, there was a distinct hole in the middle of the ear-lobe.* Even more gently, she turned the baby's face in the other direction. She bent down further and held his ear-lobe between her thumb and her fore finger. The baby made no sound. She cried in amazement, "My God! He *has* holes in both ears!"

The hospital staff within earshot gathered around the baby. The nurse who had checked the little holes in both ear-lobes shook her head in amazement and turning to the woman quizzed her, "But how did you know?"

Years earlier, even before the woman had married, her father had studied her horoscope and declared that she would have a son and two daughters. He solemnly stated that the son would have holes in both ear-lobes. "Name him

Sita Raam," he had told her repeatedly. "His name shall be Sita Raam and you must not call him by any other name; to do so would bring him bad luck."

My father, a qualified accountant had no time for palmistry and astrology. He had not studied for five long years to be led into calling his son Sita Raam, a name that would have been perfectly acceptable a few generations ago, but not in this day and age. And who was his father-in-law to tell him what to call his son?

Most relatives pleaded with him, but my father would have none of it. He felt it was an intrusion into his family and future. The more they pleaded and tried to manipulate him, the more stubborn and determined he got.

My mother explained the situation to him which had started well before her marriage and begged him to listen to the advice of the elders. "After all," she would say, "It is customary for the baby to be named by the maternal side of the family. And Sita Raam is such a good Hindu name."

"No," my father would retort, "Only if it's a girl."

My mother sulked to the extent of not speaking to him for days.

Relatives quarrelled among themselves and years of friendships were strained. An uncle of my mother came up with what he thought was the best possible compromise. He rushed into my parent's house, closely followed by two of his daughters one late evening, almost two months after the birth, exclaiming, "I have the answer. Listen to me; we can work this together to everyone's satisfaction."

"What?" my father retorted.

My mother's uncle, a small balding man with a grey moustache that almost covered his mouth, smiled and gently made himself comfortable in a chair normally reserved for my father. Taking his time, he kicked his slippers off without bending down and then proceeded to sit cross-legged in the chair, hands resting on his lap. He realised it was time to take the centre stage. Good ideas should not be hurried.

"What?" My father asked again.

The small man appeared to rise in stature. He looked around the room from one side to the other, silently seeking attention.

"Uncleji," my mother begged, "what have you to tell us?"

"Listen, child," he replied, pointing at her, "how about *you* calling the boy Sita Raam and everyone else calling him whatever your husband decides to do so." Both his daughters nodded in unison, smiling and wobbling their heads as if to indicate that the matter should be resolved immediately, there and then.

There was silence for a while. My mother started nodding, slowly at first, then empathically. It seemed that peace could now be restored to all households.

My mother, her uncle, and his two daughters seemed to take delight at the simple solution that had so far eluded all others. They all looked at my father to seal the brilliant solution.

My father stood up and took a step towards the small, balding man. "Are you out of your mind?" he shouted. "How can you suggest that my child should have *two* names, one to be answered to me and the other to be answered to my wife? What name shall be on the passport, his school books, or his medical records? This is preposterous!"

There was a long, awkward silence.

"So what do you suggest?" asked the balding man, losing patience. "What name do *you* have for the boy?"

"I don't know, yet, but I'll think of something," retorted my father.

Many months passed, my father forbade my mother to call me Sita Raam. She obediently did as requested until a solution could be found.

Then one day after analysing what my grandfather had requested, for what seemed like the millionth time, she had the answer. He had said:

"... you must not call him by any other name, otherwise that would bring him bad luck."

That is it, she thought. If I can not name him Sita Raam, I will not call him by any other name. I will not call him by any name!

She thought about this for a few days before approaching her stubborn husband, anticipating objections and rehearsing answers.

He listened without interrupting. Finally, he stood up and leaving the room shouted over his shoulder, "I need to think this over." He did not seem entirely happy, in part, cross that he had not come up with a solution.

Three days later, one evening, he held my mother's hand after the evening meal. He looked into her eyes and studied her face, thinking how troubled she must have been all these months.

They were both silent, words failed but touch compensated. He nodded the slightest of nods and smiled the faintest of smiles. She sobbed happily, uncontrollably.

A month short of my first birthday, I was given a name.

CHAPTER 2

PRESENT TIME

There are so many whys and ifs. Countless thoughts flood my mind and I am unable to piece them rationally. The throbbing in my temples grows fervently, reaching explosion point. Perhaps I was in the wrong place at the wrong time. Perhaps it was the hand of fate, *kismet*, as Paro Aunty always referred to it as. All written in the stars! If so, I was destined to end up in this mess and even if I had done things differently, the end would have been the same; divergent paths would still have led me here.

I constantly wonder, if, had I been called Sita Raam, would I still have ended up in prison?

Paro Aunty is now my only regular visitor. It is strange that for years, I had regularly visited *her* at week-ends, and now she visits me every Saturday. I have said to her on numerous occasions, but to no avail that if she is busy, she can skip a visit. I don't want her to feel that it's a compulsion. "What compulsion? I look forward to these visits. What else have I got to do with my life? You and Liz are the only ones I regularly see and talk to. Don't even think of keeping me away."

I know she is right, but I feel that I should make it clear that if she is ever in a position that she can't come, she needn't.

"Liz came last month," I informed her when she last came. She brought photographs of Florence and Rimini. They are as beautiful as Liz used to be years ago."

"Did she tell you that Florence won the Inter-schools Piano Competition?" Paro Aunty asked, wiping her glasses.

"No, I'd love to hear her; music is so soothing."

"I'll bring some more photographs of them next week." She balanced her glasses on the bridge of her nose and immediately took them off, wiping them again. We both plunged into silence while she continued looking down, holding her glasses in her hand, fidgeting with the nose-clip. Her shoulders were hunched forward and the upper back arched outwards almost in a semi-circle. The hair which had been dark and shiny when I had first met her, was now grey and limp, with specks of silver, tied hurriedly in a pony-tail with some strands sticking out carelessly. Suddenly, without looking up, she spoke hoarsely but softly. "I'm selling the house."

I knew something was bothering her. "Why?"

She continued looking down and fidgeting with the glasses and then spoke in a small tender voice, "Too big."

"What, the glasses?" I teased.

She looked up, bearing a tired smile, her eyes twitching nervously. "When Paul...and even when you were around, I never thought about it, in fact, I remember saying to Paul that we should extend it, but—"

I finished the sentence for her. "But you think that now it's too big for just you."

She stared at me for a long time, searching for the right words. "Why do I need a three-bedroom semi for? It is big and empty, and so quiet. Do you know something? A quiet house is so distracting; it's difficult to concentrate. People yearn for peace, but I've now realised that in my own house I don't feel peaceful."

"So, what are you going to do?" I enquired out of concern.

"O-ho," she replied with mild irritation, "move to an apartment, perhaps two bedrooms, with concierge and amenities."

I raised my eyebrows, chuckling wryly, "Where?"

She looked directly at me and spoke slowly, "I was thinking of moving nearby, perhaps Bicester—"

"No!" I said sharply. I knew why she wanted to move near me so that she could visit me more often.

She gave me a searching, hurt look, "Why not?"

"You have friends there - Liz, the girls, the Sethis, the Mehtas. Please don't leave them just for me."

She looked down again, this time blinking to suppress tears. I placed a hand on hers.

She smiled through the tears. "We'll see."

"No! Auntyji, please promise me, you won't move from Denham, promise me, please? Promise me."

She looked up, startled. "Why? What's the matter?"

It was my turn to look down. "Nothing," I whispered.

She looked at me pensively and took my hand in hers. "Look at you, your —"

I sighed heavily. "Don't start Auntyji...."

"Your eyes are sinking, your shoulders are drooping. And your weight... you need to see a doctor."

I withdrew my hand. I wanted to tell her my planned and now imminent intention. I wanted to apologise for the future, for what she would think of me, my madness, and my guilt. Fleetingly, I wondered how she would remember me. Instead, not wanting to worry her, I replied simply, "There is a strong possibility that I... that I won't be here for long—"

She jumped in her chair. "What! Where are you going?"

I shrugged my shoulders and replied in a hushed tone, "I don't know."

"Don't know! What do you mean? I know you. You are hiding something from me, what is it? Look at me, what's happened?"

I bit my lip, feeling trapped. "I might be moved somewhere else to a different prison," I lied.

CHAPTER 3

I was admitted to City School, a popular school in Ngara, close to Nairobi town centre and to be closer to the school we moved to a relatively spacious house a mile or so away.

From my bedroom window through the wrought iron bars, I would watch children from the neighborhood play cricket in the evenings before dusk and at weekends. Never having played the sport, I did not particularly feel inclined to join them.

My routine changed one day when I returned from an errand for my mother. As I approached home, a ball flew through the air towards me. Yogurt in one hand, I caught the speeding ball before it hit the ground. It was more by luck and defensive fright than skill but it impressed the players.

"Do you play cricket?" asked the bowler. I recognised him as Sanjay. From my room window, I had often seen the players play and called by their names. Sanjay seemed to be the respected gang-leader, an excellent bowler. He was taller than most and on closer inspection, I found myself gazing into his mischievous hazel eyes.

"No," I replied timidly.

"Come, we'll teach you," someone from a different direction suggested.

Friendships developed quickly, especially with Sanjay and Munir. In the early days, Munir and I would visit each other's homes regularly. The indentations in my ears, though fainter than at birth became a constant topic of conversation. *Did your mother get them done for you? Why don't you wear ear-rings?*

"God made me like this," I would say. But no one believed me.

Munir was about my age and height with sharp black eyes under bushy eyebrows and although in a different class,

9

went to the same school. He was not studious but loved sports- cricket, hockey, and kite flying. He lived two houses away, a small place with his parents, three brothers, and a sister. It always amused me how all the male members in his family were named with the letter 'M'. His father was Maqbool Ahmed Khan, and his brothers were called Masood, Miandad, and Mirza. His only sister had been referred to in conversations as Azra. The family was always hospitable to me – more than mine was to him and I sometimes felt uneasy with that. Whenever I visited Munir at his place, his mother would insist on me having a glass of full cream milk, and some of her delicious homemade snacks. She was a tall, fair lady with copper coloured hair and eyes with a tinge of green. "Have some more," she would insist. "How else will you play cricket with a hardball?"

Maqbool Uncle, as we called him was a tall, broad man, with a colonel style moustache, the tips of which he had a habit of twirling upwards. "*Beta*," he would always say in his deep, guttural voice, "eat well, drink well, and one day I shall have to look up to talk to you."

"Uncleji," I would answer, "then my head might end up in the clouds."

One day, Munir invited me to his house. "I'll show you how to make a kite." I had never realised how easy it was to do so. He cut a piece- about eighteen inches of thin paper. "Here, make it into a diamond. Now take a thin bamboo stick running from top to bottom and tape it at the ends." I did as ordered. He then took another thin piece of bamboo-stick; made it into an arc from left to right and taped it at both ends.

"What now?" I asked.

He proceeded to show me how to thread the string at the point of intersection. "Look carefully," he said. "When you hold the kite down by the string from about ten inches, it must balance horizontally and not tip sideways. That's the secret of a good kite, one that will take to the air easily and soar high in the sky without dipping to the ground, unless you want it to."

We then embarked on grinding broken pieces of glass and mixing the result with glue. Having made a paste of ground glass and glue, we rubbed the paste with our hands on the string. I was informed that this would strengthen the string to such a degree that we would be able to cut the string of our competitors' kites. The final preparation for this cunning plan was to stretch the string from end to end in a zig-zag fashion and leave it to dry in the sun for a few hours and finally reel it.

A few days later, Munir announced a kite flying competition between us and the Dharna kids - eight boys, brothers, and cousins living in two adjoining pink houses. What never failed to amuse us was how they always seemed to stick together oblivious of other kids in the neighbourhood. Together with sisters and closely guarded relations, they formed a formidable family in Ngara.

"Will they go kite-flying with us?" I asked incredulously.

"Of course not! Not *with* us, *against* us," Munir corrected me.

I grew excited, "When?"

"Friday, after school, I've told Sanjay and Afzal. We must win," Munir declared with determination.

The next day, we all met at Sanjay's house to plan the confrontation.

Sanjay explained, "We will meet at 4.30 in the evening, behind Khanna House - the grounds between Ngara and Grogan Road. Amar and Munir will fly from the north, Afzal, and I will fly from the south."

"Is that wise?" I asked, "Which side is the breeze coming from?"

"I tossed with Ravi Dharna," explained Sanjay. "He won and elected to go east-west. Don't worry, it shouldn't make much difference. The main thing is not to get entangled with each other. Just make sure that we have enough glass-coated string."

The Dharna brothers came in force, looking supremely confident. The four of us were supported by Sanjay's younger brother, Amit, and Munir's brothers, Masood and Miandad.

Eight of us gathered at the centre with our equipment, shook hands, and wished each other good luck. "No gloves," Sanjay explained. "We will team up about 30 yards from each other."

Ravi and Shitul Dharna went east; Pradip and Neel took the west side.

Sanjay and Afzal trudged over to the south side- Munir and I took our kite and string reel, north.

Munir laid the kite on the ground and inspected it one last time while I checked that the reel was smoothly wound. "Make sure it never entangles," he warned.

Munir, Afzal, Ravi, and Pradip took the kites to a central point – almost standing back to back, while Sanjay, Shitul, Neel, and I stood around the peripheral areas holding the reel in one hand and the loose string over our index fingers. I was a bit nervous and kept feeling the stretch on my finger. The string was rough with the crushed glass bound with glue giving me comfort and confidence. Masood and Miandad sat about ten yards behind me, shouting words of encouragement. "Keep it stretched, and keep looking up," Miandad kept shouting. "Kill them! Cut them!" Masood kept saying.

One of the Dharna kids counted from ten - backwards, then four, three, two, one, GO!

Munir held the kite just above his head with both hands. I stretched the string until it felt taut. Just as Munir let go of the kite, I pulled the string towards my chest. The kite swayed to the left, threatening to nose dive to the ground. I relaxed the string slightly and tugged hard again, arching my back and taking the string to shoulder height. The kite soared up sharply just missing Ravi's heading to the right.

"Careful! Don't tangle as yet," Munir shouted to me. "Let it soar up a bit first."

When Munir felt that our kite was steady and high enough, he rushed back to me.

"Well done Amar. Keep it taut. Stay away from the other kites for a while. Their string is also coated with glass."

We stood back and surveyed the situation for a while. Sanjay and Afzal waved to us. Munir waved back, so far so good. Sanjay's kite was soaring up but kept swaying to the right now and then. The Dharna kids held their kites neatly in the air -taut and under control. Cheered by the support from their cousins, Ravi, without warning, turned his kite in my direction.

"Watch out!" Munir shouted. He grabbed my elbow and turned it gently, causing our kite to swerve to the right to avoid Ravi's aggressive move. The string in my hand tightened, digging into my fingers, grazing my palm slightly.

"You are bleeding," he informed me.

I looked down. "It's nothing, don't worry."

"Let me take over for a while," he suggested.

Just as we were switching the reel, Ravi's kite lunged at ours from the left and Pradip's from the right.

"Hell!" Munir swore, pulling the string down with a quick flick of his wrist.

"Go higher!" I shouted.

He tugged hard at the string bringing his hand well behind his shoulder, elbow facing the kite. His face was stern and lips drawn back in concentration. Sweat beads gathered on his forehead, glistening in the hot sun.

We missed Ravi's but got entangled with Pradip's kite-both heading down.

"Pull hard!" I shouted.

"Kill it! Kill it!" Miandad and Masood screamed in unison.

Dharna supporters too cried in unison, all standing up, "Pradip, kill-kill-kill! Break it, *yaar*."

Munir was tugging and giving slack to the string repeatedly- the string digging into his fingers. His index finger was white and numb, a trace of blood on his palm. I watched transfixed, fearing that our kites were about to be cut. Both kites were heading down with the strings intertwined. Ravi's kite was threatening us but Sanjay kept it at bay by teasing his kite precariously in his direction. Without warning, I intervened, tugging at the string sharply; Munir leaned back, snapping at the reel.

Suddenly there was a cheer from Sanjay and Afzal. Miandad and Masood followed. "Well done, *Bhai jaan*."

I realised that Pradip's kite had been cut. It disentangled and headed sharply down to earth.

The Dharna camp fell silent. It was two against one. As if to avenge one defeat, Ravi, partly out of desperation and partly to take advantage of the few seconds when our camps relaxed, moved his kite sharply to the left. Sanjay was holding the reel and did not see Ravi's kite denting his until it was too late.

"Bastards," Munir swore.

I saw Sanjay reeling back with the string at shoulder height. But it was too late. His kite had a gaping hole in it!

Everyone was concentrating on the incident.

"Quick!" Munir cried, "Take a few steps to the left, go for the kill!"

Before Ravi's kite got a chance to steady, Munir dipped his towards him. With the advantage of height and pre-emptive strike, our kite tore into his.

The three kites- Sanjay's, Ravi's, and ours fought each other, although Sanjay's was powerless.

The Dharna camp was cheering and jeering. Miandad, Masood, and Amit were on their feet. "Kill it! Kill it!" Sanjay and Afzal joined in, "Munir pull! Pull hard!"

He took the advice. "Left a bit," I shouted, "Left and down."

For a few seconds, it was not clear what was happening. His thumb was bleeding steadily. *Too late, victory was more important.*

And finally, it happened, suddenly. The Dharna's remaining kite entangled with ours but was cut off from its string and soon floated aimlessly in the air away from the field.

They conceded defeat, sulking.

I still remember the day, I met Azra. Of course, I had, at Munir's house seen her fleetingly move from room to room, for a second or two, or sitting at a chair with her back to me. I had never actually seen her face, never spoken to her, and never heard her speak. One day, when I was about to enter his house, she flung the door open and in her haste took a step forward just as I was preparing to step inside. Time stood still, I remember her in my arms for a fleeting second before she blushed, turned away and ran back indoors. Electrified, I stared at nothing. A spark spread like a fire all over my body. I ran back to my house, shot straight to my room, and flung myself on the bed. I closed my eyes tight, all I wanted to see etched on the inside of my eyelids was her, not the wall or the pictures hanging on it, not the sunlight or what lay beyond. Nothing! Nobody! Just Azra!

I close my eyes, a helpless prisoner of memories. I can feel Azra's presence, her softness, her scent, and her touch.

She was perfect in beauty - copper coloured hair, green eyes, heavy eyelashes, full pink lips ... always happy, always smiling.
She did not deserve a horrific death.

CHAPTER 4

Azra affected my concentration at school and home. I prayed to God that I may be married to her; I would not want *anything* else. And then a horrible thought tugged at my mind: Munir! Surely Azra would tell him. *How could I face him? What about cricket and kites?*

I would stay in my room pretending to study, much to the delight of my mother. "*Beta*," she would say, "keep it up, education is important in life, it's the only wealth that *no one* can take away from you."

"I know, Maa...I know."

Over the next few months I tried not to brood over Azra and avoided going to Munir's except when he specifically asked me over. One day I went straight from school to Munir's as agreed to oil our cricket bats. As we were doing so, after being served full-fat milk and lamb kebabs by his mother, I happened to look up, and in the mirror saw Azra. I quickly lowered my gaze lest Munir spotted me observing her. A minute or so passed. When I looked at the mirror again, I was astonished to see her still there. Our eyes met in the mirror. She lowered her eyes and left, silently.

I started visiting Munir more frequently in the hope of seeing Azra again. Luck was not on my side. I would sit with Munir or with his brothers in their bedroom making kites or discussing cricket heroes. There was no sound or movement from Azra's room. I kept glancing at the mirror or the corridor. Nothing!

What I heard next astonished me, and to this day I do not know why Munir said what he did. He was just finishing off his homework - a watercolour painting of an elephant half-covered by bushes and dust with Mount Kilimanjaro in the background. He had this habit of sticking out his tongue halfway between his upper lip and the base of his nose whenever he was concentrating. "You know something," he said casually, head bent only about six inches from the elephant. "Azra can't speak."

Munir had made the statement without a prompt, casually, half aloud. For a few seconds, I did not understand what the words signified. What was Munir saying? And *why*? I never found out why because I never gathered enough courage to ask. I just stared somewhere between his head and the elephant. Everything seemed blurred. The world stood still and silent. Nothing moved.

"There!" he exclaimed with a wide smile, holding the painting against his chest. "What do you think?"

I didn't, but I nodded as if in appreciation.

Time dulled my shock and disappointment. Initially, I got behind with my school work. But with no will to go out and play, the only way to pass time was to read. I spent most of my after-school time reading Agatha Christie or James Hadley Chase.

"What is it *beta*?" my mother constantly enquired. "You are spending all your time reading. Why don't you go and play with Sanjay or Munir? Has something happened? Perhaps you could play Monopoly with Bimla? And remember, all work and no play is no good."

"I know, Maa...I know."

Poor Maa; She did her best. She understood well. To this day, I admire her soft face and her patience. She had an elegant walk and seemed to float gracefully compared to other women. Her *tika* on her forehead was always well centered, her long black hair always plaited neatly and her nails always polished in pale pink. She was a deeply religious woman, getting up before dawn for a shower and prayers. She never had breakfast before first lighting an incense stick and listening to devotional songs. She would then walk from room to room with her prayer to purify the whole house for the rest of the day. There was a spiritual aura about her, especially after morning prayers, something I would one day witness on her untimely death.

"Always have faith in God, *beta*," she reminded me again and again, "especially in need, don't be shy to ask, His door is always open, and remember always try your best to *not* do wrong things in life. Feel with your heart, but think with your head."

"I know, Maa...I know."

The evening breeze was cool with heavy clouds, it grew dark quickly. We were at *Mwangi's Duka*, a small corrugated stall, resembling a shack, for hot mogo chips and chili corn. We often had a bite at *Mwangi's* after playing in the evenings. The menu was limited to just mogo chips, corn, boiled beans, and soft drinks. For students, it was extremely affordable and to top it, Mwangi offered a generous supply of red chilies and fresh lemon to rub on the corn.

"*Jambo*, Mwangi," Sanjay greeted the lanky Kikuyu man.

"*Jambo Sana.*"

The stall was made from faded wooden planks of different sizes with irregular gaps and a tattered tin roof that let in small beams of the street light. There were a few low-level stools and a battered old table scratched with hearts and names. Mwangi lit a kerosene lamp and switched on the radio, loud hip-vibrating music blared into the dusky evening.

"Mwangi, *pole- pole*, we are not deaf. I'm sure that even Jomo Kenyatta can hear it in his State House." I shouted. "*Ume Elewa?*"

Sanjay joined in, "Not just J K, even Neil Armstrong can hear it as he takes his first step on the moon."

"*Ehe Wahindi, Indian*, but we are an independent country now, what does it matter?" Reluctantly, slowly moving his hips in small circles he reduced the volume, a bit but not enough. "*Kufurahia, Enjoy.*"

Within minutes, dusk had turned to nightfall, the breeze picking up. Except for the occasional car passing by, the croaking of frogs and the crick-crick of insects, it was very quiet. I sat balancing myself on a three-legged stool, making sure my feet were away from the muddy puddles.

"It feels cold here," I remarked.

Sanjay laughed. "That's because your zip's open, *yaar*."

I looked down.

"Just joking *yaar*," Sanjay smirked.

It was at a cricket match on Saturday that I first met Mrs. Webber. Looking back, I wish I never had, but sadly I have never been able to dictate events in my life. Her husband, Wayne played for the Gymkhana for four years until a tragic car accident caused mainly due to the bottle and a half of whisky he had drowned one fatal evening to celebrate the Gymkhana winning the Nairobi Railway Cricket Trophy.

For a year or so, Mrs. Webber stopped coming to the Gymkhana, but so keen was she in the sport of cricket that she found it difficult to keep away, indeed it eased her pain to be at the club. She would help with the sandwiches and drinks and exchange news and gossip with the few women who occasionally came to support their husbands.

Papa was a keen cricket player and a member of the Railway Gymkhana Club. It had a colonial feel to it and had a good reputation for cricket and hockey.

The Pavilion was painted brilliant white with a green sloping roof, polished wooden floor, and a long balcony with green chairs. I would often slouch in one of the chairs, and cheer Papa when he was batting.

He was a keen batsman and with his height and broad shoulders found it easier than most to hit the ball to the boundary. After a few months, I realised that he was referred to as *Khatra, Danger*. On one occasion, he hit the ball so hard it went over the Pavilion into the bushes never to be found again.

I remember an occasion when the Gymkhana was playing against Parklands Cricket Club, and I was lounging in a comfortable chair sipping Coca-Cola and munching a samosa, a voice interrupted my unimportant thoughts, "Hello, meet Ribena." I nearly choked on my Coke and almost fell from my chair, partly because I had been brought back to earth from miles away and partly because I had never imagined that Mrs. Webber would approach me to converse.

"My daughter," explained Mrs. Webber with a circular wave of her hand and displaying a proud smile.

I was amazed at how alike the two were, they could have been sisters. Mrs. Webber certainly didn't look like she would have a teenage daughter. I took a fancy to Ribena without even trying. She was a couple of inches taller than me, slim but with breasts bigger than any of the girls in my school, complemented by long dark hair and innocent blue eyes.

I said something, mumbled perhaps with my gaze focused on her.

"Do you play cricket too? Perhaps you can teach me the rules. Mum's *so* into it."

I mumbled something incomprehensible by way of a reply, half to myself and half to her.

"Why don't you two help me with the sandwiches?" Mrs. Webber suggested.

Silently I followed the two into the kitchen.

Mrs. Kapila joined us in the preparation for lunch. She was a middle-aged woman, tall and always elegantly dressed, perhaps too much, and often brought a tray-full of her homemade vegetable samosas.

"Suneeta," Mrs. Webber said many a time, "you do make the *most* delicious samosas. You simply *must* give me the recipe."

I had heard the same sentence said the same way so many times, each time wondering why the recipe had not been insisted on and also, why Mrs. Kapila wanted to keep the recipe so secret.

The sandwiches were a success with the players and the guests. At the close of play, Mrs. Webber thanked me for helping her. Unexpectedly, she leaned forward towards me and with one hand on my shoulder, gave me a quick gentle kiss on my cheek. After regaining my composure, I looked Ribena directly in the eye hoping that she would follow suit. She merely extended her hand and as I held it, briefly, she said, "Bye Amar."

I looked forward to Saturdays, but Ribena was not to be seen at the Pavilion. There were times when I thought that I might have upset her. I did not have the courage to ask Mrs. Webber and she never mentioned her, except once, in passing when she proudly told me how good she was in tennis. "Ribena has reached the Nairobi Inter-schools semi-finals – I'd be surprised if her school does not win the trophy again, this year."

It is surprising how quickly days turn to weeks and weeks to months. I had almost given up hope of seeing Ribena again and had almost forgotten her smile, her walk, her voice. However, hope endures for good or for bad. When I least expected to see her again, she turned up at the rematch between Railway Gymkhana and the prestigious Impala Club. The two clubs were great rivals and at the previous match at the club, the visitors won by just two runs, scored off the last ball, and with just one wicket to spare.

Papa had sworn revenge and on Friday evening, the day before the match most of the players had managed to find time to get together at Mohinder's Corner Bar to discuss strategy over the finest lamb curry served in Nairobi.

The day began well – Impala Club announced that Paul Wilkinson, their key bowler was not well enough to play.

Furthermore, the ground was hard and dry, ideal for spinners, which Gymkhana excelled in, and as luck would have it, Papa's team won the all-important toss and elected to bat.

Gymkhana started well against Impala's fielders. The score had moved to 94 when the first batsman was bowled by an in-swinging ball. The previous evening's strategy seemed to be paying off. After that, however, due to the eagerness to take revenge Gymkhana lost two quick wickets, so it was left to the batsmen on the crease to steady the ship, which caused the run rate to drop. With the pressure from the Pavilion, to accelerate the run rate, Patel, normally a cautious batsman was run out trying for a suicidal quick run. At 206 for 4, when a batsman was caught at the boundary, trying for a mighty six, Papa took the crease. "Come on *Khatra*, on with it," was the unanimous cry from the Pavilion. Papa took two overs to accustom himself to the wicket and started a blitz of boundaries and the occasional six. The Pavilion came alive, all at the balcony focusing on the pitch. Ribena came and stood by my side. "He's excellent," she said of Papa. "You must be very proud of him."

"Yes," I said. "When he gets going, it's difficult to dislodge him."

Suddenly, he hit two successive sixes. Everybody clapped and cheered, some whistled. I almost failed to realise that Ribena was not only cheering like the rest but also clutching my arm. She was certainly enjoying the game. My pulse soared with the realisation of her so close to me.

"This is *incredibly* exciting." We stayed close to each other for a long time when without warning, she exclaimed. "Amar, you have a hole in your ear." She then turned my face gently, to see if I had one in the other ear. "Wow, how wonderful!"

The score had moved to 320 with 4 overs to go, when Papa was declared Leg Before Wicket. He was cheered all the way to the Pavilion.

Gymkhana eventually scored 354, a formidable score for Impala – and they knew it!

During the change-over, Ribena asked me which team had the advantage.

"We, I suppose. Firstly, Impala will be daunted by the high score, secondly, the pitch is deteriorating fast, and finally, the evening light can play tricks on the tail-enders.

As it turned out, Impala put up a great fight, and at one point, with 288 for 6 – with nine overs to go, the home team looked worried. Impala players cheered noisily and Ribena kept looking at me as if to say, *you might be wrong*. An additional factor was the dark clouds moving fast from east to west. There was a possibility that rain or bad light could bring an early termination to the match, resulting in a draw. Mrs. Webber looked cool as ever, in her simple white floral cotton dress. "We'll win, wait and see," she said with confidence.

As if to prove Mrs. Webber right, Impala immediately lost a wicket, a careless leg stroke, the ball just toppling the bails. After that Impala lost the will, not helped by the combination of spinners and accurate medium pace bowling that Papa's team decided as their attack strategy, and were 14 runs short of victory at the close of play.

By late evening, some players and visitors had taken leave; others were either enjoying cold beer or tea with buns and cream. I had two Sprites with a ham sandwich and went looking for Ribena. She was nowhere to be seen. I ventured away from the crowd and found myself in some sort of changing room with cricket gear thrown around. This was probably where players changed into pads and body protection. I was about to leave when, on a stool, I saw a magazine – the cover displaying a woman with little to hide.

Not having seen such a magazine before, I flicked through it and was rewarded with pages of naked women in various poses.

For a minute or so, I was oblivious of the outside world. I turned the pages and focused on a woman with her full glory on display.

It could have been the breeze, or some movement in the room– I knew something was wrong. I raised my eyes from the magazine and to my horror, found myself looking straight into deep blue eyes.

Death would have been preferable! At that moment, I wanted to leave the room, the Pavilion, the country, the earth! To be looking at such a magazine in full view of the world with the door half open was madness enough, but to be caught red-handed was inexcusable, down-right carelessness! My lips moved as if to say, *Mrs. Webber?* But no sound came.

She stood still, staring at my face, not moving a muscle. She did not look away or down. I mirrored her motions.

"I'm sorry, I just..." my voice trailed away, a raucous whimper.

"Shhh," she whispered. Without taking her eyes off my face, she turned her body to one side and stretching one arm, bolted the door.

I stood frozen, terrified. *What was she going to do? What if she told Papa?* I would not be allowed to cricket matches. I would never be able to face her or Ribena again.

As if sensing that I was beginning to shake, she moved closer. My mind went blank. Slowly, without taking her eyes off me, she took the magazine from my hand and dropped it on the floor. It fell with a deafening thud. Her dress rustled as she positioned herself against me.

"Mrs. Webber, I..." again my voice trailed away.

Her response was short, "Shhh."

I tried to turn around, but she held me firmly. "It's okay Amar," she whispered, her breath warm in my ear. I stood helpless, glued to the floor, hypnotised. When I tried to turn a second time she pinned me against her. The heat passed through her dress into every part of my body. My eyes were closed, my lips sealed, and my body rigid. All I heard was the gentle rustling of her dress. I was in her hands.

CHAPTER 5

Papa had to miss a few of his cricket matches due to the wedding preparations of a friend. Secretly, I was relieved. I had a notion that if I kept away from the matches and Mrs. Webber, the incident between us would somehow disappear from my mind or that with time Mrs. Webber would forgive me for it.

However, the inevitable is only delayed, never erased. One cold Saturday morning, when I was having a strident row with Bimla over whether Michelangelo or Leonardo de Vinci was the better painter, Papa decided that peace could only be maintained by dragging me to his cricket match.

The visiting team from Mombasa won the toss and elected to bat. They needn't have bothered, for after only two balls, with the score at zero for no wicket, the heavy, dark clouds let loose their bladders. The two batsmen and the fielders scrambled back towards the Pavilion. Everyone gathered inside, soaking the polished wooden floor and giving their own version of the sudden downpour – none audible amongst the chatter echoing in the Pavilion.

"Amar!"

I turned around to see the caller, almost bumping nose to nose with Mrs. Webber.

"Mrs. Webb—"

"Amar, how are you?"

"Fine," I murmured, barely audible, worried. Then, realising that she couldn't have heard me clearly, I spoke louder. "Fine, Mrs. Webber."

She placed a hand on my shoulder and gestured me to follow her. I had no option but to obey her meekly through the crowded room. She was wearing a pink, flowery dress that swayed slightly in the breeze.

As we entered the kitchen, she held my hand and facing me, said, "I haven't seen you for a few months, you seem to have grown so much. How handsome you look, just like your father."

I wasn't sure why I was here, or for that matter why *she* was here.

"Amar, we must talk."

Panic gripped me. "Why? I mean, about what?"

"What happened between us is *our* secret. *No one* must ever know. Promise me." Her voice was firm, her eyes glued on mine.

I breathed out audibly. My shoulders felt lighter than they had for months. I nodded a few times before opening my mouth, "Yes, I mean, of course. Thank you, Mrs. Webber."

From thereon, I saw and looked upon her differently- not as *Mrs. Webber*, but as a woman who I realised was beautiful, even sexy.

"How is Ribena? I haven't seen her for a long time?"

Her eyes narrowed and her expression hardened. "Amar, let's not bring her into this. She won't be coming here again, cricket is not her scene."

"Will I see her again?"

"No!" she replied sharply. Sensing that I was hurt by the manner of her reply, she softened and added, "Maybe; it's up to her whether she wants to come here or not."

I moved closer to her. She moved back a few inches and extended a hand towards me, "Friends?" And without waiting for a reply, "You'd better go before your dad misses you."

One afternoon, Sanjay was at my house. We were just talking about this and that, nothing meaningful. I was bored and he was killing time. At some stage, the conversation turned to girls. "Do you know that Afzal is secretly seeing Samita? Don't tell anyone *yaar*. I'll get into trouble."

I was surprised. "Afzal's so timid, and Samita's always being followed by so many boys every evening. What's he got to offer her?"

"Maybe he's got a big *danda, yaar*."

We both laughed.

"Do you know who I fancy?" Sanjay asked. Without waiting for a reply he volunteered, "Anita. It's her eyes, *yaar*, they seem to look right through you, never miss a thing."

"Lovely eyes," I mumbled.

"Tell me, Amar, do you have a thing with anyone?"

I hesitated for a while. "Sure you won't tell anyone?"

"By God, *yaar*."

"I... I like Munir's sister... you know..."

"Azra?" He asked incredulously, sitting up and facing me. "Are you mad?"

"Why? I was surprised at his surprise. What's wrong with her?"

He gave me a sharp look. "She's a mute."

I was stung by his choice of words. "Mute? So? How did that happen?"

"Not sure, *yaar*. A couple of years ago, she developed some throat infection. The family didn't pay much attention to it, neither did the doctor. When the specialists discovered the problem, it was too late. They had to remove some part in her throat to stop cancer or whatever it was from spreading..." He ranted on. I was lost.

After a long silence on my part, I asked, "Is she deaf as well?"

He shook his head, "No, *yaar*, nothing wrong with her ears. Haven't you ever spoken to her?"

I shook my head.

He stood up and slapped my back, gently, "Do you know that she's off to Pakistan soon to get married?"

I was stunned! "Get married? What do you mean? Is she old enough for it?"

"Don't know *yaar*. But, hey, my mother got married when she was even younger. And who's going to marry Azra here? She doesn't even go to school nowadays. No friends, no suitors, no prospects." He looked at me thoughtfully. "She is beautiful though; lovely pouting lips. I wouldn't mind putting my *danda* between her legs."

I was used to his crude remarks. "Sanjay, why does God make someone so beautiful and then take away her speech?"

"It must be something to do with her previous life, *yaar*. Some sort of punishment."

"But then, why make her so beautiful?"

He stared at me for a while. "Double punishment," he replied, pensively.

I wasted no time; I had to see Azra. The very next day, I visited Munir after school. Her mother gave me her customary welcome. "Amar, why haven't you been for a long time? Come in, come. Munir is in his room." As I went past her, she shouted. "Azra, come, give me a hand in the kitchen."

Azra rushed out of Munir's room, heading in my direction. As she brushed past me, I tried to hold her hand – waves of electricity rushed through my body. I do not know what she felt, but her blush and flickering smile were in no way hostile. A few seconds later, we both turned around for the briefest of moments. She walked slowly into the kitchen.

Munir was reading *Cricket Today*. "Amar, where have you been, haven't seen you for a long time? Sit here, do you know, Hanif batted for sixteen hours? It's a world record, *yaar*."

"Brilliant," I said. "Munir, I hear you are going to Pakistan soon?"

"*Na*, not me, *Abbu* and Azra are going on Sunday"

Sunday! In two day's time! "I didn't know."

"Oh, it's nothing, *yaar*. *Abbu's* trying to find some nice man for Azra."

"Does he have someone in mind?"

"No, but we have a few cousins in Lahore who might be a good match.

"Has she seen them or their photographs?"

"Probably not, but *Abbu* knows the families well. They are well-to-do. He knows what's best for her."

"Does she want to marry?"

"She won't say," he replied casually, flicking through *Cricket Today.*

It was some days later that I realised the irony in Munir's answer.

CHAPTER 6

In my final year at school, a trekking trip to Mount Kilimanjaro was arranged. All the senior students were excited about the challenge. Fearing that I might not be allowed to go on account of my unsatisfactory academic results; I held back raising the subject until the deadline to seek parental consent for school. I needn't have worried. Papa was all in favour of me going. "It will do you good, son. Get some fresh air, but, make sure you are on top of your studies."

A month or so before the trip, around twenty-five of us, aspiring to climb Kili started a fitness regime three times a week after school. Mr. Slater worked us hard – starting with stretching exercises followed by running around the track, a 110 yards competitive run with rucksacks filled with forty pounds weight, and running up and downstairs repeatedly until only five of us would remain. The first two sessions were difficult for me. I suffered from cramp in the legs and blisters around my toes as a result of ill-fitting army boots that I had bought in Kariuki Market. Mr. Slater advised me to wear two pairs of socks- light cotton next to the skin to absorb the sweat and heavy wool on top to absorb the shock. The problem was soon solved.

A fortnight later, the selection for the twenty students was made- Sanjay, Munir, and Afzal were selected at a very early stage. I feared that I wouldn't until Sanjay, who was of course extremely fit and fast, gave his name as Amar when spotted by one of the teachers. The twinge of guilt was short-lived, overcome by the euphoria of being included for the trip. After that, I was indebted to him - a penalty I would pay many years later. My soul was ransomed.

During the practice sessions, I got to know and admire Rajesh, a fellow student with whom I had had little dealings before. He was short and stout, and much fitter than I. With his broad shoulders and muscular arms, he was a strong candidate for the trip right from the start. We were often teamed together and built an amicable relationship. On a few occasions, he coaxed us to join him at *Dil Bahar* restaurant for sweet lassi and spicy pakoras. After a vigorous workout, nothing tasted better.

Finally, the day arrived. We gathered at the school forecourt with our rucksacks, army boots, and heavy jackets, eager to leave. We piled into the coach cheerfully for the half-day journey to the border with Tanzania. All the way we sang unforgettable songs by Elvis Priestley and Cliff Richard until our voices were hoarse.

As we approached Loitokitok, I caught my first sight of Kilimanjaro. It was breath-taking, rising above the clouds, displaying a table of brilliant white snow against the clear blue sky, proud and majestic.

We pegged tents for the day and prepared the evening meal – tinned beans, boiled carrots, and *ugali* after which we all took stock of what we were to carry with us over the next three days.

And all this time, the snow on Kilimanjaro, *shining mountain* as it is called in Swahili, shimmered white and pure in the moonlight- majestic, timeless. I recalled how Ernest Hemingway had described it: *Wide as all the world. Great, high, and unbelievably white in the sun.*

The next morning, after tea and biscuits, we gathered around Mr. Slater and Mr. Townsend for a pep-talk.

"Now, remember, this is not a race to see who gets there first. Please walk in your chosen teams, drink lots of water, and don't be shy to rest if tired. Ask for help if in trouble. Your level of fitness will bear little relation to your susceptibility to mountain sickness. Even if you are physically fit, you can get mountain sickness during rapid ascent. Early signs include nausea, headache, and vomiting. If that happens, you must prepare to descend; not doing so can be grave. Please keep well hydrated and avoid strenuous exertion. Walk *pole-pole,* slow and steady, as they say around here. Between the two, they ranted on about respecting the locals, the vegetation, and not to throw litter around. We, of course, were all itching to go.

We are at about six thousand feet above sea level, so you have another thirteen thousand feet to go over the next two days. It sounds easy, but, the oxygen gets sparse as you go higher, especially after the Mawenzi peak. Please pace yourself-do not run out of steam. It may be just trekking all the way, but bear in mind that you will be going through five different climate zones and face acute altitude sickness. The ultimate aim is to reach the summit- Uhuru peak and witness the magnificent sunrise from the roof of Africa, over the crater, and the distant plains."

The first few hours seemed easy- just a leisurely walk, joking and greeting the mountain dwellers with *Jambo,* to which they would reply, *Jambo, pole-pole(slow and steady).* By mid-afternoon, the legs felt considerably heavier and the difference in the oxygen level was noticeable. The terrain gradually turned uneven and the loose gravel caused the feet to slide a bit at every step.

"Can't see the peak, *yaar,*" Sanjay said, slightly out of breath.

"It's above those clouds to the right. Let's have a little rest, shall we?" I said, lowering my rucksack.

Rajesh wasn't keen on it. "It's better to slow down and keep walking than rest. That way, the muscles don't contract; resting only makes it difficult to restart. Rember what Martin Luther King said?"

"What?" I enquired feebly.

Rajesh stood tall before reciting:

If you can't fly...run
If you can't run...walk
If you can't walk...crawl

But keep moving!

Munir was the first to respond. "Okay, but I'm sure he wasn't walking up a mountain when he said all that."

"Oh, shut up, keep moving, Munir."

"Rajesh the bull, always charging," commented Munir, good-naturedly. "Do you know, we've walked non-stop from seven this morning? That's six hours without rest! And we've got another three to four hours of walking to do!"

"And the gradient will get steeper!" I added.

An hour later, we all took off our rucksacks and leaned against some large boulders, gazing below and far.

"I wonder how the other teams are doing." Rajesh muttered. "I saw Harinder's team a while ago. They were taking lots of photographs."

"We'll get better photos as we near the top," Munir commented.

The sun gradually lost its brightness and the grassland turned crimson before changing to grey. Some clouds drifted past. Even at this altitude, there was little sight of any man-made invention. Truly wonderful, I thought and wondered how many had stood at this very spot a million years ago and gazed at the sight that we were smitten by.

We spent the night under some large boulders jutting out and providing shelter from the mist and cold. Munir spread a large plastic sheet to stop the dampness seeping into the sleeping bags. Except for the little light that the stove provided, it was pitch black. We ate a mixture of rice and boiled beans while the wildlife made unidentifiable sounds in the cold darkness. Too tired to talk, we slid into our bags and drifted into darkness.

Dawn always broke with incredible beauty and freshness. The grassland turned from gold to different shades of brown and the valley below us burst into green with drifting clouds covering it, as if from evil eyes. We set off energised. The first three hours passed by with little effort. Later the terrain got rougher and we treaded on stones rather than pebbles. With the air thinning, we needed a small rest, every two hours or so.

The next day proved more difficult with some of us complaining of blisters and breathlessness. The pace was slower and conversation more sombre.I can recall little of where and how we slept.

The saddle between Mawenzi and Kibo proved difficult. The sun blazed but the temperature was low and the wind howled with biting ferocity. The terrain was rough, loose gravel, stones, and sedimentary rocks. Every step took something out of me. Sanjay offered to carry some of the weight from my ruck-sack. I kept refusing, pride kept me going although I knew that in time I would have to seek help. I was drinking a lot of water to just focus and avoid the stones. As if sensing my weariness, Rajesh called a halt. "We have to trek as a team *yaar*. Amar has some problems if we ignore it; it will only make matters worse later. Sanjay is right, let's share his rucksack weight for a while. I'll take the sleeping bag, Sanjay, you take the stove and spare boots, Munir, take the food. If we see another group, we'll ask for assistance. Amar, please sip water regularly, but don't gulp. You'll be okay soon, you'll see."

Over the next few hours, I only got worse, throwing up at least three times. My stomach felt hollow, and I followed the team in a daze. Focusing became difficult and my forehead throbbed persistently, while my head ached from inside out. Deep inside the pit of my stomach, waves of nausea traversed my body like a tsunami. I cannot recall how I managed to reach Kibo hut. What I do recall is being put on a hard bed in one of the huts, Mr. Townsend giving me some tablets with soup and some water.

I woke up around midnight, disturbed by the commotion and everyone loading their warmest clothing for the final ascent.

"Afzal," I managed to shout weakly, "Where's everyone?"

"Gathering outside for the ascent, we thought you'd be better off here. Townsend said not to take you. Some of Harinder's team are staying back, looks like they got lost, and have just arrived. They are too exhausted to make the final ascent. We are lucky we have Sanjay in our team."

I was in a rage. How could I be left out like this? "Afzal, help me with my gear..."

"Amar! Are you sure? Better have a word with Slater or Townsend."

"I'm going," I said, standing up. "I feel better now. See?" I placed my rucksack on my sore back and ventured out to be greeted by an amazing sight. It was dark; some were shining their torches for fun. But the snow! It was everywhere!

"We had a lot of snow while you were resting. You okay to go?" Townsend asked.

I nodded.

Townsend asked the rest of my team to keep an eye on me. "I'll be around, give me a shout if you need help," he said reassuringly.

We set-off in our teams just after midnight. The gradient was steep and we kept slipping after every few yards. Breathing became very difficult. "Breathe gently in from the nose and out from the mouth," Rajesh kept saying, helpfully.

After two hours, we got engulfed in a snowstorm. Visibility got poor and, as advised many times before, we moved slowly, following the person immediately ahead. The wind howled and stung our faces despite the goggles and scarves. My ears ached and the feet and hands were totally numb.

"You okay, Amar?" Sanjay kept asking through heavy breathing.

"Sure," I lied, "You?"

"Not sure, *yaar*."

"What's the matter, Sanjay?" Munir asked, between deep breaths.

"I've lost it, *yaar!*"

"Lost what?" Rajesh asked, now really worried. We all stopped in our tracks.

"Can't feel my *danda*, it's gone!"

I was too weak to laugh but it made me feel better.

Foot by foot, we moved forward. At one point, I stopped in my track and looked up to see how much more we had to climb.

"Don't look up," Sanjay scolded. "Keep walking, think of something nice."

Nothing but snow, cold numbness, fatigue, and altitude sickness hit us all. After another four hours, we passed Stella Point at 18.650 feet above the sea level. I felt emphysemic. Rajesh saw me shaking my head in despair, bent forward, hands on knees.

"Keep going, *yaar*. Only another half hour to the summit, it will all be worth it."

Taking his advice, I forced myself to think of other things: kites, cricket, Ribena, Mrs.Webber, Azra...would I see her again? I was breathing with difficulty, head down, bringing one foot forward then the other. I was on the brink of turning back when Sanjay held my elbow, helping me upwards.

Munir held my other elbow as we trudged snow foot by foot. My head weighed a ton and I was having trouble focusing. Suddenly, I heard shrieks of joy. Rajesh hugged me and was thanking Sanjay for his superb leadership. There were about a dozen students on all fours clapping and cheering. Mahesh, one of the tallest students in the school came towards us, "Well done guys, you did it!"

The snowstorm had abated, giving in to light flurries of snow beating into my chapped lips. It suddenly dawned to me that we were at the top of Africa- at Uhuru Peak, 19,340 feet above the sea.

"Look!" someone shouted, "Over there." I followed the direction. An orange light was emerging in the east. Sunrise!

"Wow!" Munir exclaimed. "Seen anything like this before?"

I shook my head, tired but elated. This was a sight to relish. I put an arm around Munir and pointed towards the plains where the rising sun was coating it in gold and orange.

We sat there until the snow changed from blue to crimson to white. I could have stayed there for hours watching the sky meeting the horizon many miles away and the clouds floating away as if frightened by the rising sun.

"Time to head back," Mr. Slater cried. "Well done chaps."

Going down was not as easy as I had imagined. Having achieved our mission, we tended to rush down, sometimes slipping in the snow or bumping into others. We walked, half trotted for hours.

At dusk, we stopped at about 15,000 feet and lay our sleeping bags between boulders. As we sat sipping hot cocoa with the lights of some town shimmering miles below us and the firmament crowded by a bright canopy of stars, I was reminded of the nights when I used to sleep outdoors back home, listening to Dipti's stories. Everyone seemed content sitting in the dark in silence staring at the snow above or the town lights miles below. High above, the stars twinkled brightly with no dust or pollution to tarnish their purity. Orion's belt seemed within reach. I sat mesmerised by the enormity of the galaxy, marvelling at its creation and perpetuity.

"Did you know?" I asked, "The three stars in the belt of Orion belong to the hunter who was killed by God for being too boastful of his heroics."

There was no response; everyone was too absorbed in scanning the night sky. We sat in peace for a long while.

"Do you believe there's life somewhere up there?" Rajesh asked, almost to himself.

"No, it's just us, *yaar*," Sanjay replied with a slight shake of his head. "If there *was* life out there, they would have contacted us by now, especially the women.

Rajesh was a bit more thoughtful. "Surely we can't be the only ones in the universe. Just take a look- it's so vast, there must be some sort of life, somewhere."

"So how come they haven't found us, or we haven't found them?" Munir asked. "Look what the Americans found when they landed on the moon – nothing. Complete waste of time and money. Their only consolation is that they beat the Russians to it."

Rajesh gave up. "Yup, you can say that again."

"They beat the Russians," the rest of us obliged flatly in a chorus.

The next morning, we started our final trek to the base camp. The gradient was not so severe and the going was easier. With mission accomplished and the worst over, we got a bit careless. The plan was to assemble at Loitokitok by dusk.

We talked happily about this and that and took photographs. Sanjay and I were discussing what we wanted to do at university. Rajesh and Munir were walking faster as if racing each other.

Suddenly, I heard Munir scream, "Rajesh! Rajesh!"

To my horror, I saw Rajesh stumbling downhill, uncontrollable, with loose stones and dust flying around him. Sanjay and I quickened our pace.

Munir was shouting, "Rajesh, stop!"

"Grab him, Munir," Sanjay shouted loudly, running now. The echo came back, *Grab him, Munir*.

What happened in those few seconds haunts me to this day. Rajesh had disappeared from sight!

Munir was the first to scream in horror, followed by Sanjay. I rushed to witness the accident. Rajesh had fallen over the edge! His carelessness and the sudden slope with loose stones and gravel had made it difficult for him to stop in time.

On approaching the edge, we saw the extent of Rajesh's misfortune. He was a good fifty feet below, crying out in agony.

"Rajesh," I shouted, cupping my hands by the sides of my mouth, "are you alright?"

He was writhing in pain, lying on one side, knees bent to his chest, hands covering his eyes.

"Rajesh!" I shouted again. "Are you alright?"

He said something which we did not understand. Clearly, he was in agony.

"Oh God! We'd better go down," I said, dropping my rucksack on the ground.

Sanjay started inching down with fingers digging into the edges. I hurriedly followed the narrow path curving a bit further where the gradient towards Rajesh was more moderate.

We both reached Rajesh at the same time. "God, God!" he kept saying. Both arms were bent at the elbows and his wrists covering his eyes.

"You are bleeding, Rajesh!" I said, bending over him. His face was covered with blood. *Hell! Where was the blood coming from?* I recoiled in horror at what I saw. A twig was logged in one of his eyes! I took his wrists in mine and held them in silence.

Sanjay took a sharp breath. "What do we do?"

"Mustn't touch the eye," I shouted, turning towards Munir. "Sanjay and I will stay here. Can you head towards the base camp and get help? Get hold of Slater and

Townsend. Tell them to get some rope and maybe even a stretcher.

Sanjay placed a hand on Rajesh's shoulder. "Now listen to me, Munir is going to get help. Can you see clearly?"

He angled his head slightly and mumbled something, his lips barely moving.

"What?" Sanjay asked placing an ear close to his mouth.

"Only with my left eye," he whispered feebly with twisted lips.

"Can you stand up?"

He shook his head, "No, I think I have broken my left ankle, the right one hurts too." Sure enough, his ankles were badly bruised.

On further examination, I discovered that his trouser around the right thigh was soaked with blood. Panic gripped me. We had not been trained for such an accident. Sanjay, more composed than I carefully cut Rajesh's trousers with a pocket knife to reveal a nasty gash in the middle of the thigh, probably cut by a sharp stone as he tumbled down.

"Got some rope or string, Amar?"

I shook my head. "No, but tell you what, let's join handkerchiefs," I handed mine to Sanjay.

The handkerchiefs were tied tightly around the thigh, just above the wound. I then took a spare tee-shirt and pressed it on the wound.

"Shit! I hope this is what one is supposed to do," Sanjay snarled, expressing annoyance that no training had been given for such accidents.

Hell! I thought. The sun will be setting soon. What if help does not arrive before dusk?

"Rajesh, you need to be strong, okay? I'm going to wash a bit around your eye but I don't think we should remove the twig. Does it hurt?" Stupid question! I regretted it the moment my words left my lips.

Rajesh smiled wryly. That was answer enough.

We sat and waited in silence. I suddenly realised that his hand in mine had turned cold. "Do you want a sleeping bag over you?"

His eyes were closed but he managed to nod.

Dusk came quickly, without warning, as it often does in Africa, and darkness followed within a matter of minutes. Sanjay lit a stove for some light and heat. We crept in our bags up to the waist. A few birds overhead screeched, perhaps feeling Rajesh's pain. Frogs and crickets stopped their muttering for a while, confused by the unwelcome commotion.

"Do you feel like eating or drinking something?" Sanjay asked Rajesh.

The reply was feeble, "Water."

"What about you, Amar?"

I shook my head, too tired and worried to talk, eat, drink or sleep. We sat like that for a few hours, each wondering where Munir was and how long before help would come.

A group of foreigners, German, I think passed above, chattering happily. I called for help.

"God!" said one shining a powerful torch at us. "He needs to be taken to a hospital!"

As if we didn't know!

They followed the path I had taken earlier and making a wide U-turn approached us. I asked for a torch and someone from the group passed me one. A woman in the group offered some pain killers which Rajesh refused to take.

Just when I had given up hope of help, I saw torch lights in the distance accompanied by muffled sounds, which gradually grew louder and clearer.

Rajesh! Amar! Sanjay! I sprang to my feet. "Here," I shouted, flashing the torch around. Sanjay joined in the chorus.

Munir, Mr. Slater, Mr. Townsend, Afzal, and two residents of Loitokitok who had helped us at the base camp scrambled down towards us.

Slater and Townsend bent down to observe the situation, the latter swearing under his breath. Afzal was stunned to see the twig pierced in Rajesh's eye. Slater had a quick chat with the local residents, who in turn had a calm discussion among themselves – not a word of which I understood. One of them explained to Slater in broken English that Rajesh, who by now was unconscious, needed to be taken to hospital as soon as possible, quickly! The nearest one was in Arusha.

The man speaking in broken English said something to his friend who checked that Rajesh's spine was okay and gently picked Rajesh in both arms, before placing him on his shoulders.

Checking that we had got all our belongings, we prepared our journey to the base camp in utter silence.

The guide who spoke broken English walked faster and soon disappeared out of sight. "He's going ahead to arrange for a local doctor and a jeep to take Rajesh to the hospital," explained Mr. Townsend.

We reached base camp in a few hours, exhausted but thankful that Rajesh could now be attended to. A doctor, Mr. Slater, and the two local residents climbed into a waiting jeep to take him to the hospital.

Some details of the trip were announced at assembly on Monday morning, after which, Mr. Slater and Mr. Townsend gathered all who had gone to Kili.

"I have some disturbing news," Mr. Slater started. "The hospital just rang... "

My heart sank. I feared the worst. I saw Munir looking at me in apprehension.

"Rajesh has lost a lot of blood, but he is going to be alright," Mr. Slater continued.

I let my held breath out. *Thank God!*

"However," I heard him mention, "Poor Rajesh has lost an eye."

There was a sharp intake of breath in unison followed by a deafening silence. It took a while for the news to sink in.

Mr. Townsend stepped forward. "Thanks to the help of you chaps, we saved his life. Another few hours and he could have... died. One of his ankles is broken, but that will heal in a few months."

CHAPTER 7

1972

I arrived in England on 4th August 1972, the day President Amin of Uganda announced the expulsion of 50,000 Asians to Britain. It was the height of summer; daylight and sunshine from five in the morning to ten at night. No potholes, no dust, no overflowing gutters, no slums, very unlike Kenya.

A cousin of my father, who had left India for the good life of England, greeted me affectionately at Heathrow Airport. "Amar! Amar! Over here!"

I gazed at the smartly dressed, slim, middle-aged man with a wide grin rushing towards me, arms wide open.

"Uncle Paal? Uncleji?"

"Yes, yes!" he yelled. "Paal Nath."

He hugged me tightly and locking his hands tightly behind my lower back, lifted me a few inches above the ground in typical Indian style.

As we drove home towards his home in Ealing, he chatted breezily. "Oh, it's so good to meet you. You are most welcome here. How is *Bhai Saab?*"

"Papa is fine, thanks, and Maa too. They are very grateful to you for accommodating me"

"*Aray nei,*" he tutted. "It's our pleasure. There are so few Indians in England- sometimes we don't meet any for days. Paro will be thrilled to see you. Just look at you, so much like *Bhai Saab.*"

"And how is *Bhabiji?*

"Very well, thanks. She has sent some Kenya *chawra* for you." He beamed in delight.

"How is Auntiji," I enquired. Maa was telling me that she's recently had an operation."

"It was just appendix, nothing to worry about. Paro's tough as boots."

I had never met Paal Uncle or Paro Aunty before, only seen them in photographs. They were extremely amicable, always addressing each other as *aap* rather than *tum*, the equivalent being, in French, *vous*, rather than *tu*. Their resemblance to each other was uncanny, similar height and profile, oval faces with identical beaming smiles, and for good measures, similar rimless spectacles. *Made for each other!*

Over the next few weeks, before the start of my University, I had seen all the usual tourist attractions in London-Buckingham Palace, Trafalgar Square, Madame Tussauds, Big Ben, and so on. I liked Madame Tussauds best- especially Gary Sobers, Elvis Priestley, and Richard Burton.

One day we went for a day trip to Oxford, where I was to commence my studies in a few months.

"Ah, Oxford!" Uncle Paal said with pride. "Great people have studied here-Prime Ministers like Indira Gandhi, Harold Macmillan, Edward Heath, Harold Wilson, and authors like VS Naipaul and Oscar Wilde. And, you know, Albert Einstein also spent some time here. Christ Church must be the best."

"Why *must* be?"

He beamed, "Because *you've* chosen it!"

I was easily smitten by Christ Church on St. Aldates-the university's largest college, Oxford's Cathedral. It was so close to the town centre, yet, within minutes we were in the Christ Church meadow by the River Cherwell. The college's walls seemed strong and ancient, almost black with pollution, yet timeless and majestic. In the quadrangle, the grass was immaculately kept, displaying a large circular pond with healthy lilies. It all seemed so inviting! I wished Papa and Maa were with me.

We had lunch at a pub by the river, my first visit to a pub, and watched punters glide by as I had seen in movies. With the summer sun and clear sky, I was thinking how picturesque it all was. My mind harped back to those lazy picnics we used to enjoy so much at Naivasha, a few hours drive from Nairobi, and then tea and scones at Lake Naivasha Hotel and the picnics by Fourteen Falls near Thika, where we used to cook and eat by the thundering waterfalls. My thoughts were interrupted by Paal Uncle. "Amar, would you like a beer? I am going to have another."

"No, Uncleji, I don't drink, thanks."

Paro Aunty beamed proudly. "Amar, don't listen to Paul, you stay away from that stuff. Paul, you get yourself a Double Diamond and two soft drinks."

A few weeks later, Paal Uncle and I visited Oxford again, this time to finalise my accommodation. The college had given me a list of landlords who were willing to let rooms to students to supplement their pensions. I was keen on something close to the college, the idea being to save time and transport costs. After viewing three properties in Headington, I selected a room in a house on London Road. Mr. and Mrs. Woods kept an immaculate three-bed semi-detached property with a garden to match those in Christ Church College. We had tea with them and listened to Mr. Woods' recollection of his contribution to not just the Second World War but the first one as well. He apologised for his failing memory each time and Mrs. Woods corrected him for the mix-ups between the two wars.

"No dear, not the second, that was the *first* world war... Hitler was responsible for the *Second* World War... Churchill was too young for the first war...." She looked at Paal Uncle seeking praise for the heroics of her brave husband and at the same time, understanding for the inevitable mix-ups in the mind of an old man."

My attention turned to a photograph on the mantlepiece of two men, both of whom looked vaguely familiar. As I took a few steps to inspect the photograph-only to quench my curiosity of the identities of the two men, Mrs. Woods, said proudly, "That's Henry, with Mr. Macmillan, who was the Prime Minister many years ago."

I gazed at the black and white photograph from a foot away. Mr. Woods and Mr.Macmillan were standing side by side, both in smart suits, smiling congenially. I was struck at how handsome Mr. Woods looked, standing a good three inches taller than the Prime Minister, eyes alert and a full crop of dark hair blowing gently in the breeze. Mrs. Woods and I sighed at the same time.

Paal Uncle thought that the rent of six pounds a week was a bit steep, but on being reminded that all meals were included, he consented. On our way back he added, "Make sure you have *all* your meals with them, don't go around wasting *Bhai Saab's* hard-earned money eating outside. And no need to be shy, ask for food if you are hungry – six pounds a week is not a joke!"

About a month after arriving in England, I received a letter from Munir. He must have got the address from Maa. I felt a pang of guilt for not writing to him first for I had promised to do so as soon as possible upon arrival.

Dear Amar,

You must have settled there by now. We all miss you so much, yaar. I thought you'd like some habari ya Kenya. (In case you have forgotten Swahili, habari means news.) Well, you know we parted at the airport at dusk. After that Sanjay, Afzal, Rajesh, and I had a few beers at Simba restaurant. Sanjay drove us to Ngara and we sat at Mwangi's and had some corn, which we rubbed with chilies and lemon thinking of you.

All your friends send you their best wishes.

Your friend

Munir.

P.S, I shall be re-sitting my Economics exam soon. Liverpool University has offered me a place if I get a "C" or better. Keep your fingers crossed for me. Abbu is still not keen on me going to England. He maintains that the money spent over the next three years could be ploughed in the family business. He's promised me a car if I join his business. Good mechanics are so rare, who better to train me than him, he says.

Sanjay has got confirmation from Nottingham University for Aeronautical Engineering. Afzal is planning to fly to London and try for a place somewhere- he thinks he may not get a place at a University but can find some course at some Polytechnic- he has an uncle who is very influential in some place called Ilford. Rajesh left for England two days ago with his father, who has made arrangements for a glass eye to be fitted at Guy's Hospital. You know, we were recently talking about this and that and someone jokingly said that the positive thing about having one eye is that he will only see half the bad things going on in the world, well let's hope so. He will contact you soon. Please make time for him. Richard Misisi has been accepted for Medicine at Nairobi University – free of all fees and accommodation.

All well at home, Masood was hit by a Matatu van a few days after you left. Luckily, he was only slightly hurt, could have been very serious.

Abbu and Ammi both miss you and are always telling me to be as bright as you. They want to know what your Papa and Mama used to feed you! By the way, they are fine. Your Mama was talking to Ammi about you a few days ago and burst out in tears. Have you upset her, or does she merely miss you? Do you miss us, or get upset or cry?

Sanjay, Afzal, Rajesh, Mitin, and I recently went to see Sholay at the Fox Drive-In. It's Dharmendra's best film to date, don't miss it. Amitabh is superb of-course. We took some chicken and samosas and heated them on a stove as we watched. Really missed you, yaar! Sorry, forgot to mention Samita, she came too, super-glued to Afzal.

Azra has got engaged to a cousin of ours in Lahore. I don't know when the wedding will be- Abbu and Ammi will be going to Pakistan and I might join them there.

And how is England? Is it cold? Have you made any friends (girls?) I hear Tiger (Pataudi) gave England a tough time at cricket. Just shows, even with one eye, if a person is determined, he can do well.

I believe Edward Heath is not very popular- planning on taking Britain into the European market. Do you think he will survive much longer as the Prime Minister? And why is he still a bachelor? Someone told me that he doesn't have showers because he can't bear to look at the unemployed!

We must get together before we disperse to universities, etc. and regularly afterwards, of course.

Well, I must be off. We are all going to Dil-Bahar for lassi and pakoras- wish you were here. See you soon.

In the cosiness of my room, I switched onto Radio 4 and listened to Week-Ending, a hilarious, fun- recap of the week's main news. It seemed extremely witty, though some of it was lost on me due to my unfamiliarity with British politics. I re-read Munir's letter and stopped after reading the part about Azra. She would get married, we would probably never meet... two paths, two different worlds, she in the east, I, in the west... never the twain would meet. I switched off the radio and picked up a magazine, one of many stacked neatly on a cupboard shelf. I flicked through...Dean Martin- a cigarette dangling between his lips, Marlon Brando-looking angry in a tight, muscle hugging tee-shirt, Elizabeth Taylor- immaculately dressed with tantalising eyes, Charlton Heston standing next to four handsome white horses, Raquel Welch- in a scanty bikini, lips pouting, Ursulla Andress- with little on, emerging from the sea... As I turned more pages my mind went back to that evening at the Impala Club where I was flicking through a magazine only to be surprised by Mrs. Webber. Hurriedly, I put the magazine down, as if by just turning one more page, someone might walk in. I went over to the window and gazed on Paal Uncle's garden, small but adequately kept with a neat patch of close-cut lawn, bushes along the fence and a few rocks at the far end. At one point, I saw my reflection in the window and found a flicker of a smile on my lips. *I was thinking of Mrs. Webber.*

Towards the end of September, we arranged a boys' night out in London. Rajesh, Afzal, Sanjay, and I met in Leicester Square. Munir was sorely missed. He just missed the grade for admission in England. "No bad thing," he wrote. *"Abbu's* business is booming. He's bought a franchise with Agip at Westlands and promised me a Ford Capri within six months. This time next year, I shall be running the Agip operation. Hope you guys come here for your summer holiday; it would be great to meet again."

Rajesh looked well and relaxed. His glass eye was the spitting image of the other. "Rajesh you look good, *yaar,"* Afzal screamed.

"Afzal, you rascal!" I teased, "I hear Samita is pregnant with your baby."

"Haven't you heard the good news Amar?" Sanjay joined in the teasing. "No more pregnant- the twins were born *yesterday!"*

Rajesh joined in, "Can I be the Godfather of one? I can't handle two, *yaar."*

"Shut-up you lot!" I don't even know where a *danda* goes." Afzal retorted.

"Our innocent little baby; tell him someone," Rajesh requested, one arm over Afzal's shoulder.

"Now let me see," Sanjay pretended to be thinking, scratching his chin. "If I recall correctly, according to page 343 of the Kama Sutra you stick it in the hole in the stomach- it's called the navel."

"No," I said, "That's if you want twins, otherwise you just let her hold your *danda* for a few minutes." We roared with laughter, ignoring Afzal's scowls.

"Come on, *yaar*," Sanjay declared. "Let's have a good time."

We roamed around the square and ventured into Soho, laughing at the pictures of scantly clad women advertising live shows, discos, and strip shows.

Sanjay held Afzal's hand and lifted it to a brightly lit picture of a nude woman advertising a peep show. "Now, pay attention Afzal, this is where the *danda* goes."

Rajesh slapped him lightly on the back. "If you want to see it in detail, just go inside."

"Shut-up, *yaar*, I'm not wasting two pounds for this nonsense."

We debated for some time as to what to see and finally agreed on *Oh Calcutta!* It was the naughtiest show in London and left little to the imagination. Afterwards, we continued teasing Afzal until we ran out of appropriate dialogues.

"Shall we try a pub?" Sanjay asked. In the jovial mood that we were in, it was difficult not to concur.

I had my first taste of alcohol- a pint of Double Diamond. Afzal didn't like it and after a few sips switched to a soft drink. Sanjay drowned his easily but kept complaining that it wasn't civilised to drink warm beer. "Why don't they drink chilled stuff, as we do in Kenya?"

"We'll teach them," I volunteered. "Here's to cold beer, hot women, and fast cars."

CHAPTER 8

I slept badly, tossing and turning all night. At one point I woke up, covered in sweat. My mind wandered back to Nairobi. The last few days in Nairobi had flown-by, mainly shopping for cold British weather. Streams of relatives, friends and well-wishers dropped-by. They advised me to work hard and keep away from girls, especially the *gori* (white) ones. *'Once you get in their clutches, you'll never come back home.'*

On the day of departure, the family was exceptionally quiet, even Bimla and Nita. Maa hardly said a word and twice burst into tears, sobbing words which were incomprehensible but which I alone understood. Papa was quiet but pragmatic, ensuring that I wouldn't forget anything. "What's this?" he asked checking my suitcase for the umpteenth time. I looked sharply at the object in question, a leather-bound book, *Hundred Great Places to see in Britain*, a present from Mrs. Webber with a message on the inside cover-*Best wishes, love Anna.*

"Oh, it's nothing," I lied. "It's a present from my friends."

"Always remember PMT," he advised quietly as we were about to leave for the airport. "Passport-Money-Tickets- most important for any trip. Three things you must never forget before a flight."

As I waved good-bye to friends and family at Jomo Kenyatta International airport, I was tearful, Papa's eyes were moist as he first shook my hand and then hugged me tightly, Bimla and Nita wet their faces and tugged at my sweater until the last second and Maa hugged me for a long time, kissing both cheeks. "Go," she whispered, "make us proud, and never let yourself down." Her eyes were dry as she met mine. I knew the flood would start later.

The college year was split into three terms, each term constituting just eight weeks with twelve hours of lectures per week. I seemed to have a lot of free time each day, which I was supposed to utilise for research. Even with some additional time at the library, I found myself lost and with unwelcomed time on hand. Autumn, lovely though it was, brought constant drizzle and increasing winds. Most students joined some sort of activity, and Oxford was not short on them- fencing, debating, rowing, music, photography and so on. Unfortunately, hockey and cricket were not on the agenda until early summer. I, therefore, found myself more and more in my room a few miles away in Headington.

The novelty of newfound freedom slowly evaporated, and I found myself day-dreaming of family and friends in Nairobi, I rang Paal uncle almost every evening. "You'll be okay, Amar. Soon you will make friends and have a great time." On another occasion, he said, "Why don't you come here for the weekend? It's Paro's fortieth. We can surprise her!" At last, something to look forward to!

One day, after an extremely dull lecture on how each entry either ended in a Profit and Loss Account or a Balance Sheet, whereupon our lecturer himself got confused after an Iranian student kept interrupting and quizzing him, the student turned to me. "Excuse me, are you from Saudi? He spoke softly and slowly, choosing his words carefully.

"No, I'm from Kenya."

"Ken...?"

"Kenya, that's in East Africa."

He extended a hand towards me. "I'm Inayat, Inayat Shah."

His hand felt tender in mine. "Amar, pleased to meet you."

As we walked out of the main gate, I asked him if he would like to go to a nearby pub for a drink. Inayat was even thinner than me; about five feet nine, slightly balding with deep dark set eyes, very alert, almost smouldering.

"I do not drink, but okay, I'll come with you for company. I can have a Coke."

We found a quiet table at *The Old Tom*, on St. Aldates. It was named after the bell in Christ Church College's Tom Tower. The pub always attracted an even blend of students and locals. For that reason, and also its proximity to the college, I had begun to frequent it.

We exchanged more pleasantries and talked about how imposing the college was and the lecturers-especially Donald King, who most students regarded as gay.

"Iran is a long way from Oxford," I said, trying to figure out exactly where it was in relation to England. "Do you like it here?"

His quick reply surprised me. "No! I do not like this place," he replied earnestly, leaning forward and peering directly into my eyes. "I had to come."

I was curious. "*Had* to come?"

Inayat seemed a bit uncomfortable that I was seeking some sort of explanation. He fidgeted with his drink and finished it with a few long gulps. For a minute I thought he was going to make a hasty retreat.

"Would you like another drink," he asked, in a dry tone, pointing to my nearly empty glass.

Not quite enjoying a beer against his Coke, I asked for tomato juice. By this time the bar was filling up fast with students and Inayat, shy as he was, took no less than ten minutes in being served. I was beginning to regret the second round.

As he sat down, he asked me if *I* liked Oxford, the College, England, to which I replied in affirmative.

"I had to come," he repeated.

"*Had* to come?" I asked again.

"Yes, I love my country and I wanted to stay there, to go to the university in Tehran, but ..." His voice trailed into silence.

"What happened?" I asked.

"Please, do not tell anyone," he said lowering his voice. I realised that he had been bottling up something and wanted to get it off his chest. With no friends in a foreign land, his frustration was multiplying fast.

He found his voice again. "My father wanted me to leave the house – no, not just the house, but also Tehran."

"But *why?*"

He lowered his voice even more. I strained forward to hear above the cacophony in the room.

"My father was married to my mother for twenty-two years. I am one of the four sons and I have three sisters. Then one day, just like that, he said, he wants a second wife."

"Isn't that fairly common over there," I said, trying to prompt him by participation.

"Yes... no, not when a man has been married for that long. He is almost fifty! And he wanted to marry Sania, who was only seventeen years old!"

I peered at him from above the rim of my glass. "So did he marry?"

Inayat was looking uncomfortable, his knuckles white against the Coke.

"Of-course; he is very rich, and very powerful, much feared in our community. We all objected in vain."

"*We?*" I asked, coaxing him, trying to mirror some of his final words, rather like a psychiatrist.

"Mostly my mother and I. But my other brothers and sisters objected too. Other relatives and friends also did not like what he was planning to do, but in front of him they kept quiet." He shrugged a shoulder and looking down at his drink, shook his head in despair.

"But why did he want you to leave the family home, did *you* object the most?"

"Yes, I loved my father, but what he was doing was not right. Sania wanted to study Art at the university- she had a chance for a scholarship. Her dreams were shattered. Her parents were poor and in no state to object."

The tragedy was beginning to dawn on me.

"Is she studying Art now?"

Inayat's eyes were moist. He blinked a few times to dry them. "No, she is just his young wife for pleasure that my mother can not provide now. He made a deal with me- he would pay for my education and provide me with a generous allowance; but only if I left Iran!"

I was shocked. How callous. But something still puzzled me.

"Just you?"

"Yes."

"But why is it that just *you* had to leave Iran? Others objected too. So why didn't—"

He looked directly at me and spoke in earnest, "Because... because Sania was mine!"

I wasn't prepared for this. I stared at him in silence. My heart went out to him.

Inayat seemed distraught. He loosened his top collar button before speaking, "Worst thing is, my father *knew!*"

CHAPTER 9

I took a coach from Headington to London and made my way to Paal Uncle's house. They were delighted to see me. "Tell us all about your college? Are you studying hard? Do you like England? How are Mr. and Mrs. Woods?"

"Everything is fine," I replied, "I've made a few friends, please don't worry about me." Sensing something different about her, I commented, "Auntyji, you look different."

"You noticed!" She screeched, beaming and pointing to her eyes.

She looked younger somehow, but I couldn't quite pinpoint the change.

"Paro's wearing contact lenses," Paal Uncle explained proudly. Lowering his voice he whispered, "Birthday present."

"Are they safe? I've heard they can damage the eyes."

"Oh, they are okay; so many film stars are wearing them these-days," he said, not very convincingly.

She looked good in them, "Happy Birthday for tomorrow, Auntyji. I've got you a present, but it will have to wait till tomorrow."

"No no, no I want it now."

"Okay, but please don't open it till tomorrow!"

"Thank you," she said excitedly, touching my cheek with the tips of her fingers.

Paal Uncle cleared this throat. "We are going for a posh meal tomorrow."

She turned to face him, "Where?"

"You shall find out tomorrow," he teased.

At breakfast, the next day, over a hearty omelette and masala tea, Paro Aunty opened my present. "Paul, look; what a lovely watch! *Amar*, you shouldn't have!" She squeezed my hand firmly.

Paal Uncle came around the table to examine the watch. "It's lovely; wear it tonight, for dinner."

The day flew by. A couple, Mr. and Mrs. Mehta, who I had briefly met once before, came with a bunch of red roses for *the birthdaygirl*. We watched a bit of the Dick Emery Show and after tea drove towards London, in Mr. Mehta's car, as Paal Uncle had made it known that he would be in no state to drive after 'the birthday meal'.

"Oh, come on Paul, tell me where we are going," Paro Aunty asked, punching him lightly.

"Wait and see; I'm sure you'll like it."

It was only when we turned into Regent Street that she guessed correctly, "Veeraswamy!"

Everyone cheered.

We enjoyed it- the food, the service, the company, Mr. Mehta's jokes- some new, some old and heard many a time, but it was the way he told them.

Paul uncle drank twice as much as Mr. Mehta, who drank twice as much as me. The ladies had about half as much as me. During the three hours in the restaurant, I managed two glasses of red wine and only stopped when I realised that on my way to the loo, before the dessert, I was a bit unsteady. I was terrified of saying or doing something silly in front of the others.

The Mehta's dropped us home amid singing and laughter and repetitions of "Bye", "Ta-Ta", "Sweet dreams" and "Don't do anything I wouldn't." I was feeling happy and light-hearted.

Paal Uncle gave me a hearty hug and declared that he was retiring for the night *tout suite.*

"*Lala Salama,*" I said, knowing full well that he didn't understand a word of Swahili.

"Lal— what?" he enquired, turning around.

"Sleep well," I replied, suppressing a laugh.

Paro Aunty asked me if I wanted some hot chocolate. I declined and she shouted to Paal Uncle as he headed for the bed, "Paul, I'll get you a hot chocolate, okay?"

"Sure Paro, and a glass of whisky as well," came a reply from the top of the stairs.

"Whisky? In your dreams," she shouted back, laughing, "and brush your teeth before crashing on the bed."

I was about to slip into bed when I heard a gentle, almost timid knock at my door. Surprised, I opened it a few inches. Paro Aunty was standing against the light with a mug in each hand, the smell of hot chocolate drifting towards me.

"Fancy a hot chocolate?" she asked softly, uncertain as to whether she should be doing this at all.

"I... I didn't... I thought this was for you and Uncleji."

"Yes, yes," she spoke in a low voice, leaning forward. "He's fast asleep, snoring like a drunken sailor. Would you like his drink?"

In the few seconds that I took to reach a decision, she entered the room and made herself comfortable at one end of the bed.

"Here," she said handing me a mug. "No point wasting it."

I took the steaming drink and sat at the other end of the bed. The room grew small. "Uncleji had a great time today, so did I, of course. Hope you enjoyed your birthday?"

"Yes, and I'm glad you came" she said sincerely. I noticed, paying more attention to her on a one to one conversation, how even and white her teeth were when she smiled.

"Food was excellent."

"Yes."

"The Mehtas are nice."

"Yes."

"I hope you liked the watch."

"Yes... I do."

We both took a few sips. The house was quiet. Somewhere, downstairs, I heard a few chimes.

She was silent for a while. "Are you happy in England?"

"Yes, although I do sometimes miss everyone at home."

"Do you like coming here to us?"

"Yes, of course, thanks. If it weren't for you and Uncle, I'd probably have returned home by now. "

We continued talking about college, my friends, my accommodation and so on. The conversation wasn't really taking any direction. Suddenly she moved nearer and surprised me with a direct question, "Do you have a girlfriend?"

I was taken aback. "No," I answered, flustered.

"Not yet, you mean," she said, leaning back. "A handsome boy like you, it won't be long before you have girls queuing for you."

"No, no, I'll be lucky to have just one," I replied laughing nervously.

She took another sip from her mug. "We've never had children, you know," she said softly with a far away look.

I had often wondered why, but didn't think it was my place to enquire.

"We didn't want to start a family for the first few years we were married. Then, one by one our friends started having babies. We would be invited to parties or dinners and they would talk endlessly about their wonderful babies, the nappies, the first words, the first walk, nursery schools, on and on, Paal and I felt left out and gradually our links broke."

"What about the Mehtas, do they have children? You seem to get along with them very well."

"Oh yes, they are lovely. They have one child, a boy about your age." She grew quiet as if trying to imagine what the boy looked like. Shaking her head slightly and sighing she said, "He was a lovely boy, full of life, always running up and down the stairs. You know, he was the junior tennis champion when he turned sixteen..."

I was puzzled. "You said, they *have* a child, yet you say he *was* a lovely child?"

"Oh yes," She replied with a far away look. They still have him... but they don't *have* him."

Her smile was a mile away.

"Is this some sort of puzzle?"

She shook her head. "No, you see one day, he was hit by a car at a zebra crossing. The car never stopped, and the driver was never found. Ajit, poor Ajit, he not only lost both legs but also his speech and memory."

"That's awful! Where is he now?" My heart went out to the Mehtas.

"Ajit was in hospital for months. Then they brought him home. Nirmala gave up her job to look after Ajit. They struggled for four years. But Shatru was very busy making ends meet and poor Nirmala had a nervous breakdown. They moved from a three-bedroom house to a smaller place and Shatru still had to work all hours to make ends meet. It was only when, Shatru started suffering from angina that they decided to send Ajit away."

I was horrified! "Send him away? What do you mean?"

"Nirmala's parents live in India- Shimla. They took him over there and left him with the grandparents. I know it sounds callous, but the arrangement works well. Nirmala started working again and sends all, every penny of what she earns to her parents. Her parents in India are poor, and with Nirmala's money, they can afford to have a full-time nanny to look after Ajit. They have even extended their house from two bedrooms to four. Nirmala may not earn much by our standards, but in Shimla, her one month's salary is what two doctors would earn there."

I could see the pragmatism in the exchange between money and care.

"And what about you? Why no children?"

She put a hand to her forehead and moved it all the way to the back of her head. I noticed how fine and shiny her hair looked. As she released her hand, some strands of hair fell sideways, slightly covering part of her face. With the contact lenses, she looked even prettier, the lack of make-up accentuating to her good looks.

"Well," she sighed audibly, "we just couldn't. When all our friends had their *betas* and *betis*, we thought we would join them. We had our own flat, car and money left over for holidays- what next? Babies of-course. After two years of trying, we went to our doctor for advice. He recommended all sorts of tests and gave us dozens of leaflets."

I shrugged my shoulders in a helpless gesture, "Then?"

"Paul and I had a tête-à-tête. In fact many serious talks, here, Athens, Rome- wherever we travelled to. What was the point? Either Paul couldn't, or I couldn't! What would be the point of finding out who was the guilty party? Perhaps we are both incapable! What good would it do to go through life blaming the other, or ourselves?"

"So you never had the tests?"

"No, we tore up the leaflets and never talked to the doctors about it."

I was seeing my aunt in a different light, the get-on-with-it-woman. "No regrets?"

"Well... they say, a woman is not complete unless she's had a child... you probably wouldn't understand it. Paul doesn't. But you know; I have now accepted life as it is."

"*Accepted* life?"

"Yes, it is very consoling. Accept everything that happens, like what happened to Ajit. Why are some born in royalty and others in slums? Why do some die in childhood and others live to hundred? In death, why do some go in seconds while others linger in pain for years?"

"You seem to have a lot of faith in God," I said encouragingly, "but don't you think kismet is merely a residue of our deeds?"

"Call it God, kismet, deeds or some force, whatever. I have merely persuaded myself to accept what happens." She remained silent for some time fidgeting with a ring on one of her fingers and looked at me with a smile. "Meanwhile, I believe in enjoying each day as it comes, for who knows if tomorrow will ever come."

I took my last gulp and exulted in the concentrated, sweeter chocolate at the bottom of the mug. "That was lovely, Auntyji."

"Must you call me Auntyji? It makes you sound too young and me too old. Aunty will do." She finished her drink and walking past me said gently," I enjoyed our little chat. If there is anything you need, don't be shy to ask." Just then her perfume, worn generously for the birthday treat, hung sweetly in the room.

"I'm fine; you are most kind, Uncleji too."

She stretched her arm towards me. I thought she was doing so to take my mug. Just as I proceeded to hand her my mug, she ruffled my hair lightly, and said, "Good night Amar."

CHAPTER 10

A flurry of snow greeted me one evening as I stepped out of college. Despite the cold wind beating against my face, I enjoyed my walk up Gipsy Lane to Headington, much of it uphill. It reminded me of Kilimanjaro. I then thought of Rajesh's accident and my mind went back to what Paro Aunty had said about accepting life as it comes. I missed my friends, a penalty to be paid for gaining further education.

By the time I reached my room, I was slightly out of breath. The long walk in the snow against the cold wind had numbed my ears and feet, and my nose looked like a ripe tomato. Even with the protection of the military-style overcoat which I had recently bought, my bell-bottoms were soaking wet. Whilst changing into a pair of dry jeans, I heard the customary pre-dinner knock at my door. "Dinner's almost ready, Amar."

"Thank you, Mrs. Woods. I shall be down in a few minutes." I took a deep, appreciating breath, "Roast lamb?"

"Yes, I know you like that."

A few minutes later, I sat at my usual place at the dining table facing the garden. The snow was gaining momentum and beating softly against the French doors. "What's this, only two for dinner?" I remarked, observing the two plates opposite each other. There was no plate for Mr. Woods.

"Henry doesn't feel too good, been in bed since breakfast."

"I'm sorry, nothing serious I hope. Has the doctor been?" This wasn't the first time that Mr. Woods had been unable to join us for a meal. He sometimes felt poorly as a result of his asthma and a weak heart.

Mrs. Woods continued bringing the lamb and gravy to the table. "He'll be all right in a day or two," she said casually.

Of all the meals Mrs. Woods prepared, roast lamb was the one I liked most. She bought a good cut from a butcher on London Road near the Polytechnic, juicy and without the grizzle. The gravy was always rich and dark. "Mrs. Woods," I had often remarked. "I have eaten roast lamb in two continents in fine restaurants, but yours is out of this world."

Prunes and custard followed the lamb. I loved custard but not so the prunes. Some time back, Mrs. Woods had noticed this and remarked, "They are good for you- eat up. Just three prunes a day give you your daily intake of iron, and they help in the mornings. You might not appreciate them at your age, but wait till you are my age- you'll be crying out for them."

"Mrs. Woods, can I have *two*, until I am your age?"

I studied for an hour or two, before going down for my usual tea and biscuits and to watch the News at Ten. It was the one time that we all assembled in the lounge, which was warmed by a log fire, throwing shadows on the heavily patterned wall-paper, the pattern almost matching the flowery pattern on the carpet.

Alastair Burnett, Mrs. Woods' favourite news-reader became part of our evenings.

"It's always the same," she remarked, "IRA bombings and soaring unemployment. We should pull the troops out and let them sort out their mess. And as for the unemployment, I always said it was a mistake joining those Europeans! We've got this decimal system which I do not understand, some tax on sales..."

"VAT," I interrupted. "Value Added Tax."

She ignored me. "You mark my words; it's only a matter of time when we will have litres instead of gallons, grams instead of ounces and kilometers instead of miles!"

"And Centigrade, instead of Fahrenheit," I added, rubbing salt to wound.

Again she ignored me.

"Teddy's government is doomed, you'll see, the Tories will be out next time, and Wilson will be back. "You mark my words, one day we'll be fed-up of Europe and leave it."

"How is Mr. Woods?" I thought it would be wise to change the topic, and simultaneously, seem interested in home matters.

"I left him some soup and rolls, but he hasn't touched anything."

"Shouldn't we fetch a doctor?"

"No, he'll be alright."

I was fast asleep. "Amar! Amar! Wake up..." The voice sounded familiar but apologetic. *Was I dreaming?* Suddenly I detected the urgency in Mrs. Woods' voice and her hand on my shoulder.

"Mrs...?"

"Amar, I knocked... It's Henry..."

Tears were flowing down both cheeks.

There was no time for questions. I jumped out of bed and rushed to their bedroom. Mr.Woods was lying still, eyes closed, straining to breathe. "*Thank God he's alive!* We need to call an ambulance!" I shouted. I needn't have, for Mrs. Woods was standing right behind me.

I rushed downstairs and rang 999. After what sounded like minutes a voice asked politely. "Which service please?"

"Ambulance! Rose House, London Road, Headington, please hurry!"

Mr. Woods was admitted to Radcliffe Infirmary within an hour, just as dawn broke, revealing a fiery red sky. Mrs. Woods was still distraught. "You were right," she kept telling me, "We should have called a doctor last night."

It was my turn to say, "He'll be alright." I hoped there was enough conviction in my voice to soothe away some of her distress.

The doctors and the rest of the staff were courteous and extremely attentive. They attended to Mr.Woods immediately and kept us informed of his state. We were offered tea or coffee at regular intervals. I had heard how good the National Health Service was and this only confirmed the public belief.

A smartly dressed man in a starched white coat beckoned us into an office along the corridor.

"Good morning," a young man addressed Mrs.Woods looking up from the paperwork. "I'm Doctor Manning. Your husband will be fine, he's developed severe bronchitis and is in a mild form of coma, but he'll live. Good thing you called the ambulance in time, another hour and...." He shook his head.

"Thank you, Doc..." Mrs.Woods broke into a quiet sob, clutching my elbow tightly.

Mr. Woods stayed at the hospital for six days before returning home. He had recovered enough to eat and drink, though weakness caused him to stay in bed almost all the time.

One evening, I popped into his bedroom for a brief chat. "How are you feeling today, Mr. Woods?"

For a few seconds, he looked blankly at me. Just when I thought he had lost his senses, his eyes lit up. "Graham, you've come back!" he seemed pleased to see me and extended his hand slowly in my direction.

I held his hand, puzzled. "I'm here. Can I get you something?"

"Tell me about the war."

"What war?"

"Did we win?"

I looked at the helpless man lying before me. What was he living for? Did he realise the fine line between life and death, between hope and despair?

"Yes," I whispered. "We won."

Later, over dinner, I asked Mrs. Woods who Graham was. She fell silent. We continued eating, occasionally discussing the weather. Later, I helped her wash the dishes, silently, wishing I hadn't asked the question.

Later still, I joined her for coffee and a biscuit over News at Ten. Without saying a word, she passed me some photographs- black and white fading at the edges. I could tell they had been preserved carefully, lovingly, for many years. All the photographs showed a person that I could not identify. I scanned the faded grainy photographs and lay them on the table. "Graham?" I asked, pointing to a young boy, no more than twenty by the entrance of a building, which looked remarkably like Christ Church.

She dabbed her eyes with a tissue, nodding gently, "Our son."

I took a closer look at one of the photographs. Graham was a tall, slim young man with a boyish freckled face. As with the other photographs, he was smiling, seemed like a happy, fun-loving boy.

Mrs. Woods cleared her throat. "Graham studied History at Christ Church. He loved his books and had no desire to join the war. But Henry... he insisted that Graham fight for his country." She pointed to another photograph. "That's him at the station. He boarded the train five minutes later and..." She wiped a tear. "We never saw him again."

I was deeply saddened and took little interest in the television, beaming pictures of a building blown-up by the IRA.

Christmas holidays were very quiet in Oxford. Despite the decorations and lights, the city seemed deserted with most students leaving it in preference to their hometowns and families. Paal Uncle rang me during the break and said I would be most welcome to spend the next few days with them. They had taken annual leave until after New Year. Not wanting to impose, I made an excuse that I had to finish a college assignment. "Amar, you can finish it here, we won't disturb you," he insisted.

"No Uncleji, I need to look up books in the reference library," I lied, hating to have to do so.

"Oh- ho look, speak to Paro."

"Amar? Why don't you come? It will be fun, your first Christmas! You are supposed to spend it with your family, not with your landlord."

"Auntyji, I have some work that I need to finish."

"Okay, okay, study these next few days and come for Christmas, okay?"

"Okay, thanks, I'll be there on Christmas Eve."

Just as I put the phone down, it occurred to me that I should be buying Christmas presents. The next morning before lectures, I walked over to Marks & Spencers at Westgate Shopping Centre in Queens Street and bought leather gloves for Paal Uncle and Paro Aunty- black for him and buff for her. That didn't take long, but then I was at a loss as to what I should get Mr. and Mrs. Woods. I walked aimlessly from section to section. Christmas! My frustration must have shown, for a charming shop floor girl approached me and asked if she could be of any help. She introduced herself as Gina.

"Sure, I'm looking for a Christmas present for my landlord and his wife."

She cocked her head to one side. "Now let's see, how old?"

"Nineteen,"

"Very funny, how old?"

"Around eighty."

"Would you consider a combined present, or do you wish to give each a present?"

"Separate, please."

"May I suggest bedroom slippers for both, or one of them?"

"Excellent, slippers for both- black in men and... brown in ladies." I made a selection in less than two minutes. "You've saved me from a lot of headaches, thank you so much."

She smiled; genuinely glad to be of help.

"Thanks, you've been most helpful," I said, relieved and grateful for her assistance and the time she had devoted to me.

"Do come again," she said, smiling.

Just before I exited the store, I turned back to spot her. She was talking to some customer. *Very pretty*, I thought. A second later, I almost fell over a guide-dog.

CHAPTER 11

I arrived at Paal Uncle's place late Christmas Eve. He and Aunty were delighted to see me. "Amar, *beta*, why didn't you come sooner, we've missed you."

"Course work," I lied, stepping into the warm lounge. "Oh, what a lovely tree!" In the far corner stood a five-foot Christmas tree covered in tinsel and little white lights.

"Have you had dinner?" Paro Aunty enquired. "There's some lamb biryani in the fridge."

"Thanks, Aunty, I'm famished."

The biryani was excellent, succulent lamb pieces with coloured rice, roast potatoes and fried onions. I tucked in with gusto.

"It's Hyderabadi."

"What?"

"The biryani, it's the Hyderabadi recipe, cooked slowly, for hours in an air-tight cast iron pot," she explained.

It reminded me of home. Maa cooked something similar, but I just took food for granted back home. I made a mental note to compliment her in future. "I'll have some more tomorrow if there's any left."

"Oh no," Uncle cut in, "tomorrow, we are invited to the Mehtas for roast turkey. We always do that, Christmas lunch at their place and New Year's lunch at ours. You'll love it there." As he said that he winked at Paro Aunty, the significance of which I would discover the following day.

As I came down the stairs, Paal Uncle and Paro Aunty greeted me warmly and we exchanged Christmas Greetings. I handed them the gloves, "Merry Christmas."

Paal Uncle smiled broadly but made a face. "Why have you spent so much money? Thank you; I've always wanted leather gloves."

Aunty joined in. "You shouldn't have!" Leaning forward and standing on toes she kissed me lightly on my forehead.

"And now," Paal Uncle announced, "something for you." He handed me a carefully wrapped package. "What is it?" I enquired.

"See for yourself," he answered, beaming.

I ripped open the package quickly. "A tape- recorder; thank you so much."

"Let's ring *Bhai Saab*," Paal uncle suggested, excitedly walking over to the phone by the dining table.

We tried several times without any response. "Perhaps they've gone to Mombasa for a short holiday," I explained.

Over breakfast, Paro Aunty asked me if I had given any presents to Mr. and Mrs. Woods.

I recalled the events this time the previous day, "Mrs. Woods something for you, for Christmas." She was touched and she asked me to give Mr. Woods his present in person.

Mr. Woods was lying still in bed, curtains half drawn. He looked paler than usual, staring at the ceiling, but probably not looking at it. As we approached him, he smiled feebly.

"Amar's got you a Christmas present," she explained. "We'll open them tomorrow, Christmas day."

He blinked a few times. "Christmas, tomorrow? Thank you, Graham, God bless you," he said weakly. "What is it?"

"Slippers," I said, taking his hand. "Hope you like them, they are fleece-lined, to keep your feet warm."

His eyes moistened visibly and he pursed his lips, trying to gain some strength before saying something, "Slippers? When shall I wear them, Graham?"

"Tomorrow," I said, "Christmas day." I was still holding his hand, which was turning cold. Noting that the other hand was under the sheets, I slipped his cold hand under the sheets too.

After lunch, just as I was finishing packing, Mrs. Woods handed me a package. "Merry Christmas, tomorrow, it's not much; these too keep feet warm." I felt the package and guessed that they were socks. "You shouldn't have Mrs. Woods; you have so much on your mind."

She waved a hand to dismiss the suggestion. "You are so good to us, God bless you."

Lunch at the Mehtas was not what I had expected. I had been informed that it would be just us and them, even at that I had resisted going.

"Come on, Amar, Mr. Mehta *specifically* requested that you come along. Isn't that right Paro?"

She nodded, "Absolutely; and what would you do sitting by yourself? It's Christmas. You need to be among friends and relations."

The Mehtas greeted us warmly and made a great play that I had come. "Doc and Laura will be here any minute. And Liz too," Mr. Mehta explained after the formalities were over. Paal Uncle gave me a sideways look, smiling mischievously.

"You have a lovely house Mr. Mehta, and an equally lovely garden," I said politely accepting a beer.

Paro Aunty joined in, "You know what? They have just bought a *beautiful* villa in Spain. We might be going over there next summer." The Mehtas beamed with pride.

I spotted a shiny black Mercedes approach the drive-way and park alongside Paal Uncle's Cortina, crunching the gravel audibly.

"Ah, Doc's here," Mr. Mehta sounded delighted, "always on time."

When greetings and handshakes between the three couples were over, I was introduced to Doctor Ramesh Sethi, his wife Laura and their daughter Liz.

I shook hands with all of them and noticed Mr. Mehta wink at Paal Uncle when I held Liz's hand.

I learnt that Doctor Sethi had finished his MBBS in India and was now comfortably settled in London with Laura, who was a practicing nurse at his clinic. I felt they were slightly over-dressed for the occasion. Liz seemed to be about my age, simply dressed in flared jeans and a tight mohair sweater clinging suggestively to firm breasts. She had inherited the best qualities from each parent- her height and slimness from her father together and a rosy complexion with sharp grey eyes from her mother.

"Liz is studying pharmacy at Bristol University," Doctor Sethi explained, a hand on my elbow. "She had five A' Levels, and could have gone for medicine, but it's her choice, pharmacy."

"Have you been to Bristol, Amar?" Mrs. Sethi asked.

"No," I answered. "I have heard of Brixton but don't know where it is!"

She burst out laughing.

"*Bristol*," Mrs. Sethi emphasised. "You must spend a weekend with us; we'll show you around Bristol and Bath- beautiful cities."

"That will be nice, won't it Amar?" Paal Uncle asked, mischievously.

"What's great about Bristol?" I enquired feebly.

Mrs Sethi took a deep breath. "Well, let's see... the University of course, and then there's the wonderful town center with cobbled streets, and oh, the world-famous suspension bridge..."

I raised my eyebrows.

"She took a step towards me before adding, "It is on the cliffs of the Avon Gorge. The views are simply..."

Realising that I had been set-up, Liz butted in, "Not as nice as Oxford, though." Then, to halt my embarrassment and change the topic, "Something smells nice, I'm starving!"

I gave her my thanks-a-million look. She smiled back, understandingly.

Drinks flowed freely and food arrived in abundance. Not surprisingly, I was seated next to Liz at a large dining table running along the garden, the winter jasmine spread on each side like wings, displaying bright yellow flowers.

Doctor Sethi quizzed me at length about Kenya, Nairobi in particular. He had never been there, but a friend of his had left India many years ago to settle over there. I wondered if that person might be none other than Papa. Laura joined in. "I've heard lions and tigers sometimes come into residential areas, isn't it dangerous out there?"

"Only rarely," I answered, then added, "We don't have tigers in Kenya or Africa for that matter."

Liz, perhaps embarrassed at the unwelcome attention I was receiving, came to my rescue again. "What are you planning to do after Christ Church- stay here, or go back to Kenya?"

"Oh, if I could get a job there I'd go, but jobs for non-Kenya citizens are not common. I'll see if I can find something here, otherwise, I might try America."

Paal Uncle was discussing house prices with Mr. Mehta and Laura, sitting opposite him... "Three bed-houses... £6,000... prices are likely to shoot up." Mrs. Mehta was explaining to Doctor Sethi and Paro Aunty how she spent all her time maintaining such a large house and garden "... It takes so many hours *each* day... back hurting... Mr. Mehta works such long hours... could do with some help..."

Liz was talking to me "... car..."

I was startled. "Pardon, sorry, I was miles away."

She leaned closer to me, "I said, do you have a car?"

"No... there's been no need to so far. Do you?"

"I'm taking lessons; dad's promised me a Golf if I pass."

"Lucky you."

The food was excellent. We stuffed ourselves with roast turkey, salmon and vegetables; drinks kept flowing.

After lunch, the ladies gathered in the kitchen to help Mrs. Mehta with the washing up.

The men sank themselves in comfortable settees sipping brandy and discussing what they thought the ladies were chatting about.

I didn't feel I belonged to either camp and hung around by the dining table, trying to keep a steady conversation with Liz. We were discussing the economic effect of joining Europe when spotting her father light a cigar, she went over to him, and to my amazement, came back with a cigarette between her lips.

"Hope you don't mind?"

I didn't answer.

Going back, Paal Uncle hit the kerb within minutes of leaving the Mehtas' residence and after another ten minutes drove through a red light.

"Paul!" Paro Aunty shouted. "I really think you should cut down on the drinking. It affects your..."

"Have I ever had an accident?" he shouted back. "Have I? There's no law as to how much I can drink, is there?"

"Okay, but it's dangerous, you could kill someone!" Paro Aunty was trying to control herself.

"Kill someone! Kill? I've been driving for twenty years, have I even hit a fly?"

I felt the tension rising and wished she would not pursue the matter; it seemed futile to do so after the event. As if my thoughts had been transported to her mind, she decided to remain silent.

As we approached Ealing, Paal Uncle sensing familiar territory lost some of his sullenness. "What did you think of Liz, Amar?"

"She's okay." I answered.

"Just okay?"

"Well, she's a bright girl, but—"

"But what?"

I felt a bit reluctant to answer. "I didn't like her smoking so openly, especially in front of her parents."

"Neither did I," Paro Aunty added crossly. "I didn't even know she smoked."

"She's probably picked the habit at university," he said in her support.

No excuse, I thought.

Indoors, Paal Uncle announced that he was going to have a little nap.

"Paul, aren't you going to give Amar company? Why don't we watch T.V, I'm sure there's Morecombe & Wise or something good today."

"You stay, I'm tired."

"Auntyji, you don't have to stay on my account. Why don't you have a nap too, it will do you good."

"Amar, it's only four in the afternoon. If I sleep now, I shall lie awake all night."

Paal Uncle gave aunty an affectionate hug and squeezed her waist playfully before departing upstairs. "See you later, Amar. Paro will keep you company," he shouted from the landing upstairs amidst hiccups and giggles.

Paro Aunty and I stood awkwardly in the middle of the lounge and for a second I thought she was going to follow Paal Uncle upstairs.

"Would you like some coffee, or tea?" she asked.

"Coffee would be nice. Look, you stay here and watch T.V; I'll make us some coffee."

"Oh, you are so sweet, thanks." She dug into the settee and dragging the coffee table closer to her, put her feet up, carefully avoiding the magazines.

I had almost finished making coffee when I heard her say, "Nothing good on TV. All three channels are showing rubbish." I turned around and almost bumped into her.

"Oops. Sorry Auntyji," I said, at the same time as she said, "Small kitchen."

"Let's take the coffee into the lounge," I suggested. "It will be more comfortable there, here's yours." I handed her a mug.

We settled down and talked about television programmes – seemed a good starting point. I then proceeded to say how wonderful the Christmas decorations were. She talked a bit about the sales which normally follow Boxing Day. We carried on talking about this and that not always looking directly at each other, followed by silences and hmms. She cupped her hands around the mug and looking into it allowed the steam to coat her face before taking a few sips. Finally, she said, "This is good, where did you learn to make such tasty coffee?"

I smiled but did not answer. "They are nice, the Sethis. Have you known them long?"

"Oh yes, and we've known Ramesh for a long time. In fact, when he came from India to study medicine, he stayed with us for a few weeks until he sorted out his accommodation."

"A bit like me."

She laughed. "He was so skinny then, and shy, extremely shy. He would look down at his feet when talking to me."

I laughed, "Really?"

She sipped her coffee for a few seconds and gave a giggly laugh. "Yes. Laura's had a positive influence on him. They worked together in some hospital in Liverpool for a while you know; she was a nurse and fell for him head over heels." She gazed beyond me for a few seconds as if she had spotted a spider or some stain on the wall. "He hurt his parents though."

I looked directly at her, "In what way?"

"Well... his parents who lived in Punjab were not well off. Ramesh was their fourth child, the other three girls. As you can imagine, he was their pride and joy. They gave him the best education they could afford... on borrowed money, sacrificed a lot to send him here to study medicine, and dreamed of the day when Ramesh would go back and make them proud. When he was in his third year, they even selected a girl for him."

I thought of Papa and Maa - always hinting about marrying in Nairobi after my degree. "That sounds familiar."

Ramesh went back home and got engaged to some Punjabi girl of a well to do family over there. There was no undue pressure; he *liked* the girl, showed us photographs and regularly exchanged letters with her. His family was ecstatic, over the moon, and ..."

"So what happened?"

She laughed lightly. "The usual, Ramesh met Laura and before they knew what was happening, a seed called Liz started growing..."

"Really? *Before* marriage?"

"Yes- part two of the story began. Ramesh was distraught. On the one hand, the parents and the girl back home and the family honour —"

I interrupted, "And on the other hand, a pregnant English girl."

Her eyes shone. She slapped her thigh, "Exactly! What to do now? Laura refused to have an abortion and in the end, he did the honorable thing, got married."

I exhaled. "Ah well, a good ending."

"No! The story has a final part!"

"I thought it had finished... happy ever after."

"Not quite; his parents disowned him!"

That startled me. "What!"

"Amar, you do not understand how it is in India. Our forefathers took such things very seriously. Once people gave their word, *vachan* as they called it, then they had to live or die by it. The family honour was at stake. They wrote to Ramesh to say that they had disowned him and he was never to return to their town in Punjab." Paro Aunty finished her drink and took a deep breath. "He was distraught, and you know, he hasn't been back -not just his hometown but India."

"That's sad," I said softly, "Their only son."

"*C'est la vie*, as they say."

We fell silent for some time; Aunty reflecting on past days and I wondering if Dr. Sethi had done the right thing.

I swirled my mug about to stir the last bit of coffee in it and finishing it in one long gulp placed it carefully on the edge of the coffee table. "How did you meet Paal Uncle?"

She looked surprised. "Don't you know? I thought *Bhai Saab* might have mentioned it."

"No," I said, encouraging her. She closed her eyes for a minute or so as if to recapture the bygone days, a smile flickering on her lips.

In that brief moment, it occurred to me that she was an attractive woman, very little make-up, yet very presentable, her movements always so graceful, her voice slightly nasal and very soothing.

She opened her eyes slowly, and taking her feet off the coffee table, sat up-right. "You know, we had a strange union, Paul and I- somehow or the other, we were destined to be together."

"Destined?" I was slightly puzzled and very curious.

"Paul and I were in the same college in Bombay, both studying literature. He was so dashing, still is I suppose, and in his cricket gear he had lots of girl-fans. Once, I was going to college on my bicycle and a cricket ball-you know how hard it is, hit my cycle. Down we went, cycle and I. Next thing I remember, Paul standing over me, apologising profusely. It was love at first sight."

Nothing new, I thought as if reading my mind, she said. "It wasn't plain sailing." His parents had already chosen a girl for him! Not just that, Paul's father had already given his word to Mr. Dhanraj that Paul would be their son-in-law and that their daughter would be *his* daughter-in-law. And a priest, who had been asked to check on their birth signs, had declared that the couple was ideally suited.

"Who was, or is Mr. Dhanraj?" I asked.

She moved closer to me. "Ah, I was coming to that. Mr. Dhanraj was a good friend of Paul's father. They had been buddies since childhood, but after college, Paul's father stayed in Bombay whereas, Mr. Dhanraj moved to Bangalore."

"So when did Paal Uncle's father see the girl?"

"You see, one day Paul's parents visited a relative of theirs in Bangalore. They took this opportunity to drop-in at their old friend, Mr. Dhanraj, who happened to be looking for a suitable husband for his daughter. Paul's parents took one look at the girl and were smitten. Good friends, a good family background, a beautiful girl, homely... what more could one want for their son? On arriving back in Bombay, Paul was ordered to go to Bangalore to see the girl."

"Then?"

"He refused, coming clean at last that he was in love with a college friend and wished to marry *her*" His parents, especially the father would hear none of it. Love marriage? No one in their family, going back generations had had a love marriage! Out of the question! What would everyone say? No such thing as love before marriage. Love was sacrosanct and supposed to develop and bloom *after* marriage. And furthermore, Paul's father had given his *vachan* to Mr. Dhanraj! His word! Did Paul understand the meaning of giving-a-word? The last breath can be sacrificed, but not a given-word! Oh no, a *vachan* once given can not be retracted."

The feud continued for almost two years, while Paul and I kept meeting each other at college. Paul was scared stiff of introducing me to his parents. And then a compromise was reached, during the Diwali holidays, Paul would at least go and have a look at the girl- if he didn't like her, then the matter could be reconsidered and some sort of excuse might be invented.

"So Paal Uncle didn't like the girl." I concluded.

"Wrong! Paul was head-over-heels in love with the girl. He spent a few days in Bangalore and wanted to marry her straight away."

I was confused, "So why didn't he marry her- what happened?"

Paro Aunty sat up straight, looking at me with amusement. "He *did* marry her!" she said laughing. "*And what's more, with the full consent of his parents!*"

I was lost. "So when... I mean why... what happened to her?"

"Nothing! I'm sitting in front of you!"

It took me a few seconds to put two and two together. I sat up straight. "Ah-ha, so *you* are Mr. Dhanraj's daughter? That's incredible!"

She laughed. "Elementary, my dear Watson!"

The next few days were spent indoors watching a lot of television from *Nai Zindagi Nai Jeevan* to Dad's Army, Steptoe and Son and News at Ten. When we got tired of television, we shopped for clothes at the Christmas sales. Sometimes we went for groceries at the Asian shops in Wembley. Paal Uncle was in high spirits and insisted on buying Paro Aunty a gold chain from one of the jewellers in Ealing Road. She objected outwardly, but checked at least twenty chains before selecting one. Later she confided in me, "I suppose he's feeling guilty about ignoring me lately, especially after the lunch at the Mehtas."

I sought clarification, "You mean the long nap?" If so, that was an expensive nap.

"He always does that you know, whenever he feels guilty about his behaviour, he buys me things. Depending on the level of guilt, the presents range from flowers to... oh, I don't know."

"Gold chains?"

"Oh, no, I've had more exotic presents," she said laughing.

"The mind boggles." Months later I mentioned a money-saving scheme to Paal Uncle- not drinking too much- not having naps – not going to bed alone – not ignoring Paro Aunty and not having to buy her expensive presents. He laughed at my suggestion. "Amar, you've got a lot to learn. Look, what's the problem? I have my fun- food, drinks and women." He shrugged, "Men *do* these things. As for the presents, what does it matter, it's all in the family!"

"What about the expense?"

He sounded a bit exasperated. "Take flowers for example, what's the problem? Paro's happy to arrange them in the vase, *I'm* happy to see and smell them. Now, take a necklace- she wears it, I look at it. So who gets more pleasure out of it, her or me? And as for the money, it's all in joint names."

There was no arguing with Paal Uncle.

Laura Sethi rang on New Year's Eve. They discussed what Paro Aunty was planning to wear that evening and what she herself should wear I could see from Paro Aunty's expression that Mrs. Sethi was not a regular caller and that there was some other reason for the call. I didn't have long to wait. A minute later, I heard my name mentioned. "Oh, yes, yes he's here... just a second, I'll call him... Amar!"

I approached the phone. She swung the phone behind her and whispered, "Liz wants a quick word with you." I pulled a face. Paro Aunty mirrored my expression, handing me the phone.

Just as I put the receiver against my ear, I heard what I assumed was the last bit of the conversation between Mrs. Sethi and Liz, "... but Mum, what do I say to him..."

"Liz?" I said

"Oh, hi Amar, h-how are you?"

"I'm okay, you?"

"I'm okay too, just fine."

"Good to hear from you," I said. "Busy?"

"Yes, yes shopping and lunches, you know." She had regained her composure. "I just thought I'd have a quick word with you- just to see if you are coming this evening."

I knew what she was talking about, but thought I'd make her suffer a little bit longer.

"This evening? What's happening this evening?"

"New Year party. Aren't you...?"

I pretended ignorance. Turning towards Paro Aunty and deliberately not covering the mouthpiece, I shouted, "Auntyji! Am I invited to the party this evening?"

She was having trouble keeping a straight face. I resumed my conversation with Liz, "I guess I'm invited."

"Okay," Liz tried to sound casual. "Well, see you tonight."

"I'll look forward to that," I said, displaying some enthusiasm before putting down the receiver.

Paro Aunty pulled a face.

CHAPTER 12

The New Year Party was, by today's standard, a fairly amateurish affair, a hired hall full of balloons, a tape recorder, admittedly with big loudspeakers, paper plates and food prepared by a local caterer, who also provided the drinks. But credit where credit is due, everyone worked hard to make it a success. There were at least a hundred people, representing three generations- four if the toddler in the mosses basket could be included as an invitee. It seemed that people had come more to meet others than participate in singing or dancing. The elders were greeted and hugged by the younger generation, out of respect, enquiring about their health and well-being. That over, the younger men lost no time getting drinks and chatting about work prospects while their wives engaged themselves in showing off their jewellery and clothing, and all this time young boys in smart flared, velvety trousers and girls in frilly dresses chased after balloons and drowned soft drinks from plastic cups.

Paal Uncle introduced me to some new faces who politely asked me what I did, where and why- only half interested, and moved along. The tape recorder started playing songs. No one paid any attention, the talk grew louder. After some time the music got louder, everyone raised their voices accordingly. After another half hour, the music got even louder. Still no dancing. Some people complained that the music was too damned loud... *can't have a decent conversation*. I spotted Liz at the other end of the hall and decided to swallow my pride and make the most of the evening. Paal Uncle stopped me en route. "Come, join us, Ramesh has brought some Champagne."

"I don't drink the stuff. You go ahead, Uncleji, I'll join you later." I looked around, no Liz.

Soon the elders sank in chairs at one end of the hall, the men took off their jackets and undid their stifling ties and the women placed their shawls and handbags on unoccupied chairs. Idle conversation flowed over samosas, pakoras and kebabs. Somehow, without prompting, the dancing began. It was fun- no rules, any movement sufficed. I gave Paal Uncle and Mr. Mehta company. Soon, Doctor Sethi and a few others joined in. Paro Aunty dragged Paal Uncle aside and the two danced more or less in tune with the music. Laura Sethi and Mrs. Mehta joined our group and after some time, Liz appeared from nowhere, quite unsteady and joined us. Other groups formed on the dance floor.

Someone shouted that there were just twenty seconds to 1973. Whistling and counting began- Twenty, nineteen... the music got louder, so did the whistling and the chorus-count... nine, eight... I spotted Paal Uncle holding Paro Aunty close to him... three, two, one... *Happy New Year!* I joined in the cheering and shouting. People hugged and wished each other Happy New Year. I joined in and at some stage felt a tap on my shoulder, "Happy New Year, Amar," Paal Uncle shouted, "And the same to you Uncleji." Arms and hands were everywhere! Paro Aunty approached me with a big smile and gave me an affectionate hug. Amidst the pushing and shoving, she raised her face and kissed me on my cheek, then wished me a Happy New Year. Later I went over to the Mehtas and the Sethis and shook hands with them. A few people I had been introduced to earlier, wished me well and an elderly lady that I had never seen before wished me good health and good luck. Two hands from behind me grabbed my waist. I turned around but didn't get a chance to see who it was. A mouth found mine, the tongue playing against my lips. I leant back regaining my composure. "Liz! Happy New Year!"

Mrs. Woods was cleaning the staircase when I opened the front door. She stopped the moment she saw me, "Happy New Year, Amar!"

"And to you, "I hope you and Mr. Woods are well."

She shuffled downstairs and arched her back to loosen the stiffness. "Yes, thanks. Did you have a good time? How are your relatives?"

"Fine," I replied. "Too much eating and drinking though. And how is Mr. Woods?"

"Much better, thanks, he gets about, though still not well enough to come down."

I put an arm around her shoulder. "Something smells nice."

She smiled. "Chicken and mushroom pie, will you be eating with us?"

"Not this afternoon, but tonight, yes."

"Go upstairs and say hello to Henry," she whispered as if Mr. Woods could hear her. "That will cheer him up a bit."

Mr. Woods was sitting in a chair by his bed, his shoulders bent forward and his chin almost touching his upper chest. I approached him quietly and placed a hand on his shoulder. "How are you feeling, Mr. Woods?" I asked gently.

His eyes looked up at me, and his chin moved forward just a bit. Smiling wearily, clearly pleased to see me, he whispered. "Graham, I'm...." He paused for a while, probably trying to string an audible sentence from the few entering his mind. "Better... did you see Churchill?"

"Church-? No, the war's over, we won, you need to rest and get better," I advised.

He gave me an appreciative look, eyes smiling more than the lips, "Good, that's good," he whispered.

"Don't forget to take your medication."

He closed his eyes and nodded faintly.

"I'll see you later. I need to unpack. Can I get you anything?"

He shook his head, chin pointing down eyes still closed.

My room was exactly as I had left it a week ago, everything seemed still, too quiet. I took off my shoes and lay on the bed, knees up, feet flat and exhaled loudly. Glad to be back, I closed my eyes. Pictures flashed by, in reverse order- the Goodbyes to Uncle and Aunty – Liz's kiss- blaring music- the gold chain- lunch at the Mehtas – the coach trip to Ealing.

The room was very warm and I was beginning to dose off. Mr. Woods made no sound; everything in the house was still, not a sound. Ten minutes later Mrs. Woods resumed the hoovering.

Over the next few days, I lazed around the house. With the College still closed for the Christmas holidays, there was little to break the monotony. I re-read some articles on Accounting Standards and the Impact of Inflation on Company Accounts., which did little to mollify the boredom I was experiencing. The tape recorder that Paal Uncle had given me helped until I listened to the few tapes I had at least three times.

One afternoon, Inayat called and we went for a long walk in the meadows and sat by the riverside watching some ducklings obediently following their mother around. Later, following Inayat's suggestion, we ended up in a cinema. I wasn't too keen on watching A Man Called Horse a second time, but at least it was warm inside. We enjoyed the film, especially Richard Harris' performance. It was refreshing to see a film where Red Indians talked in their own language.

"How about a bite?" Inayat asked afterwards. I knew Mrs. Woods would have prepared dinner, so I declined, still not over the post-Christmas lethargy.

After dinner, I had some time to kill before the News at Ten. I decided to write a letter to Munir.

Dear Munir

Many thanks for your recent letter. I hope you received mine, which I posted just before Christmas.

I was delighted to learn that you are enjoying and progressing well in the family business. You always were a fast learner. How's your car? I still haven't taken any driving lessons.

In the last letter from my parents, Papa mentioned that you helped him change his tyre. Thanks- I hope you were adequately rewarded.

I have just returned from a few days with relations, and had an eventful time- tell you more sometime!

Rajesh is doing well and went to Paris for the Christmas break (wouldn't tell who with). From what I hear, Sanjay loves it here and works in some pub on weekends and holidays. Afzal is enjoying his studies and is currently in Bradford, visiting relations.

I was sorry to learn that Azra's engagement broke-off, better now than after marriage, I suppose.

The weather is atrocious. The novelty of snow, frost, and fog is long over. I yearn for the bright sunshine and bougainvillea flowers of Nairobi. Do you still have blue skies with cotton clouds in the horizon? Perhaps you can exchange that with the grey skies and drizzle that we have been plagued with for the last few days.

A few days ago I had sweet corn, with lunch – Yuk! I thought of the corn that we've had on many occasions at Mwangi's stall, rubbed with lime, salt and chillies. Next time you are over there, please pass my Jambo to Mwangi and tell him how much I miss those dusky evenings at his stall, seated on his battered chairs, listening to the blaring music from his radio.

How are Masood and Miandad? Do they indulge in kite flying and cricket like we used to?

Give my best wishes to your parents.

Hope to see you during the summer break. Miss you.

Amar

I sat back and thought of Azra.

The winter chill lost its bite and spring arrived drudgingly, slowly, like a one-legged tortoise unsure of whether to venture out or not. Daffodils, forsythias and green shoots were welcome sights in the small neat gardens in Headington. Dog owners spent a little longer in the parks, joggers a little longer pounding pavements and birds a little longer chirruping.

Mrs. Woods was pensive. I often, especially at breakfast caught her gazing at their beautifully trimmed lawn with shrubs on the left and the far side. The apple tree at the far end was beginning to flower. We both knew what she was thinking- could this beautiful patch be maintained without Mr. Woods' help? Once, as the wind beating against the sliding glass-doors abated, she sighed audibly. She was looking towards the garden but seeing it with a faraway look. "It won't be easy," she said in a low voice, her wet eyes glistening.

I moved closer. "Mr. Woods will get better soon," I said not too convincingly. "A bit of gardening will do him good."

She continued looking into the distance at the bushes. After a while she shook her head, ever so slightly and turning around, said. "They are like children, you know; we grow them, nourish and feed them, doing our best to make them presentable, making sure that they don't go in the wrong direction..." She stopped mid-way.

I looked into her eyes and smiled until she smiled back. "I have to be off, Mrs. Woods," I said. "Please don't worry about what you can not change." I thought I sounded like Maa. "I'll help."

I kept my promise. As the days grew longer, I spent some time in the garden, sometimes in Mrs. Woods' way and sometimes of some assistance. What was more important to Mrs. Woods was not that I should be an expert in her garden, but that I was there to give her company, encouragement, moral support, someone to talk to after a hard day with Mr. Wood —cleaning and feeding him, giving him his medication on time and still finding time to do the household chores.

The daffodils gave way to bright red tulips and then the pink climbing roses bloomed all over the fence. The Virginia creeper against the dining room wall changed from dull brown branches to a lovely green tapestry covering every inch of the wall. The Wisteria too was in full glory, magenta flowers hung all along like bunches of grapes.

One evening after I had helped Mrs. Woods with pruning the honey-suckle, I broke the news about going to Nairobi for a month. "Mrs. Woods, my Dad's sent me a ticket to visit the family... I shall be leaving in a few days."

The shears in her hand stopped and she pursed her lips. She just nodded.

"It's only for a month," I said in mitigation. "I'll be back by the time the apples are ready."

She blinked a few times and nodded.

Bags packed, I was ready to leave. It was a lovely bright morning – just like Nairobi, except that there was not a cloud in the sky, whereas in Kenya there are always scattered clouds on the horizon even if the sun is shining all day. Knocking gently, I entered Mr. Woods' room. He welcomed me with a bright smile. "I'm off for a while, Mr. Woods. Hope you are much better by the time I'm back."

"Graham," he said in a voice that was barely audible. "You will come back, won't you?"

I moved closer. "Of course, I will."

He held my hand tightly, the grip surprised me. "Win the war, Graham," he whispered.

CHAPTER 13

Papa, Maa, Bimla and Nita were all at the airport! It was great to see them again. He looked more distinguished in spectacles and the early stages of grey in the hair. Maa was unchanged, but Bimla and Nita! I couldn't believe how beautiful they were turning out to be. "Lipstick, Bimla?" I questioned, as we took to the road.

"Amar, *bhaia*," she answered, blushing, "Brother, if you can wear aftershave, why can't I put a bit of lipstick?"

"So, why can't I?" asked Nita pouting.

"When you finish your A'Levels," Maa suggested.

"Amar, we've had the whole house painted," Papa said. "You'll like it."

"Oh no!" Nita said, crossly. "That was supposed to be a surprise!"

The Uhuru highway was well maintained, lined by trees and flowery bushes, but the side roads were dusty and uneven, with pot-holes jarring the back every now and then. Perhaps I had got used to the even British Roads I thought.

It was good to be back, I felt I belonged there. My room was exactly as I remembered it to be.

Maa commented that I looked different, more mature, more confident, and taller.

"What!" I asked, amused. "In just one year?"

Bimla joined in, "I want to go to England too, but Papa thinks I should study here."

"Why? I enquired.

Papa looked a touch guilty, "Let Amar rest first, we'll discuss later."

Bimla left the room in a huff without replying.

Maa appeared from the kitchen. "*Beta*, I've made your favourite dish, guess what?"

I looked up. "Fish curry and rice?"

"That's right, and it's Tilapia."

I laughed. The smell from the kitchen was unmistakable.

Later, Papa wanted to go to the Post Office to check his mail and asked me if I felt like coming along.

Sure, I thought that will be a good opportunity to see if Nairobi has changed since I left.

"Nairobi is changing by the day, new hotels and new office blocks," he commented as we drove past Government Road.

"Where's the money coming from?" I enquired.

"Amar, don't you get Kenya news over there? The Americans are pouring lots of money here, Britain as well."

"Why?"

"To prevent Kenya from turning pro-Soviet, of-course, America and the Soviet Union are both trying to buy friends all over the world. Just look at Asia - China and Korea are communist countries, India is pro-Soviet. And in Africa, most countries are turning pro-Soviet too. Kenya, at the moment, is neutral. America desperately wants access to the Indian Ocean and Kenya is ideal—"

I interrupted. "So, by pouring money in Kenya they gain friends here and have uninterrupted access all the way to the East."

"Yes, the Americans have extended their naval base in Mombasa. Kenya is flourishing. Oh look, that's Hotel 680, nearly complete, it wasn't there last year."

Nairobi had certainly changed - City under the Sun, trees and flowers everywhere.

Later, driving back, I asked what Bimla's plans were. She had done well in her A' Levels and could easily get a place at a university in England. "What does she want to do?"

He was silent for a while. "She wants to be an accountant, which of-course is commendable... very commendable, and she does have the brains for that."

"So what's the problem, Papa?"

"Amar, you probably won't understand. It's—"

I interrupted, "Try me."

He remained silent for a while. Knowing him, I realised that he was choosing his words. "Well, firstly, money. Do you know the fees for a foreign student is three times more than for a UK student? If Bimla goes to study overseas, in two years' time, Nita will want to go as well- it would be difficult to afford the fees—"

Again I interrupted. "So why did you send *me* overseas?"

Papa's voice took a stern tone, "You are a boy, our *son*."

I was amazed. "Papa we are in 1973, Kenya has been independent for for ten years, boys and girls are equal. Go to England, you'll see how girls are outperforming—"

This time he interrupted me. "Amar, we are Asians- whether you like it or not, girls are *not* equal. It's a fact. And this is not England. I can't afford to spend so much money on a girl's education, only to then get her wed as soon as she's gained some qualification."

"But Papa, that education surely will get her a better, more qualified husband."

"Who knows? The money we spend on her education can be used for her wedding. Imagine how much we are talking about. It would be enough to buy a house *and* a car, and more."

"So it's all about money, is it?"

He was getting irritable, not usual for him. "Isn't everything in life about money? And anyway, she can study Certified Accountancy here in Nairobi, why go all the way to England?"

"The experience, Papa—"

"What bloody experience?" he demanded harshly. "Are you suggesting I spend five times the money for her to be an accountant in England when she can get the *same* qualification in the warmth and safety of her family? And following that pay as much in dowry?"

"Papa, I see that... but living independently does make a better person of —"

"Better? What does better mean? Do you know how many Asian girls in the West never come back or never get married? Do you know how many British girls end up divorced? Did you hear of Pandey's daughter- qualified as an Architect in Edinburgh- married a local *gora*- two kids in three years? Where is she now? I'll tell you, back in Nairobi with both children! Who will marry her now? You tell me. Have you heard of any Indian divorce in Nairobi? No! Zero! Shall I tell you why not—?"

"Okay, Papa, you do as you please." We drove in silence for a while. On reflection, I saw his point and realised that he would never see mine. So why argue and spoil everyone's mood; after all, they were his daughters and his responsibility.

I placed a calming hand on his shoulder. "You are right."

The next morning after breakfast, I decided to visit the town centre with Bimla and Nita. Papa had a meeting with the Tax Inspector and Maa preferred to stay at home and cook. "Don't eat any of the fried rubbish there," she warned. "I'll be cooking chicken in thick coconut milk just the way you like it, Amar."

Bimla and Nita exchanged glances. "*I* don't like chicken," Bimla shouted, mocking.

"And *I* don't like coconut milk," added Nita, proffering a mischievous smile.

The town centre shops were very much unchanged except for the face-lift at Woolworths. We ordered drinks at

Rendezvous, a popular spot for mid-morning snacks and drinks. "Please add a small pinch of salt and black pepper in my passion fruit juice," I requested the waiter. I scolded my sisters for ordering fizzy drinks. "What's the point; you can buy that *anywhere* – it's just a bit of gas and sugar!"

They giggled. "How do you know? Have you tried Sprite in Kenya?" Bimla protested, poking me in the ribs.

I merely shook my happy head.

"Can we please order samosas?" She leaned towards me and spoke contendely,"And let's go to Kit-Kat-Cafe tomorrow. I love their faludas, but don't tell Maa."

We sat out in the sunshine and watched people walk by, men clutching briefcases, glancing at their watches- women killing an hour or so before dashing home to prepare lunch for their families, tourists in safari gear and zoom lenses. I just loved mid-mornings in Nairobi.

"Oh, look," shrieked Nita, "Balwant Aunty!" She was pointing at a middle-aged woman with a large zebra skin handbag across the road walking towards Macmillan Library.

"Who's Balwant Aunty?" I asked only half interested.

They looked at each other and burst out laughing at the same time. "You'll find out," Nita replied amidst uncontrolled laughter.

"No, tell me now."

Still unable to suppress their laughter, Bimla managed to say mutter something.

"Meal?"

"No, M-I-L."

"MIL? What's that?"

Bimla pretended to give the matter some thought. In mock seriousness, she said, "FIL's wife."

"Bimla, be serious," I said. "What's FIL?"

They both pretended to be deadly serious. "FIL is BIL's father," Nita replied, trying to keep a straight face.

"Is this some silly joke? What's BIL? Or rather, who's BIL?"

"Calm down, Amar brother," Bimla shrieked, placing her hand on mine and supressing laughter. "We thought everyone knew - don't they teach you that in England? BIL is SIL's brother of course."

Nita nodded emphatically, trying to keep a straight face.

It was sounding like some sort of puzzle. "So who is SIL?"

Bimla crossed her arms across her chest. "SIL? MIL's daughter!"

Nita whispered something in Bimla's ear. Bimla was thoughtful for a few seconds. Once again they both burst into uncontrollable laughter.

It struck me how lovely they both looked, laughing heartily with not a care in the world. The mid-morning sunshine fell on their faces, radiating warmth, and fun. They epitomised innocence and happiness. In that instant, I thought that perhaps Papa was right to keep them in Nairobi.

When we reached home, Maa greeted us at the door. "Amar, you have a visitor," she whispered secretly.

"Who?"

Before she could answer, I heard a voice from the lounge, "Amar! Come here, *yaar*!"

"Munir! How are you, you rascal?" We shook hands and hugged. "You look well."

Maa stood nearby, smiling. "Now come on, lunch is ready."

"Amar," Munir said in mock seriousness, "try the fish, I helped Aunty cook it, just the way you like it in rich coconut milk."

"Have you ever been inside a kitchen, Munir?" Bimla enquired.

He made a face. "Funny."

Over lunch, I told Munir a bit about Oxford and my college, how Rajesh, Afzal and Sanjay were doing. "Life is tough, but rewarding. In the winter, I used to leave home in the dark and come back in the dark. There are times when we don't see sunshine for days! But then in the summer months, there's sunshine from five in the morning to ten at night!"

"I'd still like to go there," Bimla interjected.

"Bimla, the grass may be greener over there, but remember for a few months in the year it's covered in cold frost."

"I'd rather be here," Munir said thoughtfully.

I studied his face, taut with a firm jaw and deep piercing eyes. "Tell me what you've been doing, Munir."

"Oh, I like what I'm doing. The first few months were a bit tiring, taking orders from everyone, but I soon got the hang of it. I suppose I can repair any car now. I've bought a Capri- goes like a bullet, *yaar*."

"Wow!" Bimla exclaimed. "Perhaps you can give me a lift to town, sometimes."

The conversation flowed with ease from one random topic to another. There was a question at the tip of my tongue several times, which I failed to ask, but luckily in all innocence, Maa did. "How is Azra, Munir?"

I sat still, not wanting to miss a single word.

"She's okay, Auntyji."

"Where is she now?"

"Oh, she's still in Pakistan, with our relations in Lahore."

"Why doesn't she come back?" I asked, trying hard to sound casual.

"*Abbu's* relations are convinced they'll find her a nice boy." I could tell that Munir was not enjoying this bit of the conversation. We continued eating for a while.

"That was delicious, Auntyji," Munir said finishing off, and holding out his plate devoid of a single grain of rice for Maa to see.

"I liked it too," I said. "Munir, you really must give me the recipe."

During my visit, I met Munir a few more times, but briefly. He worked long hours at his father's garage. Once we met late afternoon and took a long walk around the school and decided to have some corn and tea at Mwangi's.

Mwangi was overwhelmed to see me again. "*Bwana! Jambo,* It's good to see you again."

"*Jambo* Mwangi, *Habari?*" I said, happier to see his happy face.

We sat on his uneven-more-battered stools and enjoyed the steaming tea and corn. I dipped my half lime into a mixture of salt and chillies and rubbed it all over the corn. "This is delicious!"

Mwangi smiled his thanks, "How about some music, *bwana?*"

"Don't call me *sir*, Mwangi. I may be from England, but I'm still your friend- just call me *Rafiqui*. Have you forgotten?"

I looked around. Not much had changed, the pot-holes seemed a bit bigger and the roads, dustier. I commented on this.

"You've got used to English roads and streets," Munir remarked.

"True," I said. "Kenya's not doing too badly though- a lot of foreign money pouring in."

I wasn't ready for Munir's reaction, "Foreign money? Where? Do you see any? Is Mwangi going to see any?"

I was taken aback. "I hear the West is planning a lot of investment here- hotels, offices, hospitals, schools—"

Munir interrupted, "Nobody is helping the average man. Look around you. Do you see any change? I'll tell you what's really happening? The Americans are merely handing money to the politicians- just so they can keep them happy! Nothing goes to the poor! Corruption is a creation of the West!"

"But, the new hotels and—?"

Munir interrupted my protest. "You think the poor are going to stay in those hotels? Look Amar, all the West is interested in is to keep the Ministers happy, to keep Kenya away from the Soviets. They don't give two hoots what ultimately happens to the money. Most of it ends up in Swiss banks, accounts owned by Ministers."

I thought for a few seconds. "Okay, but if the West wasn't giving money to the Ministers, no one else would- so what's wrong? At least Kenya will remain democratic."

He looked at me incredulously. "What democracy? This is a one-party state. Does the average man in the street give a hoot whether he has a say in Government policy? All the poor want are a roof over their heads, food, electricity and some clothes. The average man here is not even interested in knowing *who* their leader is. Ask Mwangi. Tell me, Amar, do *you* have any say in how the British Government is run?"

"Yes," I replied, "I could vote if I was a resident of Britain."

"Sure, you put a cross on a piece of paper. But do you determine the policies? Do people have a say in whether the West should be in Vietnam, or whether Britain should be investing in nuclear arms, or whether—?"

"Hey, cool down Munir, perhaps you should enter politics." I tried to laugh but failed.

Munir exhaled to dispel his anger, but he wanted the last word. "Amar, the poor are getting poorer, the rich, richer. We could be heading for a civil war, or a coup."

"Mwangi, some mogo-chips, please?" I asked, hoping to diffuse the tension.

The days flew by. One afternoon, Maa answered the telephone and conferred with Papa in low tones. Bimla suppressed a laugh, placed a hand on her mouth and left the room. Nita followed suit.

"What's going on?" I asked.

Papa acted casually, "Oh, nothing, just a call from Jaspal."

"Who's Jaspal?"

"Just a friend, we are planning to buy some flats in Westlands together."

Maa decided to join in, "The Panesars are very rich, *Beta*. You should see their house as big as your Buckingham House."

"Palace," I corrected.

"Yes, yes, it's like a palace. And they've just bought a Mercedes from Germany."

I was getting a bit bored with this. "Not many mangoes in the garden this year."

"Amar, how do you fancy dinner at the InterContinental, this evening?"

"Papa, I'm free."

"That's settled then, dinner with the Panesars."

"Settled? No, they are your friends. I'll stay indoors."

Maa gave me a sharp look. "*Beta*, what will you do at home by yourself? Come along, the Panesars are paying."

"Settled," Papa declared. Then turning to me, "Wear something nice, that brown suit you brought from England." I thought I heard a squeal from my sisters' room.

We arrived at the InterContinental ahead of the Panesars. "Let's wait in the lobby," Maa suggested. She looked around nervously. "Bimla, tone down your lipstick."

A woman entered, accompanied by a smartly dressed boy of about sixteen and two even more smartly dressed girls around twenty looking remarkably similar. The woman saw us and rushed towards Maa. I was sure I had seen her before.

And then I spotted the zebra skin handbag. Bimla followed my gaze, "Balwant Aunty." She pinched my elbow and whispered, "Good luck." Only then did I realise the purpose of the meeting.

Introductions took place. The young boy was Bitu and the glamorously dressed girls were Billie and Bilo. As all this was going on, a smartly dressed man in a striking red turban made his way in our direction.

"Jaspal!" Papa greeted him. "Meet Amar, you know the others."

At about six feet four, he towered over me and almost crushed my hand. "Nice to meet you, young man, I've heard a lot about you."

"Only the good things as yet, Uncleji," Bimla added, pinching my arm.

Mr.Panesar put an arm around my shoulder. "Let's have dinner. I hope you are hungry."

During the lavish meal, I tried my best to differentiate between the Panesar sisters, but without success. They were both fair-skinned and had dark, soft fine hair practically down to the waist. They both had oval-ish faces and big bright eyes. I concluded that they must be twins. One of them seemed more relaxed and talkative, though when I spoke to the other, she was not hesitant in replying. I kept wondering which one I was supposed to impress. Bimla and Nita realised my difficulty and enjoyed the show even more.

Later, back in the car, I thought of protesting at the whole setup. Realising that that would only amuse Bimla and Nita and give Papa and Maa a chance to lecture me about my future, I decided to play things by the ear.

At last, Bimla found my silence annoying. "Well, Amar brother, did you like her?"

I decided to have a bit of fun. "Oh, yes, she's very nice, but I didn't like the zebra skin handbag."

"I'm not talking about Balwant Aunty!"

"So who are you talking about?" I asked in mock innocence.

"Bilo!"

"And which one was Bilo?"

"The one sitting opposite you," Nita said, throwing her hands in the air.

"No," I said, slowly. "I didn't like her much; I thought the other one was better looking."

Maa intervened trying to explain in her customary calm manner, "*Beta* they are twins. Bilo is the—"

"He *knows* that, Maa," Bimla said, exasperated. "He's just being silly."

Papa attempted to explain, "Amar, Billie does not wish to marry yet and they are looking for a nice boy for Bilo."

"So where do I come into all this; when did I mention marriage?"

"Families meet; boy and girl get to know one another. The rest is up to God."

"These things take time, *beta*," Maa cajoled. "No hurry, if you both like each other, you two can meet as often as you like and —"

"And next year you can get engaged," Bimla interrupted.

"And a year later you can get married," Nita added.

"And a year after that you can have a child," Bimla advised.

Nita covered her mouth trying to suppress her laughter, "And a year after that—"

"Okay, okay," Papa said hastily, realising that we were not getting anywhere. "Leave it now, we will talk tomorrow."

We drove in silence for a while. I wound the window down a few inches and breathed the fresh warm Nairobi air. I closed my eyes and took a deep breath. Bimla began humming something. I wound the window up. The humming became clearer. "FIL-MIL-BIL-SIL- la la la la." Nita joined in. "FIL-MIL-BIL-SIL- da da da da."

Maa seemed pleased. "That's a nice tune, what film is it from?"

Bimla and Nita giggled and joined in chorus "FIL-MIL-BIL-SIL..."

In that instant, it dawned on me what had been bugging me earlier. The references were to in-laws- Father, Mother, Brother and Sister. I decided in joining the fun half laughing, half-singing and shaking my head.

"FIL – MIL – BIL – SIL – no, no, no, no."

Bimla's jaw dropped. Nita bit her lip.

Papa didn't play cricket on the Saturdays that I was in Nairobi. He felt obliged to spend his available time with the family, especially as I was going to be there for just a few weeks. With only one Saturday before my departure, I coaxed him to play. Secretly, I half wanted to see Mrs.Webber; and perhaps Ribena again. Maa also thought that the exercise would do him good. Reluctantly, he rang the Club Organizer and made arrangements to play, which was to be against a team from Nakuru. Bimla and Nita were disappointed that I was going to be away all day.

"Why don't you *all* go," Maa suggested. "I will cook in peace."

"But Maa, we can't just take over the Pavilion, it's not a family game," I protested.

"Oh, don't worry; you can all help with the sandwiches."

Decision made, we accompanied Papa to the Gymkhana on Saturday morning. Just as we parked, Mrs. Webber came from a side door, waving. She must have recognised his car. On seeing practically the whole family, she expressed surprise. I wondered if she had met Bimla and Nita before. She looked no different and approached us graceful as ever.

"Amar! So good to see you again," She extended a friendly hand, which I held, briefly. It felt cool and soft in mine but stirred no special emotions. Giving Papa a friendly pat on the back, she exclaimed, "My, my, what angels do we have here?" He introduced his daughters to her and she gave them a gentle hug. "The family resemblance is striking."

We trotted off to the Pavilion balcony. Papa greeted some players and headed for the changing room. I felt good being on familiar territory with the past behind me. "You haven't changed a bit, Mrs. Webber."

She smiled, taking it as a compliment. "*You* have." She paused for a moment, "For the better. Just look at you, and such lovely sisters!"

"Not so loud, they'll get big heads," I joked.

Bimla decided to join in the conversation. "Can we help you with anything, Mrs. Webber?"

"Oh, you are such dears, yes, later, with the sandwiches and drinks. Mrs. Pereira will be helping too." Looking at me again, she said softly. "Amar, you must tell me *all* about Oxford. Your Dad occasionally fills me on some of the little details."

"Of course, but there's not much I can tell you that you don't already know. How's Ribena?"

She appeared slightly flustered. Answering as casually as she possibly could, she said, "Oh, she's fine. She's engaged to a Dentist and living with him in Lower Kabete."

I was taken aback; Ribena didn't appear to be of marriageable age when I last saw her a year ago. I felt I should say something. "Congratulations. Please pass that to Ribena when you see her next."

She smiled her thanks and gave a small nod.

Nita, perhaps getting bored of adult talk asked Bimla if she wanted to look around, and they both excused themselves, walking towards the other end of the Pavilion, Nita reaching for Bimla's hand.

Mrs. Webber watched them for a few seconds, and then placed a hand on my arm. "Are you happy in England?"

I answered flatly. "Yes, looking forward to finishing my studies."

"Would you settle there?"

"I suppose so, if I can get a good job there, otherwise America."

We talked about the weather, the changing seasons, television programmes, films, Paal Uncle, Paro Aunty, the shopping malls, cars, houses, Mr. and Mrs. Woods... She was touched when I described how Mr.Woods kept mistaking me for his dead son, Graham.

"And girls?"

I looked at her blankly, "Pardon?"

She dropped her voice. "I said, have you got a —?"

"No," I interrupted, and dropped my voice to match hers. "I'm friendly with one or two... but nothing serious."

She laughed. "Give it time. A fine boy like you... Oh look, they are on the field." The players were making their way towards the pitch.

The fielders and the two batsmen took their positions, Papa's team fielding. Sensing that the match was about to begin, Bimla and Nita turned around. Nita was still holding Bimla's hand. Watching the two of them walking towards us, Mrs.Webber waved to them to come and join us. "They are such lovely girls."

"Yes." I was thinking of how much they had changed in just one year, especially Bimla. I wondered if girls matured more quickly. Or perhaps, in my absence, they had taken over more responsibilities leading to more confidence and ability in conversing with people of all ages.

I briefly explained the cricketing rules to my sisters but it was clear that they were never going to be cricket fans. About an hour later, with the score at 64 for no wicket,

Mrs.Webber asked them if they could help her with the food. They were happy to leave the newly polished balcony.

I continued watching the match though my thoughts were mixed up- the pace of life seemed so much relaxed in Nairobi. The weather was always so inviting for outdoor activities and people had so much time for anything, be it relatives, friends, idle chat or sitting at a restaurant with a glass of beer and some snacks. I felt a tinge of jealousy for the residents. My thoughts were shattered by a surge in clapping and whistling. A player had just been caught at the boundary.

Over the next two hours, I chatted with a few familiar faces from the past who seemed impressed that I was studying in Oxford. "You must be brilliant, young man... Well done son... Make your Dad proud... Get a degree from there and you'll be made for life...Wilson studied there, you know..."

The Nakuru team was all out for 202. Papa was confident that Gymkhana would beat them, and so they did with four wickets to spare, Papa scoring a quick 33 off just 24 balls before he was clean bowled.

Just as we were leaving, I again asked Mrs.Webber to congratulate Ribena on my behalf. Jokingly, I said that I expected to be invited to the wedding. She in return wished me luck in my studies and "other things."

What other things? I wanted to ask, but didn't.

Maa was excited as she opened the front door. "Balwant rang."

Bimla pushed ahead brushing me aside, "What did she say?"

"Bimla," Papa said quickly, "let your Maa speak."

"What's all this about?" I enquired.

"Did they like Amar?" Nita asked excitedly.

I was half annoyed and half puzzled. Surely last night's dinner was no pointer to a marriage proposal. There was no indication from my part that I had any intention of looking for a life partner.

Maa seemed pleased with recent events. "Balwant was saying that they *really* enjoyed dinner last night." Then turning to Papa, "She and Jaspal both thought how nice our son is."

"What did Bilo think of Amar brother?" Bimla demanded to know.

Yes, I thought. What *did* Bilo think of me? How strange - parents seemed to have more of a say in selecting a son-in-law or a daughter-in-law than the two who would be spending their lives together!

Maa was taken aback, "I didn't speak with *Bilo*, only with Balwant."

I was now ready to protest. "But Maa, I do not want to marry as yet. I've still got to get my degree and after that, find a job."

Papa cut in quickly." Amar, no one is forcing you to marry. These are just discussions. Ultimately, you and the girl will make the decision. All we are suggesting is that you select her for your future."

"*Select* her?" I couldn't believe my ears. "Papa, she's not some object, like a... like a *car*, that I select and place an order for. Firstly, all this is too early. Secondly, we don't even know what *she* thinks of me. For heaven's sake, this is 1973. Things have moved on since your days."

"But, *beta*," Maa said quickly, "we are not asking you to marry her *now*, just say that you also like her and then you two can be engaged. Marriage can take place when you are both ready for it, maybe next year or when you finish your degree."

Papa came to Maa's support. "Amar, you don't know how much responsibility a daughter's parents have. The sooner the daughter gets engaged and married the better. Bilo is such a sweet little thing. She will be a good daughter-in-law to us." A sudden thought flashed in my mind - DIL. Bimla and Nita had forgotten to mention Daughter-in-law.

He was still speaking, "And Jaspal is such a decent chap. He and I are planning a big business deal..."

Another thought flashed in my mind. Was it the big business deal that was spurring the marriage deal? Was there a link? Surely, Papa and Maa did not think that marriage was a barter of some sort?

"Please listen to me," I said hoarsely. "I do not, as yet, have the slightest intention of getting married until I've—"

Maa interrupted me quickly. "*Beta*, there you go again. We've said so many times that we are not talking about marriage, just see her again - after some time, if you like each other, get *engaged*. Marriage can be later when you are both ready. Such good families and such nice girls like Bilo do not fall from the sky every day. Please *beta*, think of our responsibilities and also the Panesars."

For a minute, I thought that Maa was right. I saw the point that Papa and Maa were trying to make. No, I thought, it was *my* life and I had a right to decide when I wanted to marry, and to whom!

"Sorry Maa, Papa," I said as softly as I could to hide my anger. "I have given you my answer." I left the lounge. As I was walking towards my room, I heard Papa say, "He's now thinking like an English *Saab*."

CHAPTER 14

It was raining as the plane touched down at Heathrow airport at six in the morning. Why are week-ends always wet? I asked myself. As I exited terminal three a man with every inch of his arms covered in tattoos approached me, "Taxi?"

I nodded and gave him Paal Uncle's address. The driver took an unusually long route to Ealing. I was again struck by the smooth wide roads and discipline at traffic lights and roundabouts. The cars zooming past were in good condition and reliable. In a funny sort of way though, I missed the dusty, pot-holed roads of Nairobi with the old bangers and the occasional broken down car by the roadside.

Paro Aunty answered the bell, "Amar!" She instinctively put her arms around me and hugged me affectionately. "How are you?"

"Great. How are *you*? Where is Uncle?"

"Oh, he's out, getting his car fixed. He'll be back soon. How is everyone at home?"

"Just fine, they talk highly of you both. You must visit them sometime."

"Yes, I'd love to see Africa, and *Bhai Saab* and *Bhanji*, of-course. Have some tea."

"I'll just have tea, please. I had a full English breakfast on the plane. Can I have a quick shower though, if there's hot water?"

"Of-course; go upstairs."

I freshened up and went down. Tea was ready and a mushroom omelette was just coming off the pan. The kitchen was filled with an inviting mixture of smells- fresh tea leaves, eggs, and spices. Suddenly I was hungry. "I'll have a tinsy-minsy bit of the omelette if I may."

"Anything you like, Amar."

I handed her two elephant hair bracelets. "One for you and one for Uncleji. Kenyans believe that it brings luck and good health."

The doorbell rang. "See? Didn't I say this would bring you luck?"

She laughed a happy throaty sound. "It's Paul. I bet he forgot to take the key. Go and surprise him."

I flung open the door, "Uncleji!"

"Amar! How are you? When did you come? We weren't expecting you until next week. Why didn't you let me know? I would have picked you up from the Airport." He gave me a tight hug.

"And how?" shouted Paro Aunty from the kitchen. "How's the car?"

"What happened?" I asked.

"The gearbox, it's gone. I left the car and my keys with the mechanic and took a bus home. No need to worry. Tell me; how's *Bhai Saab*? And everyone else?"

"Very well," I answered. "You really must visit them sometime and see Kenya."

"Yes, when Paul's car is fixed," Paro Aunty said.

Paal uncle breathed in deeply, exaggerating the delight in the smell from the kitchen. "Your perfume smells lovely, Paro."

The days flew by. We took buses to the shops that afternoon and on Sunday, the tube to Marble Arch, where we spent mid-morning gazing at the paintings on Bayswater Road and then walked around aimlessly in Hyde Park. Seeing a crowd at the Speakers' Corner we hung around listening to various speakers insulting all sorts of politicians, especially Americans and British. Voices were turning hoarse at the criticism vented towards President Nixon for America's interference in Vietnam and Prime Minister Heath for his stand against the Unions in Britain. Paal Uncle was critical of the speakers. "In their own countries they would be thrown in prison for speaking against their leaders, we are too liberal here, democracy and secularism gone mad!"

I remembered something Munir had said to me a few weeks ago. He had asked me if democracy really gave people a say in how the Government was run. Whether or not it did, at least it gave one the chance to vent one's anger in public.

Another speaker was shouting at how all western women who chose to wear hot pants and mini skirts were mere prostitutes and would go to hell, where they would burn together with their disgusting clothes. Paro Aunty said in a low voice, "I bet his daughter goes to parties in a mini."

"Stand on a box, Paro," Paal Uncle suggested. "Speak your mind."

A few weeks later, I was reading an article on emerging markets seated in a deck chair in the back garden. Though small, the garden was well maintained. The fence at the bottom of the garden displayed pink roses as if they were at the Chelsea Show. The quiet in the hot sunshine would have long sent me to sleep had a bird stopped its continuous chirruping. Perhaps it was showing off some new song it had learnt this summer. Paal Uncle and Paro Aunty were both at work and were not expected back for another few hours. I had offered to cook rice with peas to accompany the chicken leftover from the previous evening.

I was halfway through the article and was just starting on my drink, a mixture of chilled milk and cream soda when the phone rang. Reluctantly, I put the magazine and drink down and made my way to the dining room. "Hello...." The phone went dead. On my way back the phone rang again. I hurried this time. "Hello."

"Amar?" a voice screeched in my ear.

"Yes, speaking."

"Guess who?"

"I'm sorry, I... I can't..."

"Liz."

"Liz?"

"Yes, Liz, you know?"

"Good of you to call, Liz; how are you?"

"I'm fine, thanks. Listen, if you don't have much to do, why don't we go out for a meal or a movie, sometime?"

I was taken aback but I could do with some company when Paal Uncle and Paro Aunty were at work.

"Sure, we could meet for lunch tomorrow... where?"

She answered quickly. "There's a good pasta restaurant near you, Ealing Broadway, close to the Odeon. We can meet outside the restaurant at... 12.30?"

Paro Aunty was not too pleased with Liz's invitation, "I just don't think she's suitable for you, Amar. Be careful of such girls, they'll take advantage of you. And tell her not to smoke in public, it's disgusting."

Paal Uncle was more relaxed with the whole issue. "Don't fret, Paro. Amar's not a child, I'm sure he can handle himself." He leaned closer to me and whispered, "Go for it, man, while you are still single."

Liz was dressed in a skimpy denim skirt and a loose low-cut cheesecloth shirt, her long slender legs ending in casual 'V' leather slippers. The sunglasses held casually above her forehead, supporting her wavy hair gave her a model-like appearance.

I couldn't help wondering why, when she was trying to be so friendly with me, I was finding it difficult to reciprocate. Was it because she was open about it? Was it because I perceived her to be *too* good looking for me? Or was it because she kept making the first move?

Ealing Broadway was at its busiest. Shoppers strolling with store bags, business people rushing towards their favourite lunch spots, not bothering to wait for the green man at the traffic lights.

It was a lovely day, sunny, blue sky with a faint hint of a breeze. I felt light-hearted. Liz smiled cheerfully, holding on to my arm as we stepped into *Bella Venue*. Lots of heads turned towards Liz as we waited by the door.

A minute later a waiter approached us. I stepped forward and was about to say something when he threw up his hands and beamed at my companion. "Lizee, Lizee, *Buon pomeriggio, signorina.*"

She responded accordingly, "*Luigi, come sta oggi?*"

He smiled broadly. "*Sto bene, grazie.*"

Liz pointed me to Luigi. "Meet Amar, a very good friend of mine."

He made a small gesture of a bow and greeted me extravagantly. "Amaro, is-a nice to meet you." Then turning towards Liz again, he waved a hand. "Lizee, I have the besta table for you."

We were seated by the window and presented with large leather-bound menus. "*Grazie, Luigi,*" she said.

I feared that this was going to be an expensive meal. "I take it you come here often?"

She replied hastily. "Not as much as I'd like to. Dad has an account here. All we need to do is order and eat."

"Hey, that's not on, I should pay at least my share," I protested, perhaps not too convincingly.

She laughed. "Tell you what, I'll pay today, you pay next time. No, better idea, why don't we see Bobby sometimes, you pay."

"Bobby? The Indian film? Is it good?"

"So I hear. It broke all records in India."

I realized that I was about to commit to another meeting with Liz, but felt trapped and concurred."

She grinned, "*Quid pro quo!*" Seeing my puzzled look, she laughed. "Latin - one doesn't get something for nothing."

"I'm impressed with your Italian... and Latin. Where did you learn—?"

She waved a hand and replied quickly. "I'm fairly fluent in French and Italian... As for Latin, I just know a few phrases. Do you speak any languages?"

I thought for a second or two, "*Si*, English."

She laughed, I joined in. "Very good, *molto bene*." She was thoughtful for a while, then added. "But you do speak fluent Hindi and Punjabi, unlike me."

"You seem to understand Hindi fairly well." I said encouragingly.

"Yes, a bit from listening to relatives and watching Hindi films, but it's not the same as speaking it confidently. I suppose you grew up listening to Hindi?"

"No, Punjabi. Like you, I picked up Hindi from movies. Most Indian languages are pretty flexible and easy to learn."

"How so?"

"Take for example... for example: *I am going to the shops.* In English there is only one way of saying that; subject-verb-noun. But in *desi* lingo one can start with either the subject or the verb *or* the noun."

Two bowls of pasta arrived, mine with chicken and broccoli, Liz's with roasted aubergines, sun-dried tomatoes and salad. She ordered a bottle of Chianti for us.

"Ah, back to *desi* lingo, so what would one say," Liz enquired, picking a fork.

"Well, one can either say: *Main dukono pe ja raha hoon* or *Dukono pe main ja raha hoon* or *Ja raha hoon ma dukono pe*, or a combination of these. There are many... at least nine ways of saying the same sentence."

"Amazing!" she declared, pointing her fork in my direction. "It must be easy to rhyme sentences."

We chatted happily over a sumptuous meal and excellent service. Conversation came naturally to Liz and I was jealous of that. Several times, at the table, I wondered why I wasn't attracted enough to a girl who was beautiful, happy, intelligent, and could converse so easily. Sure, she was loquacious but she talked sense. And above all, she liked me! Most young men would go out of their way just to talk to her. I couldn't answer my question, perhaps the chemistry was lacking between us. I was thinking for a while when I heard my name.

"Amar?" Liz was talking, "You seem miles away. Are you okay?"

I felt embarrassed. "Sure, I was just thinking."

"Wow! What?" she asked, eyes laughing.

"Oh, nothing... so when do you start driving lessons?"

"I've started!" she said proudly, raising clenched fists in the air.

Luigi approached us quietly. "Everything all right?"

Liz replied quickly, smiling, "*Grazie, il cibo era delizioso.*" We ordered coffee.

"*Eccellente*, Lizee." With a slight professional bow and a pleasant smile, he left us to continue.

"What was I saying?" Liz asked, blinking a few times and smiling broadly.

I returned her smile. "Driving lessons."

"Ah yes, I've had a few. When I pass, I'll get a car."

That was another thing with Liz- not *if* I pass, but *when* I pass. She was always optimistic. It was that trait in her that I was jealous of. I would have said, *if* or *if and when*.

I was impressed. "So... lessons, car, exams, what then?"

She chattered gaily, "Then? Then I'll get my own pharmacy... make money... lots of it, see the world... enjoy life." After some thought, she added, "I suppose I'll get married at some stage."

"When; before seeing the world or after?" I asked laughing.

She laughed too and joked, "Once *before* seeing the world, and again after that, with some reliable sort."

"My parents are already putting pressure on me to get married," I said with a hint of annoyance.

She smiled knowingly. "They are probably under pressure from girls' parents. Why are boys regarded as some sort of God in Asian societies? Parents having to run around hunting for sons-in-law, it's crazy!"

"SILs," I said remembering Bimla's and Nita's abbreviations on relations. I explained the various terms to Liz but it didn't seem funny without my sisters' hysterical laughing and giggling. *Bella Venue* was crowding and so was the Broadway with cars now bumper to bumper. The sun changed direction and was now on one side of Liz, revealing her firm, high breasts through the thin cheesecloth shirt. Her perfectly shaped collar-bones swooped sideways languorously with a hint of perspiration on them. I had to make an effort to keep my eyes locked with hers and stop them from wandering down.

"Things are changing," I said, "slowly."

Liz was not impressed. She sighed impatiently, "Too slowly. When I qualify, I don't want Dad and Mum begging for a boy for me. I want boys running after *me*."

I nodded my understanding. "You'll break lots of hearts."

"So what are you planning to do after Christ Church, Mr. Oxford?" she asked, leaning forward and looking directly into my eyes.

"Hmm, haven't thought much about that," I replied honestly. "I might study Accountancy or Law, go around the world begging for some girl to marry me, settle down in Oxford and have enough children to produce a cricket team..."

"Oh shut-up," she snapped in harmless annoyance.

We finished our coffee and Liz asked for the bill. Much against my protests, the bill was charged to the account of Doctor Sethi. Liz reminded me that I could pay for Bobby.

Luigi was impressed. He took Liz's hand and planted a loud kiss on its back. "*Ciao*, come again. Iza always good to see you. And you too Amaro." Liz's smile and blush made his day.

"*Benissimo. Ciao*, Luigi," Liz said, with an aristocratic wave. "*A presto.*"

"Thank you, bye Luigi, and 'bye." I added.

Once outside I asked curiously, "What's Bobby all about. Everyone was talking about it in Nairobi."

She wasn't quite sure. "I think it's about a college student who falls in love with some poor girl—"

"Let me guess," I interrupted. "The boy is rich, the girl poor. His parents object – the boy persists- and finally, the families agree- the boy and the girl get married."

"Something like that; sweet don't you think?"

"I've seen dozens of films like that. What's special about this one?"

"Haven't you been listening to the songs? Everyone's singing them- especially, *Hum tum ek kamara ma baand ho, aur chabi kho jaye...You and I locked in a room, and the key is lost.*"

I laughed, "Liz, your Hindi is pretty good."

"Shut up Mr.Oxford. Look, if you have time, can you please help me choose a birthday present for a friend of mine."

"Sure, I'm free."

We wandered around, window shopping. Nothing caught her fancy.

"Why don't we try Bentalls?" I suggested. "It's the biggest store around here."

We entered the store and walked aimlessly for a while. Then, to my surprise, she headed for the Men's department. She looked around, missing nothing. Finally, she held a cashmere sweater wide in both hands. "What do you think of this, Amar?"

It was a lovely navy blue sweater, soft to the touch. I glanced at the price tag and bit my lip, glad I wasn't paying. "It's lovely, who is it for?"

"A friend of mine... John. It's his twenty-first."

I forced a smile.

CHAPTER 15

Oxford hadn't changed a bit except that it appeared to me to be sun-baked, sunny and happier! The coach had broken down en route and I was an hour late arriving. Mrs. Woods was not in, perhaps she had gone shopping. I went up to my room and unpacked. Strangely enough, the room seemed smaller, claustrophobic. I suppose I had got used to open-air and larger premises. I opened the window and breathed some fresh air. The house seemed quiet, even allowing for Mrs.Woods' absence. I lay on the bed and closed my eyes. Not a sound. Everything was still, devoid of movement.

Suddenly, I sat up in bed. Mr. Woods! Where was he? Was he alright? Despite the heat, I felt cold. I leapt out of bed. His door was shut. I put an ear against it- silence. "Mr. Woods, are you alright?" I asked in a low voice. There was no response, but that was not unusual. After two quick knocks, I opened the door and peered inside.

He was there. I tip-toed to the bed and stood by the base for a while, studying his face. It was as white as the sheet that covered him up to the chin. The veins in his white hands, jutting out from beneath the sheet were blue and protruding outwards from his shrivelled skin. His face seemed smaller than what I could remember. There were blue circles under his closed eyes and the skin below the cheeks was shrivelled and hollowed. Purple veins ran from both cheeks down to the hollows of his cheeks. I took a step forward and froze. He was staring directly at the ceiling, eyes sunk in deep sockets, mouth open, jaw drawn back. I held his hand; it felt cold. "Mr. Woods!" I shouted.

I heard a voice coming upstairs. "Amar?"

"Mrs. Woods!" I shouted. "Please come!"

In a few seconds, she was beside me. She held his hand. "Henry! Are you alright?"

I was in a cold sweat. Looking sideways at Mrs.Woods, I saw that she was shaking. "Henry?" We both feared the worst.

A slight sound escaped his open mouth. I couldn't believe it! He was alive! I exhaled loudly. Mrs.Woods brought her face next to his and a tear rolled down her cheek onto his cheek and finally dripped down on his pillow.

Mr.Woods was still staring at the ceiling. Was there a sound from him or had I imagined it? I wasn't sure.

The sound came again, faint, forced from deep down his throat and out from his lips, "Jane...Graham."

We stood by him mesmerized. It was then that his jaw dropped further.

CHAPTER 16

College started a few weeks later. The green leaves of summer were turning red and gold and the sun lost much of its warmth. Some of the loss of cheer was replaced by a letter from Liz. She had a free weekend, and would I mind if she came to see me and Oxford for a day I had mixed feelings about Liz's request. Of-course she was welcome to come and see me, I was always willing to show Oxford to friends. I was also always happy to meet friends, old and new and make time for them. But, what was Liz's intention? What did she *really* want from me? However, it would have been rude to turn down her request; after all, I did enjoy her company. I rang to say that I was looking forward to seeing her on Saturday.

Liz's coach was supposed to arrive at 10 A.M. I was at the coach-station, a good half-hour early and decided to get myself a coffee from a nearby café and sat at the steps of the coach station sipping my drink. The morning air was refreshingly cool and the sunshine just warm for me to enjoy the coffee. Peace was periodically broken by coaches coming and going. I wondered why coaches left engines switched on for ages before leaving. What a waste of fuel. Half a dozen or so cars waited nearby to collect arriving friends or relations. A shiny black Rover turned the corner at exceptionally fast speed with the radio blaring and abruptly stopped, taking two parking spaces. I was thinking about how inconsiderate some people could be. Was he showing off his shiny Rover? Was he some spoilt brat? Deaf? Perhaps plain stupid!

A shadow fell over my face and a voice interrupted my train of thought. "Excuse me..." A girl around twenty was standing by the steps with a fiver in her hand. She looked like a typical Oxford student - loose jeans, a cheesecloth shirt and a large bead necklace. "Do you have change?"

I fumbled my pockets. "Sorry, just notes, some coins amounting to two pounds." I shrugged my shoulders.

She seemed disappointed. "Can you believe it? The café doesn't have change."

"They probably want you to buy something," I said, speaking from past experience.

"Doesn't buying a coffee count?"

"It happens," I answered. "Look, it's just coffee, why don't I get you one?" I took some coins from my pocket and half got up.

"That's okay, I'll get it," she said, taking twenty pence.

The Rover was still there, windows down and the music louder than before. Presently, a coach came and I wondered if it was Liz's, arriving early. No, I thought, they do not come early.

My thoughts were interrupted once again, by the same girl. "Mind if I sit here?"

"Not at all, this is a nice sunny spot." I moved sideways making room for her. "Thanks for the coffee," she said sitting down and raising her drink in salutation.

"Think nothing of it as long as you repay me by Christmas. After that, I'll charge you interest."

She laughed aloud. In the light from the sun, her face took a tanned appearance, complimenting her straight blonde hair, falling all the way to her slim waist. "Okay," she said, teasing, "Meet me here at noon, Christmas day."

"We need to have that witnessed by someone with sound mind and body," I suggested.

She laughed again. "You won't find anyone like that around here. Sound mind, maybe, sound body? Definitely not!"

"Christmas day is fine by me," I said. "And wear a red rose."

A coach was approaching in the distance. "That's probably the one I'm waiting for," I said.

"Me too, and it's on time!"

We got up and walked to the stop to greet our respective guests, scanning the faces stepping down. When I could make out only a handful of figures in the coach, walking towards the exit, I got concerned. None of the remaining figures looked like Liz. Nevertheless, I stood my ground, scrutinizing the passengers as they stepped down... until the coach emptied out and the driver walked to the end of the coach and back to ensure that all was well. Finally, he closed the door and walked away.

Damn! Where was Liz? The letter did say 10 A.M Saturday. With the letter at home, I couldn't even contact her. With a mixture of disappointment and anger, I debated my strategy. Do I go home and ring her? Why the hell didn't she let me know if she had changed her plans? I was pondering when it struck me that she must have missed her coach and that she would have taken the next one. I walked over to where a timetable was displayed. The next coach from London was not due for another fifty minutes. The place was looking deserted and quiet; the shiny black Rover had gone. Spotting a vending machine near the ticket office, I decided to buy a hazelnut chocolate. I managed to get the right combination of change and coin by coin dropped them in the slot. The last coin was swallowed by the machine but did not dropdown. I banged at the machine. Nothing! I banged the button for the chocolate. Nothing! The machine rattled with money but refused to drop any chocolate. Not my day, I thought. But then, why was I wasting time and money using a machine when there was a decent enough café nearby.

With another forty minutes to go, I ordered a coffee and a hazelnut chocolate at the café. The place was a bit dingy and needed some paint to cheer it up. Although not crowded, some of the tables needed clearing up. The coffee did not taste as good as the first one, though the chocolate made up for it. I was about to go when I spotted a familiar face in the corner. The straight blonde hair was unmistakable. I wondered what she was doing here on her own? I walked over and tapped her shoulder. She looked up recognising me instantly gave me a friendly smile. "Hi, we're not supposed to meet until Christmas. What are you doing here?" She looked around me. "And why are you alone?"

"Why are *you* on your own?" I asked.

She laughed when I explained what had happened. "Snap," she said, showing more concern than I was experiencing." I hope John's in the next coach, else..." She didn't finish the sentence.

"Who is John?" I asked and immediately wished I hadn't. "Sorry, none of my business, I was just..."

"That's okay. He's my boyfriend. John's coming for the weekend, from Hayes. I don't understand; he's never been late before."

"Always a first time," I said, trying to sound sympathetic.

"And your guest?"

"Liz, she must have missed the coach."

"So, who's Liz, your girlfriend?"

"No!" I said quickly. "She's just a friend, a family friend. Oh, by the way, I'm Amar."

She extended her hand for me to shake. "And I'm... oh look, there's the coach."

Through the bay-window, we spotted a coach heading towards the station. She gathered her handbag and we headed for the terminal.

This time we waited together for our respective guests to step down from the coach. Surely Liz must be in this one. By 11.00 all the passengers had gone. No Liz. No John. We stood there for a while, both embarrassed. I threw my hands in the air and tried to underplay the episode. "Well, maybe something came up. What are you planning to do?"

"I'll wait for the next one," she muttered, visibly disappointed.

"Good luck. I'll head home; perhaps she left a message with my land-lady." I stood up, preparing to leave, "See you around."

"Sure," she muttered, trying to put a brave face and smiling stiffly, "Christmas day."

Liz had not called and there was no answer from her phone. I decided to leave the whole matter for the time being.

A few days later, as I came home in the evening from a late session at college, Mrs.Woods informed me that a lady called Liz Sethi had rung for me to say how sorry she was for not being able to make it on Saturday. Something important had come up and the lady was profusely apologetic.

Inayat, Robin Stone, a fellow student and I went to see the Guy Fawkes fireworks on 5th November. It was a great display in an open field near Cowley. Inayat and I were impressed, though Robin said he had seen better ones in his hometown, Birmingham. Compared to the small, poorly organized fireworks that I had sometimes seen in Kenya, this was splendid. Inayat was particularly impressed by how much care was taken to ensure that no one got hurt. Apparently, a cousin of his was badly scarred in the face during a firework display in Tehran when he was just eleven. "Back home," he said, "No one bothers how close children get to the fireworks. They occasionally *hold* fireworks in their hands. It's fun, but there are some tragic stories."

Robin thought it would be a good idea if we had a drink or two in some pub nearby and then got some fish and chips to take away. I was all for that- I felt like a cold beer and I loved eating fish and chips with lots of salt and vinegar in a newspaper in the open air. It vaguely reminded me of eating mogo chips and corn rubbed with salt, chilies and lime in Mwangi's stall.

We stopped at the Crown Inn at Cornmarket Street.

"Did you know?" Robin asked, "William Shakespeare used to drop by here."

"But I thought he lived in Stratford-upon-Avon," Inayat stated pointedly.

"Ah yes, but legend has it, he used to break his journey between his place and London by staying here. It is commonly believed that he was on exceptionally good terms with the landlord's wife, Jane Davenant."

I was interested. "They could have made love in this very room!"

Robin enjoyed the attention. "Talking of love, it is commonly believed that in this very pub, Mrs. Davenant, fathered Shakespeare's son."

"I'm not sure, sounds like a lot of gossip to me." I said.

"Ah, there's a lot of truth in gossip," Robin said indignantly. "My mother always used to say that there's no fire without smoke."

We stared at him. "Surely," Inayat stated, shaking his head, "you mean there's no *smoke* without—"

Robin grinned, "You know what I mean."

"Ignore him Inayat, he always talks like that."

The music got loud and we had to shout above the cacophony to hear what was being said. Most of the tables were taken by groups that had been to the fireworks display and some had glow-sticks which they waved around for fun. Everyone seemed to be enjoying themselves. I heard someone call my name. It sounded like a female voice. And then I saw her. In an instant, I recognised her as the owner of the straight, blonde hair that fell to her waistline. She was coming towards us, "Amar, small world."

I got up from my seat. For a few seconds I desperately tried to remember her name, but then realized that she hadn't told me. "Hi, it's good to see you again - before Christmas!"

She laughed, audibly, happily. "You look good." Seeing my friends, she raised a hand in salutation, "Hi all, I'm Jennifer."

I introduced Robin and Inayat to her. "Why don't you join us?" I suggested.

"Thanks, but no. I'm with friends over there," she said pointing to a table where a few girls were rocking their waists and being merry. Upon seeing Jennifer talking to us, a few of the girls shouted noisily, one or two whistled. "I'll see you before we go."

"Sure," I said, "take care."

We stayed for another half hour or so. The place was getting too crowded and noisy and Inayat was getting restless after three soft drinks. "Come on chaps, I'm dying for some fish and chips"

We got up, Robin reluctantly, draining every drop from his glass. As we fought our way through the crowds, I made a quick detour to say bye to Jennifer. Approaching her, I raised a hand and made a *see-you* with my lips. She stood up and gave me a light hug. Her friends and a few others joined in a chorus of oooooohs and whistling, Robin and Inayat too.

Robin was a bit unsteady and Inayat and I provided the occasional support from opposite sides, but once the smell of fish and chips made way in his direction, he regained his balance. I sprinkled extra salt and vinegar on the fish and chips. Eating as we walked back to the city centre in the cool November night, I felt happy to be in good company, despite their jovial remarks about Jennifer. "Look here," I protested, "She's just someone I met for a little while recently, nothing serious."

"She likes you," Inayat prophecized, his expression midway between a smile and a laugh. "I can tell."

"Inayat, until an hour ago, I didn't even know her name!"

"You don't have to know someone's name to fall in love," he replied.

"You've hit the nail on the hammer," Robin exclaimed, thumping Inayat playfully. We turned to look at him. He shrugged good-naturedly, "You know what I mean," he said sheepishly.

I laughed, "Love? That's going too far. And I don't like the idea of *falling* in love, maybe *being* in love, but certainly not falling."

Inayat was in no mood to give in. "The only way to *be* in love is to first *fall* in love."

"Oh yes, you are an expert, aren't you?" I snapped and immediately regretted my choice of words.

"Hey, hey," Robin cut in, "I can tell when someone is in love!"

"Oh yes? Have you got a love-meter or something on you?" I demanded.

He handed me his bag of chips. "Hold this, now in a minute, I shall be able to tell you the truth. Don't move, both of you." He blew into his palms, rubbed them against one another and placed one palm on Inayat's chest and one on mine.

"What are you playing at?" Inayat chuckled.

Robin was serious. "Stay still both of you, just for a minute."

We obeyed out of curiosity until Robin gave a loud howl. "You are in love Amar, your heart's beating faster than Inayat's."

I returned him his bag of chips. "Oh shut up."

CHAPTER 17

It wasn't until I put my hand in my jacket pocket for the front door key that I saw a little piece of paper fall on the ground. I picked it up, opened the door and popped my head into the lounge where Mrs.Woods was watching the last few minutes of the News at Ten. Arab producers had announced a 25 percent cut in oil production. "News gets worse and worse. There's some coffee if you feel like it," she said. I declined but proceeded to watch the closing headlines and the weather forecast. I went on to describe the fireworks to Mrs.Woods.

"Henry and I used to take Graham there every year, until..." her voice trailed off with a faraway look.

"I'll take you there next year," I volunteered.

"Oh, I'm too old for these things," she said, forcing a laugh.

Suppressing a yawn I bid her good night. "It's been a long day."

The next morning, at breakfast Mrs.Woods handed me a scrap of paper, which seemed vaguely familiar. "You left it on the coffee table last night," she explained.

I recalled how I had left it on the table with my keys without much thought while watching television.

It was a small piece, torn in a hurry with a number on it and the letter 'J'. I read the numbers aloud- 76232. My puzzlement was partly solved by Mrs.Woods. "It's a telephone number." I still could not understand why or how a scrap of paper should have been in my pocket. I put it back in my pocket, not quite sure what to do with it.

"Ring her," she said in a matter-of-fact tone, placing a bowl full of cereal under my nose.

"Pardon?"

"Ring her, Miss 'J'," she said enjoying my naivety.

I thought for a few seconds and wondered if it was Jennifer's phone number. Concluding that to be the most likely explanation, I still could not work out how and when the piece of paper got into my pocket.

"I will, thanks," I said, still not convinced. I wondered if this was some sort of joke that Inayat and Robin were playing on me. The more I thought about it and the events of the previous evening, the more convinced I got that indeed my friends were having fun with me. I'm not falling for that, I thought.

At college, I tackled Inayat and Robin about the telephone number on the little piece of paper. Initially, they were confused, then, Inayat suggested that Robin had written the note. Robin, laughing hysterically, accused Inayat of it. I was beginning to see the funny side of the event and I tore it into small pieces and deposited them in a public bin upon which, Inayat and Robin screamed together.

"Don't!" Inayat cried, rushing towards me.

"Oh no, it wasn't us," shouted Robin, "We were just joking!"

"Well, I just believed you," I shouted with some annoyance.

"Amar, you should have belief in yourself. Believe the believable, don't believe that the the unbelievable is believable unless you believe in —"

"Shut up Robin, be serious for once," I shouted over his words. Seeing their serious faces, I realized my mistake. I should have listened to Mrs.Woods.

"Quick! Collect the pieces," Robin shouted. "Where there's a way there's a will."

We scrambled for the little pieces, placing our hands one by one in the bin. After several minutes I declared that we must have every piece. Inayat, out of guilt, stuck his head inside the bin to check that no piece was remaining inside.

We laid the pieces, ten in all, on a nearby bench. "What goes where?" I demanded to know, losing hope. "There can be so many combinations."

After several minutes, we realized that the number began with 7 and ended with 2. But what lay between? One of the numbers had been torn so badly that it was difficult to decipher it, let alone decide on where it belonged.

"I feel bad about it, Amar," Robin said, apologetic.

"It's okay," I murmured. "It's not meant to be. Perhaps *she* was joking. And what I can't understand is how the paper got into my pocket."

We were silent for a while, Inayat still trying to work out the number, shaking his head every now and then.

Suddenly, Robin thought that he could unravel part of the mystery. "You know, when she hugged you, just before we left, she must have slipped the note in your pocket."

I thought about it for a few seconds. With the noise and the crowd, it would have been difficult for me to notice that happening. "You're probably right."

We made one final attempt to work out the number before giving up.

That evening over dinner, Mrs.Woods asked me if I had rung Miss 'J'. Embarrassed, I explained the comedy of errors and events of the morning.

To my astonishment, she said excitedly, "Oh, I remember the number."

"What!" I cried, "How?"

"I saw the note, remember?"

"But that was ages ago!" I said, with some hope. My heart was beating faster.

"I never forget numbers!" she exclaimed.

"So what is it?" I asked quickly.

"I'm sure it was 7623...2."

"Mrs. Woods, you are a genius!" I scribbled the number on a paper napkin.

"Ring her, straight after dinner."

I had trouble concentrating on food and she realized that. "Ring her now."

Trying not to be too excited about the whole event, I dialled the number. It rang! And rang, and rang."

"Perhaps she's not in tonight," she concluded.

"Yes," I added, trying to hide my disappointment. "I'll try tomorrow."

I rang the next day, mid-morning... lunchtime... mid-afternoon. A soft voice answered the early evening call. "Hel-hello," I stammered. "Can I speak to Jennifer, please?"

"Speaking."

After all the delay, this was happening too quickly. With heart-pounding, I searched the depths of my brain for something appropriate to say. So much time had been spent on deciphering her number; I had not rehearsed what to say. Should I make it clear that she had given me the number? No, I thought that might embarrass her. I wasn't even absolutely certain that the number had been given by Jennifer. What if a friend of hers had played a prank? My knuckles were white against the receiver.

"Jennifer," I heard myself say. "This is Amar. I was given this number ... I'm not quite sure how I got it... I..."

"It was me."

The matter-of-fact reply stunned me, "Pardon?"

"Why didn't you ring earlier?"

I was taken aback. "Well, you didn't sign the note, I wasn't sure. Anyway, it's a long story." I wondered for a moment if I should ask her why she had given me her number then, decided against that strategy.

"Shall we go for a drink sometime?" Her directness was unsettling. I was beginning to think that unlike me, she had had enough time, and sense to rehearse.

"Sure," I replied, with a mixture of excitement and loss as to what to say. "There's a nice pub by Christ Church, The Old Tom, perhaps we could meet there at seven tomorrow."

"Ah, tomorrow is the one day I can't." She seemed genuinely disappointed, "How about Friday?"

"That's good," I replied hastily.

Friday proved to be a long day, minutes seemed to be as long as hours. Inayat and Robin gave me all sorts of advice on what to wear, what to order, how to behave with Jennifer, and so on. "You be the boss," Inayat advised me time and time again. "Don't seem too keen. And don't touch her."

Robin sounded more pragmatic. "Compliment her on her clothes, smell, and sense of humour. Make her feel important."

Inayat wasn't convinced, "You are the man, act like—"

"I don't agree," Robin butted in. "The most important thing—"

Inayat opened his mouth to protest.

Robin raised a hand to silence him even before he had uttered a single syllable. "Don't talk when I'm interrupting."

We stopped to check his sanity.

He shrugged his shoulders, smiling at the same time. "You know what I mean."

I found it difficult to concentrate in the library so I went home after lunch. There was a letter for me. I instantly recognised the Kenyan stamps and Munir's handwriting on the air-mail form.

Dear Amar

Thanks for your letter. Sorry, I couldn't write earlier- we all had to dash to Pakistan to attend Azra's wedding. It was all too sudden. We didn't even have time to get the wedding cards printed in Kenya. Everything was organized by Yusuf's (Azra's husband) relations. The wedding went well.

Sanjay was here for a fortnight to help his father in disposing some properties in Westlands but I could only meet him once, briefly, as he left soon after I came back. He looks great, seems to have a great following of girls in England as well as in Nairobi. Take some lessons from him.

Any news of Afzal or Rajesh? I haven't heard from them for ages. Tell them to write when you see them next.

I bumped into Bimla the other day in Curry Pot. She's enjoying her accountancy course and has aspirations of joining your dad's firm when she qualifies. She has a great sense of humour. Take some lessons from her too.

It's really hot at the moment and there is a shortage of rice and bread with prices rising by the day, who can afford these things anyway? There is also a severe water shortage and supplies are cut-off between 10 and 11 each morning. Most people end up storing bucketfuls of water before 10 A.M for washing clothes and courtyards. Another Government cock-up!

Crime is on the increase, especially in Nairobi. The other day a friend of mine, who had stopped at a traffic light was ordered to leave his car at gunpoint in broad daylight. The two thugs not only took his car but also his clothes, leaving him standing in Uhuru Avenue in his underpants.

Amar, remember how we often used to take late-night buses from the city centre to Ngara? Well, no one does that now, it's not safe.

In your letter, you mentioned that it was getting cold in England. Here, it's the opposite- Abbu has fitted ceiling fans in all the rooms at home, but the air in the rooms still feels warm, making nights very uncomfortable.

I must be off, yaar, please keep in touch, it's always good to hear from you. Best wishes from all here.

Your friend
Munir

I started reading the letter again and stopped after Azra's news. My heart went out to her, fearing for her, hoping that her disability wouldn't spoil her future with her husband.

Standing by the window, I looked out for a few minutes not watching anything in particular. There was a faint hum of the traffic, the rest was quiet. A sparrow moved from branch to branch in a rose shrub, moving its neck in different directions until it spotted me looking directly at it. It stood still, cocking its head in one direction, then another as if trying to read my mind. I angled my head and we looked into each other's eyes like two people meeting after a long time, content to just gaze. It flew away just as I blinked. At that moment I wondered if I would see Azra again.

I bumped into Jennifer just outside the pub. Approaching the meeting place from opposite directions, I turned a corner and, overtaking a group of Japanese tourists, practically walked into her arms. "I'm sorry..." I started apologizing, but broke off when I realized it was her. She just laughed then instinctively, put her arms around my neck and kissed me lightly. It happened so quickly and naturally as if it was always meant to be, that we both accepted the event without much thought to it. "Jennifer, you look lovely."

She eyed me from head to toe, "You look good," she said softly.

Her long straight hair was pony-tailed neatly behind her, blending with the cream coloured blouse that stretched tightly over her upper half and tucked in blue jeans.

"Shall we go inside?" I asked. "It's freezing out here."

"Sure."

We reserved a table and I got drinks for us. "Well..." I said, just as she said, "So..." We laughed. "You first," I said.

"So we meet again," she said softly with amusement, "before Christmas."

"We nearly didn't. You should've given me your number more formally."

"You should have asked," she said quickly "Everyone else does!" Then seeing my strained expression she added, "But, I've never given them my number, don't worry."

"And why not?"

"Well," she appeared thoughtful, "didn't really like them, or their motives."

"Why me?" I enquired.

She angled her head, narrowed her eyes and waited a while before answering, "There's... something about you." After a brief pause, she added, "You seem so... so trusting."

I was completely lost. "Trusting, just that?"

"Never mind," she said abruptly. "Tell me, did you ever hear from your friend who was supposed to come in that coach from London?"

I had completely forgotten the incident, it seemed so long ago. "Yes," I replied simply. Something important came up, she said. What about your date? John, wasn't it? What happened?"

"He never rang. I did, a few times, left messages, he hasn't rung back."

"His loss," I said flatly.

She raised her glass in saluation, "Her loss."

Jennifer asked me what I was doing in Oxford. After answering, and telling her briefly about my Kenyan background I told her in more detail about Inayat and Robin, Uncle Paal and Paro Aunty, Mrs.Woods, and what I planned to do after my studies, she told me a bit about herself.

She had lived all her life in High Wycombe, a little town in Buckinghamshire and was now studying Politics at St.Hilda's. "You know, until I came to Oxford, I had never been outside Buckinghamshire."

I was interested and puzzled, "Why not?"

Her expression grew stern. It seemed that she was uncomfortable harping back; clearly, she did now wish to talk about the past.

"I'm sorry, I didn't wish to... pry."

"That's okay," she answered, smiling wryly. "It wasn't easy. My father left us- my mother and three children when I was only four. One morning, my mother got up and saw a note from him. Apparently, he could not cope; felt constrained with family life and wanted to go it alone. He wanted to go to South Africa and make a better future, have fun, make money and *live*.

I stared at her, "What! Just like that?"

She nodded in dismay. "Yes, here today, gone tomorrow. Of course, I was too young to understand the significance of the implications. I kept thinking that he would come back in the evening, or breakfast the next day, or in a few days' time. Sometimes, I went to bed convinced that he would be at the breakfast table the next morning. The expected arrivals kept changing, the gaps widened. Perhaps he'd come for Easter or Christmas, or my birthday..." Jennifer's eyes moistened and she blinked a few times to block the tears.

"I kept a doll he had given me for my fourth birthday by my pillow for three years until I realised that he was never coming back. Then, one day, I cut the doll into little pieces and buried it in the garden. I never played with dolls or toys after that."

I stared at her in silence for a few seconds. "How did your mother cope?"

"Badly... She had a nervous breakdown and was incapable of properly explaining to us that Dad was never coming back. She was so reliant and in love with him that she kept thinking he would come back, she still does! As if he will come galloping on some white horse one moon-lit night, with a bunch of flowers and throw himself at her feet, begging for forgiveness!" Jennifer looked down at her hands in her lap and grew silent. For a while, neither of us wanted to break the silence. I waited for Jennifer to finish her story. "It must have been difficult for all of you."

She gave a slight nod, "Yes, though Tom, a year older than me quickly adjusted to the new environment and carried-on as if nothing had changed. And Milton, two years younger, never really got to know Dad."

"Where are they now?"

"Oh, Tom runs a small florist's shop in Beaconsfield and Milton is studying mechanical engineering in Manchester. They are both doing well."

"And your mother?"

"She's okay. She works part-time in a pharmacy in Chaltfont St.Peter."

I placed a hand on hers. "Well, you've made her proud."

She shrugged. "I decided a long time ago, perhaps when I was around sixteen that the only way to get out of the rut was to study hard and be someone. Only then would I be able to take care of me and Mum."

"You are right. You will gain respect and reward. My mother always tells me how important education is, the only wealth that no one can take away from you."

She smiled. "You know, Amar, I haven't talked about my family for a few years. How did this topic start?"

CHAPTER 18

I saw more and more of Jennifer. The winter jasmines gave way to the forsythias. With each week, the breeze grew weaker, the air clearer, and all this time she and I grew closer, our relationship, like spring, grew warmer.

Occasionally, we went out with Inayat and Robin for a drink or a meal, and a few times we all, including Jennifer's friends went out for drinks.

One day I asked her if she would mind coming to dinner at my place. "Mrs. Woods keeps asking me to bring you around. The poor dear is partly responsible for bringing us together."

Jennifer laughed and in her casual manner remarked, "I suppose she wants to meet her future daughter-in-law."

"Yes," I replied, "there's a ring that has been in our family for generations, which she would like me to slip on your lovely finger."

"It had better have a diamond in it."

"Oh yes, a big one."

Mrs. Woods was pleased to meet Jennifer. She remarked how lovely her straight waist-length hair was. "Amar has told me *so* much about you."

"Good things, I hope," Jennifer said laughing.

"I'm sure there are no bad things to be said about you," Mrs. Woods assured her.

The smell of freshly brewed tea and homemade scones drifted all around the dining room. "Can I give you a hand with the tea?" Jennifer offered.

"Oh dear, no thanks," Mrs. Woods replied quickly. "You two sit here and talk. It's no trouble."

We talked about how long Mrs. Woods had lived in Oxford, how it had changed over the years, how immaculate the garden was and other things. Conversation always flowed easily with Jennifer; she was so quick to seize on any words that hung suspended in the air for more than a few seconds.

We all enjoyed tea and later Jennifer successfully insisted on helping her host with the washing.

When it was time for Jennifer to depart, she gently kissed Mrs.Woods on the cheek and thanked her graciously.

I lived and breathed Jennifer, her voice was always in my ears, her smell in my nostrils. I wanted to be with her every minute of the day. Did she feel the same way about me? I frequently asked myself. Robin was sure that when two people are in love, the feelings of one are mirrored by the other. "Ask her," he advised. "Tell her how you feel, she'll be honoured and flattered." Inayat was not sure of Robin's advice. "Don't let her know you are head over heels about her. You'll be playing in her hands." Robin protested in disagreement, "I'm sure *she's* head over heels about Amar!" he shouted. "Go for it man. A bird in the hand will keep the doctor away."

We stopped in our tracks. "And I suppose an apple a day is worth two in the bush?" Inayat asked.

Robin tried to answer, but instead, ended-up shaking his head, confused.

"Well, I'm seeing her soon. I'll find out." I announced.

We met Saturday evening for a drink at The Old Tom. I had been waiting a while with a pint of larger when Jennifer rushed in. The chatter in the bar grew significantly lower and most men gave her a second look as she approached my table. Her long, flowing dress rustled as she bent down to kiss me lightly. "Sorry I'm late darling, the child-minder was late and the children were *so* restless today."

Her light-heartedness never ceased to amaze me. "Oh yes?" I enquired, "All *four* of them?"

She seated herself beside me. "Yes," she sighed and rubbed her stomach in a circular motion." And this one has been kicking me all day."

"Well, in your state you shouldn't be drinking. Shall I get you some juice? I asked getting up.

"Okay, with a bit of vodka."

"What's the vodka for?"

"Gives my hair a shine," she teased.

We stayed for a while and had a few drinks after which we went for a pizza at a small restaurant that we had been to a few times, where the dough was thin but heaped with toppings. "Fancy a film?" I asked munching a bite.

"What's on?"

"I wouldn't mind the James Bond film, at the Odeon."

"Live and let die? Roger Moore?"

"Yes," I replied. "Although I hear he's not as good as Sean Connery."

"*I* like Roger Moore, let's go see him," she said enthusiastically.

By the time we were ushered in, the film had started, just. As we took our seats, Jennifer said she fancied an ice cream. I tutted, "Can't we wait until the interval?"

"There may not be an interval," she said quietly.

Reluctantly I left my seat. Viewers in our row did not seem amused, despite my apologies.

When I came back with the ice creams threatening to drip down my hands, Jennifer was not where I had left her. Damn, I thought. Perhaps she's gone to the wash-room. I shuffled to my seat much to the annoyance of the viewers. A few minutes later, she approached the row of seats and stood there beckoning me. In return, I waved to her and pointed to the seat beside mine. She just stood there for a while and walked towards the last row. I felt a hand pat my shoulder from the row behind. A voice hissed, "She wants you back there." A few heads turned towards me visibly annoyed. I got up with the two ice creams now beginning to drip towards my wrists. Yet again I apologised to each person as they got up to let me pass. I was thoroughly puzzled by Jennifer's antics. She was sitting smugly in the last row by herself.

"What's the meaning of this?" I whispered, leaning towards her ear.

She leaned close to me and spoke softly, "I was feeling claustrophobic over there. Much better here, don't you think?"

I wasn't amused. "My hands are all wet and sticky," I said, handing her an ice cream. She started licking it quickly and settled down.

The name's Bond, James Bond, Roger Moore was saying in his smooth tone, an eyebrow arched.

Jennifer concentrated on her ice cream until it was all gone. A car chase started, the music got louder. Suddenly she took my hand and started licking it.

"What—" I started saying, then stopped, enjoying the tingling. My ice-cream was nearly finished. Bond was smashing his fist in some villain's face. Jennifer tugged at my shirt pulling me forward at the same time sliding down from her seat towards the floor. "Jennifer, no..." I whispered.

She was on the floor, tugging at my shirt more strongly. I felt myself sliding off my seat.

"We will be thrown out; do you realize —?"

"Be quiet, there's nobody here at the back," she whispered in my ear, brushing my ear-lobe with her lips. I lost control bending on top of her.

"I could be expelled from college!" I protested. "Why don't we go to your place?"

In the semi darkness she was wriggling to make herself comfortable. I was almost on top of her. The music got louder again. I got a fleeting glimpse between the seats. "I want to see Bond jumping over crocodiles," I whispered but she was paying no attention to anything I was saying. Her skirt was pulled up. The music boomed around the auditorium. She grabbed my belt and pulled me closer. I decided not to resist anymore. The music got louder. Bringing her lips to my ear, she hissed sharply, "Live and let die!"

"Amar?" the voice at the other end of the telephone sounded anxious.

"Yes, speaking."

"It's Paro. Have you forgotten us? We've not heard from you for ages. Are you all right?"

I felt a tinge of guilt. For some time, I had been meaning to ring them. "Sorry Auntyji, I've been a bit busy at college. I was planning to ring some time today," I lied.

"Are you alright? You are not getting bored there on your own, are you?"

"Yes, no, no, no. I'm fine. How's Uncleji?"

"That's the reason I rang. Paul's alright, it's his father." She hesitated, choosing her words. "His father's passed away. We got the news last night."

For a few seconds, I was lost for words, the receiver tightly gripped in my hand. When I spoke my voice sounded gruff. "I'm really sorry, is he okay? How's he taking it?"

"He's fine, a bit shocked though. We are trying to get him a flight to India as soon as possible."

"Auntyji, I'll be there by the evening. Will he—?"

"You don't have to rush," she interrupted.

"That's okay, I must, I mean, I'd like to. Can I have a word with him?"

"He's just popped out with Ramesh - he knows a travel agent in Southall. Our car's broken down again. Everything is happening together. It's Paul's birthday in a few days…" her voice was breaking down.

"Oh, I'm sorry. Look, Auntyji, I'll be there as soon as I can, please don't worry."

"Are you sure? What about college?" she was genuinely concerned.

"It's okay, I won't be missing much."

"All right, see you later." She sounded relieved.

Paal Uncle was in, trying to close a bulging suitcase as I entered their house. He immediately straightened himself and his arms went wide. We hugged sombrely. "I'm so sorry, Uncleji."

"What can one do, Amar? These things are in God's hands. Thanks for coming."

"What was the cause of death?"

"Heart attack. Thank God he didn't suffer, went quietly just after breakfast. He was a good age- 81 next month."

Thanks for coming," Paro Aunty said, as we all sat down. "The Sethis and the Mehtas will be here shortly."

"What time is the flight?" I enquired, not quite sure what was happening.

"We've got to be at Heathrow at nine, the plane leaves at eleven," she replied.

For some time we sat in silence. Thoughts froze in the air. Uncle and Aunty were probably thinking of bygone days and when their last encounter with his father was. The bell rang. I jumped up and instinctively went for the door. The Sethis and the Mehtas greeted me sombrely. Mrs. Mehta was carrying a cardboard box from which drifted the aroma of curried vegetables.

"Everything ready, Paul?" Dr. Sethi asked in a matter of fact tone.

"Yes, thanks Ramesh. We'd better leave soon."

"Eat first," Mrs. Mehta suggested. "There's time."

The ladies gathered in the kitchen to arrange a quick meal.

"Got your passport?" Dr. Sethi asked of Paal Uncle.

PMT, I thought. Papa was always reminding me – Passport, Money, Tickets, most important. I kept quiet. As if reading a bit of my mind, Mr.Mehta said. "Don't forget your tickets." I wanted to add money to the brief list, but kept quiet.

Presently, we helped ourselves to some rice with curried potatoes and peas that Mrs.Mehta had brought with her. Paal Uncle barely touched his and although I was hungry and found the food tasty, I thought it best not to have too much.

When no one wanted any more, Paro Aunty suggested that we make a move. Mrs.Sethi and Mrs.Mehta volunteered to wash the dishes and pans before departing.

We left just after eight. I sat in the Sethis' car while Paal Uncle and Paro Aunty went with the Mehtas. Dr.Sethi suggested that we follow the Mehtas and meet at the terminal three departure lounge.

"How's Christ Church, Amar?" Mrs.Sethis asked after a while.

"Fine, Mrs. Sethi," I replied. "This year seems easier than the first. How's Liz doing?"

"She seems to be enjoying herself."

"Too much," Dr.Sethi added. "I worry, sometimes."

"Oh, stop fussing, Ramesh. University days are the best days in one's life. Have you forgotten?"

"Laura, I'm not saying that she shouldn't have fun. I do wonder sometimes whether she is concentrating enough on her studies!"

"She got through the first year without any hitch, didn't she?" Mrs.Sethi demanded.

"I *know*." He sounded exasperated. "Until she qualifies, it's not over. She can't relax just because she's got through the first year. Have you forgotten what happened to Potter's daughter? Sailed through the first three years in medicine and then gave up. She was so into boys, parties and booze. What's she doing now? Nothing! "

Mrs.Sethi was not to be defeated easily. "Jill's doing something. She's got a *good* job in Ealing Hospital."

"Huh, doing what?" he demanded.

"*I* don't know. She drives a BMW, so she must be doing all right."

"You know very well the car's not hers, probably paid for by some doctor that Jill's trapped with her looks."

"Well, there you are - not only has she got a BMW but a doctor too!" Mrs.Sethi declared triumphantly slapping the dashboard.

"Yes, but for how long? If she gets ditched, she loses all."

"With her looks, who's going to ditch her?"

"You are missing the point," he said, almost shouting and slapping the steering wheel. "What I'm trying to say is that one should be qualified enough to be able to stand on one's own feet in the face of adversity. God knows, so many marriages fail and I feel that if a woman is qualified enough, she can then take care of herself and any children she may have dumped upon her."

Mrs. Sethi kept silent, pondering on her husband's last point. I could sense the tension in the car and had a feeling that Mrs.Sethi would want the last word. She exhaled audibly.

"Relax darling, Liz will be okay. She's a sensible girl."

Dr.Sethi kept silent and shook his head slightly knowing that the argument was going nowhere.

We approached the car-park.

Paal Uncle had just checked in when we dashed into the departure area. "Gate 18," he was saying to the Mehtas and Paro Aunty. "I'd better rush. Will you be all right, Paro?"

Before she could answer, Mrs. Mehta, cut in, "No need to worry Paul, we are here for her."

"Yes, of course," Mrs.Sethi added. Then turning to her she added, "If you like I can get Liz to come over for a few days and stay with you."

"No," she replied hastily. "No need, thanks. Amar's here for a day or two. I'll be fine. Anyway, Paul will be back within a week." She took my hand in hers and squeezed it firmly. "Thanks, Amar."

"Now, Paul, have you got everything?" Dr.Sethi asked holding him by the elbow. "There's nothing to worry about. I've asked my brother, Trishul to meet you at the airport in Delhi. You'll have no problems in the customs."

"Thanks Ramesh," Turning to all of us, Paal Uncle said, "I just don't know what I'd have done without you lot."

"Don't worry about a thing," Mr.Mehta announced. "You just take care of your family over there." He grabbed Paal Uncle's hand luggage. "Let's get you to the departure gate."

Paal Uncle hugged us and thanked us all for our support. Paro Aunty was a shade tearful. "Take care of *Mataji*; bring her here if she's up to it." Paal Uncle nodded and passed through the departure gate. We stood quietly, half waving until he disappeared.

Dr Sethi suggested that we all have some coffee but Paro Aunty was feeling tired and declared that she just wanted to get home.

"Ramesh," Mr.Mehta announced, "We'll drop Paro and Amar. You can go home."

"Thanks, Shatru," Dr.Sethi said. Turning to Paro Aunty, he said, "If there's anything we can do, just ring, it's our duty."

"Thanks, Ramesh, I'll be fine. You and Laura have done so much already."

CHAPTER 19

Back home, Paro Aunty was very quiet. I offered to make tea with cinnamon and cardamoms. "The house seems so quiet," she commented. "I'm glad you are here. Are you sure you can stay for a couple of days?"

"Please don't fuss. It's nothing."

She curled up on the settee and flicked through a magazine. "God, my shoulders ache."

I offered to get her some pain killers. "This will do you good with a hot drink"

"No, I don't take pills unless I really have to, they upset my stomach."

"Have a hot drink anyway, it won't harm you. I wouldn't mind some biscuits myself," I shouted from the kitchen.

"Sorry, I've run out of biscuits." After a few seconds, she shouted, "There's some *chewda* in one of the cupboards. And oh, can you please add some ginger in the tea."

We sat in silence for a while, sipping tea and looking at different bits of the room. Suddenly, we both broke the silence at the same time. "I hope Paal Uncle ..." I said. "You've put ..." she said. We both laughed, "You first, Auntyji."

"It's nothing... I was just saying that you've put on some weight." Reading my expression she added, "I meant it as a compliment. You look ... more handsome, a bit more broad-shouldered than when you were when you came from Kenya."

I wasn't quite sure how to take that. I merely smiled my thanks and searched for the invisible spider. To rid the embarrassment hanging in the air, I added, "The contact lenses suit you."

She looked me directly in the eyes, and asked, "Do you have any friends?"

"Of course," I replied.

"I mean girls in Oxford or elsewhere?"

I instantly thought of Jennifer. Even before coming to Ealing, I had made up my mind not to mention her to relations. That way, life would be less complicated. I didn't want to be pressured into bringing Jennifer here or cajoled into marriage. "No," I answered, "don't really get time for girls." I hated myself for lying to Aunty because she was always so frank with me.

She threw her head back and finished her drink. "You do make the nicest tea. Here, be a dear and take my mug."

I reached over and grabbed the mug. "Would you like some more?"

"No thanks. That was lovely. I vote you as the best tea-maker in Ealing."

"That's no praise," I protested. "Ealing's a small place."

She spread her arms wide over her head. "Okay, the best tea-maker in the *whole* wide world. Oh, my shoulders do ache."

"Shall I massage them? It might help," I volunteered.

Her eyes lit up and she shifted cheerfully in the settee. "You are such a darling. Perhaps the best shoulder massager in Ealing, sorry, the world." She bent her neck forward and with the swipe of her hand moved her hair to one side.

I stood behind her and held her shoulders firmly before squeezing then about. Digging my thumbs against her shoulder blades I moved them around, haphazardly. Her soft, shiny hair fell back on my hands.

"Sorry," she said. Without waiting for a reply she moved her hair to the other side, slightly forward. "Is it still in the way?"

"That's better," I replied. Her shoulders were rounded, feminine but firm. I moved my hands gently to rub the far ends of her collar bones and the dimples just above them. Her skin was firm and my fingers glided easily around her shoulders.

"Oh, that feels so nice, you are good at this. Have you done this before?"

I laughed, "It's my part-time job, pays for the college fees."

She laughed. "Hope you are not planning to charge me, I've no money."

"The first massage is complimentary, next time I shall want my fees in advance."

"Hmm, can you do a complimentary neck massage as well?"

"Of course," I moved my hands against the back of her slender neck.

"Amar—"

She was interrupted by the chimes of the clock. As if on cue, the phone rang. She sat up straight, her hair falling back on my hands. I let go off her neck. She shifted about and got off the settee. Taking a few steps she reached for the phone.

"Hello," she spoke softly sounding half asleep. I could hear some crackling coming from the phone. Her expression changed instantly. "What!" she exclaimed. "There's no point. Come straight back." More crackling. "Get a taxi or something." She was talking loudly and fast now. "Your brother can sort things out." She then proceeded to listen.

She kept listening for a while longer, then in exasperation, interrupted the caller. "Have a word with Amar." She handed me the phone. "It's Paul."

"Hello... Uncleji, something wrong?"

"I'm still at Heathrow beta, no planes to India."

"Why, what's happened?"

"Looks like a plane's been hijacked in Delhi and India can't guarantee landing rights to any planes at the moment."

"God, that's terrible, what about other cities in India? Can't you—"

Paal Uncle interrupted me. "All other major airports are clogged up. One option is to wait here and see what happens."

"I think Auntyji's right. Take a taxi and come back. When flights resume the airline will ring us and you can assess the situation accordingly."

He was thoughtful for a few seconds. "Okay, tell Paro that I'll be home in about an hour. See you later."

We waited for Paal Uncle to come back.

Months flew by. The cold brisk wind from the Arctic came with a vengeance. Diwali, Christmas and New Year came and went. Because of Paal Uncle's father's death, we had a quiet period and kept away from parties and celebrations that year. I had spent Christmas with Jennifer and Mrs.Woods, who insisted on cooking a full celebrity lunch. For New Year, I visited Paal Uncle and Paro Aunty and we all went for a quiet Chinese meal on New Year's Eve. The next day, in the evening, the Sethis and Mehtas visited us and we had a few drinks with lamb kebabs and *pakoras*. Liz couldn't make it as she was holidaying in Paris with a few friends.

Jennifer and I spent more and more time together. We were beginning to read each other's behaviour better and there were times when we were content just to be together, each immersed in our books or coursework for hours on end without feeling the need to partake in the conversation.

One cold evening after some fish and chips, we were in Jennifer's room. It was smaller than mine and the clutter of photographs, posters and books stacked on the floor made it appear even smaller. What I did like was the sink in one corner, it was unsightly but practical. I was slouched in an armchair, feet on the bed, going through some coursework on *Dividend Restrictions*. Jennifer was propped up in bed against a few pillows, her feet over mine.

The music changed to Simon and Garfunkel. *Bridge over Troubled Water* was followed by *Mrs.Robinson* and then *The Sound of Silence*. She withdrew her feet and squeezed them under mine, tapping them in tune with the music.

"Ouch," I said.

"What?"

"Your toenails are digging into my heels. Can't you do that gently?"

She ignored my question. "I like all their songs, especially this one. Did you ever see the film?"

"The Graduate? Yes, Dustin Hoffman was fantastic, and of course, this song was brilliantly played in the film. He won an Oscar for his role I think."

She propped herself straight and stretched her long shapely legs forward, again squeezing her feet under mine. "Did you know that they wrote the song to capture the emotional trauma felt by many in this world when John F. Kennedy was assassinated on 22nd November 1963?"

I put my book down and lifted my feet off hers. "No, I didn't, but what I'm impressed by is that you remember Kennedy's assassination date so clearly."

"I'm not just a pretty face, am I?"

"Well I'll be the judge of that, but tell me why you remember the date—"

"First tell me that I'm not just a pretty face," she demanded, lips pouting.

I sat back and put my feet on top of hers. "Okay."

"Okay, what?"

"Okay, you are not just a pretty face."

"That didn't hurt, did it?" She made a face and settling back, put her book in front of her face. After a brief pause, she said flatly, "Easy, I was born on 22nd November."

"Oh! You know what, Jennifer? I think you *are* just a pretty face."

With her face still hidden behind her book, she ignored my comment and we both continued reading. After a while she raised her head over the book, her forehead furrowed. "Do you like my breasts?"

I was taken aback and did not reply for a while.

"Well?"

"Ya...Yes."

"Just *yes*, what sort of answer is that?"

"No honestly, I like them, you know that," I replied defensively.

"They are not big, are they? I thought men liked large breasts?"

"Is that a question or a statement?"

She screwed her nose and replied, "A question." For a few seconds, she paused, watching me put my book down - carefully, flatly on the bed. Without warning, she unbuttoned her top and pulled the collars out wide. "Well?"

I narrowed my eyes deliberately, "Ten-out- of- ten."

"*Amar*, tell me the truth, wouldn't you prefer them to be bigger?"

I picked up my book. "Well... yours are not exactly small, and I'm no expert, but from what I gather, large ones are visually more pleasing to men—"

"Oh! So you *do* prefer—"

"No," I said sharply, holding up my hand. "You didn't let me finish. When it comes to caressing and holding them, men would prefer yours; large ones flop around too much."

That pleased her. "So you like mine as they are?"

I picked up my book and searched for the paragraph I had last read. "Yes, of course."

She flashed a quick smile which slowly faded as her brow furrowed. "How do you know so much about breasts?"

"God, Jennifer!" I scratched the back of my neck for an appropriate answer. "Robin told me," I replied hurriedly.

"Robin? How does he...?" Seeing my exasperation, she stopped midway. "Okay, fine, tell me, do you prefer them pear-shaped or apple-shaped?"

"Look, I'm trying to read." I allowed my eyes to linger at her chest. "I don't know what shape yours are."

She lowered her chin and examined them as if for the first time. Her forehead creased. "I guess they are somewhere between apple shape and pear shape," she declared with some certainty.

I leaned forward. "No, no they look more like apples to me. Now can I please continue? I have to summarise six chapters by next week."

She shifted against the pillows and buttoned her top slowly, humming some tune. For another ten minutes, we read in silence. I was in deep concentration when I felt her eyes on me.

"Amar...am I your first love?"

"Huh?"

"You heard; am I your—"

"I heard."

"Well?"

"Yes... and no."

She narrowed her eyes. "Don't avoid the question. You can't say Yes and No. That's like saying that someone is half pregnant - impossible! One is either pregnant or not pregnant... full stop. Now tell me, have you ever loved anyone before?"

I put my book back on the bed. "There was a girl back home..." I mused. "I was in my teens—"

She pulled a cushion against her chest, eyes smiling mischievously. "Oh, tell me about her! What was she like?"

I shrugged my shoulders and picked up my book. "Nothing came out of it. It was ... it was just love from a distance. Her parents took her to Pakistan to get her married—"

"What! How old was she?"

"She was in her teens as well and because of her disability... she was mute, her parents wanted her married off as quickly as possible."

"I don't understand—"

This time I interrupted her. "You wouldn't, Asians are different."

She placed the pillow behind her and leaned back. "Was she beautiful?"

I nodded, closing my eyes. "Yes, very."

"If she were to come into your life tomorrow would you choose her or me?"

"Jennifer! This is preposterous!"

"Well?"

"Well, what?"

"Well?"

"Well, *what*?"

"Well... would you choose *her* or *me*?"

I puffed air, "You." I replied, flatly.

Jennifer cocked her head sideways, "Sure? You aren't just saying that to make me happy?"

I put my book down. "No."

"No what?"

"No, I'm not just saying it to just make you happy."

We looked at each other for a while.

She walked on her knees making the bed creak. "What was her name?" she asked playfully.

"Jennifer, do we have to... it was a long time ago. I've got to finish my reading."

"Okay, just tell me her name and I'll shut up."

I picked up my book and placed it between us. "Azra."

"Az—"

"Azra."

"What does it mean?"

"Oh, for heaven's sake, I don't know! I was too young to look for meanings. I think it means *Pure*."

She was quiet for a while, "What does Amar mean?"

"Amar?" I asked, puzzled. "Why do you ask?"

"Yes, Amar. What does your name mean?"

"Why do you want to know?"

"You seem to be answering every question with a question; are you pretending to be a psychiatrist?"

"What's wrong with that?"

She ignored my question and instead shrugged her shoulders. "Amar, I'm just curious, does your name mean something?"

I put my book down. "I'm not quite sure; it's either 'forever' or 'immortal'- same thing I suppose."

She half jumped up. "Forever? I like that. *Amar... forever*; I think I'll call you Mr. Forever from now on. And you two would have been Amar Azra, Forever Azra, *Forever Pure*."

I smiled, blowing air from my nostrils, "You know, I was supposed to be named Sita Ram, not Amar"

Her forehead creased. "So why aren't you called *Sita Ram?*"

"It's a long story. I'll tell you some other time, please not now. I have to read."

Jennifer pulled a face. "Sita Ram...Sita Ram. No, I prefer Amar, Mr. Forever."

I picked my book and held it a foot from my eyes. It was no good. I couldn't concentrate.

"And what does Jennifer mean?" I asked, trying to gain advantage over her.

She stuck her tongue out, "None of your business."

An hour later I finished reading and closed the book loudly, deliberately. I stretched and stood up. "How about a bite, I'm starving?"

She continued reading and mumbled, "There's some chicken in the fridge, make yourself a sandwich or something."

I thought about it. "No...I don't fancy chicken."

She peered at me from the top of her book, "So what do you fancy, Mr. Forever?"

I looked directly at her, "Do you know what I'd really like to have right now?"

She raised an eyebrow.

"A couple of apples."

She eyed me quizzically until my straight face cracked, then throwing a pillow in my direction she shouted amidst giggles, "Grow your own!"

PART 2

CHAPTER 20

1979

I married Billie in July 1979.

Bilo had fallen in love with a handsome mechanic close to home and despite family, protests had proceeded to marry him. Her marriage lasted just eleven months and she separated from him a few months before Billie and I tied the knot.

We had a simple temple wedding where we took our marriage vows in front of close relations. Mr.Panesar and Papa commenced the ceremony by garlanding each other followed by Mrs. Panesar and Maa.

The *pundit* (priest), in a simple white *dhoti* and *kurta*, whispered in my ear, "A Hindu marriage is not just between a groom and his bride. Just as importantly it is between two families."

Billie appeared from another hall, head and face covered by a *chuni*, and adequately supported on each side by aunts. As she stopped a few feet away, facing me, head and face covered, *punditji* requested garlands.

Mrs.Panesar stepped forward with two huge African marigold garlands, "Here *punditji*, the *jai malas*."

Upon his instructions, Billie first placed a garland around my neck and amidst much cheering and clapping, I around hers. Following that, I drew back the *chuni* from her face leaving it to cover just her head. She looked more beautiful than I could remember, her almond-shaped eyes rose to meet mine.

We were all ushered to the *mandap* where we sat cross-legged around a small fire, Billie and I closest to it, *punditji* facing us on the other side. He gathered several items near him, a copper bowl filled with water, a steel plate with sacred earth, ghee and flowers. "Who will do *Kanyadaan?*" he enquired, looking around.

Mr. and Mrs. Panesar stepped forward to give away their daughter, placing Billie's hand in mine.

"May the fire, water, air and earth bear witness to this auspicious occasion," he muttered. The next hour was totally lost on me. Most of the ceremony was in Sanskrit, the world's oldest language and only *punditji* among those gathered really understood it. Why, I wondered, did Hindu ceremonies have to be in Sanskrit? Why couldn't a Hindi or Punjabi version be used to conduct a marriage? But traditions prevail! Billie and I cast sideway glances at each other until the ceremony was deemed complete when we went around the small fire seven times, Billie following me six times and I her once, its significance being that the husband is supposed to protect and lead his wife, however, there are times that the husband may be hesitant or uncertain, whereupon the wife has to take the lead. And finally, 'the blessings'. Everyone stood up and showered us with rose and marigold petals. I heaved a sigh of relief. The end of the ceremony was in sight. Mrs. Panesar cried profusely as she again placed Billie's hand in mine and stepped back to let Papa and Maa hug their 'new' daughter-in-law.

She looked lovely in her red *Salwar-Kameez* and gold *Chuni*, which she had used to cover her head at all times in the temple and later also in the *Gurdwara* where we were showered with blessings from a Sikh *Garanthi* who read passages from the religious book which washed over me but which Billie followed and acknowledged with great devotion.

Later that evening the Panesars held a lavish reception at the Kenyatta Conference Centre for over twelve hundred guests, among them Daniel Arap-Moi, the President of Kenya, who had succeeded Jomo Kenyata after his death the previous year. All persons of any influence or importance in Kenya were present.

"Your FIL does not miss mixing business with pleasure," Bimla teased me on two occasions.

"And doesn't your MIL look important, surrounded by those pampered coffee-club housewives?" Nita added.

"Hush," Maa scolded her, "You mustn't talk like that about his in-laws. If Billie hears a word of this, there will be a calamity!"

"Maa looks lovely, doesn't she? Just like Meena Kumari," I commented. "I bet she feels relieved, now that we're all married."

"She does seem so relaxed," Nita agreed, "except for the twitch in the chin she has developed lately."

"Oh, probably the stress of getting me married off."

Bimla joined in. "I hope so. Oh I do so love marriages; they bring families together like no other occasion."

Bimla and Nita were both married off a few years ago, Bimla to Rajesh's cousin, Rahul, and Nita to Peter Towgood, a US resident she had met while working at the American Embassy in Nairobi a few years ago. They had made a special effort to attend my wedding, coming all the way from Los Angeles.

Papa and Mr. Panesar did an excellent job welcoming and thanking the guests. He had put on a fair bit of weight since giving up cricket and had developed lines running from his nose to the sides of his lips. Faint wavy lines on his forehead were visible too, just edging the grey beginning to appear at the temples. Mr. Panesar looked suave in his trimmed beard and maroon turban. They got along so well together. Months later I would discover that with the marriage they had sealed a business partnership in developing a block of seventy-four flats in Lower Kabete, a leafy part of Nairobi.

It was a joyous occasion, perfectly timed and executed no doubt with plan Bs for all events. It was good to see the Maqbools, especially Munir, and other friends - Afzal, Rajesh, Inayat and Robin. Sanjay couldn't make it because he was recouping from a knee operation, necessitated by a heavyweight which he had accidentally dropped on it at a gym he had recently joined. There were relations that I hadn't seen for years and some that I didn't know existed. Munir had recently been engaged to Rehana, a charming girl from England, visiting relations in Nairobi. "One look and I was smitten, *yaar*," he confided in me.

"Surely," I corrected him, "One look and *she* was smitten. She's not likely to get such a catch in England, you know."

"There's just one problem, Amar."

"What? Is she already married?"

"No ..."

"She has children?"

"No *yaar*, she doesn't want to leave England, and my roots are firmly fixed in Nairobi."

"Oh no, take my advice Munir, forget marriage, just be her pen-pal. There is much joy in letter writing."

"Shut up *yaar*, "he said indignantly, punching me lightly on the arm.

Paal Uncle and Paro Aunty made it too and planned to spend the following week in Mombasa by the beach. They loved every minute of their stay in Kenya and my happiness doubled seeing them enjoying themselves.

There were so many friends, relations and guests to meet that Billie and I had no time to tuck into the mountain of food that everyone raved about.

"Amar!" I turned around to acknowledge the voice though even before facing the person I realized who it was. "Mrs. Webber."

"Congratulations! You two make such a handsome couple." She placed her hands on each side of my face and kissed me affectionately.

"Mrs. Webber, you look lovely. I hope you are having a good time." She looked no older than she did when I first saw her, except for the rimless glasses, which only went to enhance her dignified poise. "Thanks for coming. And how is Ribena?"

"Oh, very well, she's around somewhere, among the crowd here. You'll probably bump into her in a minute. She has two children now, a boy and a baby girl." She turned to Billie. "*Balv*inder, you look *so* radiant. Trust me, you have found yourself a perfect husband."

Billie blushed and later confided in me, "I don't like her. There's something about the way she talks to you, do you know her well?"

"No... not very," I replied, wondering if I was lying or being truthful.

Late into the early morning the drinks and music continued. Most guests had departed in small trickles leaving close friends and family members. I started dancing with Paro Aunty. Bimla and Rajesh joined us. Within minutes, Munir, Afzal, Inayat and Robin were all trying *Bhangra*. Papa led Mrs. Webber to the dance floor and she danced with a grace that many others, watching, envied- a natural. Perhaps she had been to *Bhangras* before, I thought.

We danced to all sorts of music and film songs- Punjabi, Hindi and English. Munir was particularly energetic and seemed inseparable from Rehana.

Paal Uncle emerged from the shadows, beaming and swaying. "Having a good time Uncleji?" I shouted over the music.

"Faaantastic! This beats India or England." He stumbled towards me and gave me a long tight hug. It was then that I saw his collar smeared with lipstick, a colour very unlike what Paro Aunty was wearing on her lips. I called Inayat and Robin over who gently escorted him away from the dance floor. About ten minutes later they were back with Paal Uncle in a clean white shirt and Inayat in Paal Uncle's lipstick smeared shirt. The day was saved!

The two-week honeymoon was exhilarating- a week on the island of Lamu tucked away in a quiet village by the name of Shela where the ocean was crystal clear, with an abundance of swaying coconut trees. There was not a car engine to be heard on the heavenly island, donkeys being the only mode of transport. The locals of Arabic origin were the friendliest people I had ever come across, many insisting on Billie and me eating with their families at their homes. Billie was a good swimmer and we both soon lost the pounds we had gained eating *ladoos* and other sweet dishes before the wedding.

We would lie on the powder white sand, under swaying trees watching the dhows glide by. In the evening, we would wonder where the day had flown by and at night we would walk hand in hand on the beach and most nights make love in some secluded corner. She was good.

We spent the second week of our honeymoon at Treetops and Mount Kenya Safari Club, where the air was cool and fresh.

"Do you know, Amar?" Billie reminded me on a few occasions, "It was here that your Queen was informed of her father's death."

"I know darling, 1952."

We lost count of how many elephants, wild-beasts, and buffalos we saw that week. The highlight came when a leopard pounced upon a gazelle by the water-hole and brought it down in seconds. It then grabbed the poor creature by the neck and dashed away into the dark just as quickly and quietly as it had appeared. Except for a half-hearted, helpless shriek the gazelle offered no resistance.

Billie pursed her lips tight and I put an arm around her to comfort her. Outdoors, upon a tree, watching the way of the wild, she yielded to my touch and clung to me for affection. The cool air merely added pleasure to the warmth of her body and the yielding lips.

Early next morning, Billie stirred, perhaps sensing the sweet memories that were flooding my mind.

"What time is it?" she murmured, her voice thick with asleep, eyes closed.

"About six."

She put her head on my arm and snuggled against me. "I thought so."

"Thought so? What do you mean?"

She giggled softly. "A woman can tell when it's six."

I was mildly puzzled. "What, how—?"

She pressed her thighs against mine. "That's when the clock hands are up and erect," she teased."

I was happy, but little did I know at that moment that after the close of the year my life would change... for the worse.

Back in Oxford, months flew by, days seeming like hours. I had not experienced bliss for such a long stretch of time. Our first mild disagreement came one winter evening in England as we sat to watch The News at Ten. Islamic militants had taken American hostages in the US embassy in Tehran. I was glued to the television.

"Why don't we buy a bigger house?" she asked in a matter-of-fact tone.

Something in me stirred, perhaps without reason. "Why? What's wrong with this place?"

"Nothing... it's just a bit small. I thought that we could—"

"Small?" I interrupted. "A three-bedroom house for the two of us, how can that be small?"

Billie was taken aback by my outburst. For some time she was silent, though I wish she wasn't for it only increased the tension between us. For a while, we watched the news without seeing or hearing much. After a long silence, I cleared my throat and without looking at her said, "I have fond memories of this house."

"I understand, sorry darling. Let's retire to bed."

"Sure," I muttered. "You go ahead. I'll be along shortly."

I sat alone for a long time, staring at nothing. I had fond memories of the house. My first abode in Oxford, Mr. Woods' departure and then, just last year, Mrs. Woods' unexpected death. My mind went back to that summer day last year when we both spent the afternoon mowing the lawn and later pruning the Forsythia by the rockery and the Wisteria above the dining room French windows. I was up a ladder and carelessly throwing down the young stems which Mrs. Woods was gathering with a rake.

"Have a break, Amar. I'll get us some lemonade."

"OK, you do that; I'll be down as soon as I finish pruning."

The Wisteria was intertwined with the television aerial wire and the Virginia creeper and took longer to prune than anticipated. In my enthusiasm to finish the job, I did not realize that the sun had been beating on my back, which was now drenched in sweat, shirt clinging to my body. As I stepped off the last rung and placed my feet on the ground, a shiver went through my spine, despite the heat.

I gathered some more cuttings with the rake then took off my shoes and entered the dining room. It felt cold and dark inside, a stark contrast to the bright sunlight in the garden just a few feet away. I made my way to the kitchen, where a glass of lemonade awaited me on the worktop. In a few steps, I approached Mrs.Woods seated at the breakfast table.

"This is the life Mrs. Woods, hot summers and cold lemonade." I slumped opposite her and finished my drink in a few long gulps. She was seated in her favourite chair with a glass of lemonade on the table in front of her and eyes wide open. There was a drop of blood by the corner of one side of her lower lip. I froze at the sight and sat staring at her, mesmerized, knowing that she had gone but not knowing what to do. *Only a few minutes ago, she was alive, walking and talking!* After a while, I leaned forward and felt her hand. It was cold. I remember thinking how strange it was that a person could get so cold in just a few minutes.

The subject of moving house was not mentioned for months, until Billies' cousin called from Dubai to say that he was en route to Singapore and would very much like to stay a few days with us if it was no trouble. Jagmohan was a property magnate with hotels all over the Middle-East apparently used to the luxuries of life- large spacious houses, expensive hotels, fast cars and so on.

"What will he think?" Billie enquired in an accusing manner. "We've only got one bath-toilet. Amar, can't we..."?

"No," I shouted, flinging the newspaper across the room. If this is not good enough for him, he can stay at the Waldorf."

"Amar, you don't have to act like that, all I'm saying is that..."

I interrupted her again. "I know what you are saying. You want a bigger house just because you are used to such luxuries in Kenya. For heaven's sake Billie, you are now married to *me* – for better or worse. I can't afford to provide you with the luxuries that your dad did. Be thankful for what we have got, there are thousands worse-off than us. God knows where we'd be if my landlady had not left me this house in her will."

"But we *can* get a bigger place. *Babaji* can lend us some money."

"Billie! I am *not* going to accept any charity from your dad. For God's sake, please remember, you are not a Panesar anymore. You are now Balvinder Dushant. We have to live within our means. If you really must have a bigger house, why don't you get a job?"

My question inflamed her close to hysteria.

"A job? You want me to work *and* look after this house? Am I a servant to cook, clean, sweep *and* go out in the miserable weather for a few shillings?"

"Pounds," I said under my breath.

"What?" she glared at me, her eyes glinting in the light.

"Nothing, look, why don't we save some money for a while before we talk of a bigger house, OK?" She sat erect on the edge of the settee for a good few minutes in silence staring at some invisible spider at the far end of the wall, head turned away from me, sulking painfully. Finally, she muttered without conviction, "If you say so."

CHAPTER 21

After obtaining my degree at Christ Church, I had accepted a job with a medium sized, but fast growing company in Cowley- Tab Foils Limited, which manufactured foil for sealing tablets. It was a low risk, high turnover sector and the monthly profits kept growing. I worked hard and transferred most of the manual records onto computers. Within two years, I was producing Management Accounts detailing turnover, cost of sales and profits, not just by month but also by product. Any product not producing sufficient profits came under scrutiny and corrective action was instigated. Christopher Skinner, the Managing Director was quick to recognise my potential and dedication.

At one of the Board meetings, it was suggested that we should have a slogan for the company to cut down waste and improve efficiencies. I came up with M3 - *Measure, Monitor and Manage*. I explained that what we can't measure, we can't monitor, and what we can't monitor we can't manage. It wasn't entirely my slogan; I had read about something similar at college. At the final stage, the majority of the directors chose my slogan in favour of the Sales Director's *Seek Customers' Requirements*.

Tab Foils became a household name in Oxfordshire and turnover, profits and rewards kept growing. I was becoming a popular figure within the company until I suggested a plan to take over one of our rivals, Oxfo Foils, another medium sized company near Oxford, much against the resistance of all directors, especially the Finance Director, Duncan Dunhill. Although I had no axe to grind on this matter, Duncan was annoyed that I had taken the lead on the takeover debate, much against his recommendation. He would sometimes pass me in the corridors without acknowledging my greeting.

"Why engage in a costly and hostile bid when business is booming?" he directly enquired of me at a departmental meeting.

"Precisely, it is *because* we are growing so fast. We can't just stand still and be the subject of a takeover bid ourselves. By taking over Oxfo Foils, we would be a larger organisation and in a better position to resist bids against us. Also combined, we would control foil manufacture from one end of Oxford to another."

The takeover debate continued for months until rumour spread that Alum Foils Limited, a subsidiary of a Canadian organization based in Greater London was planning a bid for *both* Oxfo Foils and Tab Foils. We moved fast, working on figures late into the nights. Oxfo Foils had a sound Balance Sheet and a robust Business Plan. We had to make sure that our bid would be acceptable. The Board decided to pay a premium of twelve percent and secure the bid. Negotiations were long and rough. I attended a few of the meetings and in the end we had to settle for fifteen percent goodwill. Alum Foils backed off, unsure of how the new structure would pan out in Oxfordshire.

The result was that Duncan was proved wrong and his strategy disgraced. I was promoted from the position of Management Accountant to Chief Accountant. A bigger office, a secretary and a fully expensed Vauxhall Cavalier SRI came with the new title. Hurt by being leapfrogged by his protégé, he took early retirement. A few months later, I became the Finance Director and a few months after that I married Billie.

Paal Uncle invited us for Diwali at his place. "It's Billie's first Diwali in England, and your first as a couple. You must come over to us." He had been very insistent when he rang a few weeks earlier. Secretly, I was pleased to be invited to spend the day with them- Diwali is such a family occasion.

They had recently moved from Ealing to a quaint little cottage in Denham, a small village in Buckinghamshire.

"Oh, how picturesque Uncleji," I remarked in admiration. "It's lovely! So, English!"

Paro Aunty held Billie by the hand. "You look so charming. Come. Amar, you too, let me show you the garden." We went through the patio doors into a large square shaped garden with rockeries at the far corners and gravel paths forking from the patio to its edges.

"You know, Amar, Denham is regarded as the best kept village in Buckinghamshire," she said, leading us to an oval pond by the fence.

Billie was holding on to me as we stood by the pond catching glimpses of fish between floating lilies. "Look! There are so many in that corner! What are they, Auntiji?"

"Those are zebra fish; they keep away from the others."

Paal Uncle was looking restless. "Come; let's go inside, we don't want Billie catching a cold."

Inside, Paro Aunty suggested we say a short prayer, as it was Diwali.

We took off our shoes and sat cross legged on the floor facing some pictures of Lord Rama, his wife Sita and the monkey God, Hanuman. Paro Aunty lit a *diya* and incense and sang '*Om, jai jadish*' whilst we held our hands together in prayer and joined in the hymn. After chanting a few more hymns, Paal Uncle stood up and stretched his back. "Come on, time for fireworks. Let's lighten the sky and drive out the demons."

Paro Aunty made a face. "Shouldn't we wait for Ramesh and Laura?"

I was startled. "Are the Sethi's coming?"

Paal Uncle laughed teasingly. "It's all right *beta*, she won't eat you." From the corner of my eye I saw Billie's brief bewilderment. Paro Aunty said quickly. "Yes, Just some friends and their daughter."

"Are the Mehtas coming as well?" I asked.

"Alas, no, they are in India. I'll tell you about it later," she replied quickly. The tone in her voice suggested that I shouldn't pursue the matter any further- all would be revealed in good time.

Just as I began wondering if we were going to wait for the Sethis, a car screeched to a halt in the drive.

"Happy Diwali!" Ramesh Sethi shouted while walking inside, followed by Liz and Laura. Liz looked anxiously at Billie and me, "Congratulations! How are the newly-weds?" She hugged Billie and complimented her on her necklace. Before I could grasp the situation, her arms were around me. "Well done Amar, she's lovely."

Paal Uncle cut in. "Fireworks, everyone." He led us all to the back garden, where he and Dr. Sethi proceeded to explode loads of fireworks. "I love this bit," Liz said to me, "especially when Diwali and Guy Fawkes Day are so close to each other."

Laura and Paro Aunty went inside the house after some time to prepare dinner. Billie followed, offering to give a hand.

Paal Uncle and Dr. Sethi continued to lighten the sky with fireworks.

Liz moved closer to me. She looked beautiful. She was wearing a black figure hugging pullover and denims which did full justice to her figure.

She brushed a hand against my elbow. Her face was tilted towards me and she flicked her hair in an exaggerated movement, "Happy?"

After a few thoughtful seconds I replied, "Of course. I've no complaints with life."

"And do you have any against me?"

I gave her a slow smile, and a slow shake of the head, "No... of course not."

"You don't seem sure." She was silent for a few minutes whilst we tried to concentrate on the exploding fireworks.

Presently, I broke the silence. "How's John? Are you still with him?"

She smiled wryly. "Not *with* him, no, but I do see him frequently."

"Are you going to marry him, I mean, *would* you marry him?"

She remained silent for a long time staring at the fireworks, not really seeing them. After a while she clucked her tongue and as if on cue a voice from behind us broke the silence.

"Amar, why don't you come in? It's cold outside."

Liz turned her head. "You have a caring wife. Perhaps she doesn't want you to get into any sort of trouble."

I waved to Billie, "In a minute." I thought about Liz's choice of words. Any wife could see that leaving a husband unattended with Liz could be trouble.

As we turned to move inside the house, Liz touched my hand lightly. "We all make mistakes; I hope we can still be friends."

Billie was still standing by the doorway, waiting for us. I glanced sideways, "Of course."

Paro Aunty had made only vegetarian dishes being Diwali, and I found them refreshingly tasty. She insisted I sit opposite Billie and once everyone was seated, I realized that Liz was seated furthest from me. Clearly, Aunty wanted her Diwali dinner to go smoothly.

It was at our next meeting, a few months later at our house in Oxford that I remembered to ask Paro Aunty why the Mehtas couldn't come to her Diwali dinner. "You said that they had to go to India and you'd tell me why," I reminded her.

"Ah, yes. Amar, do you remember I once told you about their son in India?"

"Yes, the one who's severely disabled," I tried to remember, "living with his grandmother in Simla?"

"Yes, Ajit... well he died just a few days before Diwali. I didn't want to mention it that day, you know, being Diwali and Billie's first visit to our house."

"I understand. I'm sorry."

"It's not that I'm superstitious, it's just that—"

I interrupted her. "I understand. The Mehtas must have been distraught."

"Well, yes, they were. But I suppose in time they will realize what a relief it is for everyone."

After a while she popped a question out of the blue. "Have you forgiven Liz?" The tea in my cup wobbled for a second or two whilst I tried my best to phrase an answer. "It doesn't matter any more. Time and love are great teachers."

She smiled faintly and placed a hand on mine gently. "And you are a great student." After a while she asked another question. "Amar, please don't think that I am intruding, but, are you happy?"

"What do you mean?"

"Marriage, I mean... Billie and you."

My tea cup wobbled again. It took me a few seconds to realize that I really wasn't sure of the answer. She must have seen the brief hesitation on my face. "Sorry I asked. I wouldn't like to see you unhappy; I'll do anything to make sure you are happy."

Billie was more homely than I had imagined, being house proud and quite content to stay indoors for days on end. She took pride in keeping the place tidy and in her culinary prowess.

It didn't seem to matter in the first few months of our marriage. I was only too glad of a more organized home and prepared meals with little to do around the house. She took care of everything, the shopping, cleaning, washing, ironing, bills and even gardening.

Although not one to refuse or deny me of sex, she never once took the initiative.

Little by little things changed in the house. There were cushions on the settees, cushions on beds, cushions piled on a corner of the lounge. My comb, which I had for years placed on the window sill near the bath room was tucked inside the bath cabinet. Slippers which for years had lived at the foot of my bed started a new life in a closet. "Billie, what's wrong with keeping them here?" I would ask.

"They don't suit there, and it's not hygienic!"

"What! Not hygienic? Billie, this is not a temple or some... some... it's our home!"

Over time, gentle arguments grew louder and the silences between us longer. Sometimes Billie would sulk and I would then try to bring her out of her moods. These periods gradually increased and the discomfort grew heavy in the house.

I found myself with more spare time than I had for months. A few times, I had made excuses when Inayat or Robin had asked us to go out together. We understand, they had said, "Newly weds, eh?"

Inayat rang me at the office one morning. He sounded extremely cheerful. "Hello, love-bud, forgotten me?"

"Inayat! How are you? I was about to ring you," I lied, feeling guilty that I hadn't contacted him for a while; it was always him ringing me.

"OK then, I'll put the phone down, you ring me," he chuckled.

I laughed. "How are you? It's so good to hear from you."

"Amar, there's a new Lebanese restaurant opening just off Queen Street on Friday, shall we try it?"

"*Shall we try it*? Of course! Is there any restaurant in Oxford which we haven't tried? I was feeling a surge of excitement at the thought of meeting friends again, "Who's coming?"

"The usual circle of friends, your house is on my way; we'll pick you around seven, OK?"

"OK Inayat, I'll look forward to it."

Billie threw a tantrum at the invitation."You should have asked me before agreeing. Why don't we stay at home, just the two of us and watch a film?"

I thought she was being very unreasonable. "We've nothing planned for Friday. I knew that, so I didn't see the point of asking you. Furthermore, you didn't mention anything about a film."

She marched out of the room, banging the door on her way out. "Next time..."

"Next time, what?" I shouted, following her.

"Next time, *ask* me!"

I was furious. "Ask you for *what?*" I bellowed, "To get out of this house? And *stop* walking about!"

She turned around, fists clenched. "I am your *wife*. You are *married* now. You can't spend all your time with your friends," she shouted back.

"*All* my time?" I yelled. When was the last time I went out with them? And they are *our* friends, not just mine." I was having trouble controlling myself. "Don't walk away! *Billie!*"

She vanished into the kitchen. "Well, I don't like them!" she shouted.

"What!" I followed her into the kitchen where she was standing looking at the garden with her back to me. "What's wrong with them?"

Her jaw clenched and unclenched. "I don't know," she screamed, turning around. "What's wrong with *me?* Why can't you spend the evening with *me?*" Her voice choked with anger.

"Nothing," I replied, trying to lower my voice. "But we spend a lot of time together, what harm will there be to go out with friends once in a while? Be reasonable, Billie."

She rolled her eyes and marched past me in a rage. "So *I'm* unreasonable? *I'm* wrong? Why did you marry me then?" The words screeched through clenched teeth, stinging my ears.

I did not answer. I stood still, out of breath in the middle of the kitchen, which seemed to have shrunk, closing on me from all sides. She thumped up the stairs to the bedroom, dislodging a painting in the process. It swayed and fell with a loud thud, cracking the frame. Neither of us made any attempt to clear it from the foot of the stairs. I shuffled to the lounge. The damned curtains had changed again for the third time in as many months. Billie's question was biting my skull. *Why did you marry me?*

I slouched into an armchair and closed my eyes. A few seconds later, I stood up, shaking with rage. I could not stay still and slouched into the chair again. *Why did I marry her?* I had no answer.

Reluctantly, after some persuasion and flowers, Billie agreed to go to the restaurant that Friday. Inayat came dead on time with his girl friend, Saira, a pretty girl who was in her final year studying Hotel Management. She had large shy eyes and hardly ever spoke unless spoken to. At six foot, she was a good three inches taller than Inayat, though neither of them thought that was a problem. Most acquaintances ended up asking Saira of her height at some stage or the other to which she would reply, 'five foot twelve'.

Robin, minus his ginger beard was waiting by the restaurant with Cheryl, another pretty girl, with the slimmest waist and the widest smile in Oxford. She had long dark hair; the length sometimes reminded me of Jennifer. Cheryl was chatty and could end up giving minute details of physiotherapy sessions she gave at a local clinic.

We greeted each other warmly even Billie made an effort. The restaurant was very Middle-Eastern, with copper lamps and bright chandeliers everywhere. Compared to the winter chill outside, it felt warm and welcoming. The place was covered with damasks and gaudy brocades, the ceilings dripped with shiny lanterns. The smell of spices and mutton was unmistakable. Sizzling dishes were expertly carried on flat palms at shoulder height by smartly dressed waiters. Some customers, having finished their meal were contendedly smoking shisha pipes.

"Looks lovely in here," Cheryl exclaimed, rubbing her hands. "The food smells good."

"Let's hope it tastes good," Robin added.

The food *was* good, and the waiters, dressed in Arabic flowing gowns were discreetly attentive, serving excellent meze, kebbeh meshwiyeh and endless kebab dishes with fragrant rice and naan bread.

Expectedly, the conversation turned to married life to which I had to give positive replies as Billie's expression took that far away look which I was now getting used to. Cheryl and Saira exchanged knowing glances and I thought of turning the topic around. "So, who's next?" I poured more wine all around. In recent months Inayat had decided to stop fighting the custom and had taken to wine in small quantities.

Robin shook his head. "No hurry here, not until I find the right woman. I never chew more than what I can bite." Everyone laughed at his habit of deliberately mixing words. Cheryl gave him a hard punch on his arm. "No darling, the biting comes first. And consider yourself lucky, you've found *a* woman, right or wrong, you're unlikely to find another."

"*Touché!*" I shouted.

Robin mused over his drink for a while. "Perhaps I should marry; afterall happiness is not the only thing in life." He received another friendly punch on the arm from Cheryl.

We were silent for a while and then turned to Inayat. Saira blushed, dimpling in both cheeks and lowered her eyes. Robin thumped the table, "Inayat! Do you have something to declare?"

Cheryl joined in, "Out with it, Inayat."

"Steady on, Cheryl, not in a restaurant!" Robin exclaimed.

"You've got a one track mind." Cheryl retorted.

"But it's a good track- and you know it," came the swift reply.

Amidst laughter all eyes were on Inayat, "Well?"

He stretched out a hand and held Saira's. "Shall we tell them now?" he asked her softly.

Robin thumped him on the back, "Out with it, man!"

Inayat took a sip from his glass and moved closer to Saira. She raised her eyes looking into his, "We've decided to tie the knot."

We all cheered and clapped. Some of the customers joined in. "Bravo!" shouted a voice from a nearby table.

"Inayat, this is great news. Saira, you two will be perfect for each other," I said. "Waiter, champagne please!"

Billie, seated next to Saira, offered congratulations.

"When Inayat? When do you get married?" I asked excitedly.

Inayat spoke in a lowered voice, "It will have to be soon, very soon."

"Good," Cheryl said, raising her glass, "the sooner the better."

I leaned forward, not comprehending Inayat's expression. "What do you mean; it will *have* to be soon?"

Once again, all eyes were on him, then on Saira. He cleared his throat. All eyes moved back to him. "Well..." No one made a sound. "You see, Saira and I... I mean we... What I'm trying to say is that in another seven months, there will be *three* of us."

Had we not consumed any alcohol, we would have grasped it instantly. It took a few seconds for the penny to drop.

Robin half stood up. "Inayat!" he shouted, thumping him on the back. "Well done man! Congratulations, Saira."

I looked around for a waiter, "More champagne, please."

Winter did not agree with Billie. She was content to stay indoors, tidying, cleaning, tidying again and cleaning again. She spent hours cooking exotic dishes, trying to improve on previous attempts and relishing on compliments, which over time seemed too formal between the two of us. Attempts to socialize, even just the two of us brought excuses- too tired! - too cold! - not in the mood! I found myself spending more and more time in front of the TV and she in the kitchen, with Hindi songs from films she had grown up with in Nairobi.

One evening, I was watching *Yes Minister*, a comedy programme on TV when Billie came and sat next to me. I looked sideways and smiled. "Finished with the dishes?"

"Yes, I thought I'd see what you are up to."

I threw my hands up, "Nothing really."

She stretched her legs forward and dug her back deep into the settee. Her legs were long and shapely. I leaned to her side and placed a hand on her thigh. "Tired?"

"Uh-huh." Her sigh lingered for a while. "Amar, why don't we start a family?"

I was taken aback. I had sometimes wondered how or when couples bring up the subject about starting a family; Billie's approach seemed a bit abrupt.

"A family?"

"Yes, you know, children."

I asked, teasingly, "How many?"

She met my eyes and realized I was not being serious, "Four; either all together or singly."

She hadn't joked about anything for months and her remark was very welcome. Without replying, I moved against her and unbuttoned her blouse.

For many months Billie talked about little else but babies. She bought baby books, videos about babies, catalogues about babies, went window-shopping for push chairs and brought up baby names, even choosing a school for the baby.

"Steady on, Billie, one step at a time," I cautioned on several occasions.

"Amar, guess who I bumped into at the Supermarket, this afternoon?" she asked me one spring day.

"God?"

"Be serious. *Saira*. She's in her *fifth* month. She looks *so* radiant and happy."

"Is that so, in that case she'll have a boy."

Her tone softened, "A boy? How can you tell?

"Well, I read somewhere that if after some months, a woman looks radiant and happy; she always has a boy, especially if the blood-pressure increases." I was doing my best at keeping a straight face.

"Oh, I wish I had known, I would have told her so."

"Why don't we invite them over for dinner, then you can surprise her with the news?"

It took a second or two for Billie's eyes to light up, "Yes, I'll ring her tomorrow."

"Can you also ring Cheryl and invite her and Robin too. We haven't seen them for a few months."

"OK," she replied, but not so enthusiastically.

It was close to midnight in late June when Inayat rang us of the news of the arrival of their baby son, Mahmoud. I was quick to congratulate him heartily. "I hope Saira and the baby are doing well." Inayat couldn't stop talking, much of which didn't make sense for in his excitement he was tripping over his words.

From thereon, Billie went into a state of mild depression, sometimes tantrums. "Hey, our turn will come," I tried to reassure her on many occasions. She would turn her face away and blink away the moistness in the eyes. "Billie, these things take time. Please don't despair; it will only make matters worse."

"But we've been trying for months. If it was going to happen, I would have been pregnant by now. Maybe there is something wrong with me."

"It's nothing of that sort, just a question of time."

She retorted sternly, "It might be *you*."

I was stunned. "*What!*"

"I *said*: it might be *you*! I... I..." she screeched. In her angry state she stammered over her thoughts and words.

The venom hurt. I tried to control myself. "It may be both of us, or neither of us, or one of us. I don't care! Just wait another month."

"That's what you said last month," she shouted, in despair.

We sat in silence for a while. Her hands in her lap folded, unfolded and folded again. She focused on some imaginary spider on the facing wall. "Amar, why don't we have a check-up?"

I was deeply annoyed. I recalled a conversation I had with Paro Aunty some years ago. She had said that Paal Uncle and she had accepted God's decision and they did not wish to know which partner was incapable. Did I really want to know which of us could not conceive?

"No!" I said sternly. I will not have doctors checking our private parts- not yet! If God wants us to have children, we will."

She stood up in a shot. "Then *I'll* have a check up," she screamed. "You can wear bangles, bracelets, whatever and stay at home. Pray to your God and see what He does!"

"*Billie!*"

"Oh shut up! And go back to your friends."

"*Billie*! That's enough!" I screamed taking a step towards her, my ears ringing in pain with her words. "Be reasonable, whenever I offer you an olive branch you just... just set fire to it and throw the ashes in my face."

"I can't stand it *anymore*." She stepped back and rushed to the spare bedroom slamming the door behind her.

CHAPTER 22

Our second wedding anniversary passed fairly peacefully. Paal Uncle and Paro Aunty came for Sunday tea and we all went for a walk by the river. Billie was quiet but happy. I had bought her a white gold ring, which she genuinely liked. She in turn surprised me with a soft leather wallet.

The meadow was lush and a few cows grazing nearby gave us a congratulatory look. Paal Uncle and I were walking a few steps ahead of the ladies, who kept getting distracted by the punters.

I mentioned Billie's longing for a baby to Paal Uncle. "Have you had tests done?" he asked.

"Billie has. I don't see the point."

"I see. Yes, I suppose if one partner gets the result, then you'll know the full story."

"Not really, Uncle, I wasn't in favour of either of us having tests. *Que sera sera*, I say."

He was quiet for a while. "Amar, we went through something similar. But Paro and I both agreed not to know who was infertile. What's the point? And unlike some people, we did not wish to adopt. Paro always said that if God wished..."

We walked in silence for a hundred yards or so.

"Paul." We stopped and turned around.

It was Paro Aunty, standing still and shielding herself from the sun with a hand on her forehead. "We'd better head back; I've had enough exercise for a day."

Paal Uncle whispered in my ear, "Shall I have a quiet word with Billie?"

I hesitated then nodded.

He took Billie's arm, "You look lovely today. Can I walk with my favourite neice?"

I walked alongside Paro Aunty, trailing the pair in front of us by about ten steps. She stooped down to pick a little stick. "You know something Amar, your wife needs a holiday. Why don't you take her back to Kenya for a week or two, it would do her good to see her family again."

The suggestion made sense. If Billie had mentioned her predicament to Paro Aunty, she made no mention of it. I didn't feel like asking. "Perfect, I'll work on it."

The next day, just as I was about to get in the car for work, the Postman, walked up the drive with a few letters. "I'll have them," I said casually.

The letter on top arrested my attention. It was addressed to Mrs. Balvinder Dushant and marked 'Private'. My heart skipped a beat. I didn't bother to check the other letters.

I went back indoors. "Billie," I shouted, "letter from the hospital."

She rushed down, "Must be the results." Her hands were shaking as she opened the letter and read it, lips trembling. I waited anxiously.

"What does it say?"

She handed me the letter. "Everything is normal."

The first word that came to my mind was, "Good."

She went pale. "So what do we do now?"

I gave her a clumsy but gentle hug. "I'm not sure, Billie, I've got to get to work. We'll talk when I get back."

Before I got a chance to open the door, her words stung my back, "You and your precious work! Go!"

"Billie, be reasonable, I'm already late for a meeting. I was supposed to..."

"Yes, yes, go. Never mind me." She forced the words through clenched teeth.

"OK," I shouted. "So I'm the incapable partner. Does that make you happy? Maybe we can adopt."

"I don't want *someone else's* baby sucking my breasts!" she screamed.

"Well then," I screamed back, "find someone who can fuck you!" We both recoiled at the words that I had uttered. I hadn't meant to say that, it just came out and despite my anger I felt ashamed and hated myself for it. We fell silent for a while, I not trusting myself to open my mouth and she not quiet believing what I had said. I faced her and shook my head."I'm sorry, I didn't mean that."

She was shaking in disbelief. For a few seconds, we stared at each other, hating the other. She narrowed her smouldering eyes and hissed at me, "I *will!*" Her lips trembled, her mouth gathering more venom to spit at me, "You will rue this day!"

The annoyance within me reached the tip of my tongue, which I bit to contain the situation. The briefcase in my hand felt heavy. I debated for a few seconds whether to continue talking or leave. Realising that we could argue till nightfall and still not get anywhere, I flung open the door and left her at the doorstep. As I pulled away from the drive, in the wing mirror I saw her slamming the door shut.

CHAPTER 23

Two weeks in Nairobi did Billie a world of good. She was destressed and felt quite at home with her family.

Papa's business deals were taking fruition and he proudly displayed his new gleaming white Mercedes to go with his not so old Peugeot 404. He even hired a driver to take the congestion strain. Traffic in Nairobi was getting unbearable. "Discipline is lacking," he complained. "People overtake from either side, they don't stop at traffic lights - that's if the damn things work. Some drivers even go over the roundabouts."

"Why don't the police do anything?" I asked.

"Police?" he laughed, "Give them fifty shillings and you can get away with murder. You know something, a client of mine rang the police one night to inform them that burglars were breaking his front door, and their reply? *Hakuna petroli.* Can you believe that? *No petrol.* "

"Papa, you've got to take it easy, you've lost a lot of weight. Have you had a check up lately? And have you noticed the twitch Maa keeps having in the chin?"

"Amar, there's nothing wrong with us. You chaps in England have a habit of visiting doctors at the slightest problem. That's why they do so well there. Here in Nairobi, they drive little Nissans."

There was no arguing with him, or for that matter with Maa either. "Just my age, Amar, you think I'm going to change?"

"Maa, no one else has that kind of twitch, doesn't it bother you?"

"No," she replied flatly, "*Beta*, you look after Billie."

There was no point arguing with either of them. They were gradually changing and adjusting to each other's habits and ways. I found them more and more talking to each other while moving around, even walking away. Many a time, a sentence would start in one room and finish in another, the listener only hearing half the words. And yet, they were blissfully happy.

One evening, when Billie had gone shopping with Bilo, I met Munir for lunch at Dil Bahar restaurant. It brought back sweet memories, even though the hygiene factor bothered me. "Don't they ever wash the aprons here?"

He laughed. You are talking like a *wazungu, European.* Oh, that reminds me, do you remember Mwangi?

"Of course I do. Corn with lime and chillies, why?"

"Poor chap, he died a few months ago. Syphilis; couldn't afford the medical treatment."

The suddenness of the news saddened me. "That's a shame; we had some great times at his *Duka.*" I shook my head. "A lot of people here leave their wives and kids in the village *shambas* and come to the glittering city lives thinking money is easy to make here. Their only evening pleasure is finding some prostitute."

He grimaced. "Nairobi is crawling with prostitutes. Even the best hotels keep a supply for tourists."

"Munir, it happens all over the world."

"Maybe, but what I find obscene is seeing old haggard Americans and Europeans picking up girls young enough to be their grand-daughters for what they would pay for a packet of cigarettes back home."

I stared at him. He certainly had something against the Western world. "Sad," I said. "Poverty is tragic." Then, to change the topic, I asked, "How's Rehana?"

His eyes lit up. "She's the best thing in my life, *yaar.* Mind you, she keeps talking about moving to England. Every time she mentions England I take her shopping, that shuts her up for a few weeks."

I laughed. "You fool."

He shrugged his shoulders. "Whatever. Her happiness is my happiness."

I felt a pang of jealousy.

The sweet *lassis* arrived. I took a long sip. "Wonderful!"

The *pakoras* came next, followed by chic peas curry and *puris*. Munir ordered two mango and almond *kulfis* - that way, they would be softening by the time we were ready to have them later.

"Good thinking, Munir."

Billie and I went swimming a few times at Serena Hotel. She was relaxed and happy, with no mention of babies. I wondered why, but dared not ask, afraid that the mention of the "b" word might spark a tantrum waiting to erupt. Even when we made love she never mentioned that word, yielding willingly. I wondered what had caused this welcome change. Was it merely being back to her motherland, or had her parents had a pep-talk with her? I was grateful to Paal Uncle for suggesting the holiday. "We must come here at least once a year," I once suggested.

To my surprise she remarked, "Don't you want to see the rest of the world?"

Back in England, Billie gradually went back to the routine- cleaning, tidying, cooking, cleaning, tiding, cooking... I once suggested house help for cleaning and ironing. "There's a lady in my office whose sister does this sort of thing."

She turned to face me. "Amar, are you suggesting I can't cope?"

"No, what I meant..."

Her lips quivered. "You mean I don't clean and iron well enough?"

"Billie, *no*! What I meant was that you'd have more spare time to go out and meet friends. Visit Saira, she's at home full time now." The moment I said that, I bit my tongue.

She stood still, absorbing the stinging words. "I hate you," she finally hissed, narrowing her eyes before averting mine.

I took a step towards her. "What did you say?"

Taking a step back she murmured, "Nothing." Her lips pursed and after a brief silence she said as calmly as she could, "Saira's too busy with her baby."

I wanted to argue and discuss, but dared not. Silence is golden.

CHAPTER 24

Autumn arrived in its full glory of red and gold. The leaves looked spectacular against clear blue skies, the fresh cool air blowing them down with soft kisses. I loved walking on crisp gold leaves in the parks around Oxford, the fresh breeze biting softly into the eyes.

Billie however withdrew more and more into the house. Too cold outside!

It was a lovely Saturday morning when the phone rang, the call to change my life.

"Amar?"

It took me a few seconds to identify the caller. "Sanjay!" I shouted down the line, "How the devil are you?"

"Hey, I'm fine. Listen, I've been offered a posting in Oxford; isn't that great?"

"Really? That's wonderful! When do you start?"

"That's up to me. If I like the setup, I could start in a month's time. But, hey, I'm coming next week-end to sort out some accommodation."

"You can stay with us, what's there to sort?"

"Lots, I'll explain when I see you; how about lunch-time this Saturday?"

I was thrilled. "I'll look forward to that. Have lunch with us."

"No, no lunch, I really don't know what time I'll reach you guys. See you Saturday."

A bright red Mustang graced our drive around noon that Saturday. As I opened the front door, Sanjay waved to me. "Hey Amar, I have a surprise for you."

I took a few steps towards the car; going around it he opened the passenger door. With a bow and a wave of an arm he introduced me to a woman getting off the seat. "Meet Carla, my brand new wife."

I was dumbstruck. Billie joined us and looked equally puzzled. She had met Sanjay a few times, but neither of us was aware that he had married.

Shaking hands with him, I said. "What, when...I mean, congratulations...you never mentioned..."

Carla appeared to be a few years older than Sanjay, and didn't seem his type at all. He was tall and trim and she the complete opposite. To top it all, she wore a short skirt which did no favours to her short plump legs. Her short hair made her face seem more rounded than it was.

Sanjay seemed happy. "Surprised, eh? Sorry to spring it on you. Hey, we only got married two months ago. It was a quick Registry wedding with only three witnesses."

"Well, come in. Lunch's nearly ready," I suggested.

One question was soon answered when I saw the six huge diamond rings- three in each of Carla's hand. Over lunch, Sanjay explained that he was being transferred to the Oxford branch of Standard Bank. He was going to be the Chief Manager with relocation and removal expenses all paid. His plan was to stay at the Randolph Hotel until he could find some decent accommodation.

"I'm sure you can find something good in Oxford. What's your price range?" I enquired.

He glanced at Carla. "Something spacious, at least four bedrooms, with a large garden, I just love gardening- up to £300,000." Carla nodded.

I nearly fell off my chair. "For that price you could get a *six* bed house here!"

They *did* buy an expensive house in Kidlington, a few miles north of Oxford town centre. I never asked him how much he paid for it; a six bedroom house with a garden that seemed to have no end and large remote controlled gates. Our three bed semi could have fitted comfortably in his drive.

One day, a few months later over a few beers in a pub, Sanjay confided that at his salary he couldn't have afforded the luxuries that he was now taking for granted.

"So, has Santa Clause showered you with money?" I asked.

He laughed, "Something like that; he brought Carla into my life."

"How did you meet her?"

He leaned forward, serious, "Come on, Amar, would I go around meeting someone like her? No, *she* sought me out." Seeing my puzzled expression, he clarified, "Hey look, I was just a junior bank manager with Standard, Carla was my boss." He took a long sip from his glass and smacked his lips. "Between the two of us, Amar, she wasn't getting anything between her legs; I certainly paid little attention to her. But, she's clever. As far as foreign exchange transactions are concerned, she was the best in the bank. Her Christmas bonus alone was more than my annual salary. What she didn't know about Options and Forward Rate Agreements is not worth knowing. She would keep me late at work on some pretext or the other, then take me for expensive meals, the finest wine, drop me home in her Porsche, give me expensive presents ... I was hooked!"

Shocked, though not surprised, I said, "Damn it, Sanjay, that's harassment! You could have taken action against her."

He laughed, his hazel eyes lighting up. "Amar, this is strictly between these walls. What would I have said? Carla makes me work late sometimes. Damn it, the bank would have congratulated her for increased productivity. And if I went around saying that she was taking me to expensive restaurants, I would only have looked foolish in court. *But Your Honour, Miss Carla Shepherd never forced the plaintiff to eat the food or drink the wine!*"

I scratched my head. "Did she ever make sexual advances?"

"Ah, ha, she's too clever. She made *suggestive*, not sexual advances. She knew that in time it would happen." Sanjay was looking a bit subdued.

Having known him since childhood, his cheerful, carefree nature, I felt hurt that he had been entrapped in such a way that would affect the rest of his life.

"So, did it ever happen, before marriage I mean?"

"Oh yes," Sanjay said quickly, smirking, then falling silent for a long time, staring at the top of his drink and replaying the event. "Oh, yes, at the last Christmas party. Hey, you know how it is. She made sure the drink had gone to my head." He lifted his eyes to mine, "and to my *danda.*"

I laughed, "What happened?"

"Some other staff members were kissing and cuddling. That turned me on. I was having a good time with some mates and had just finished a dance with a pretty girl working in Loans, when Carla brought a bottle of Champagne for all of us and sat next to me, one leg practically on my lap."

I thumped the table. "That's sexual harassment!"

"Come on, Amar, it was a Christmas party. Everyone was either at it, or pissed. She knew I was drunk and hungry, later she offered to give me a lift home. Only, I didn't go home."

"Good for you," I said softly.

"No, *bad* for me; we ended up at *her* place!"

"Oh shit!"

"Amar, have you ever played a game called, *Shock Me?*" From my expression he knew that I hadn't. He waved a hand in a dismissive gesture. "I think it's Carla's invention."

I was interested. "What's the game?"

"Dirty, very dirty. One partner says something dirty, the other has to match or better it, and so it goes on, until...you know." He looked at me and laughed. You should try it sometime, it's crazy.

"I don't quite—"

He interrupted me. "Let's say, one person says, *I'd like to kiss you on the cheek,* the other has to be more vulgar, and might say something like *I'd like to kiss you on the lips.*

"And do they?"

"They do. The first person then has to say something more shocking..."

I got it. "They take turns to upstage each other. So one might say something like... *I'd like to undo your bra* and the other—"

"Not so fast, Amar, the game's got to move slowly, can't go to bra so quickly.Maybe something like... *shirt.* It can take hours if one wants to. You can guess how it ends."

"So you were hooked from there on? Sanjay, if you are not in love with her, how are you going to...?"

"Hey, love, life, sex - what are they? Mere instruments! Just because I'm married to Carla, you think that's the end of life? You think I can't have these pleasures any more, elsewhere?" He leaned forward and lowered his voice, "Because of her, I've got this promotion in Oxford, because of her I have a lovely house, because of her I drive expensive cars." He paused, "I could go on."

"How can you, if you don't love her?"

He sounded slightly exasperated. "Oh, come on, two can play this game of life. Carla's not the only one who can give me a good time is she? Just because I like blue suits, doesn't mean that I can't try brown suits?"

The penny dropped. He drained his glass and keeping it in front of his face eyed me through it for what seemed like minutes. "Hey, what about that girl you used to fancy in Nairobi?"

The sudden change in conversation startled me.

"What girl?" I asked quickly, frowning but knowing full well who he was referring to.

He placed the glass on a stool shaking his head. "I've forgotten her name... the mute one, Munir's sister."

"Azra," I said simply.

He leaned forward, eyes smiling, "Boy, she was something, those pomegranate lips. What happened to her?"

Seeing me shrugging my shoulders, he continued, a mischevious smile playing on his lips. "You fancied her, didn't you? Boy, she could have broken a million hearts if only—"

"If only she wasn't mute," I finished his sentence. "She's in Pakistan, either engaged or married, I'm not sure."

He smiled again, made a face and clucked his tongue, "Another drink?"

There was no mistaking that smile. His lips curled down before widening into a smile, creasing on side of his face. It was almost a wicked smile.

"No, I should be heading home."

"Back to Billie, eh?"

I nodded and we stood up. As we exited he commented, "You've done well, she's beautiful."

I never mentioned my meetings with Sanjay to Billie. She and Carla became good friends, improbable though it seemed at the time. I suppose, Billie was taken in by Carla's spending power and she enjoyed shopping with her for their new house. She was probably also taken in by the huge house and the Porsche. Carla was new to Oxford and was content with Billie's company and her contribution to the selection for house contents. Occasionally, they went over to see Saira, who being shy and more down to earth kept herself to herself. There was also little Mahmoud, who needed constant attention. Knowing Saira, as I did, I knew that she didn't like venturing out unless she was accompanying Inayat.

Who was I to complain? Billie had a friend, she went out more than she ever did, and got some fresh air. We argued less and sometimes ate out by ourselves or with Sanjay and Carla. On a few occasions Robin and Cheryl joined us for a meal or drinks. Life ticked by- work, home, friends - I was content. As Sanjay once put crudely, "There are five Fs that are important in life - Fun, Food, Family, Friends and..."

"And what?" we dared him.

"Can't say in front of the girls" he laughed.

"Is it the four letter word?" Robin asked, pretending to be innocent."

"*Yes*, Fish!" Sanjay teased.

"Talking of letters," Inayat said, "there are five Ws we must be careful of."

After a lot of guesswork, laughter and arguing, we agreed on Weather, Wives, Wine, Water and Whores. Carla wasn't going to take it lying down. "You men," she said, "you are the problem of this world. What about the five Ms?"

We all looked at each other. "What Ms; never heard of them?" I declared.

Carla exchanged glances with Billie. "Well, how about *M*ental, *M*eningitis, *M*enstruation, *M*enopause and *M*en!"

"Yes," Billie added, "I could add Manchester United to it as well."

I threw my hands up in the air, "Touché!"

Peace was shattered on day when Carla informed Billie that she was expecting.

Billie rang me at the office. "That's great!" I said. "I'll ring Sanjay straight away to congratulate him." It was only when I put the phone down that I realized I had detected a certain bitterness in her voice.

Sure enough, in the coming weeks, she brought up the topic about babies numerous times.

"We've been through this before, Billie, we can't have children- it's not the end of life." The discussions grew longer until they turned into arguments.

"Why is it only me?" she said bitterly on one occassion.

"Billie, it's not you, it's *me.*"

"So why is it just *us?*" she demanded in loud frustrarion.

"It's me," I half whispered.

She rattled the kitchen drawers with exaggeratred speed, clanging the cutlery. A knife spun and fell noisly on the lino. She banged the drawer shut, pushing her hand against it until it would go no further. The knife shuddered in defiance but settled quietly, defeated. Neither of us made an attempt to pick it. Wheeling around to face me she shouted, "I know, but it still means that it's *me* who can't have a baby.Because of *you.*"

I willed myself to be gentle. "We can adopt, you know."

"Don't patronize me, Amar! I've told you a million times that I'm not having someone else's baby sucking my breasts."

"OK, calm down. There's nothing we can do."

"*Don't!*" she forced the words through clenched teeth. "Don't *ever* tell me to calm down. You don't understand. I don't feel like a *woman!*"

Billie withdrew into her world of housework and made excuses when Carla invited her over for coffee or shopping. I found myself watching TV by myself again. One night I went upstairs and found her sleeping in the spare room. Standing in the doorway, I wondered if this was the beginning of a breakdown of our marriage.

Next morning, she was relatively sedate and asked me what I would like for dinner.

"Daal and rice would be nice."

"OK," she smiled. "We haven't had that for a while."

I thanked my stars that she seemed calmer, until...

"Amar, why don't we get a bigger house?"

"What? Why?"

"Everyone else does," she replied in a shrill voice.

"Billie, it's just the two of us..."

"That's not the point. Look at Sanjay and Carla, Paal Uncle, the Mehtas, the Sethis..."

"*Billie*, I have to get to work. Can this wait?"

"Work,work,work! It's either that or your friends." She was beginning to shake with rage. "You just live in the shadow of your friends, especially... especially Sanjay. You are just his little poodle!" Her almond shaped eyes turned into balls of fire.

That hurt. "*Poodle?*" I shouted in anger.

"Yes, *yes*," she screeched, with clenched fists."

With that she turned away from me and stormed into the kitchen.

For a while, I stood frozen in silence, her words stinging my ears.

As I closed the front door, I heard shattering of glass in the kitchen.

I mentioned brief details of what Billie was going through to my friends over a few drinks at a local pub.

Inayat was of the opinion that I should have a check up. He knew a very good doctor. Robin agreed, "Nothing to lose. Doctors can only help, maybe there's a blockage somewhere. A simple operation..."

Sanjay, casual as ever said how lucky I was. "No pills, no condoms, blank bullets with all the pleasure."

"Billie's getting a bit depressed. Sometimes I have difficulty concentrating at work."

Inayat made a suggestion, "Have you considered artificial insemination?"

It was like a brick hitting me. "Having someone else's sperms inside my wife? Not keen on that."

"First things first, man, see a doctor," Robin concluded.

"About the house," Sanjay said thoughtfully, "I think Billie's right. Hey, you can afford a better place."

"Maybe, but then I'll have to cut down on other things- eating out, holidays, and so on. Anyway, it's big enough for two." After a few sips, I added, "And it has happy memories."

"Sanjay's a bank manager, take his advice man," Robin suggested.

"If you need financial help, you've only got to ask, you know that, don't you?" Inayat said, touching his glass against mine.

For once Sanjay was serious, "Amar, you've lived in that house long enough. Sell it; there will be no Capital Gain Tax. You will have a substantial sum to put forward as deposit for a much better place. I can get you the maximum mortgage possible at a reasonable rate."

I wasn't sure. "With one salary, that's not going to be easy. I don't believe in struggling in life."

Sanjay was getting excited. "Amar, your house is probably around £35,000. Sell it; keep £10,000 for luxuries and so on. With a deposit of £25,000 and a mortgage of around, say, £30,000 on your salary, you could buy a four bedroom house without any problems. Property values, especially around here are going to double within the next five years. By the time you retire, the house will probably be worth around £800,000."

Robin slapped my back. "That's settled, man. Toast everyone." We all raised our glasses. "Here's to four babies... sorry, bedrooms."

I could see some gain in this. Perhaps I could reach a compromise with Billie!

I decided not to discuss the matter with Billie until I had done some research on property values. I got some local papers and contacted two estate agents. Sure enough, my house was worth around £35,000. Most four bedroom detached houses were around £45,000 and Charles Church were selling a new phase of five bedroom detached houses with double garages for £52,000! To make sure that I could comfortably afford the mortgage payments I approached my manager at Barclays Bank. He called me at the office within twenty four hours. "Mr. Dushant, we'd be delighted to offer you up to £28,750."

I rang Sanjay and gave him my salary details. He offered me £30,000 at a quarter percent less than what my bank was offering. "Hey, you won't get a better rate than this, Amar. I'm bending some rules here, for you."

I worked out the mortgage repayments. No problem!

Sanjay was right. Had I been blind? An accountant unable to set his own house in order! And if an average house had increased from £6,000 to £35,000 in just over ten years, then surely prices would keep going up.

Until I was sure, I was still reluctant to discuss the matter with Billie. The Charles Church homes were ideal but the estate agent advised me to see a few others for comparison. "Older properties have more character, Mr. Dushant. Check them out." He shoved a few leaflets under my nose. I flicked through them. Most looked like they needed some repair work.

"No, Mr. Deery, I'll leave these."

"Have a look at 15 Churchill Garden. It's been reduced by £5,000 to £49,000 for a quick sale."

I wasn't sure and made an excuse, "Looks like it needs a new roof."

"Not yet, that will last for another few years. A new roof would set you back no more than £900. Take a look at the garden, there's potential for a decent size extension."

I still wasn't sure. The house seemed too big, "So why the reduction in price?" I enquired.

Mr. Deery lowered his voice. "I shouldn't be telling you this; between us two, the husband's left his wife and she's desperate to sell and move to a smaller dwelling. She can't afford the mortgage. Keep this to yourself, eh."

I wondered how many of Mr. Deery's clients had heard that story.

I took another look at the house in the leaflet. It certainly had character, and potential. A large Chestnut tree stood on one side and Rhododendrons lined the other. The drive was large enough for six cars. I cocked my head to one side and studied the leaflet in detail.

"Fine," I conceded. "I'll see this one. Unfortunately, I can't do so for another two days."

"Shall I make an appointment for Thursday? It's a Mrs. J. Rowan you'll be seeing."

"Yes, OK," I replied. "After work, around 6:30"

The following day, Sanjay and I met for lunch at the Randolph on Beaumont Street. It's a magnificent 1864 gothic designed hotel overlooking the world famous Ashmolean Museum and within minutes of the shopping centre, colleges and theatres.

"You stayed here when you first came to Oxford, didn't you?"

He was impressed. "Yes, you don't forget anything, do you?" He gazed in all directions, "Lovely place, I believe it was built by the famous Randolph Churchill."

I shook my head. "No, that's the common belief. In actual fact the name comes from its close proximity to the Randolph Gallery, which—"

"Really? So I've been giving incorrect information to my clients?" This time he shook his head. "Anyway, we are not here to talk about this place but the one you intend buying-unless you want to buy this hotel."

"Wish I could." I dug out the leaflet for 15 Churchill Garden. He scrutinized every detail. "Hey, if you can get this for anything less than £55,000, you'll have done well. Don't lose this, it's a bargain. Do you want me to come with you?"

"Not this time, it's only a preliminary visit. Besides, she's on her own; you might get the hots for her."

Sanjay laughed in anguish. "Hell, with Carla close to delivery, I'm getting the hots for anything in a skirt. I've been bone dry for a few weeks."

"When the time comes, call Pizza Hut."

He screwed his face. "What's Pizza Hut got to do with it?"

"They are doing free deliveries."

CHAPTER 25

Close to 6.30 PM, I approached 15 Churchill Garden. It looked better in bricks and mortar, freshly painted in white towering up to the attic, majestic in structure. The front door was large, purpose built in heavy walnut wood with metal studs. Reaching for the illuminated bell, I subconsciously crossed my fingers for luck. The front door opened wide.

"Mrs. Row—" I froze. A bolt of lightening struck me. She was the last person I expected to see. There was no premonition, no feeling that I would be seeing someone from my past...

"Jennifer!"

"Amar!" she uttered my name instantly.

We stood still for almost a minute, eyeing each other with incredulity. She hadn't changed much. Her hair was shorter and the waist not so small, but still curvy. The breasts were fuller and her face more dignified, probably due to the emergence of a few thin lines by the eyes. She stood straight and tall in a white silk blouse and a slate grey knee length skirt, her shoulders in line with her ears.

"Jennifer, I had no idea. The estate agent—"

"Won't you come in, Amar, or is it Mr. Dushant? At least, that's what the estate agent said."

I forced a laugh, "Amar."

She looked at me from head to toe, taking her time, as if she still had every right to do so- for old time's sake. I wondered what she was thinking of me.

A smile flickered in her eyes, "Amar... *Forever*." Her smile widened. "You never did tell me your surname."

I laughed awkwardly. "You never asked," I replied, also observing her from head to toe, unashamedly. "You look the same as when I last saw you, more distinguished perhaps."

We stood in the hall for a while and gazed at each other with a mixture of nervousness and excitement. Later, I followed her across a wide hall into a spacious square lounge overlooking a large sloping garden through leaded glass French doors.

She reached for my hand. "Come, let's sit down. I chose a comfortable settee opposite her as she sat straight and crossed her legs. "You haven't changed much... a bit more in weight perhaps, for the better."

I was still not completely relaxed. "It has been a few years." I looked around the room, paying special attention to a large silk tapestry showing a hilly landscape, probably somewhere in Devon. "Nice."

She sighed. "Where does time go? It seems like yesterday that we first met."

"The coach station," I murmured.

We looked at each other, beyond at the walls, then around the room and finally back at each other, smiling uneasily, together.

"Would you like a drink? Please say yes, I'm dying for one."

I nodded and blew out the breath caught in my chest for the last few minutes, "Yes."

She laughed to release the tension. I joined in, thankfully.

"Come, choose." I followed her to an adjoining room, an L shaped dining room with a large mahogany cocktail cabinet, under a wide tapestry of a woman breast-feeding her baby.

"Vodka and ice, two cubes please."

She opened the cabinet and proceeded to make the drinks. Her back still had that lovely S curve. "I think I'll have the same," she said, without turning around, probably aware that I was observing her.

Presently she turned around with the glasses in one hand and an ice cube in the other, which she threw out of the window. "Now that we've broken the ice..."

I laughed. "That's *my* line."

She came closer. "How have you been, Amar?"

I shrugged my shoulders. "I have no complaints, got married to a girl in Nairobi. Still living in Headington; you remember the house?"

She narrowed her eyes as if to picture the house. "Sure. And who's this lucky girl you married?"

"Balvinder... Billie. Our families have known each other for years. *I'm* the lucky one."

She smiled with a far away look. "Wow." She was thoughtful for a few seconds and her forehead furrowed, remembering, "And that lovely old lady, Mrs. Woods?"

"She passed away," I replied, "peacefully."

Jennifer bit her lower lip, "Sorry, she was a charming lady."

"Yes... and you? Did you —?"

She shook her head as I was talking "It's a long story. John never really wanted me. He was seeing someone else – some stupid Pharmacy student." She waved her hand in mock anger. I decided not to bring Liz into it. "After we broke up, I went back to Mum. A few months later, I met Alex. He was a jet setting Marketing Director working for Dell Computers. I accompanied him on some of his visits. He promised me the world. About eight months ago, he decided to set up on his own in Banbury and we bought this place."

I looked at some invisible spot on the wool carpet. "Where is Alex now?"

She waved her hand again. "Oh, he's always jet-setting, you know how it is? We've decided to sell this place and move to Banbury. Not as historic as Oxford, but at least we'll be nearer to his office."

Why was she lying? Pride? I couldn't think of any other reason.

I finished my drink. "I suppose, I should be seeing the rest of the house."

She stared at me for some time, in a far away look. "Amar, I'm sorry about that night. It was a one off, a moment of weakness. A few drinks, candlelight... you know how it is?" She pursed her lips to stop them from trembling.

I nodded. Scrambled eggs can not be unscrambled, I thought.

She got up slowly. "It's a *magnificent* house; all the décor is mine."

"I realized that," I said softly as I walked by her. She was lightly perfumed and her blouse swished gently as we glided from room to room. Every room was done tastefully, in pastel paint or wallpaper exuding capaciousness with decorative statuettes in the right places.There was no evidence of Alex - no photographs, no clothing behind doors, no trace of men's lotions in the bathrooms. Mr. Deery was right.

The bedrooms were luxuriously done but sparse to give an air of spaciousness. We stood by the window, looking at the garden below. It was dark but in the security light I could see that it had been lovingly cared for.

"Jennifer, I have to go soon."

She turned around to face me, "Do you? And the house, do you like it?"

"It's a lovely house, and I can see you've put a lot into it. And that Chestnut tree at the front, that's really something. I've not seen many as big as that one."

She smiled wryly. "It's close to hundred feet, and, according to the previous owners, almost a hundred years old. The chestnuts are tasty, perfectly edible."

"So it's been here before the house was built?"

"Oh, Goodness yes, history has it that at that very spot, before there were any houses around here, a jilted bride-to-be committed suicide and her father planted that tree in her memory. It's the only Chestnut tree around here."

I stared at her, in part because she looked lovely and in part because of the sensitivity of what she had just told me. "Yes," I mused, "it's indeed a fine tree. And I love this house. I'd be tempted to call it *The Old Chestnut* or something like that."

"Perhaps your wife would like to see it?"

I nodded.

We made our way to the front door. Jennifer leaned forward and kissed me lightly, her lips parted, lingering against mine. Her hair had a hint of fragrance that I hadn't detected earlier. Her perfumed neck rubbed against mine. "Why don't you come for lunch sometime; we'll talk, for old times sake."

I studied her face. Her eyes were still sharp, now eager. My hand moved to the small of her back. "That would be nice."

"When?" she asked softly.

Her breath was warm against my lips. "Soon, Jennifer, no..." Patting her gently behind the shoulder I pulled back. "I have to go."

That night I tossed and turned in bed. Things could have been so different. Jennifer and I had shared so much and I had forsaken her for that one fallacy of hers.

It came back to me so clearly. We had gone out together almost every day for months. I had asked her to meet me outside the college at six one evening. She had made an excuse- it wasn't the excuse but the way she had said that she had something to sort out that puzzled me. I could read her so well. One half of me wanted to preserve her privacy, to trust her; the other half realized that something was not quite right. By eight my head was exploding. Something was wrong. Jennifer was never good at lying. Perhaps she was in trouble. I had to find out. I just had to. Truth was more important than a jealous intrusion.

I walked the two miles to her flat. For almost twenty minutes, I stood outside in the cold, not daring to knock. Why didn't she want to see me? *Why?* My heart wanted me to rush in. My mind exercised caution. If she was not in, she would never know that I had called. But I had a feeling that she was in. The curtain was lit by the light from the table lamp by the bed. My heart was pounding. Even knowing that I could be making a complete fool of myself I knocked. After a long silence, the door opened. She was draped in a night gown. *She hated wearing a gown!*

"Amar, this is not convenient... I can't—"

"Jennifer, can I come in, please."

"No." Her voice was sharp but hushed with a mixture of anger and fear.

"Why not, what's the matter?"

A voice called from inside. "Jen, is everything all right?"

"Amar, please, it's John... he... please leave, please. I beg you, please... I'll explain tomorrow."

That was the last I saw of her, until this evening.

Many weeks after my intrusion she had rang me, "Amar, I'm sorry about John... It was nothing. My ex-boyfriend —"

"He's not your ex. any more, is he?" I had bellowed, forgetting that Mrs. Woods was around.

"Amar please, it was a one off. I've broken off with him now. We just needed to sort out—"

"Sorry Jennifer, please don't contact me again." In that hasty moment of madness and without hearing her out: I slammed the phone down. A few moments later, it dawned on me why that day, at the Coach Station, John and Liz never made it to Oxford.

"What's the matter, Amar?" Billie whispered dreamily, her voice thick with sleep. "Can't sleep?"

"I'm fine," I whispered back. "Sorry I woke you."

She turned her back to me and pulled her knees up. I curled myself closely against her back, moulding my body to hers. She was warm and her hair smelt nice. With a swift movement I turned her on her back and before she had a chance to get her breath back I was inside her.

"Amar, slow down, what's come over you? Amar! *Stop!* You're hurting me!"

A few minutes later we were both panting, covered in sweat.

I stared at the ceiling for a while before closing my eyes. Jennifer's perfume was still lingering around me.

CHAPTER 26

We moved to our new abode during the Christmas break, but not before I had taken a cutting of the Wisteria from our house. I couldn't possibly erase the memory of Mr. and Mrs. Woods and in years to come the Wisteria would resemble its parent in Headington. The house looked so empty, almost feeble, devoid of all the furniture and photographs. I touched the walls as I roamed the rooms. What sounds and laughter were they hiding? What births and deaths had they witnessed in all the years they had stood, lips sealed? Billie was waiting in the car while I studied each room, my footsteps echoing around me. Just as I closed the door for the last time, I thought I heard a voice call me from inside, 'Graham?'

Sanjay and I met often, mostly for lunch at one of the many restaurants and coffee houses springing-up in Oxford. Carla had given birth to a handsome little howling infant. They named him Neel, after a small blue spot on his heel.

Sanjay was always talking money. Some of his clients were among the richest in Oxfordshire and they exchanged valuable information not privy to most people. Somehow or the other, he knew which companies were doing well, what stocks and shares were about to soar in price, which residential locations were producing high yields, how sterling was going to fare against the dollar.

"Sanjay," I would ask, "if you know all this, why aren't you a multi-millionaire by now?"

He would throw his head back and laugh. "Hey, I will, soon. I'm sick of making clients rich, those stuck-up dumb assholes. All I need is capital to start off with."

"Why don't you play the market a bit at a time and build your empire?"

"Hey, I don't want to waste my time penny building; time is precious. I want to go for the *kill*."

Sometimes his talk frightened me. He was too ambitious for his age. Perhaps Carla was the reason for his obsession, I thought. He was competing with the wealth that Carla's family had built up and wanted to show her that he could do better.

One morning, he rang me at my office and asked me to meet him for lunch at his house. Why not some restaurant? I asked, and why put Carla to the trouble of cooking for us?

"Hey, listen, I want to discuss something important with you in private, no waiters, or interruptions. And don't worry, Carla and Neel will be at Saira's. I'll get some pizzas."

"What's so urgent? Can't it wait —"

"Trust me Amar, see you at one, sharp, razor sharp."

"OK," I said, "I'll be there on time." And I was.

He opened the containers. "Amar, we can make a killing, I need your help."

I hadn't the faintest idea what he was talking about. "Sanjay, what are you—"

He handed me a slice of pizza. "Roast pork OK?"

I nodded.

"Hey listen; I have a client, a property developer. He's in the middle of converting an office block in Watford into forty two residential flats. The job's nearly done and the bugger's run out of money. You with me?"

I nodded.

"I arranged a large loan for him; I can either give him more or call the loan."

"Isn't that a bit callous?" I asked, referring to the second option.

He ignored me and continued talking passionately, not once taking his eyes off mine. I was seeing him in a new light and not liking what I thought was coming.

I helped myself to another slice of pizza. "What's this got to do with me?"

Sanjay took a bite from his slice. He waited a while before answering. "Amar, I can make you rich." He munched his pizza before continuing, "Very rich! Don't you see—"

I interrupted him quickly, "Sanjay, I do not wish to get involved in anything dodgy."

He totally ignored me, eyeing me simultaneously in a cautious and teasing manner. "Would I do that to a friend? I, we can help this chap, everybody wins- the developer, the tenants, you, I, everyone!"

"Where do I come in?"

He leaned forward, excited, eyes piercing. "Hey, why don't *you* finish off the project?"

This was incredible! I half laughed, ending in a coughing fit. "Sanjay, I've just about raised enough money to buy a house and you are asking me to finish off building forty odd flats!" I shook my head. "I can't do this."

He shook his head emphatically. "Just bear me with. Money is not the problem. It's simple. I pull the plug on the developer, my bank gives *you* a loan and out of that you pay off the developer, he pays back the loan to my bank, you buy and sell the flats, and we make a killing."

I was having difficulty with Sanjay's reasoning, "How can *I* get a loan; on what security?"

He clucked his tongue. "That's where *I* come in. I'm a senior manager at Standard, remember? I sanction the loan to you."

I gave him a quick glance. "On what security?"

He answered with a half smile on his face, "Amar, you leave that to me."

"Surely even your bank gets checked and audited. You and I, both, will be in trouble."

He was losing his patience. "I can make sure that certain transactions are kept quiet. Very soon the loan will be repaid to the bank. Hey, that's my prerogative. Stricter laws are being imposed on banks all the time, but believe me there's nothing wrong with what I am suggesting. You don't want to stay Mr. Average all your life. Look at opportunities, challenges... feel your heart beat. Breathe the excitement. Be a hero, not a zero."

"What about the poor developer?"

"What about him?" Sanjay shouted. "He is a crook, I know him well. Don't feel sorry for him. That bastard's got enough stacked up in offshore banks. He'll get his share and move somewhere else."

I breathed out. My head was buzzing with conflicting views. I was quiet for a long time. Sanjay watched me intently but kept quiet, knowing that I was thinking, hooked. "I don't know, Sanjay. I need time to think."

"Damn it! If we don't move fast, others will. Amar, we'll never get an opportunity like this again. This is win-win, no risk!"

"Look, I'm just not sure. And what's in it for you?"

He hid a smile. He *knew* I was interested. "You sell the flats and we split the gain."

I sighed heavily, chest feeling like a ton in weight. "How much can we make?" I asked softly.

He leaned forward, only a foot away from me. "Forty two flats at around £25,000 each. Pay off the developer's loan of £550,000 and another £100,000 for professional fees and contingencies. Make an allowance for marketing and estate agency fees, say £50,000."

I did a mental calculation. Surely not! "That's a gain of around £350,000!"

Sanjay leaned back, smirking. "You can buy three 5 bed houses in Oxford with £175,000. Hey, you and I, we could go places. In four months you can make more that what you earn in four years!" Leaning back further, he placed his hands behind his neck, fingers locked. "Well?"

I stared at him for a good minute or two before blinking my agreement.

Billie kept herself busy and in charge of decorating the new house- not that there was that much to be done. The curtains and carpets were in excellent condition, and all fixtures and fittings were of the highest quality. She was happy but surprised that I was leaving everything to her. At times, she asked for my contribution: Will a cream settee go with the curtains? Should she get leather? Was I sure? A *chaise longue* against the bed? More lamps? Cushions with beads? Indian beads? Small beads? Red beads? I gave her complete freedom. She enjoyed the shopping, often taking Saira or Carla with her. They would meet Cheryl near her place of work for coffee and snacks. Her excitement was my peace – the calm before the storm.

Suddenly, I had a lot on my mind. The year end accounts had to be finalized and Board reports had to be prepared. Our auditors were due in a few weeks and on top of it all, forms to be signed. No sooner had I signed one, Sanjay brought another. I saw the Watford site, a smart block with landscaping, a café and a grocery store. I met the developer, who thanked me a dozen times for rescuing him. We met Norton and Sons to discuss marketing and selling the flats. The costs came to about £15,000 more than what Sanjay had anticipated but as Sanjay assured me, Nortons were the best in the business. It was better to pay a bit more and be sure of selling quickly. And Nortons were reliable- they had a reputation of never going back on their word.

"You've been seeing a lot of Sanjay lately," Billie remarked one late evening, after he and I had spent a few hours with decorators.

"Just exploring a business proposition," I half lied, not wanting to reveal too much.

"Be careful. I wouldn't trust him."

I was astounded. "Why, what's he done?"

She made a face. "I don't know; just a woman's intuition."

"What if I were to go into some major business deal with him? Lot of money involved."

"Just be careful. I know he's your friend, but where money's involved friends are only friends until they can afford to not be friends.

Everything comes at a price. After the euphoria of moving to Churchill Hill, and after organizing the furniture and décor, Billie resumed concentrating on the household chores-dusting, cleaning, cooking, and so on. A bigger house meant more housework. She refused my offers of a cleaner-the house was hers and *she* would keep it clean, though she did, after a while, through coercion, agree to the services of a gardener for two hours a week- as long as he didn't enter her house!

I noticed that if I was in the family room, watching TV and Billie upstairs, the distance seemed too much. We couldn't talk to each other, even by shouting. Either I had to cross the wide hall and go upstairs or she had to make her way downstairs to the room at the far end and communicate with me. As a result, certain things were either half discussed or not at all.

Our protracted silences over meals grew longer and eye contacts shorter. I often caught her looking at me when I was concentrating on my plate and I grew a habit of observing her when her face was lowered or turned away from me. Over time, without complaining we developed a way of communicating without facing or even looking at each other, eyes fixed on the television screen, a book or office notes. She would reply through the steam rising from a sizzling frying- pan, wiping the work top or just staring out onto the garden. It's difficult to pin-point when it started, so gradual and at the time, so natural was the transformation that we were unable to reverse the change. It just happened. The rooms grew taut with tension, to the point of appearing alien. Our marriage was turning into nothing more than a prosaic companionship.

Billie, never having been fond of television, began spending more and more of her time upstairs listening to Hindi film songs. I encouraged her to read books but she found them a strain on the eyes. Besides, she didn't want to wear spectacles like I had just started doing. The arrival of video recorders helped in that she would often watch films.

One day, she rang me at the office to say that she had borrowed *Silsila* from someone and would I come home on time so that we could watch the film after dinner. "Amar, don't be late. Amitabh and Rekha are both superb in the film."

After a meal of Jeera chicken and rice, she cuddled up to me on the settee and started the video. "I just love Amitabh; don't you think he's the best actor India has ever produced?"

I thought for a few seconds. "He's got a great, deep voice and he's certainly very good looking—"

"But?"

"I still don't think his acting is in the same class as Dilip Kumar or Raj Kapoor."

"Oh, Amar, he's *so* versatile. Not like the lemon-faced Dilip Kumar or the funny looking Raj Kapoor."

"OK, OK, let's watch."

I did enjoy *Silsila.* It was a bold story. Amitabh gets married but later has an affair with Rekha, obliviou of his suffering wife. What made it even bolder was that, that is what happened in real life to the three stars.

CHAPTER 27

From the day we moved to Churchill Garden, I knew the time would come when the euphoria of moving would drain away, bit by bit, and Billie's craving for a child would resurface. I began to dread the day when the furniture would all be bought and put in place, the day when the painting and decoration would all be complete, the day when the garden would be to her satisfaction. It dawned on me that the only way to postpone that day was to keep surprising her with holidays, expensive presents, films or some other means. But for sure, that day would come – the storm after the calm!

Fred Norton requested a meeting at his office. I was terribly busy with auditors and suggested that he meet just Sanjay. "No can do," Fred said in his calm, silky voice. "I've asked Sanjay as well as your solicitors. My solicitors will certainly be present. Lots of documents need signing."

I flicked through my desk diary. "This week's very difficult for me, Fred, how about Wednesday morning?"

"Amar, I don't mind, but from Monday, everyday will cost you chaps £2,000 a day. Our bit is done. We have potential buyers waiting to pay deposits; it's your call."

I checked my diary again, "How about Saturday morning?"

I could hear him having a quick discussion with someone. His voice crackled over the line, "Saturday, 10 A.M."

Sanjay picked me up from Churchill Garden at nine Saturday morning. As the Mustang roared down the A40, he turned his head and winked at me. "In two months, you'll be driving something like this." He patted the leather steering-wheel. "Hey, what would you like?"

I thought for a while, Porsche? Mercedes? "Let's not count our chickens before they—"

"Amar!" He mocked. "Stop being the cautious accountant. Live man, live."

The A40 was clear that time of the day. The Mustang stayed in the fast lane most of the time. I gazed sideways at the countryside. This part of England was so green, I loved it.

Sanjay broke the silence, "How's work?"

I wondered what he meant. Did I like it? Or, was I busy? Or, perhaps, was the company doing well? I shrugged, "It's OK."

"How profitable is the organization?"

The figures were fresh in my mind. "We're likely to make a profit of over two million. There is no end to the demand for foil."

"Where do you get the raw material from?"

"Oh, most of the paper," I replied casually, "comes from Sweden, some from Norway."

"Who is your main supplier?"

"It's a medium sized company by the name of Swenberg AB. You know in Sweden AB is equivalent to 'Limited'.

"I know," Sanjay was thoughtful for a while. "And how do you pay - by cheque, telegraphic transfer, or what?"

A black Golf GTI flashed its light at us repeatedly. "Asshole!" Sanjay cursed, glancing at the mirror.

"Let him pass," I suggested casually.

Sanjay moved into the middle lane. As the Golf roared past, the driver showed two fingers and cut into the middle lane perilously close to the Mustang. Sanjay swerved sharply. "Asshole! I'll show you!" He shifted into a higher gear and pushed the accelerator hard. The tyres screeched. The car surged forward and Sanjay charged into the fast lane. Within five seconds the Mustang was parallel to the Golf, whose driver, in dark glasses, showed us two fingers again. Sanjay kicked the accelerator hard. I glanced at the speedometer- 110 miles per hour! I was on the edge of my seat but decided to keep quiet. Knowing Sanjay, I was sure that he wasn't going to listen to me in his excitable state. He was leaning forward, teeth clenched, jaw protruding. The knuckles holding the steering wheel were pale. Suddenly the Mustang shot forward as if it had been pushed by a rocket from behind. Sanjay lifted his hand, two fingers straight up and cut in the middle lane. The Golf decided to switch into the fast lane but Sanjay had anticipated that. He swerved into it just ahead of the Golf, which conceded defeat and decided to remain safely behind.

We remained silent for some time.

"By cheque?" he asked.

I expelled air from my lungs, replying curtly, "Yes."

"Do you pay in sterling or Swedish Kroner?"

I was puzzled at the constant questioning, "Sterling. That way, we don't bear the currency risk, a simple way of hedging. Why do you ask?"

He shrugged his shoulders. "Just interested, oh, we'd better change here."

There was more traffic on the small roads and Sanjay kept a slower pace.

"Carla tells me that Billie wanted to see *Silsila*. Have you seen it?"

"Yes, we saw it last night. Good stuff," I said. "I felt sorry for Jaya -in the film and in real life. To be cheated openly like that, and for the whole world to see the story."

Sanjay tutted, "Hmm, and if, just for argument sake, Jaya was not aware of the affair, would you feel sorry for her?"

"You mean, if Amitabh and Rekha had a *secret* affair?"

He nodded. "Yes, if he had an affair but loved *both* women, would that be OK?"

I shook my head. "No not really. That's still cheating!"

He gave a loud laugh. "But if his wife doesn't *know*, and he cares and loves both women, what harm is he doing to either of them. Hey, the man's happy, his wife's happy, his mistress is happy; what is the problem?"

I licked my lips, "Human beings shouldn't be that way. Unlike animals we have a conscience."

Sanjay ignored what I was saying. "Amar, you like that blue suit you are wearing?"

"What's that got to do with—?"

I was interrupted, "What I'm trying to say is that just because you like, or love that blue suit, it doesn't mean that you can't like another suit- grey, brown, whatever. By the same token, if you like, or love one woman, it doesn't mean that you can't love another, just as passionately."

I didn't agree, but decided not to argue anymore.

Sanjay gave a loud howl. "Hey, life's too short; live, love, learn."

Fred Norton ushered us into a large room with a large round mahogony table.The room was luxuriously decorated, heavy marble wallpaper, carpeting up to the ankles, with a huge crystal chandelier directly above the table. Our solicitor, Kevin London was already there, sipping tea. Within minutes of our arrival, a solicitor for the Nortons entered the room, led by a charming, busty middle aged woman, who I took to be Fred's secretary but Sanjay later informed me that she was his wife. In his controlled, silky voice Fred took us through the glossy brochure and the details of the potential buyers. "Well, gentlemen, of the forty two flats, eighteen have been reserved by commercial businesses for their executive staff and the rest by private tenants. The last reservation and deposit was paid on Tuesday."

Sanjay had a quiet discussion with Kevin. Clearing his throat, he asked when contracts were likely to be exchanged.

"We are ready," Fred explained, "to exchange in the next three weeks, with completion a fortnight or so after that."

Matters were moving fast. I leaned forward. "Do you have assurance of the availability of funds?"

Fred's eyes moved from person to person. "Sure. There are at lest a dozen reliable, buyers on the waiting list if anyone wants to pull out. However, *I'm* quietly confident that there will be no complications."

Sanjay had another short discussion with Kevin. "Fred, what are the figures looking like?"

Fred licked his middle finger and flicked through the brochure, stopping at a page. "Gentlemen, if you turn to page twenty six, you will see a detailed breakdown, of the deposits paid to date and the remaining balance receivable. Please note that the south facing flats are a thousand pounds more than the rest and for each floor above the ground floor, the balance increases by eight hundred pounds. The summary on page twenty eight shows the total due to you as £1,070,000. Out of this, you will need to pay our fees, which amounts to £56,400." He leaned back, satisfied, smiling. "It's all there," he said confidently, tapping the brochure.

I perused the marketing and sales breakdowns and did some quick calculations. £1,013,600 less £100,000 for legal costs and £550,000 to the vendors would give Sanjay and me a profit of £363,600! We exchanged quick glances. He closed the brochure and turned to me. "Hey, are you happy to close the deal or do you have any questions?"

My head was spinning with the bottom line. I shook my head.

Sanjay turned to Kevin. "Kevin, you have our authority to close the deal with the Nortons and their solicitor. We can sign the forms anytime you like." He stood up and everyone followed suite. We shook hands all around, satisfied. "You have a very shrewd partner," Fred said quietly to me as I shook hands with him.

CHAPTER 28

The next few days passed in a whirl. Sanjay and I met everyday for lunch, mostly at the Red Lion on Abingdon Road. We both liked to stroll by the river after a light meal and a pint of beer. Most days, he would bring some document along with him for me to sign. On one occasion, I suggested that we ought to tell Carla and Billie of the Watford flats. "After all, completion is imminent," I said.

He moved his fingers back through his long wavy hair. "I was thinking the same. Hey, why don't you come over to my place for dinner tomorrow and we'll break the news to the girls."

"Come to us," I suggested," Billie is not as busy as Carla is with Neel around- she can cook with ease."

Sanjay smacked his lips. "OK." Then he shook his head, "No, you'd better come to us. Neel needs to be put to bed at eight."

"Fine, I conceded, "we'll be there at just after eight. Keep it simple, just one dish."

Carla was very welcoming. She was still retaining a lot of the weight that she had put on during her pregnancy and her face which had always been fairly full appeared to take an even more rounded appearance. "To what do we owe this pleasure?"

Sanjay winked at me and placed a finger on his lips. Billie gave her a hug, "I hope you did not go to a lot of trouble."

Carla beamed. "You are worth it," she replied simply.

Sanjay handed us all drinks and Carla some home made pakoras.

"We have wild mushroom soup and roast chicken. I hope that's OK? I know Amar likes his chicken that way."

"Yum," I said. "My mouth is watering already!"

We sat around dining table number two, it seated up to eight, compared to the bigger one which could seat up to fourteen.

I commented on the new rug in the room. "It's a gift,"remarked Carla, waving her hand in mid air, "from a rich client of Sanjay; some Saudi prince."

I bent down to feel the texture- pure silk, soft and smooth.

"Sanjay was saying that it's probably worth two thousand."

I was astonished but kept quiet, wondering what other items in the house were gifts of some sort or the other.

"Talking of gifts," Billie said, raising her voice, "Look!" She waved her hand to reveal a new ring I had bought her earlier that day. Carla held her hand. "Is this from some Saudi prince as well?"

Billie snatched her hand back. "No!" she pouted. "It's from Amar."

All eyes turned to me.

Sanjay broke into the conversation. "What guilt are you hiding, Amar?"

"Yes," Carla added, "be very careful of men bearing gifts."

Billie looked directly at me, "Tell them, Amar."

I looked blank. "Tell them what?" I shrugged my shoulders. "I just —"

"Let's," Sanjay interrupted, "eat first; we can discuss gifts later."

Carla winked at Billie. "That will give Amar time to think of a good excuse."

I dug into the chicken. It was generously coated with masala and cumin, spicy without being it hot, and grilled ginger and tomatoes- just the way I liked it.

"This is delicious."

We were all silent for a few minutes, paying more attention to the food amidst the clatter of cutlery.

"Do have some more chicken," Carla said after a while but no one had space for more.

"More wine, anybody?" Sanjay asked, half standing up and leaning towards the bottle.

I picked up my glass. "Just one more. What's this?"

"Chablis, Premier Cru," Sanjay read from the label. "Who's driving?"

I swirled the wine in my mouth, glancing at Billie, "It's your turn, isn't it?"

She pulled a face. "It usually is."

Over coffee, Sanjay, sitting opposite Billie, said casually, "Amar's soon going to be rich, very rich."

Billie put her cup down. "I hope so; he's been working very hard recently. Perhaps they'll promote him to Managing Director."

"Maybe that's why he's bought you that ring; Amar, out with it," Carla added, pouring more coffee.

Sanjay cleared his throat. "No, I didn't mean that. Amar and I have bought some flats in Watford which we will be selling in a few weeks. We stand to make a handsome profit from that."

Billie waved her hand casually. "Amar's blown his profit on the ring." She looked at her hand approvingly.

I leaned forward, "Sanjay's right. We should make close to three hundred sixty *thousand* soon."

Carla lowered her cup by an inch from her lips and spoke in a rasping whisper, "Do you mean real money, three hundred and sixty thousand *pounds*?" Seeing me nod, she put her cup down, "*How?*"

Billie looks around, very puzzled.

Sanjay leaned back, hands clasped behind his neck, "I'd better explain."

It was a lovely, crisp autumn day. The sky was clear bar a few cotton-wool clouds. I hurried to the pub, hands in my trouser pockets to keep them warm. Sanjay was seated in a far corner with Kevin. They both stood up as I approached. Kevin extended his hand towards me, smiling broadly. "We completed early today," he shrieked, punching air.

"Thanks Kevin, you've been wonderful," I said in appreciation.

Sanjay gave me a tight hug. "And you doubted me, eh? I'll get you a drink, the usual?"

Before I had a chance to say a word, Sanjay had hurried to the bar.

"So what happens now, Kevin?"

He shrugged his shoulder and looked at me over the rim of his glass. "The money's in. Your share will be transferred into your account by close of play today as per the agreement."

I lowered my voice. "Kevin, how much do I get?"

He checked a thin file of summary transactions before replying, "Just over one hundred and eighty one thousand pounds."

I sat quietly for a good minute, staring into his grey eyes. In a hushed whisper I asked, "What do I do with it?"

He laughed. "You could always give it to me."

Sanjay came with a pint of pale ale. "Let's order lunch."

"Fish and chips, two slices of lemon, tartar sauce and lots of vinegar," I said, without even looking at the menu.

"Kevin and I chose steak and kidney pie with mash before you came," Sanjay said. "I'll go order."

Food finished, I thanked Sanjay with a smile. "I still can't take it in. All that money—"

"Spend it, you'll get more." There was a twinkle in his eye.

"What are you going to do with yours?"

He threw his head back and laughed. After a while he said laughing, "Food, clothes, wine, women..."

CHAPTER 29

"Amar, have you robbed a bank or what?" Robin was asking. We had thrown a party to celebrate our success. Robin and Cheryl had just arrived and were admiring the shining new BMW Sports with the personal registration: AD 2.

"It's all His doing," I said, pointing to the heavens above, "Come, let's go in, it's getting a bit chilly here. Robin, you've got glasses too!"

He smiled, "Should have eaten more carrots when I was young."

"I thought you did," I joked. "Isn't that why you've got ginger hair?"

Inside, they shook hands with the others.

"Late as usual," Inayat said, balancing his drink.

"Wow, this is something!" Cheryl exclaimed, noticing the marquee next to the lounge, where two caterers were preparing naan and kebabs in the clay *tandoor*. The air was thick with the smell of meat and spices, "A real clay oven!"

"We think Amar has robbed some bank," Paal Uncle whispered, winking at Cheryl.

"That's *exactly* what Robin said!" shrieked Cheryl, giving Saira a tight hug. "And how's little Mahmoud?"

"Fine, he's sleeping upstairs, next to Neel."

Sanjay, Carla and Paro Aunty were in the marquee tasting chicken wings. They entered through the French-doors and greeted the newcomers.

"You simply must try the chicken wings. Those chaps in there will char them according to your taste," Paro Aunty said, holding a well charred piece.

"Why is there no skin? I prefer chicken with crisp golden skin," Cheryl commented.

"Oh, no dear, we always remove the skin before cooking chicken," Paro Aunty explained, taking another bite. "The skin is all fat and high in cholesterol. I thought everyone knew that."

Cheryl wasn't convinced. "Really, but I always feel that the skin retains the succulence. What's a bit of fat? It's not as if it would do *you* any harm, Paro."

Carla, coming closer, joined in the debate. "I much prefer flesh to slimy or even crackly skin. Anyway, one can never be too careful." She went through the French-doors to refill her plate.

Robin followed her. "Must see what this tandoor thing is." One of the caterers explained that the naan- bread was placed against the clay walls whilst the skewers could be placed all the way down to the floor of the tandoor. The hot coal at the base heated the clay walls to such a high temperature that naans were ready in less than a minute. He came back with a plate heaped with chicken wings, lamb kebabs and naan. "Wow, that thing beats a barbecue any day!"

"Hey, Robin, use your fingers," Sanjay teased him as he picked some cutlery.

Robin gingerly held a chicken wing between his thumb and fore-finger. "I don't like my fingers getting greasy."

"Oh, don't be a wimp! God made them before forks and knives were invented."

"Do you know something?" Paro Aunty said breaking her conversation with Cheryl. "Food always tastes better when eaten with fingers."

"How so?" Robin asked respectfully.

"Because by doing so we use all our senses. We listen when food is being cooked, we hear it sizzling and spluttering, right?"

Robin nodded.

Paro Aunty continued. "So we use our sense of hearing. The second sense we use is seeing the food being cooked, the third sense, of smell comes into play when the food is being cooked—"

"The fourth sense is that of taste," I added, "when we put the yum-yums in our mouth."

Robin looked puzzled, "What's the fifth sense?"

"Touch!" Paro Aunty said triumphantly, one hand flying in the air. "When we hold the food." She lifted a piece and bit into it. "So, no cutlery for the chicken wings or the kebabs!"

Robin tried the chicken wings using his hands and nodded appreciation. "It's good, I like it."

"You really do, or are you just saying it?" Paro Aunty wanted to know.

"I mean it, heart on hand!"

"You mean, hand on—"

I stepped forward, breaking into the conversation. "Don't mind him; he always mixes up his sentences.

Presently, Sunny Singh, the chief caterer, came over to announce that the main course was ready. We assembled in the dining room. Among the cacophony and chatter Saira bumped into me. In her inimitable soft spoken manner she asked me something which I couldn't make out.

"Pardon, Saira?"

She smiled, cheeks dimpling, "Do we sit anywhere?"

Before I could reply, Sanjay cut in, "Sit next to me Saira; Amar will just bore you to death."

Paal Uncle was trying to find a position from where he could look into the garden. His hesitation proved to be unfruitful for in those few seconds all but two chairs were claimed. "Here, Uncleji," I said, "you take this chair. I'll sit nearest to the kitchen."

"Ah, that means I'll be sitting next to Paro."

"What," I asked, "is wrong with that? After all, you two do eat from the same plate at home."

"That's different," Paro Aunty said, joining in. "We are not going to economise on the crockery and cutlery here, Amar."

Robin, sitting at the other end was curious. "Do you really eat from the same plate?"

"We've done so ever since we got married. It runs in my family," Paal Unle said, smiling, quite proudly.

"That's rather sweet," Carla added.

"That reminds me of the old couple who go to the restaurant on their sixtieth wedding anniversary—"

"Oh Sanjay," Carla interrupted, "you're not going to tell that joke now, okay?"

"Why not?"

Inayat raised a hand. "Go on, tell us."

"Everyone's heard it," she protested, frowning.

"I haven't," Inayat and Robin shouted together.

Sanjay cleared his throat. "As I was saying, this old couple arrived at the restaurant." He looked around to make sure that he had everyone's attention. "They order a few dishes. First the wife eats while the husband watches. The waiter observes the couple. Then the husband eats while the *wife* watches him lovingly. The waiter is mesmerized, but puzzled. Presently he approaches the couple and asks why, when they are so much in love, they don't eat together. 'Son,' replies the old woman, her mouth wobbling. 'If only we could. You see we only have *one* pair of dentures!'"

Robin guffawed and thumped the table. The infectious laughter lasted a while. Sunny Singh brought the dishes to the table, trying to keep a straight face.

"Well let's tuck in while we still have our own teeth," Billie urged, passing the mutton biriyani to Saira. "Please help yourselves."

"Yes, also, while we still have use of our fingers," Paal Uncle joked, glancing at his wife.

For some minutes everyone was quiet, busy with filling their plates and bowls. Forks, knives and spoons chinked the crockery. Bowls passed from person to person. Music was drifting from the lounge.

"This is lovely Billie," Saira said enthusiastically. "You shouldn't have gone into so much trouble."

"You don't mean Billie. Surely you mean, Mr. Singh!" I corrected.

"Oooh, the panir, is *delicious*," Cheryl said, licking her lips. "You must give me the recipe."

"Only if you finish it," I said simply.

We ate without interruptions for a while.

"I haven't heard that song for ages," Paal Uncle said suddenly, turning towards the lounge from where a tape was playing.

"What song?" Paro Aunty asked.

"Shhh... listen."

Everyone stopped and sat stiffly, trying to make out the lyrics.

Paal Uncle had his eyes closed, head slightly back, delighting in the music and lyrics, "*Chaudvin ka chand*."

"What a beautiful song," Paro Aunty murmured. "It's from *Pyaasa*, one of the best films India's ever made. And considering that it was made such a long time ago—"

"1957," Paal Uncle said. "They don't make them like them any more."

"My favourite is *Guide*," Saira added. "Wow! That had Waheeda Rehman in it as well. Didn't she get some award in America?"

"Truly great," I said beginning to eat again. "In my books, Mother India, Guide and Pyaasa would rank as the best three films from the sub-continent."

"Just listen to the words," Paal Uncle suggested. He was concentrating hard.

Chaudvin ka chand ho, ya afataab ho

Jo bhi ho tum khuda ki kasam, laajawab ho

"I don't understand the words, but they sound nice," Cheryl said simply. "What do they mean?"

Paal Uncle was savoring the song, eyes closed, thinking back to younger days.

Saira cleared her throat. "The male singer is admiring a woman."

> *Are you a full moon or the sun?*
> *Whatever you are, I swear by God, you are matchless.*

"Carry on," Inayat whispered.

> *Locks of your hair fall over your shoulders like clouds*
> *Eyes like full cups of wine*
> *You are the liquor intoxicated with love*
> *Face like a lotus in full bloom ...*

Everyone clapped.

> *Lightening from your smile plays on your lips*
> *Rainbows bow before you ...*

"Saira, you say it so beautifully," Sanjay said, clapping.

She smiled shyly, "Of course, one looses the rhyming in translation."

"Like making love to a woman over the phone," he said, crudely. Saira made a face.

"Indian songs have a certain melody which we don't seem to appreciate in the West," Paro Aunty said. "Don't you think?"

Cheryl had been listening intently. "Now-a-days there's more emphasis on rhythm rather than melody."

Robin nodded in agreement.

"You know, Inayat," Paro Aunty said, "a lot of Indian songs originate from Persian poetry - perhaps the greatest contribution the Mughals made to India."

"And the Taj Mahal," Inayat added. "Didn't most of the marble and jewels come from Persia?"

I nodded, "You are probably right."

Billie turned to face Paal Uncle, "What is your favourite Hindi song?"

He stared at her for a while and narrowed his eyes, thinking. Paro Aunty broke the silence. "I know, it's from that old film, *Mela*, you know—"

"Aaaaah, yes," he said enthusiastically, "*Ye zindagi ke mela*...sad song, very sad." He wobbled his head sideways as if the words were floating in his mind.

"My mum used to love it," Saira said. "Come to think of it, *her* mother used to sing it as well. How old is it?"

Paal Uncle leaned on both elbows, hands clasped. "1948, Mohammed Rafi's golden voice enchanted the entire subcontinent in those days."

"Paul," Paro Aunty said, "Sing a few lines."

"Oh no, it's too sad; we're all having fun here. It's probably the saddest song that I know."

"Oh come on," Carla, Billie and Cheryl urged together. The others joined in. "Just a few lines."

We fell silent; he was concentrating, mentally, reciting the first few lines.

> *Ye zindagi ke mele*
> *ye zindagi ke mele*
> *duniya main kam na honge*
> *afsos hum na honge*
>
> *ek din padega jaana*
> *kyaa waqt kyaa zamana*
> *koi na saath dega*

sab kuch yahi rahega

jaaenge hum akele
ye zindagi ke mele
duniya mein kam na honge
afsos hum na honge ...

He pursed his lips and fell silent. We were all struck by the sadness in the lyrics.

Inayat broke the silence, "It's amazing. I understood a lot of it."

Sanjay nodded. "There's a lot of Urdu in Hindi songs and a lot of it comes from the Persian language. Paul, you sing with such emotion! There seems to be so much pain in the song."

"Ah, pain, my dear, is the inspiration of poetry," he replied, philosophically.

Presently, Robin cleared his throat. "Could you translate some of it, please?"

Billie half raised a hand. "I'll try, shall I?"

Paal Uncle nodded vigorously.

The funfairs of life
will always remain
sadly, I won't
One day I shall have to leave...

She looked around, confused. Paro Aunty came to the rescue:

No one will accompany me
My possessions will remain behind
I will go alone
Leaving the funfairs of life

Everyone cheered and proceeded to concentrate on eating, the only sound came from cutlery chinking on plates.

Presently, Sunny Singh came over to Billie. "Shall I serve desert?"

Billie nodded and he made his way back to the kitchen.

Sanjay leaned forward and spoke in a hushed voice, "Did he mean desert as in wasteland or dessert as in sweet?"

"Shut up, Sanjay. You *know* what he meant," Carla said, voice equally hushed. "It's not his fault he doesn't know French."

"Okay okay, just joking," Sanjay spoke with some irritation.

"Well, what *is* for dessert?" Robin enquired.

As if on cue, Sunny Singh brought a bowlful of *rasmalai* and a bowlful of rice pudding with grated carrots, almonds and pistachios.

"This is my favourite," exclaimed Paro Aunty, helping herself to two pieces of *rasmalai* and a generous helping of the rich creamy milk.

"I'd like a bit of both," Inayat said.

In the end, we all ended up having both, eating and talking noisily.

Sanjay finished his and leaned back, hands clasped behind his head, "This is the life, eh, Amar?"

I nodded, smiling. "I could get used to this."

Later, Billie offered to make us all some *masala* tea.

"Hey, I'll give you a hand," Sanjay said, standing up and following her into the kitchen.

"I love Billie's spicy tea," Robin said leaning back in his chair. "What do you put in it?"

"I'm not sure." I confessed. I turned to Paro Aunty. "Do you know?"

She had been quiet for some time, "Oh, a mixture of cinnamon, ginger, cardamoms, cloves, fennel and black pepper, all very good for digestion."

"Not just digestion," Paal Uncle added, smiling, "also, good for —"

She interrupted quickly, "Don't!" Everyone gazed at her. "That's all he thinks of," she explained, slightly embarrassed.

"Eh?" Robin enquired innocently, amidst much laughter and giggling.

"My dear," Paro Aunty said softly, "you don't need to know until you are married."

"I think I'll have *two* cups," Inayat said, "Mahmoud could do with a brother."

Saira blushed. "No masala tea for him for another year or so. Give his share to Robin and Cheryl."

Just as Cheryl opened her mouth to protest, Sanjay and Billie brought the tea. "What?" he asked. "Why are you all giggling?"

"We've been discussing the goodness of masala tea," Carla explained.

He threw back his head and laughed. "I have it with *gur*. Boy does that combination work? Ask Carla."

"Shut up Sanj," Carla shouted, crossly.

Robin leaned forward towards me. "What's *gur*?" he asked in a hushed voice.

I replied softly, "Raw crystallised cane sugar. "Billie, can you bring some *gur* as well?" I said loudly.

All the men cheered.

Later, we retired to the lounge. Paal Uncle was the first to sink into a sofa. "Thanks Amar, Billie, it's been a lovely evening."

"Absolutely marvellous," Robin shouted, coming into the room and raising his wine glass.

Everyone settled down. I handed some more wine around.

"Paul," Paro Aunty said.

"What?"

"You've had enough—" she was clearly cross.

He turned his gaze to her, "Just one more, Paro."

"One for the road," we all chanted.

"Why don't you stay the night here, Uncleji?" I suggested. "You don't want to drive after all that wine."

"Yes, we can leave tomorrow, after breakfast," Paro Aunty suggested.

Paal Uncle wasn't sure. "Hmm, no, I'm meeting a friend early tomorrow. He's going to check the car before the MOT. But thanks for the offer."

"It's no bother, you can leave early tomorrow," I suggested.

He was not convinced. He threw his head back and finished his drink. "We'll see you all soon," he said, getting up. "Come on Paro. Thanks Billie, Amar. Good night all. Ta Ta. It's been a great evening." Hugs and hand shaking took a good twenty minutes amidst promises of further get-togethers. I escorted them to their car. "Please come again, any time."

"You too, Amar," Paal Uncle shouted and drove away waving from the open window.

It was a pleasant night, cloudless and clear, just a slight chill in the air. I lingered around, past the Chestnut tree breathing fresh air into my lungs, trying to neutralize the acidity in me. It felt good. Almost reluctantly, I walked back, kicking a few shingles here and there. Faint sounds and laughter drifted through the open front door. In the darkness, the lit windows appeared even brighter. Sunny Singh and his friends were clearing up in the utility room. Sanjay and Billie were in the kitchen, probably clearing the tea cups. I closed the front door behind me, the house felt very warm.

Robin shouted, hearing the door close, "How about a night cap?"

"I've got some nice Cointreau, will that do? Or would you prefer brandy?"

Sanjay came out of the kitchen, "Did someone mention Cointreau?"

Billie and Saira opted for some juice.

Carla screwed her nose. "I fancy a —"

Sanjay interrupted, "Not now darling. Can't you wait till we get home?" He turned to the others, "must be the *gur!*"

"Shut up Sanj. What I was saying was that I fancy some Irish coffee. Is that OK with you?"

"Good idea," I said. "I'll second that. The problem is that my cream doesn't stay on top. Who's the expert?"

Carla got up, slowly, straightening her skirt, with some effort. She was still holding on to the pregnancy fat. It struck me that Sanjay and Carla were becoming so polarized. He was tall and slim, she, short and plump. His hair was always crying out for a cut, hers, too short.

"I'll show you, Billie get me double cream and a spoon."

We all gathered around Carla. She sprinkled some brown sugar and coffee into two glasses and poured freshly boiled water into them. As she stirred the mixture, I handed her a bottle of Scottish whisky. "Sorry, I don't have any Irish whisky. Will this do?"

She nodded and poured a gentle helping in each glass. "Now then, watch carefully." She poured double cream into the glasses by tilting it gently over the inverted spoon. "Slooowly does it." The cream settled on top, forming a beautiful white head. "Success!"

We all watched in awe, "Genius!" I exclaimed. "What a concoction! Where did you learn *that?*"

Carla winked, "Now, that would be telling."

We sat down again. I cuddled my coffee, almost too good to drink. The aroma of whisky and dark coffee wafted up my nostrils, warm, intoxicating. It certainly tasted heavenly. "Have a sip Billie." She came over and bending forward, did so and licked her lips. "I could get used to this, thanks Carla."

For a while we sipped and drifted into silence.

Inayat broke the silence, "So, what do you think of Regan?"

Robin was quick to reply, "Only in America, would an actor be elected President. Ronald Regan was a second class actor and I think he'll make a second rate President."

Carla peered over the rim of her Irish coffee. "The only reason, I think, Regan's won is because the Americans wanted a change. Carter was a weak President. The slogan, ABC, Anyone But Carter, struck a cord with the public- the Democrats had no chance!"

"Well, let's hope Thatcher builds a good relationship with him." Sanjay murmured. "Our economy depends a lot on how that actor performs."

"Give him a chance," I said. "He may well be better than the previous administration—"

"Yes, ABC," Sanjay interjected. "Hey, if he can build a good team around him and delegate appropriately, he could do well. Running a country is no different to running a company- one needs a good team and management skills; leadership alone is not enough."

Inayat threw his head back and finished his drink swiftly. "Half the job would be done if Regan can bring inflation and interest rates down, what do you think?"

"Yes," Robin agreed. "And the other half, if he can control the foreign policy- less interference in world affairs."

"More coffee? Billie asked, quietly.

Sanjay and Robin shook their heads at the same time. Sanjay stood up slowly, arching his shoulders back. "We'd better get going, it's getting late." Robin stood up mimicking him.

Saira looked at Inayat. "Shall we get going as well?"

He placed his glass cautiously on a side stool. "Thanks folks, we'd better go, while I can still stand straight."

Billie walked in from the kitchen. "Stay a while- don't all go together."

"Eh?" Robin winked, "afraid to be alone with Amar?"

"You can come with *us*," Cheryl joked.

We all moved into the hall. "I hope you all had a good time," I said.

"It was *lovely!*" Cheryl said. The others nodded emphatically.

Carla and Saira went up stairs to collect the babies.

"Thanks Billie, you shouldn't have gone to so much trouble," Robin said, hugging her then shaking my hand.

I opened the front door, welcoming the cool fresh air which enveloped my face. "Wrap the babies well, it's cold outside."

"Thanks Billie, Amar- it was a great evening," Carla said, going past the front door. I waved to the crowd. "It was a pleasure, must do it again. Now drive carefully, don't forget to belt-up and—"

"Phone's ringing," Billie shouted.

"What?"

"Phone—"

"Oh, bye all," I shouted and rushed into the living room.

A voice screeched in my ear. "Amar! Amar, is that you?"

"Yes Auntyji? Where—"

"Amar! Something dreadful's happened. Paul... Paul ..."

She sounded hysterical.

"What?" I shouted. "What's happened? Where's Uncleji?"

"Amar," she said faintly. "Paul..." She was sobbing audibly now. Suddenly the sobbing became distant.

"Auntyji—"

A male voice came on the phone, authoritative and controlled. "Sir, are you Mr. Amar Dush—"

"Yes, yes," I interrupted, shouting. "What's happened? Who are you?" I was getting hysterical too. I heard Billie close the front door.

"Sir, I'm from Thames Valley Police. There's been an accident—"

"An accident?" I shouted, stupidly.

"Amar, what's the matter?" Billie was now standing beside me.

I held up my hand.

His reply hit me like a ton of bricks. "Sir, there's been a fatal accident, I'm afraid the lady may have lost her husband!"

"What! That's impossible!" I gripped the phone, now moist. "Are you sure?"

"Sir, we are proceeding to the Wycombe General Hospital. If you could —"

"I'll be there as soon as I can. What happened? How—"

"Sir, we can discuss matters when you arrive here."

Billie was standing motionless, holding on to my arm. I put the phone down, my whole body was shaking. I sank on the sofa, then immediately got up. "I've got to go; I've got to go... there's been an accident. Paal Uncle... he's..."

She stepped back, tearful. "He can't be! He was here only an hour ago, there must be a mistake!"

CHAPTER 30

1987

Another hot day, I thought. We had been sitting in silence for a while. It didn't feel awkward, sitting in silence. There was no need for pleasantries or idle conversation; both of us knew that. There was a lot to say but we didn't, the companionship was enough, more important than talking unnecessarily, just for the sake of it. We knew what the other was thinking, more or less.

I was seated in a cane chair in the conservatory, gazing, not intently, but with mild interest at the climbing roses. With the sun shining on the petals from one side, they seemed to be of two colours, pink where the petals picked the sunlight and red where the petals curled back. Their strength lay in their delicacy, I thought. Eyes could not ignore their beauty amidst the thorns that arose like the devil's claws to threaten those silky soft petals.

My gaze dropped to the lawn. "I ought to mow it one of these days," I said, almost to myself. I wasn't expecting any answer, for it was not a question or some contentious statement. There was no response.

I got up slowly and arched my shoulders back, stretching my back. "I'll make us some tea."

She was reading some article in a magazine and without lifting her head gave a slight nod. Although I didn't see it, I was sure that just then there was a smile, a faint one.

The kitchen was meticulous; everything had a proper place, either in the cabinets or the work-top. I knew where everything was. While the kettle boiled, I gathered the tea, sliced a lemon and pinched a few mint leaves. While the mint leaves floated around for a while in the hot water, I looked around for something to eat. Tea by itself just didn't seem a civilised way to relax. There were some honey glazed dates in the fridge; they would do.

"Here we are, tea and dates," I announced placing the tray on a coffee table between two cane chairs.

She shifted, and carefully put the magazine on the floor beside her chair. Straightening herself, she accepted her mug with both hands. "You are a darling, Amar, how would I have managed without you, all these years."

I said nothing. I knew she would have, somehow. She was strong willed and had always accepted fate.

I took a few sips and chewed a mint leaf. "You are a strong believer in *kismet*, you would have managed."

She smiled wryly. "What else is there to believe in? *Kismet* brings us into this world and *kismet* takes us away from it." After a brief pause she continued, more softly, "And then it reincarnates us back into this world to punish or reward us for our previous deeds."

"But don't we," I asked, "to some extent, make our own *kismet*? To a certain extent *kismet*, fate, luck, wtatever, is a residue of our hard work and deeds. Shakespeare is known to have said: *The fault, dear Brutus, is not in our stars, but in ourselves, that we are underlings.*" I agree with the great writer.

She picked a date from the plate. "I think our destiny is written in our stars, from cradle to grave. By trying hard, we may take a different route, but ultimately that route will converge to what we are destined to do or be."

"But Auntyji, people work hard for fame and fortune. Surely, they wouldn't make it if they didn't persevere?"

"Ah, precisely, the determination and hunger to succeed is predetermined- it's all in the stars."

I wasn't convinced, but decided to surrender. "I see."

"Amar, tell me, why is it that some children are born in riches and others in rags? What does a child do to deserve to be born in a slum and die of malnutrition even before its first birthday?"

I shrugged my shoulders. "That's the world we live in. There are rich people and there are poor people. A new born baby has no say in where it should be born."

Her eyes gleamed, "Precisely! It's the baby's *kismet*! It can be traced to the previous life!"

"There's no proof." I protested.

"Of course there isn't! How can there be! Babies do not come into this world with some letter or certificate to say what they had been up to in their previous life."

"So, do you not believe in dust to dust and ashes to ashes? Most people do."

"Oh I do, Amar! But I also believe that while the physical body turns to ash, the soul carries on, to reap or repent later. You know very well, the saying in *Mahabarat*, that dying is like shedding your old clothes and accepting new ones. The body sheds the old ones and the soul is given new ones in a new body. If they have done good deeds, they will come back on earth as better persons, with good *kismet. I* do not believe that when we die, we go up somewhere or thousands of feet down below to some burning place called hell. Heaven, earth and hell are all here! There are people on this planet who live a heavenly life and there are people who live a hellish life- all here on this planet! We live here and we die here. And later we come back here. No heaven, no hell... just earth!"

"Interesting," I remarked, narrowing my eyes.

She sighed deeply and leaning back, closed her eyes. "It's God's will."

"That's if there is one." I muttered, looking down at nothing."We are repeatedly told, from childhood that there is a God... and ... to our dying day we continue believing that. There could be one, or none, or hundreds of them. Whilst I agree with you that there is no heaven or hell, I don't believe we ever come back. When we are gone we are no more. No reincarnation, no heaven, no hell, no soul, no God. IF there is a soul, what is it? Where is it? Who has seen it? No one! And as for God, does he stretch from the North Pole to the South Pole and from East to West?"

Paro Aunty opened her eyes and gave me a sharp look."Don't be silly there *is* a God."

"So where is He? Auntiji, you yourself said that there is no heaven and no hell. Is it not possible that there is no–?"

Paro Aunty sat up straight. "There must be a Creator who made this universe, you, me and–"

It was my turn to sit up straight and lean forward. "So who is God? Shiva, Ram, Allah, Buddha...?" Maybe they are *all* Gods, a big happy family of Gods, different ones for creation, continuation, destruction, fire, air, soil, rich, poor, etcetra etcetra."

"Amar, stop," she cried out, banging the arm of the chair, "if... *big if*, there is no God, then there must be *some* force, the sun perhaps, or the moon. Otherwise what's the point in our existence?"

I couldn't argue.

"Amar, have you ever looked closely at the lines on your palm? Do you not feel that they are unique to you? Just imagine, all babies in wombs curl their fingers the same way, yet, when they are born, everyone has unique lines."

I had to bow to Paro Aunty's superior power of understanding and wisdom.

We fell silent for a long time. I finished my tea and sucked on the lemon slice. "It's difficult to imagine that Paal Uncle has been gone six and a half years."

She sighed heavily and placed her half drunk mug on the coffee table. "I hope he's happy," she said with softness and sincerity. "He was a good man and a good husband. I am sure he's back as a better person- someone's gain, my loss."

I didn't quite know what to say. "You've been very brave, Auntyji. I'm very proud of your positive attitude," I managed to mutter finally.

She looked away from me, towards the point in the garden where the roses mingled with the honeysuckle. "I wonder if people get some sort of inclination before... departing."

I thought about it for a while, "Coming events can cast a shadow beforehand. I suppose in some cases..."

"Amar, do you remember the sad song Paal recited that night? Just before..."

"Yes," I interrupted.

> *Ye zindagi ke mele*
> *duniya main kam na honge*
> *afsos hum na honge*

> *The funfairs of life*
> *will always remain*
> *sadly, I won't.*

"I've often thought about that. I don't think Uncleji *knew* that there was going to be an accident. It's just that we started to discuss songs and someone asked what the saddest song he knew was."

"Yes, but *why* did we discuss sad songs? *Why* did someone ask that question? *Why* did Paul sing that song? *Why* did that lorry skid into *our* car that night? *Why* wasn't Paul wearing a seat-belt? I've asked myself these questions a thousand times."

I shook my head instead of replying.

"Amar, it was Paul's *kismet*. That man upstairs with the blue umbrella, *He* had written the script a long ago."

I nodded, "Huuuuh. All I can say is that every morning when I wake up I say to myself that I should do nothing that could harm someone- mentally, physically, emotionally or financially. I strongly believe that this covers all commandments and religious teachings."

After a brief pause, and to change the topic, I asked, "How are the Sethis and Mehtas? Do they keep in touch?"

"Yes, they are *so* good. Of-course they don't call around as frequently as they used to, but they've always been so supportive. And Liz! She's wonderful! I never thought that she'd change so much. She calls in every Wednesday, after closing her Pharmacy. And you know, she won't accept a penny for all the things she gets me- some of those medicines and toiletries are expensive; even I know that."

"Does John ever come?"

"Oh, yes, sometimes, and every few months they bring the children. They are so well behaved; they call me Aunti*jee*. Oh, I wish I had a child, it would be like a part of Paul still with me." After a long pause, she said simply, "Do you know, Amar, except for you I have no relations here. If it wasn't for your support, I would have packed up and gone back to India long ago."

"Why don't you ask your parents or brother to visit you, even if it's for a little while?"

Smirking, she answered, "You don't know them. They are old fashioned and like many Indians believe that once a daughter is married off, she belongs to the in-laws. My parents are still of the belief that a girl is born in one family and dies in another."

I thought back for parallels in Kenya where it was different, not so old fashioned as India but at the same time not as liberal as England. "It will be years before things change," I sighed.

"Generations!" she mused. "A girl is still regarded as a liability over there, especially in villages. There are countless cases of new born baby girls killed off by their *own* parents- just imagine!"

I looked at nothing. "Poverty is such a curse. I suppose a lot of the poor think that their only escape is boys, who will either till the soil or work in hot sweaty factories."

"Yes, boys as young as five, perhaps even younger, are forced to work in sweat-shops. It is their *kismet*, a consequence of the deeds of their previous life, late administration of justice!"

Auntyji, we must look ahead, there is much that we have to thank God for."

She laughed, looking directly at me. "You are beginning to sound like *me*!"

I grinned, "Nothing wrong in that."

"You don't want to sound old before you *get* old."

"Huuuuh," I said standing up and stretching my back. "I'll take the mugs back in the kitchen."

Later, that night I tossed and turned in bed. It was too warm and I slept restlessly, awakening with the birds. I decided to go for a walk in the village and buy the Sunday Times. Even at six in the morning, the air was warm, but fresh. I paused at the large house by the stream, overlooking the fields. Two passers by, walking their dogs greeted me with faint smiles and nods. I quickened my pace and passed a few more dog lovers. After a while, I strolled more leisurely, admiring the robust wisteria growing outside so many homes. Denham village was at its best in the summer.

Forty minutes later, I was back. Paro Aunty was waiting – breakfast laid at the table. I put the paper down. "You needn't have waited, Auntyji."

"Oh, don't be silly. It's only at week-ends that I have company. Here, start with cereal. The eggs are done and tea is almost ready."

We sat down and I prepared my cereal, sprinkling on a spoonful of linseed, two dried figs, a few almonds and a cluster of green raisins, topped with semi-skimmed milk.

She always smiled as I went through the ritual. "I almost feel that you are going to burst into a prayer when you do that."

I laughed, "Oh, Lord, give me more of the same every day."

She laughed too and placing her elbows on the table closed her eyes and clasped her hands together. "And for me, just muesli and Amar's burnt toasts with olive oil, mint leaves, ginger slices and loaded with lots of dark organic honey."

"You don't have to be so descriptive," I said. "Just ask God for royal toast every morning."

We scrapped our cereal bowls in silence. I flicked through the Sunday Times.

"Anything exciting?"

"No, not unless you are keen on football; it's full of the FIFA World cup which has started in Mexico." I continued flicking through the pages. "My money's on Argentina."

"Amar," she said slowly, "you don't have to come every week-end you know. You have your own life. I *can* manage."

I placed both palms on the table edge and looked directly at her. "Auntyji, don't feel guilty or bad. I *like* coming here. What else would I do at week-ends?"

"Don't get me wrong. I look forward to you coming here, but... you have friends... and I'm sure you have—"

I placed a hand on hers. "Please don't think like that. If I had something important to do, I'll let you know in advance. I have so much time the rest of the week..."

"What about Sanjay and Inayat? Why don't you—"

I interrupted. I see quite a lot of them during the week-days. At least three days a week I lunch with Sanjay and every now and then with Inayat. Don't worry about me; I go round to their places quite a lot. I love the boys and once a week or so I meet Robin and Cheryl in a pub or somewhere for a few drinks."

"How are they? I haven't seen them for almost two years."

The boys are great. I take them to the park for a game of football Monday evenings. They are fond of me too. You know, it's amazing- they are the same height, Mahmoud's taken after Saira and Neel after Sanjay. Thank God, they didn't take after their partners- otherwise they would both be short!"

"And are they similar in nature?"

"Well... yes and no... they both enjoy sports and they are both mischievous, but... Neel rushes into things, he's more spontaneous whereas Mahmoud thinks things through before doing anything." I took a bite at the toast. "A few days ago, a ball rolled to the other side of the road. Both boys went for it- Neel ran after it instinctively but Mahmoud spent a second or two by the edge, looking for cars before crossing the road."

"God! That could have been—"

"Yes," I interjected. "I ticked Neel off and gave them both a lesson on crossing roads."

The toasts disappeared. "Hmmm," she said, clearing a bit of honey from the corner of her mouth and licking her finger. "Amar, you should reveal this secret to the big wide world; they don't know what they are missing." She picked her mug peering at me over the rim, "And how are the ladies?"

"Fine; Saira's still shy and soft-spoken, less so than before though, and still dimpling in both cheeks, Carla's still overweight, though less so than before and Cheryl still looks lovely, even more than before."

I stretched across the table for some more tea. "Pass me the milk, please."

"Oh, I almost forgot, Sanjay's going to Kenya in a few weeks- some bank business as usual. He wanted to know if he could get you anything from there."

"That's sweet of him, no I'm fine. Please tell him I appreciate his offer. He's quite a charmer, isn't he?"

"Yes," I replied, "and a good friend."

She eyed me silently for a while. "There's something about him that I don't like. He's a bit rash, and from what you tell me, so is Neel. Just be careful. He's what I regard as a BMW friend."

I was struck by what she had just said. Another profound statement! "A BMW friend!" I laughed. "What... what does that mean?"

She smiled secretly. "A BMW friend is one who loves you more for your expensive things or your worldly goods than anything else. As long as you are rich and sociable, he is with you-loose your wealth; you are on your own. BMW friends talk of strong friendships and bonds, but you've got to take it with a pinch of salt- it's just talk. Their self interest always comes first; they help with trivial matters when it's no trouble to them." She shook her head, "they are not *pukka* friends."

I stared at her. "Have you had any experience of these... these BMW friends as you so eloquently call them?"

She wobbled her head without replying.

Thoughtfully, I said, "BMW owners might be offended by this, you know."

"Oh, it's nothing to do with cars, it's just a term to signify materialistic people, and God knows, they are now a majority. A day will come, when we'll either have to join them or be thrown by the wayside."

I remarked, half jokingly, "How did you acquire such insight at such a young age?"

She laughed. "Life teaches. And if *I'm* young, you need to be on milk bottles."

"But why *BMW*? Why not Mercedes or... or Rolls Royce friends?

She waved a hand in a dismissive gesture. "Oh, I don't know. It's something Paul and Shatru came up with once over a few drinks. What does it matter? You know what I'm trying to say."

I leaned forward, elbow on table and chin balanced on the palm of my hand. "BMW," I mused. "Bloody Minded Weirdos? Boring Men and Women?"

"No."

"Beautiful Men and Women?"

"No," she said, half laughing, "definitely not."

"What then?"

She shrugged and smiling faintly raised her eyebrows. Then looking at me quizzically she asked, "Didn't Sanjay go to Kenya a few months ago?"

I nodded. "His bank has a branch in Nairobi and he is heading a team to see if it's feasible to open another branch in Mombasa."

"Does Carla manage when he's away, with Neel and her consultancy firm?"

I nodded. "She's amazing, what she lacks in size, she makes up in her strength and energy. Besides, they have a gardener who comes on Sundays, a cleaner who comes every Saturday and a maid who cooks week-days."

"I like her, she's so bubbly." Paro Aunty placed her chin in the centre of her palm, elbow on the table. She looked directly into my eyes soberly. "Amar...have you heard from Billie?" She must have noticed my frown. "I'm sorry to bring it up, but you need to sort —"

"Sort what?" I asked quickly, "Someone who was constantly nagging and accusing me of not being capable of giving her a child... walks out on me...?" My voice rose and I made a deliberate effort to control it. "I received a letter a few weeks ago. She is happy there, no mention of coming back."

"Why don't you go and speak to her? You two could have a whole life together. I know last year has been difficult... but the longer you remain separated, the weaker the bond between the two of you will get. And as time passes, the healing process will be more difficult. Swallow your pride and get her back."

"Get her back?" I asked sharply. "For what? Auntyji, she'll never change. After a few weeks, perhaps months, she'll revert back to her true colours." I shook my head. "You saw her the last few years, she stopped going out altogether and hated me meeting friends.... even you!"

This time Paro Aunty shook her head, slowly. "Strange isn't it? I would give anything and everything to get Paul back and you have Billie but don't want her back."

"That's not fair," I snapped. "*She* left *me*! Remember?"

"She's probably dying to come back to you."

"Then why doesn't she?"

She was silent for a while. "Women... they are different. They like to feel wanted, to be loved. Go to Kenya and ask her to move back with you, just this once, please."

"No! Matters are beyond repair. Too much has been said and done. The marriage is ... finished." Suddenly I remembered something. She must have seen my brief smile.

"What?"

"Nothing." I replied.

"I saw you smile; out with it."

"It's just what Robin once said to me." I replied. "After marriage, husbands and wives become two sides of a coin; they just can't face each other."

She chuckled, and then thumped the table. "Aha, but *still* they stay together! Why can't you and Billie?"

I shook my head in defeat and dared not challenge the dignity of her question.

She placed her hand on mine and rubbed it gently. Silence ensued for a while. "Let's leave it to Him, eh?" she said finally.

Good old Aunty, I thought. Whenever there was no solution, she left things to Him. He was her solace, her balm, the strength to move on.

We fell silent and quietly started to clear the table.

Suddenly she sat straight and thumped her thigh in triumph, "I remember now!"

"Remember what?"

"BMW!"

"What about it?"

"*BMW – Booze, Money, Women.*" That's what Shatru used to say about some people, "BMW friends. Never trust them. They are more interested in those three things than sincere friendship; nothing to do with the car, just a certain type of people."

I smirked at the idea, "That's clever, but should be used with care."

"Ya, ya, I know."

"Auntyji, I hope you don't mind my saying so," I said softly, almost timidly, "I'm probably the last person to advice... but... I must say this, it's been on my mind for months... you may want to consider... marrying again."

I had no idea what reaction my statement would have. She stood still for a while and then gently placed the plate in the dish-washer. Turning round, she gave me a tight hug. "Oh Amar, don't *you* start! I appreciate your concern, but I'm alright." She drew her head back to look directly up into my eyes. "I'm alright, really." She let go off me and continued loading the dishwasher. "I have enough of that from colleagues and friends. I'm fine, this is my *kismet* and I've accepted it. People go through worse."

I was almost annoyed. "*You* have to make your own kismet! It's now or never! You are still attractive and earning, with no children; there are dozens of men out there who—"

"Amar, I'm *fine!* I could never forget Paul." She thumped her chest with a clenched fist. "He's still here."

I was getting frustrated. "Paal Uncle was great! We all loved him- but he's not going to come back. You may be fine now, but in years to come, you'll be lonely and you'll need support and companionship—"

She closed the dishwasher with a bang. "I know you mean well... alright... let me think about it... okay?"

"Promise?"

She smiled and crossed her heart.

CHAPTER 31

Dear Munir

July 1987

I sincerely hope this letter finds you and your family in good health.

A few weeks ago I recruited a Trainee Accountant by the name of Farukh Akhtar who is also from Nairobi. He vaguely remembers your Dad as his father used to get his car serviced from your Dad's Agip garage in Westlands. He might have seen you there too.

Farukh is a bright young man and stays with an elderly couple just as I once did. And as I once did, he visits relations at week-ends. The next time he goes back home I shall send some gifts for you and of-course 'Old Spice' for your dad.

Life goes on here. Ever sine Paal Uncle died I question what existence is all about. It seems so unpredictable and fragile. I suppose we should regard each day as a bonus and carry on.

But no more of my somber thoughts. What is going on in Kenya? I hear there have been lots of political arrests and human rights abuses. Is there a lot of unrest in Nairobi?

Munir, the world seems to have changed since our teen-age days. I wonder what Farukh will witness when he is our age?

As you probably know, Billie and I are now separated. For some time our marriage was going nowhere. One day we had a quiet sulky breakfast and upon returning home that evening she was not to be found. Next morning she called me from Nairobi to say that she would not be coming back. Just like that!

Here, Margaret Thatcher has won her third successive election and is now the longest-serving UK Prime Minister of this century.

I haven't heard from Afzal or Rajesh for some time - have you?

Sanjay is my only regular school-friend contact here. It seems strange that every Tom, Dick and Harry seems to visit England but not you. Please, please try to come- it would be great. You and Rehana will of-course stay with me.

Your friend, always
Amar.

Sanjay and I met for lunch two days later. Sanjay seemed excited, but then when wasn't he?

"Amar, I received a letter from Raj."

"Raj?"

"Rajesh! Raging Bull! He calls himself Raj now-a-days. He's opened a night-club in London, Mayfair, calls it *Sili-Sili*—"

"Night club?" I enquired, surprised. "Why? I thought he was an Engineer!"

Sanjay waved a hand, "Yes, but hey, is there any money in Engineering? Anyway, we are invited; he insisted you come. I've given him your address and your office number." he threw his hands in the air, "All on the house!"

"What about Carla, wouldn't she like to—"

"Hey, don't be silly! We're talking about a boys' night out. Who takes a lunch-box to a five-star hotel?"

I shrugged my shoulders. "Okay."

He leaned forward and nudged my elbow. "I'll fix a date, next Friday okay?"

I nodded.

A neon light in red displayed *Sili-Sili* above a dark glass frontage. Two burly bouncers were stationed on either side of a high glass door. Sanjay spoke to one of them, giving our full names. As if by magic, the door opened and I followed him up a spiral staircase.

"I can hardly see where I'm going."

"Just follow me," Sanjay hushed. "Rajesh gave me instructions- up the stairs and turn right towards the Purple Bar. He's expecting us."

We turned right passing snuggling couples, men talking in earnest and young women flashing thighs and smiles. It was weired!

"It's very exclusive you know, Amar; admittance is strictly by recommendation."

We were a good ten feet from a bar dimly lit in purple when a man dressed in black, from head to toe, blowing cigar smoke advanced towards us. "Sanj! Amar!"

Rajesh had put on considerable weight all over and his shoulders threatened to rub against the corridor walls. His face seemed more square than usual as a result of his thinning hair, revealing a broad flat head.

"Raj!" Sanjay shouted, not stopping, "Good to see you again."

They embraced. Raj took a step back and spread his arms wide, "*Amar*, Amar, Amar, long time no see, *ndugu*." He gave me a tight hug, slapping my back a few times.

"Great to see you, Rajesh, nice place you've got here."

"I'll show you around in a minute, first, let's go to my office and talk."

We walked along a wider corridor with ankle high carpeting and into a brightly lit office with a dozen or so monitors. Raj pointed to a red Chesterfield sofa. "Make yourselves comfortable."

"You guys look good, *yaar*, very trim, especiall Sanj. Look at me?" Raj said, patting his rounded stomach.

We all laughed. "What do you keep in there?" I asked jokingly, eyeing his stomach.

Sanjay interjected, "All his profits."

"So, how are the families, still one child, Sanj? And you Amar? Zero? What's the matter with you guys, *yaar*? Fuck man, don't your *dandas* work any more?" He leaned back in his swivel chair. "I have four; two from my previous marriage and two from Helen. Just one more I've said to Helen- after that I'm going to tie a rubber-band around my *danda*. Tell me, do you hear from the others?"

I nodded, "I keep in touch with Munir, but I've not heard from Afzal for over a year."

"No shit, I met Afzal at Heathrow about a year ago," Raj said. "I was on my way to New York and he to Germany. He wants to fuckin live there now." We waited for more. "Forget him man, how's Munir?"

"He's very well. He sold the garage he owned with his father. But Maqbool Uncle retired some months ago and Munir and Masood are in the hotel business now- doing well."

"And what about that lovely sister of his; any news of her?"

I warmed under the collar. "Azra? The last I heard, she was married to some cousin of hers."

"Beautiful girl, pity she couldn't talk." He played around with a silver letter opener before addressing me directly. "Keep in touch, *ndugu*, we're related, my cousin's still married to your sister."

I nodded.

"Hey, you guys remember how we used to say that we should meet regularly and not like those guys in that Curry Pot joke, meeting every ten years? Remember the joke? Before we all left Kenya."

I nodded.

"I've forgotten the ending." Sanjay confessed.

"You tell him, Amar."

I recollected quickly. "There were these four buddies who happen to meet at a conference in Nairobi ten years after A'Levels and going overseas for further education. They decide to meet in Curry Pot because the waitresses were very goodlooking.

Rajesh cut in,"Fucking good looking, boobs hanging out. They then happen to meet after another ten years and *again* decide to have the reunion at Curry Pot. Why? This time because the *service* was very good."

"Ah yes," Sanjay shouted,"they go back to their respective countries and happen to meet after *another* ten years. And of course they decide to meet again at Curry Pot. But this time because they recalled that Curry Pot had a ramp for wheel chairs! But damn it, I can't remember why they go to Curry Pot the fourth time."

"Let me help you," Rajesh bellowed, "When they happen to meet in another ten years, the old foggies again decide to meet at Curry Pot, but fuck, they couldn't remember WHY!"

We all burst out laughing but after a while, Sanjay and I saw the serious side of the story and stopped while Rajesh was still howling with laughter, his shoulders and stomach wobbling in unison."Fuck man, we must meet more often."

"How long have you been open?" I enquired, trying to change the topic.

"About three months. Tell you what, *yaar* this is great business! I'm making more in one month than I was in *six* working for Smith Aero. At *Sili-Sili* I am targeting young businessmen who want fun with discretion. We've got everything- gambling, food, wine, women, hashish – you name it, we can supply it. I have a manager with fifteen years experience in this field. He hand picks women from Africa, Thailand and Poland."

"Why not from England?" I enquired.

Rajesh shook his head. Firstly, the fuckin *goris* want too much money and they don't stay long enough, secondly the *goras* themselves want something different. They can have English women at *home*. It's the same with the Indians and Pakistanis- they want to try something *different*. Then they go home to the usual! They release their full fat cream here and pump their wives with semi-skimmed milk, if you know what I mean." He stopped and winked. "Some of the people who come here are house-hold names; you'd be shocked by some of the guys who come here."

I wasn't enjoying this. Rajesh had changed and I did not approve of his open admiration of the set-up.

As if reading my mind, he added, "Fuck, business is business, or as the Gugu Nairobi shopkeepers used to say: *bijness is bijness*. If you want to make money you've got to go into it *whole*-heartedly, otherwise you're down and out in no time and the competitors throw shit all over you!"

Sanjay, cavalier as usual, asked, "Hey, do you supply hard stuff as well?"

"Sanj, who doesn't? I give my clients what *they* want! I don't force anything down their throat. Competition is fierce and these guys, especially the young Indians– they want the best. Their parents came to this country empty handed and slogged their guts off, sleeping ten to a room- you know that! They made the money and this generation is spending it like water. They want what their fathers never had; they want what the *goras* have. Tell you what, you give these guys the hard stuff and they can tell *exactly* where it comes from- at the moment the craze is for Himalayan hashish, best in the world! Want some?"

Sanjay smiled a nod just as I started shaking my head.

"Come on, Amar, a little bit will clear your head."

"Sanj is fuckin right," Rajesh added. "A little gives you a boost, too much can kill you of course."

We looked at each other slightly confused. Presently, Rajesh stood up and straightened his jacket. A shirt button against his belly threatened to pop out. "Come, I'll show you around."

We followed him back to the bar and past it towards another bar at the far end lit in blue and pink. "This is exclusive- private bookings only," he said patiently. "That door over there leads to private rooms." He winked, "They all get taken by midnight!"

"Can you reserve two for us, tonight?" Sanjay asked laughing.

Rajesh stopped and turned to look at me. He questioned me without asking.

I was on the spot. "Now look," I protested, "we only came to meet you, Rajesh; let's take it easy, okay?"

Sanjay waved a hand, "Enjoy life, Amar. It's all between friends. Remember the time we all did it with those Marabu girls in Mombasa after our A-Levels? All in one room!"

Rajesh and Sanjay broke out in a fit of laughter. "That was the best, *yaar!*" Rajesh screamed. "I can never forget that night. And Munir thought those things were fuckin *balloons!*"

"*Balloons!*" Sanjay screeched, throwing his head back and locking his fingers behind his neck.

I joined in the laughter, "And Afzal said a special prayer afterwards—"

"And that shy guy, what's his name...Anubhai...shit man, he started crying!" shouted Sanjay. "Whatever happened to him? Haven't seen or heard from him since school days."

Rajesh slapped my back, "Oh, Anu said we'd all go to hell, remember?"

Sanjay put an arm around my shoulder. Hey, let's get some girls, what have you got to loose, Amar?"

Rajesh shrieked amidst hysterical laughter, "Certainly not his virginity this time!"

The laughter subsided slowly and we stood there just shaking our heads, remembering that night in a cheap hotel.

"Come," Rajesh said when his voice was stable, "I'll show you the rest."

He led us down the spiral staircase. "The ground floor is for gambling with a bar in that corner." He waved to a few people around two gambling tables. Eight people- mostly Asian men were playing poker at the table near to us. They were all accompanied by smart young women in tight black skirts, standing near or directly behind their male partners. Some of the women eyed us through narrowed eyes but stayed with their clients, faithful for the night.

The bar had more women in tight black skirts, hanging around, just waiting for clients. A tall young man with a trimmed beard and a black turban passed us with a young Thai girl barely reaching his chest. I gazed at them as they made their way to the front door. Her perfume stayed with us even when they had made their way out.

Sanjay nudged me, "What a dish, eh?"

"A bit short," I whispered.

Rajesh gathered nearer to us. "We've all sizes and shapes here. And if you can't find the right one, I can get one from a club nearby. We have this arrangement with a few friendly clubs."

"What about food?" Sanjay enquired.

"No problem, *yaar*," Rajesh said quickly. "We serve snacks at the bar and there is a restaurant in the basement, follow me." We went down black granite stairs to a dimly lit restaurant. The place was less than half full –couples eating over candle lights in red stained vases. The ceiling, floor and walls were all black.

Rajesh waved a hand in a semicircle to cover the restaurant. "There's no electric lighting in the restaurant, just candles. We don't cook here; all the food comes from a caterer in Hounslow. We just get the stuff, heat it and serve. That way, I don't have to employ unnecessary fuckin staff."

"It's a bit quiet here," Sanjay remarked softly.

"Believe me," Rajesh countered in a low tone, "it fills up towards eleven." He then touched me at the elbow and spoke in a much lowered voice. "Don't look now, there's a man with a goatee beard, third table to our left, with a Somali woman, see him?"

I waited a few seconds before gazing in that direction. An Asian man, around fifty was chatting away with a slim girl probably half his age.

"Who's he?" Sanjay enquired with his eyes.

"Very well known, appears on television sometimes. He has a wife in Pakistan and a *gori* wife in London. He comes here once a month, always asks for the same woman."

Sanjay was staring at the couple. "She's stunning," he whispered.

"Come," Rajesh said. "Let's go up and have a fuckin drink."

We walked up the granite stairs and up the spiral stairs to the purple bar. Rajesh asked for a bottle of Chateauneuf du Pape.

As we sipped the full bodied wine, a tall lean man with sunken cheeks approached Rajesh and whispered something in his ear. He nodded a few times and frowned deeply.

"Excuse me for a while, *yaar*, some fuckin problem in the gambling room. Make your self at home. Order anything and sign R808."

Sanjay raised an eyebrow, "Anything?"

Rajesh nodded and winked before leaving us.

We remained silent for a while. "He's changed," I said, looking around.

"That's what a business like this does to people. Hey, let's have some fun, we've nothing to loose. Do you want to play cards?"

"No," I replied. "I'm not good at it. Why not stay here and have a few drinks. I don't want Rajesh to think that we are taking advantage of him."

He looked directly at me. "Hey, relax; I helped him with the loan. What we do here is peanuts as far as he is concerned."

An hour later we decided to visit the restaurant. It was getting crowded. We took a table along the wall close to the fire-exit and placed our orders. The waiter recommended grilled king prawns and I took his advise, Sanjay went for lamb dansak. The light from the candle was just enough to see what we were having. It struck me that we were the only occupants of the same sex. I mentioned it to Sanjay and he laughed lightly. He leaned towards me and caressed my hair. "Let's tease them."

I leaned back, laughing.

"Later, perhaps," he said, sitting back. "Ah look, here's the food."

Despite the awkwardness, I enjoyed the food and the service. We signed the bill under R808 as Rajesh had instructed. That impressed the waiter so much that he accepted the tip reluctantly.

It was almost eleven and I had promised to take Paro Aunty to Southall for some silk curtains next day. I suggested we head home.

Sanjay tutted and rolled his eyes, "Amar, for the nineteenth time; relaaaax, tell you what; we'll leave at midnight, OK?"

"Can we leave just before that? I don't want to loose my shoe like Cinderella did. Where the hell's Rajesh?"

"He's probably shagging some woman in his office; let's not bother him. Tell you what; let's have a brandy at the bar."

We made our way to the Purple bar and ordered two large brandies on Sanjay's insistence.

Couples came and went, some giving us discreet stares. A stout Chinese man with a very rounded face and a beaming smile approached the bar with two pretty women, one on each side- both blonde, one about his height and the other a few inches taller. He gazed at the variety of drinks on offer, pinched the tall blonde woman's bottom and they left giggling.

The barman kept glancing at us from time to time. "I wonder what his problem is," Sanjay said, frowning.

I raised my hand to beckon the waiter and as he approached us, I scribbled "R808" on a napkin and held it in front of his face. His expression changed immediately. He flashed an apologetic smile, served us and wished us a happy evening. Timidly and hastily he excused himself to serve another couple.

"It's nice here, isn't it?" The voice was soft, husky and sexy.

I turned around. Directly behind me were two amazingly beautiful women, of ivory complexion and light honey coloured hair. I assumed that the one who was smiling had spoken to us. She had short hair gathering around her neck, the other had shoulder length hair curling up at the ends. Except for that distinction they could have been sisters.

"Yes," I managed to say, "very nice."

Sanjay stood off his stool. "Why don't you join us?"

"We wouldn't like to impose—"

He switched on his charm. "Not at all; you seem such intelligent and lovely ladies." Eyeing them flagrantly from head to toe he asked, "What will you have?"

The husky voice ordered vodka with lime and ice, the other gin- neat with no ice.

We introduced ourselves. The husky voice introduced herself as Lisa and the other, Barbara. Lisa locked eyes with mine and said how distinguished I looked with the few strands on grey appearing in my hair. *She knows every trick*, I thought. Barbara rubbed her palm gently on Sanjay's shoulder and leaning forward, whispered something. Sanjay smiled and nodded. I could only imagine that Sanjay was succumbing to practiced flattery. Lisa sat close to me, her perfume drifting teasingly in my direction. When she talked or listened, she would look directly at me and by some trick, make her eyes sparkle. At first I thought that it was all pretence and that she was some dumb escort- girl. However, I soon realized that she was fairly up to date with current affairs and news. She laughed at the right time, not before or after and I began to wonder if she was one of Rajesh's women or a visitor like me. When Sanjay went to the Gents, Barbara moved next to Lisa. *Nice move; separating Sanjay from me.*

At five minutes to midnight, I directed Sanjay's eyes to Barbara's wrist-watch. He shook his head, smiling mischeviously. Lisa must have read my mind. Her eyes laughed at mine. She leant forward giving me a full view of her breasts. The low cut blouse was not accidental. She crossed her legs brushing my thighs and allowing her skirt to fall back towards her hips, a *practiced move*, certainly *not accidental*.

CHAPTER 32

Next day, I rang Paro Aunty to say that I would be late. She reminded me that I had promised to take her to buy some silk for the lounge curtains.

Parking in Southall was a nightmare. I managed to parkmy car between two vans fifteen minutes walk from the Broadway. We walked in a zigzag fashion, avoiding pavement stalls and crowds appearing from all directions. The smell of curry and spices was unavoidable, almost overpowering. Every third shop seemed to blow a mixture of smells towards the pavement- biryani, kebabs, sweet meats and naan. Hindi songs and Urdu *gazals* drifted from shops at regular intervals.

"Amar, why don't we have some snacks first, I can't resist it."

"Later, after the silk," I countered.

She pouted, "Just a plate of *Pani-Puri*. We can have something more substantial later, please?"

I gave in. We entered *Jyoti's* and shared a plate of *Pani-Puri*. Not surprisingly, we both ended up having a glass of faluda as well. It was delicious. As she sucked her last sip, she said child-like, "Afterwards, we'll have some *saag, maki rotis* and a few *kebabs*. And oh, finally some sweet- *paan* with thin *saparis*, OK?"

"And when shall we have the *rasmali*, you know I love that?"

She closed her eyes and took a deep breath. "Tell you what, we'll get some *rasmalais* and have them at home with masala tea."

An hour later we tried various shops for silk. There was an endless collection - from India, Hong Kong, Thailand. "Look, Amar," Paro Aunty shrieked, "so much variety and at half the price you'd pay in Selfridges." Finally, at Gunweet

Brothers, she found the colour that she was looking for. I admired the patience of the two women attendants, especially one who introduced herself as Manjula. They both showed us their endless collection for almost forty minutes. They showed no irritation but immense politeness, unwrapping countless rolls and expertly flinging yards of silk on the counter. They were good- looking but too heavily dressed in gold. "We will definitely be finding something for you, *mem-saab*," they insisted.

"I think this will match the carpet and sofa-set," Paro Aunty said, holding a good length of soft cream Benares silk against the light. What do you think, Amar?"

"Excellent."

"Are you *sure?*"

I nodded.

She went over to the far side of the shop to settle the bill, but not before negotiating a ten percent discount. From where I stood I could see that the woman accepting her offer, despite the strands of hair partly covering her face, was beautiful,very beautiful. Unlike Manjula and the other attendant who had shown us reams of silk for such a long period, this one was not overdressed and wore no jewellery except for a thin chain around her slim, long neck.

Walking towards *Tandoori Spice*, Paro Aunty was excited with her purchase. "Just feel this silk; it can go through a wedding ring, you know."

"Let's eat, Auntyji. I'm starving."

The *saag* was fresh and went well with the *maki rotis*. "You know, Amar, the best *and* cheapest Indian restaurants are all in Southall."

"I know, but I wish the waiters would smile a bit more. And they need to change their aprons more frequently."

"Stop fussing; are you interested in the food or the waiters? Oh, by the way, did you notice that woman in Gunweet?"

"Which one?" I probed. She nudged me gently, eyes laughing, "The pretty one! And you know what; she was watching you all the time."

My spoon stopped in mid air. "*She* was watching *me*? I don't think so. *I* could have watched her all day. Mind you, she was a bit far and kept her head down; I couldn't see much of her face. Her hair kept falling over her face."

She laughed and I joined her. Leaning forward, she pinched my cheek teasingly. "I could arrange a meeeeting."

"No thanks. Let's get some *rasmalai* and head home."

Queen Street was busy as ever during lunch break. I strolled over to the junction with Cornmarket Street just as the tower clock struck one o'clock and made my way to George Street, passing students hurrying about. I was aiming for the far end, towards a sandwich shop that was popular for its bacon sandwiches and strong freshly brewed coffee. The sound of my name stopped me abruptly.

I turned, "Sanjay!"

He closed the distance between us and touched my elbow at the curve. "Hey, have you been avoiding me, old friend?"

I had but I couldn't say it. "No... of course not; been a bit busy lately," I lied.

"Ginos?"

"Yes, I fancy a BLT sandwich."

"Amar, I have a financial proposal. It could be very profitable for you." He sounded serious.

I glanced sideways. "It's just that... I'm very busy... couple of important meetings—"

"Let's meet tomorrow for lunch at the Red Lion, it won't take long."

"O...K, fine."

We reached Ginos. The smell of fresh coffee, bacon and fried eggs blended together greeting us at the entrance.

"What are you having?" he enquired.

"One BLT sandwich and black coffee. What about you?"

Sanjay glanced at the blackboard with the specials written in yellow chalk. "Hmm, I'll have a tuna with mayo and a large espresso." Just then, a couple prepared to leave. "Why don't we grab that table?"

I nodded. "You take the table, I'll order."

I joined Sanjay in a few minutes. There were only four small tables at Ginos. The place was small but always crowded and noisy at lunch hours. Sanjay leaned forward and spoke in a low tone. "Hey, you're not regretting that night, are you?"

I was, and I wasn't. "I don't know... no... no." I knew I was lying, so did he.

"Amar, relax, enjoy life. You are single... and through no fault of yours."

I grimaced. "It was a set-up. I don't like—"

He raised an eyebrow quizzically. "What's wrong with a freebie? And *you* had the dishy one! She was good, wasn't she- you told me she was." He poked a finger in my ribs, "Admit it."

"Yes, yes," I said smiling but with a hint of irritation. "But she's not *mine*, is she?"

A waitress approached us. We fell silent while she carefully arranged our food and drinks on the small table.

"Thank you, Suzie," Sanjay said, cocking his head sideways and flashing a wide smile at her. She coloured but smiled back and made a hasty retreat. We picked up our sandwiches.

"Look, Amar, in a few years you won't be able to get it up, so why don't you—?"

"What's this proposal?" I interrupted.

"Gosh, this is nice," Sanjay spoke with his mouth full, "and so cheap too."

"What's this proposal?" I repeated.

He rolled a tongue over his teeth and raised his cup to his lips. Without taking a sip he put the cup down. "Let's talk tomorrow."

"Oh come on! Don't keep me in suspense. Why wait till tomorrow?"

He fell silent for a while, his face taking a solemn expression. "Amar, there's a prestigious development planned in London, aimed for the rich Middle-Eastern community, it's off plan at the moment…"

Sanjay must have observed my disappointment. His voice trailed for a while. "Hear me out. This is really big, I mean big. If you can raise a million pound, you could double your money in three months!"

"A *million!*" I cried incredulously, almost spurting out the coffee. In a way I was relieved. Such an amount was beyond me and I wouldn't be able to partake in this proposal. I looked around and made an effort to lower my voice. "You are joking, aren't you? Where would I get that sort of money? Sanjay, the money we made from the Watford apartments – my share, it's mostly tied up in properties and gold, which are stagnant at the moment. Even if I were to sell everything, I wouldn't be able to raise more than six hundred thousand pounds, certainly not in the next three months." I shook my head, "You need to approach someone else, perhaps a finance institution."

He leaned forward, locking eyes with mine. In a low voice he continued, "*You* don't, but your company has that sort of money."

I almost laughed. "What's my company got to do with it? It makes *foil products, not money.* It has no interest in properties. The Board members—"

He interrupted me, eyes still trained on mine. "Amar, I have a plan. You buy some of these London apartments off plan using your company's funds, just for a few months. You then repay within three months."

I couldn't believe my ears. He was asking me to steal company funds! "I can't do that! Surely you don't expect me to—"

He interrupted me again quickly. "You know you once told me that you buy your foil from a Scandinavian company."

"Ye...s, Swenberg."

"Well, instead of paying Swenberg, put the money in a bank account, buy the apartments off plan, sell within three months and pay Swenberg from the profit- you can retire after that."

I blew air in exasperation. "I don't get it. Firstly, Swenberg will be chasing for the money, secondly, nobody will sign that sort of cheque. Sanjay, my limit is only one hundred thousand pounds, anything over that- up to five hundred thousand pounds needs a second signature and any amount over that needs *three* signatures. What you are suggesting is impossible! It's fraud! I could end-up in prison! Let's just eat."

He looked over his shoulders. "Let's get out of here; we can talk on the way back."

"No!" I said firmly, "There's nothing to talk about. It's not possible."

"Amar, it's *possible*. Just hear me out."

I leaned back and crossed my arms across my chest. "Okay, I'm listening."

He leaned further forward. "I take it your payments are to Swenberg AB." He paused and licked his dry lips. "Now, instead of paying Swenberg AB, make the payments to AB Swenberg."

For a minute, I thought Sanjay had gone mad. "What difference—"

He raised a hand. "Open an account in my bank for AB Swenberg. I'll sort that out. We can say that AB Swenberg is a new employee of your company from Sweden. *You* are AB

Swenberg. Your company will make payments to AB Swenberg thinking that the funds are for Swenberg AB. *You* then transfer the funds to your own account and complete the transaction on the apartments. When the properties are sold you transfer the money to AB Swenberg's account and then pay the Scandinavia Company, Swenberg AB in full."

I licked my pursed lips, at the same time pondering over what he had just said. "Hold on, Swenberg AB will get suspicious if it gets funds from AB Swenberg, won't they?"

Sanjay shook his head emphatically. "I've thought about that. The money will be going through my bank remember. Your company has an account with my bank. I can easily get the funds transferred from AB Swenberg to Swenberg AB in Sweden."

Seeing my dubious look, he continued, "Hey, relax Amar, if ever there's a problem, I will write to Swenberg AB or *your* company and put things right. As a Senior Manager in Standard Bank, I carry a lot of weight."

I was beginning to see his plan and I didn't like it and didn't want a part in it, I probed into it, trying to find holes in the plan. "The signatories will not sign cheques made payable to AB Swenberg," I declared flatly.

He looked around. "They will," he hissed. "Just say that someone in accounts payable has written the AB the wrong way around and that you will sort it out shortly. If anyone is still suspicious, I can write on the Bank's letter headed paper to your company that the Bank has made an administrative error which will be resolved in a few days"

I looked over my shoulder and around the room, "Sanjay, Swenberg will start screaming for their money. They will contact the Managing Director sooner or later. This is theft!"

He tutted and sighed heavily in irritation. "To keep Swenberg sweet, make small payments up to a few thousand pounds every few weeks. You are the Finance Director. They will contact *you* first. Just say that the cheque is in the post or that the computer is playing up or you are short of a signatory- damn it, stall for a few weeks with small payments."

I could see Sanjay had thought it through carefully. "So every time Swenberg AB screams for the balance owing, I make a small payment to keep them happy...?"

He was excited. "Yes, yes, only for a short time," he whispered leaning further forward, elbows on table. Then lowering his voice right down he continued, "Within a few months its balance will be cleared.Three months at the most. I promise."

I picked up my half eaten sandwich and immediately put it back. "It's my neck on the line- I could go to prison for it."

He shook his head. "No, I'll take care of it. No one will see your account or your file. If your company contacts the bank, I'll explain that there is some payment delay due to the bank. I'll apologise. Amar, I won't let you down."

I looked around the small café. No one was interested in us. I pushed my plate back and said finally, "No Sanjay, it's not right, but I'll mull over it."

A few minutes passed before he spoke again. "Amar, you are *so* yesterday. Be today, or better still, *tomorrow!*" His eyes raked me up and down and he continued, "Think about it. We can make a million pounds within a few months. Swenberg will get *all* its money, albeit a bit late. I'll be fair with you, you keep sixty percent."

I shot him a glance. Was this the same Sanjay I had known since childhood?

"Look," I said softly, "I'm happy as I am. Why do I need to get involved in—?"

He slapped the table with the palm of his hand. "Happiness doesn't buy money! The world has changed. *Money* buys happiness now-a-days. Get real."

That's the kind of phrase I would have expected from Robin. I struggled to string a response. The waitress passed us and I raised my hand for the bill.

Sanjay leant across. "Amar, please at least think about it. We'll discuss it in more detail sometime, okay?"

My head was exploding. Just wanting to leave, I nodded.

CHAPTER 33

Paro Aunty spread the silk across the lounge window.

I took a few steps back and narrowed my eyes, "Looks fine to me."

"You don't think it's too light?"

From the tone of her voice, I knew that she had made up her mind. I had known her for so many years and was smart enough to realize that there was no point me trying to talk her out of it. "You want a darker shade?"

"Yes, yes, exactly, *slightly* darker." She moved her hands about trying to choose the right words. "We need more colour, something a bit intense—"

"You want to change it—?"

"Yes, can we, please? I'm sorry. It means another trip to Southall."

I nodded.

The staff at Gunweet Brothers recognised us instantly, probably guessed the reason for our reappearance. The two charming women who had spent so much time with Paro Aunty a week ago smiled brightly at us. Manjula approached us staying behind the counter and addressed her, "Nice to see you again, madam, how can I help you?"

The other woman, slightly shorter, was serving a couple and resumed her discussion with them over the length of sarees.

Paro Aunty took the silk material out of the bag and explained that a darker shade of cream would be more appropriate. "No problem," I heard the woman behind the counter say, reaching for a catalogue.

I looked around for the pretty woman who had been behind the till at the far end of the shop the previous week. Paro Aunty followed my gaze. "Is she not there today?"

I coloured and shifted my gaze to the catalogue. Two little boys bumped into me playfully. "Sorry Uncle*jeee*", one of them muttered, while the other giggled hysterically, placing a hand on his mouth.

"She's in the store," Manjula said in a low voice, addressing me without lifting her head from the catalogue.

I turned to look at her and then at Paro Aunty, puzzled. "Who's in —?"

Paro Aunty nudged me and whispered. "You know very well."

I kept my mouth shut, uncomfortable that the matter was becoming public interest.

Paro Aunty examined various shades of cream and yellow as Manjula expertly flung large pieces of material in front of her. Every now and then she would take a piece and hold it a few feet in front of her. "What do you think, Amar? Does this have a warm feel to it?"

I scratched my chin, not quite knowing what to say.

"This is very popular with our customers," Manjula said smiling breezily, displaying perfect white teeth. "It's like the morning sunlight. I'm sure you'll love it."

I nodded agreement.

Just then a middle aged woman clad in a bright red sari and a scanty matching blouse, revealing bulging layers of flab around her mid-riff entered followed by two teenage girls. Breathless, she demanded immediate attention. "Excuse me," she spoke in a shrill voice to Manjula. "Do you have any material for *salwar-kameez* in blue- navy blue?"

"I'm serving this lady," was the polite reply. "As soon as I finish—"

"How long will you be?" interrupted the woman in red.

I observed the newcomer. She was large. I reflected if my fingers would touch were I to embrace her by the waist. No, definitely not!

"I can't wait for ever—"

"I won't be long, madam."

"Isn't there anyone else who can serve me? I've been waiting—"

Paro Aunty straightened herself and turned to look directly at the woman, face to face. "I don't think a navy blue *salwar-kameez* would suit you." Just as solemnly, she went on to ask, "Do you think this shade of yellow will make good curtains for my sitting room?"

The woman in red was dumbfounded. Her eyes smouldered and bulged outwards in anger. For a second I thought that she was going to slap my aunt. She stood still for a while; eyes locked with her and then grabbing her daughters, marched out.

Amidst all the commotion I did not notice the arrival of the pretty woman. She must have come back from the store during the commotion. As I glanced in her direction she lowered her eyes and reached for a pen. I continued looking in her direction, though not directly at her. Her head was now bent quite low and she was scribbling on a note-pad. Her hair fell to one side blotting out most of her face though her long slender neck was visible from where I stood.

"OK, I'll take this one," I heard Paro Aunty say.

I turned to face her, "Which one, Morning Sunlight?"

"Yes."

"Very wise," Manjula added. She scribbled a note on a card and handed it to her. "You will need to give this card to that lady at the till and get a new receipt for our stock records, there's no extra charge."

Paro Aunty turned to me and handed me the card. "Be a dear, Amar; sort it while I get the material packaged."

I happily took the card to the pretty woman by the till. For some reason or other, the visible bit of her face turned red as I approached her. She certainly was beautiful - soft features and a lovely slender neck, ending in delicate collar bones. I handed her the card. Her gaze shifted quickly and she lowered her head to key some codes on a computer. I stared at her lovely hair, now partly covering her face once again.

She continued keying numbers on the computer, conscious that I was staring at her. With her looks, she must be used to people, especially men, staring at her, I thought.

Without lifting her head, she slid a white envelope on the counter, in front of me. I followed the movement of her long slender fingers. The two green glass bangles to match her green blouse jingled as she moved her hand back.

The name on the envelope caught my attention- it looked oddly like RAMA, the name of a Hindu deity. I peered at the envelope and realised that it was not facing me. Curiosity got the better of me and I cocked my head sideways to re-read the name - AMAR!

It was as if I had been hit by lightening! A dozen thoughts flooded my mind, none made sense. Was the envelope for me, if so, *why*? How did she know my name? Who was she? My heart was beating fast and I was puzzled, confused.

Uncertainly, slowly, I reached for the envelope. Just as my fingers touched the envelope, she hurriedly, grabbed it and turned it upside down. The writing was facing me, in bold: PLEASE DO NOT OPEN UNTIL TOMORROW. It didn't make sense! The envelope *was* for me! I picked it up and read it again.

My throat was dry but I forced the question. "Excuse me, is this for me?"

She was unmoved, head still down and remained silent. I cleared my throat. "Is this for—?"

To my surprise and shock, she nodded briefly and then handed me a receipt for the silk material.

How did she know me? "Excuse me, do I know—"

I felt a tap on my shoulder. "Everything OK, Amar?" I turned around to face Paro Aunty with two bags, one in each hand. "Here, take one."

In one swift motion, I took the bag and turned around. *Pretty woman had gone!* Paro Aunty saw the surprised look on my face. Nudging my elbow, she whispered, "She went that way." I followed her gaze and realized that she had hurried away into the little store behind her.

"Amar, are you all right? You look like you've seen a ghost!"

I remained silent.

"Oh, it's that lovely woman, isn't it?" she asked in a hushed tone. "Did you say something to her?"

I shook my head.

"Come, let's go. I'm starving."

I hastily slid the envelope in the inside pocket of my jacket and followed her towards the exit.

CHAPTER 34

Sanjay rang next morning, just as I was about to open the envelope. "Amar, meet me for lunch at the Red Lion, one o' clock, okay?"

"That may be a bit difficult, I've a meeting—"

He sounded irritable. "You remember I said I'm going to Kenya for a week? Well, I'm flying tomorrow. Can't you please spare half an hour today?"

"How about this evening?" I was annoyed that I had forgotten about his trip.

"Sorry Amar, can't meet this evening...or tonight - entertaining Carla's parents. When can you spare a bit of time for me?"

I scratched my head, trying to remember the meeting times. "How about two? We'll have to be quick."

"Two o'clock then, I'll be there. Thanks, Amar."

I glanced at my watch. Damn, I was getting late!

It was not until I was a good ten miles away from home that I realised I had left the envelope by my bedside. Damn! Damn Sanjay! All night I had pondered over the letter, meaning to open it first thing in the morning. The call from Sanjay had unsettled my focus. It would have to wait till the evening!

Sanjay was wearing a new expensive suit with not a crease. He got up as I reached the lounge and we shook hands. "We'll have to be quick, Sanjay, I've got to be in Banbury by three-fifteen."

"Sure, I've ordered the usual. You look flustered. What's the matter?"

I *was* flustered, and annoyed with myself for leaving home without opening the envelope. I hadn't been able to concentrate all morning. At the meeting earlier someone had suddenly asked me what I thought of the proposed price increase in foil and all I could reply was, "Huh?"

There was no point mentioning the envelope saga to Sanjay. I hadn't even mentioned it to Paro Aunty.

"No, I'm fine," I lied. "Just the usual office deadlines, you know?"

"Amar, you could retire in a few months. We need to finalise what we discussed about Swenberg last week."

"But... you're off to Kenya tomorrow!"

"Precisely, before I go I need to know if you can see any holes in our plan."

"*Our* plan? Sanjay, I'm not happy with it. It's immoral!"

His irritation was obvious, "For heaven's sake! Who's going to loose out? Swenberg will get every penny they are owed. Okay, a bit late but nevertheless, *every* penny. The bank does not loose out, you don't; I don't, the Arabs don't, what's the problem? We make a million pounds- look, you take two thirds."

I had other things on my mind. Sanjay was racing ahead too fast, not giving me a chance to debate the issue with my conscience. "Can't we discuss it, when you come back from Kenya?"

He threw his hands up in exaggerated exasperation. "Amar, we discussed it all last week and you said you'd think it over." He leaned to one side and lifted his brief-case to his lap. With one swift movement he opened the case and grabbed a document lying on a pile of paperwork. "Here, if you instruct me to open an account for AB Swenberg, then at least I can set it all up before I leave tomorrow. When I come back, if you do not want to go ahead with the deal, I'll cancel the account, fair enough?"

I looked directly at his hazel eyes. Where did he hide his cunning plots? "What do I do?"

He handed me a pen. "Just sign but date it, I'll do the rest."

A petite waitress, with close cropped hair brought our food and drinks. We fell silent as she carefully laid the food and drinks on the table. I studied the document that Sanjay had passed to me. No harm in signing it, I thought- as Sanjay said, if I didn't want to go ahead with the whole thing, the account would have no transactions and would stay dormant. I was the only one who would be able to use the account. My head was all mixed up- the deceit, the risk, the shame! Was it worth it? But on the other hand, a million pounds for us in three months! Could Sanjay be right? He *had* been right on the Watford apartments. I *had* gained substantially. Suddenly, my mouth felt very dry. I lifted my glass and finished almost a third of the beer in one long gulp. For a few seconds I felt elated, this was exciting, a challenge. A million pounds between us- two thirds mine! I could retire in three months time!

His face took on a supercilious expression. "Amar, believe me, it's only a timing issue. Swenberg will get their money for sure. Banks use other peoples' money all the time, yours, mine! If *they* can do that and make millions, why can't we?"

"Where do I sign?" I asked flatly.

His face softened and he leaned forward and pointed to a box in the bottom right hand corner of the form.

As I signed, he placed a hand on my knee. "Relax, Amar. This is the game all financial institutions play- using someone else's money. Money breeds money."

That evening I left work early. On the way home I stopped at Green Pearl, a Chinese take-away that I had begun to frequent. The proprietor was a middle-aged lady with a permanent wide smile. Most times when I stopped there, her two daughters, around eight years of age would be sitting behind the counter, doing their homework. They were not around today.

"Ah, Mista Ama," she greeted me warmly. "What you like today?"

I glanced at the menu. "Shredded pork and fried rice," I replied quickly.

"Good," she said. "I get for you...ten minutes." She started writing on a small pad.

I nodded and grabbed the local paper as she disappeared behind a curtain of silver strips separating the reception from the kitchen.

"Mrs Wong," I said upon her return, "I'm going to nip out next-door for some juice. I'll be back in a few minutes, OK?"

She smiled. "OK, you back soon."

At the grocery store next door, I bought some orange juice, brown bread and a pack of four beers, all of which I placed in my car boot before going back to Green Pearl. Mrs Wong beamed at me. "Food ready soon."

I observed the gold fish in the aquarium as she took a couple of orders from customers.

"Where are your daughters today?" I enquired when she seemed free.

"Ah, they working, back soon."

"Working, they are too young for that!"

She beamed proudly. "They good girls. Go school, work, then study."

I was puzzled. "What work do they do?"

Mrs Wong lowered her voice. "Baby-sit for lady nearby until she back from work."

"Baby-sit!" I was too tired to argue further. What business was it of mine to protest that her daughters were too young for that sort of work? Above all, how could someone trust a baby with two young girls! It was against the law! It then dawned upon me that like me the whole damn world seemed to be breaking laws! I was miles away when I heard Mrs Wong announce my order ready.

"You enjoy food, Mista Ama."

"Thank you Mrs Wong, see you again."

I got hold of the envelope as quickly as I could. Even after twenty four hours it made no sense. I stared at it: 'AMAR' The handwriting was simple, neat. I turned the envelope over.

PLEASE DO NOT OPEN UNTIL TOMORROW.

I peeled it from one end. The glue was strong and I didn't want to mess it up. Walking over to the kitchen I grabbed a sharp knife, which I pushed into the badly peeled corner and slid the blade sideways. Inside, there was a pale blue sheet folded in half. The take-away was unopened on the kitchen work-table. I unfolded the note. The words lept off the note:

Good to see you again

Azra

Azra! *Azra?* My heart leapt! It couldn't be! How could she be here? She was in Pakistan; otherwise Munir would have informed me, or would he? Why would he? My heart was beating fast and my body felt numb. A hundred questions flooded my mind, none of which were answered. Azra! Was she still married? Why did she write the note?

I sat down, dinner forgotten. Over the next hour or so, I read the note again and again, smelling it, studying the handwriting. Finally, unable to sit still, I paced the kitchen floor. *I must see her again*, I said to myself. Deep down in my heart, a pain began, one which I had felt many years ago when she had left for Pakistan. I wanted to see her at the earliest opportunity. It would have to be Saturday, first thing in the morning. My brain urged caution. It was just a note of recognition- no promises, no desire or invitation to meet again. She must be married now. She probably had children. Why was I getting so excited?

It was a long and uncomfortable night. True, I was honoured to have received the note, but what now? I was still legally married and she was probably married. The note merely stated: *Good to see you again.* Why was I getting so worked-up? Saturday was so far away, but a day to look forward to. What would I say to her? Suddenly I remembered that she was mute! That explained the note. I tried to brush away her impediment. It was not important. She was still the most beautiful woman I had ever seen. I tried to remember her behind the counter, her hair falling over her face, the long slender neck and those eyes. I felt ashamed that she had recognised me and I hadn't.

Saturday would take a long time coming.

Here, languishing in my prison cell in Bicester, I often rue the day I read Azra's note. On countless occasions, I have played back the sequence of events that led to our meeting and that note. But who can fight fate? All *what if* questions fall by the wayside against what is pre-written well before birth. Of all the curtain shops in England, why did we end up in Gunweet Brothers? *What if* the first curtain material had sufficed? *What if* Azra hadn't left Pakistan? *What if... what if* I had never met her again? She would still be alive.

CHAPTER 35

1994

"*Jambo Rafiki*," I said flatly to the man half asleep behind the steering wheel. *Hello friend.*

He forced his eyes open. "*Jambo Sana, bwana... unakwenda wapi?, Where do do wish to go?*"

"Parklands, near the Aga Khan Hospital. I shall tell you exactly where, when we get there.

As the taxi sped on the Uhuru Highway past the Inter-Continental Hotel, the driver asked me how long I was staying in Nairobi.

"*Sugui*," I said, *who knows*. This time I really did not. It was my third trip to Nairobi in the last two years.

"*Wewe unatoke wapi?*" he asked turning around.

"*Unigereza*," I answered. *England.*

We continued speaking in Swahili for a while.

The June morning air was cold. The driver apologised when he saw me struggling to close the window. "Sorry, *bwana*, business is bad. I mean to get it fixed but...business is bad. Tourism is down."

I half knew why but thought I'd ask anyway. "Why is that?"

He gazed at me in the mirror. "Crime and corruption; the biggest problems we have. The people at the top are fleecing the economy. Rest of the people are poor. Since the death of Oginga Odinga, the Opposition Leader in January, things have gone from bad to worse. Everyday, thousands of men are leaving their families in the villages to come to Nairobi and make some money. But there are no jobs for them here." He shook his head, "*hakuna kazi*."

"So what do they do?"

He gave me a long hard look in the mirror and again shook his head in despair. "What *can* they do? In Nairobi, nothing! Sooner or later they drift into crime - drugs, gang wars, prostitution or theft. Some just sit and stare at nothing and some stare at those who stare at nothing."

I got the drift. Crime was soaring in Nairobi. This led to a drop in tourism, which in turn led to more crime. It was a vicious circle.

We approached the traffic lights at the end of the Highway. He kept his foot on the accelerator despite the lights just turning red. I smiled wryly. It was getting pretty common not to stop at red lights - many lawful drivers had been attacked in stationery vehicle.

"Take the second turning left," I said as we approached the Aga Khan hospital.

Papa must have seen me pulling my suitcase up the drive. He opened the door when I was half way up the few stairs leading to the front door. With slow measured steps, he approached me with arms outstretched, "Amar!"

We hugged. In a few seconds I felt his wet cheeks.

"*Namaste* Papa, how is Maa?"

He pursed his lips and blinked a few times to stop the flood building behind his eyes.

"Amar." A soft voice greeted me as I entered the front door. Nita embraced me tightly. She smiled faintly but said nothing.

My mouth was close to her ear. "It's OK; we've got to be brave." I stepped back to take a look at her. There were dark circles under her eyes. "Is she awake?"

She nodded faintly and led me to Maa's bedroom. Papa followed us silently.

The room was in semi darkness and had a medicinal smell to it. Without a word, we all entered the room. Nita stood by the head of the bed and beckoned me to sit near Maa. She was lying on her back; legs stretched straight, hands by her side. Her face was taut, eyes hollow and cheeks shrivelled. Most of her hair had gone. I bent forward. "*Namaste* Maa," I whispered. I'm here."

Her gaze shifted slowly from the ceiling to me. Her eyes, which seemed dead a second ago, lit slightly. She struggled with her jaw and lips. After much effort, she whispered, "*Beta...*"

"Yes Maa, I'm here. Everything will be fine. You'll see."

She forced a wry smile. Her solemn eyes shifted to a picture of Lord Rama, on the bedside cabinet. Her lips twitched. Over the last two years she had found it difficult to move her lips. I held her hand, it seemed lifeless. I was shocked that in just three months, when I was here last, it had become so light, bones protruding from the flesh, the shrivelled skin forming tributaries. I was reminded of Mr. Woods.

Papa went around to the other side of the bed and held her hand.

"Maa, when you are a bit better, I'll take you to England. The doctors there are very good. They can cure leukaemia, you'll see, everything will be fine."

She closed her eyes. The dark crescents under the eyes fell back in resignation. After a long while she shook her head, gently.

"Shouldn't she be in hospital?" I whispered to Papa.

He sighed deeply. "Yes... but you know her. She wants to be at home in her final days." He paused for a while as I searched his face. "I think she knows..."

Nita shifted and cleared her throat. "I'll make some tea."

That evening, after dinner, we were gathered in the lounge with Mr Brent, our neighbour who had popped in to enquire of Maa's condition. She was asleep in her room.

"She's a brave woman. I know the last two years have been very difficult for her," he said softly.

I shrugged my shoulders. "What can one do? At this stage, it's up to the doctors."

"How's your other sister?"

"Bimla? She's in Los Angles, recovering from a burst stomach ulcer. She's unable to come." Nita answered.

Mr Brent puffed air. "She mentioned her ulcer to me when she was here a few months ago. I remember telling her to have lots of milk and liquorice. Natural cure; I believe in that."

"Yes," Nita agreed, "I've heard that too, they are both good in neutralising acidity in the stomach."

Mr Brent turned toward me. "And how's Oxford?"

"Oh, you know, much the same, it's hotter there than here this time of the year. The tourist season is in full swing. Everyone is excited about the Channel Tunnel between England and France"

Mr Brent scratched an ear lobe. "Ah yes, I believe the Queen and the French President, Francois Mitterand have now opened it. As for Oxford, I remember visiting the colleges a few years ago. We went from London on a week-end break. Our coach had a lot of Japanese tourists. They all had their cameras and books on Oxford." He threw his head back and gave a loud snort, slapping his thighs at the same time. "By the time they reached Oxford, there wasn't much about the city they didn't know."

"Yes," I added, "they take these things very seriously."

Maria, the maid, brought some tea and biscuits for all.

"Ah, *chai*," Mr Brent beamed, "such a civilised drink, I just love the way Indians make it- boiled with full cream milk and sugar."

Papa dipped a biscuit in the tea before managing to carry it all the way to his mouth without dropping the soggy bit. "In the winter months, I like a bit of ginger in my tea- a natural body warmer."

Back in England, I always had my tea without milk or sugar but somehow in Nairobi that just didn't work.

The days passed slowly. Although there was not much to do at home, I, like Papa and Nita, stayed indoors most of the time. He brooded often, for long periods, shoulders hunched, reading newspapers endlessly. I often wondered if The Nation or The Standard had enough news to keep him occupied all day. He would look at the clock every hour or so and go over to Maa's room, staying there a while. Most times, he gave her the medication himself, relaying fresh news to her as if everything was normal. One late afternoon, I heard him telling her about all the holidays the family had taken together- Mombasa, Malindi, Victoria Falls, Cape Town. What was her most memorable holiday? Would she like to go to Europe? England? Oxford? See Amar's home? It didn't seem to matter to him that the conversation was all one-sided. There was solace in companionship.

Nita and I took turns going out. I once persuaded Papa to go out for a drink at the Inter-Continental. He obliged reluctantly, though by the pool bar, he relaxed somehow. I ordered two cold Tuskers and grabbed a table near the bar-counter. There was a group of loquacious Germans pushing each other into the pool, shrieking with laughter each time they succeeded in doing so. We tried not to watch, with the mood we were in but after a while, with the beer and weather we saw the funny side of it. Papa smiled at their antics. There were a few more tourists lazing around the pool, most of them reading novels through sunglasses. My eyes rested on a pretty woman with a stunning figure in a yellow bikini. She was seated on the grass verge with her knees pulled to her chest and hands clasped under the knees. There was something familiar about her. I was trying to figure out what when I heard Papa asking me something.

"Sorry Papa. What were you saying?"

"I was asking," he said solemnly, "if you had heard from Billie?"

"Billie," I mused. "No... I haven't."

He took his eyes off me to some point in the swimming pool. "Nairobi is a small place..." His voice trailed off.

I sat and watched him in silence. Knowing him, I knew he would soon make his point and that if I interrupted him, I would never find out. My gaze shifted back to the woman in the yellow bikini still clutching her knees. There was something familiar about her...

"Everyone knows everyone in Nairobi and people talk." He poured the rest of the beer from the bottle into his glass, tilting it to reduce the froth, hands shaking slightly. "A few people have told me that she's seeing someone."

We lapsed into silence for a while, watching nothing. I shrugged my shoulders.

Finally, I spoke, half to myself, "It's been a long time. She's an adult and if she wants to see someone... why not?" After a few seconds I continued, speaking slowly, "And if I want to see someone, Billie can't stop me." I eyed him for a while. "Who is it?"

"What?"

"Who is she seeing?"

"Don't know; some smart looking man. They are pretty discreet but you know what Nairobi is like? It's too small for secrets. Sooner or later..."

A waiter approached us to check if everything was okay and whether we wanted more drinks. I smiled and shook my head.

"Did I tell you that I sold my share in the properties I jointly owned with the Panesars?"

I peered at his face through the top bit of my glass. He was still a handsome man. Maa's illness was a strain- made him look ten years older, but that would pass. "Yes, and I'm glad you sold out. Broken relationships do not make successful businesses." Inwardly, I thought that his future was financially secure. I hoped that he would come and stay with me in England, but knowing Papa, I knew he wouldn't. He loved Nairobi, his relations, his friends, the house, the weather- everything.

We finished our drinks at the same time and whilst I thumped my glass carelessly on the beer-mat, he placed it carefully in the middle of his, using both hands.

"Shall we go?"

Papa ignored the question. "Amar, why don't you move back here?"

"Move to Nairobi?"

"Yes... here, with us. Nairobi is such a vibrant city now-beautiful buildings, cosmopolitan food and a rich Asian community."

I smiled wryly and refrained from mentioning the gated houses, the watchmen and the guard dogs that all rich residents had, locking themselves in their grand prisons after dusk.

A German couple ran past me giggling and laughing, spraying some pool water on my back.

I had never thought of moving. It made me think of Inayat. He and Saira were planning to go back to Iran but that was because his father had passed away some months ago, and his brothers kept writing to him to help in the running of the business empire. *They want the contribution of my English qualification and business experience, Inayat had said.* I felt a pang in my heart. I would miss them and Mahmoud of course. He was growing fast and we were both very fond of each other, almost like an uncle and nephew.

How could I leave Robin, Cheryl, Sanjay, Carla and little Neel; above all, Paro Aunty and Azra? No, I had my little world in England; some part of me was embedded and intertwined with others there. It would be impossible to leave them after all this time. And being a British citizen I would not get a job in Kenya.

As if reading my mind, he said softly, "You have relations and friends here too."

I nodded and patted his hand. "I'll think about it, Papa." Even though I knew the answer, I made a mental note to ask Azra if she would ever consider moving back to Nairobi."

"Shall we go?" This time it was he who asked the question.

"Yes, let's," I got on my feet and glanced around. The pretty woman who had been clutching her knees was walking towards the pool, her long blonde hair flowing in the slight breeze. It suddenly came to me; *Jennifer!* That's who she reminded me of!

CHAPTER 36

July, as expected proved to be less cold than June. The mornings were cool but pleasant, the afternoons warm and soothing. There were flowers everywhere, particularly bougainvillea. I went out for short walks, breathing the fresh unpolluted air and the unmistakable spicy smell of Eucalyptus trees around Parklands. Sadly, pot-holes were common place- in the roads, pavements and grass verges. Government spending on such matters was low priority and the June rains hadn't helped, widening and deepning the holes.

On a few occasions, I would stop at one of the shanty food stalls that had sprung up by road sides in most of the residential areas in Nairobi. I often thought of Mwangi's duka which I used to frequent many years ago in Ngara. There was one particular stall mid-way between home and the hospital, just a few meters from the road that was clean and offered good service. Kip Kiprugut was the owner, manager, chef and waiter at *Uhuru Hotel*, which boasted two worn out tables and three chairs between them. The "hotel" was no more than ten feet by eight feet with a corrugareted tin roof and wooded structure, used for storing groceries, the kitchen by the side in the open. Not trusting the chairs or the tables, I preferred to lean against a Jacaranda tree trunk and eat standing up. He made the most delicious tea imaginable- the secret he said was in how long the mixture of water, tea, milk and sugar was boiled and at what heat. "First high heat then low and slow." he lectured.

Kip was tall and very muscular, with an old knife scar running down from the left cheek bone to the jaw. The scar gave him a fearsome look but the man was so gentle in his mannerism that I doubt if he could harm a fly. His greetings were always warm and welcoming, displaying perfect white teeth.

"*Jambo* Kip," I shouted from the other side of the road one afternoon.

He straightened himself over the stove. "*Jambo Sana, penda chai? Would you like some tea?*"

I debated for a few seconds. It was mid afternoon, tea would be nice. "*Ndio*," I said beginning to cross the road. *Okay.*

"So, how is my friend from *Uingereza?*"

"Fine," I replied, shaking hands with him, "nobody around today?"

"A few people just left. What will you have?"

"*Nitakunya chai na maziwa na sukari kidago sana*," I said, leaning against a tree trunk. *I'll have tea with milk and very little sugar.*

"Okay, have a seat; I have fixed this chair for you."

I obliged, a bit uncertainly. It seemed fine. "You need to fix the other chairs and tables too."

He grunted, "Soon, *rafiki*. Maybe, I buy new ones."

He added tea leaves to boiling water and lowered the stove temperature. "What is your business here, *rafiki, biashara gani?*"

"No business," I replied. "I'm visiting my sick mother. She's not at all well and my father can't cope by himself. She doesn't have long to live."

"*Ayee*," he said, biting his lower lip, "may God help her."

"*Ndio, mungu atamsaidia.*" I agreed

We remained silent for some time while he added milk and some sugar into the pan and decreased the temperature.

"Why don't you come and live here with your father?"

I thought about it for some time while Kip poured tea in a large mug. "My house and friends are in England," I replied. "I've lived there too long to come back. Besides, I have a British passport, can't get a job here."

He handed me the mug and took a seat next to me, balancing expertly on a three legged chair.

"This is excellent tea Kip, *nzuri sana*." I meant it.

"Do you have a wife there?"

I took a few more sips before I answered. "No."

He locked eyes with me. "No Woman?"

I stared at his innocent eyes and sighed audibly. "I don't live with any woman, but I've been seeing someone in England for a few years now. She's very beautiful. I used to know her in Nairobi when I was young."

He smiled and slapped his thigh. "Ayeee, there's no love like first love, *rafiki*. God wants you to be together."

I smiled and looked at him through the rising steam. "Yes, I love her very much."

He matched my smile. "And she loves you? Has she told you?"

His question hit me. Told me? "No, she hasn't. She can't speak. But I know she loves me- maybe not as much as *I* love her."

"Why doesn't she live with you?"

"She... she lives with an aunt. We can't live together—"

He interrupted quickly, "Why not?"

I finished my tea and smacked my lips. "Give me some more."

"Wait I'll heat it first. Why can't she live with you?"

This is crazy, I thought. Why was I telling Kip all this? Perhaps my secret would always remain a secret with him. I fell silent and he gave me time to construct a reply.

"Well, I'm still married to someone else...to someone who now lives in Nairobi and this woman, in England, my friend, is married to someone in a different country... Pakistan."

Kip shook his head, confused and I repeated what I had just said. He shook his head again. "Three people from three continents! Why isn't your friend staying with her husband in Pakistan?"

"Ah my friend," I explained, "some years ago, she ran away from her husband and went to live in England with her aunt?"

He put his mug down, "But why, *rafiki*? Why did she leave him?"

"*He* was already married and his wife did not treat my friend with respect. She was treated like a servant, did all the housework- cooking, cleaning, washing, and so on. At some stage, she had enough! She stole money from her husband, a bit at a time and went to England."

"*Ayee*," Kip said sadly, pouring me another drink, "is she happy now?"

"Oh, yes!" I exclaimed quickly, "she and I both. I want to be with her forever!"

"*Mungu atakusaidia*," he said. *God will help* His sincerity was touching.

"I could do with His help."

"Why didn't you bring her here with you?"

I sighed. "She wouldn't come. Her family lives in Nairobi, and by leaving her husband her family feels that she has brought them shame. They have disowned her." I gazed into his little eyes. "Even her brother who is a good friend of mine since childhood has disowned her!"

He poured himself some tea and offered me biscuits. He shook his head as if not comprehending how a family can turn against its own daughter. "What work do you do in *Unigereza*?"

I mused over the question, "Nothing! I don't do any work in England. Maybe when I go back I'll buy a hotel and —"

He looked at me incredulously. "You do *nothing*?"

I nodded and didn't expand on that. Suddenly I didn't want to tell Kip of the money I had made from the Watford apartments or from the Swenberg fiddle.

A few, around six men strolled into Kip's open compound and conversed in rapid Swahili, most of which I failed to understand. He poured each person tea and some of them asked for boiled maize and beans. Two of them grabbed chairs and the rest squatted on the ground, feet flat, arms balanced lightly on the knees. Kip stood near them for a while, listening to their stories, occasionally shaking his head then left them to converse among themselves.

He came and sat down next to me. "Ayee, things are not good, *rafiki*; lots of problems in Nairobi."

"What's happened?"

"These men," Kip replied, pointing in their direction, "have lost their homes, furniture, savings, everything!"

I sat up straight, not understanding. "How did—?"

"Their houses, together with dozens others were bulldozed at dawn today, without warning, without notice. Their furniture, whatever little they had was flattened to the ground." He shook his head in dismay. "And you know what? The police raided their cash-boxes and beat-up anyone who dared to confront them."

I was horrified. "The *police*? Surely they wouldn't—"

"*Ayee*, the police, they rape and rob too, what can we do against their guns?" he said in despair, spreading both hands sideways, palms upwards.

I stared at him, speechless.

Presently, one of the men came over and exchanged words and shook hands with Kip. The others stood up and thanked him in a chorus. "*Kwaheri kwa sasa.*" *Goodbye for now.*

"*Karibu*," he said after them. We sat in silence watching them disappear in the distance.

"Where will they go?"

He sighed. "They'll move to some other slum. And when that is pulled down to make way for some new development, they'll be on the move again. They are city nomads, they'll survive."

"Kip, are things better or worse than they were years ago?"

"It depends, *rafiki*. Those who are part of the corrupt regime are better-off, others..."he shook his head. "Ever since the *wazungus (Europeans)* left, the rich have grown richer and the poor, poorer. There are too many problems in Kenya- aids, drugs, prostitution, crime, poverty and slums... who can tackle all these? The biggest problem is corruption."

"I hope *you* are OK," I muttered encouragingly.

He laughed. "Ha, one day I feel good, next day..." He shrugged his shoulders and spread his hands out wide. "But you know, *rafiki*, we laugh and we cry, but we are independent – that's the main thing. "Kenyans got their independence- for better or for worse. We can walk on the road; go inside a hotel, cinema, school, train... whatever."

I was curious and I craned forward, waiting for him to continue.

He smiled with his eyes. "Do you know the story about the wolf and the dog?"

Leaning back again, I shook my head.

"*Rafiki*, listen. My mother used to tell me this story when I was little. There was a wolf that lived in the wild. For many days, he couldn't find any food and was extremely hungry. The farmers had locked up their cattle and goats and chicken. The wolf was starving, it's ribs showed and the limbs became weak. He walked for miles in search of food, day after day. Then one day, he came upon a dog." Kip paused to see if I was following him. I was, and signalled it with a nod.

"The dog was healthy and well-fed. The starving wolf told the dog of his predicament. '*Why don't you stay here with me?*' the dog asked. '*My master is looking for someone like you. He is very kind and will feed you well.*'

The wolf couldn't believe his ears. '*Would he really?*' He asked. '*Then I will stay.*' But just then, the wolf noticed a collar around the dog's neck. '*What's this?*' He asked. '*And what's that chain for?*'

'*Oh, it's nothing,*' explained the dog. '*My master ties me with a chain so I do not run away but stay here to guard his house.*'

'*Can't you go where and when you please?*' asked the wolf, saddened by the dog's answer.

'*Alas, no,* replied the dog, *but I am well fed, three times a day.*'

The wolf stared at the dog for a long time. Finally he spoke. '*I might be starving and weak, but I am free to go where I want to and do what I want to. My freedom is most important to me.*' And so, the wolf said kwaheri to the dog and continued his search for food."

I was enthralled. "Kip, that is beautiful. *Kipaji.*"

Presently an old lady came with a little girl and asked for some tea and bread.

I straightened myself. "*Kwaheri*, Kip, see you soon, *asanta.*"

"*Asanta rafiki, kwaheri. Rudia.*"

I crossed the road to make my way back. "Sure, I'll come again."

"*Mungu atakusaidia mama,*" Kip shouted. *God will help your mother.*

That evening, as with previous evenings, after dinner, we gathered around Maa. She liked having us around her bed in the evening for a while. Most evenings we would convey some sort of news or reminisce. She would listen with glazed eyes and flicker a small smile at being reminded of happy days and events. I told her of Kip and his Hotel, though I kept silent on how good his tea was. Papa and I between us talked about the world cup football matches that were being staged in America. Brazil and Italy were going to be in the final in a few days. Papa favoured Italy despite my protestations that Brazil had been more impressive so far. Nita and Maria between them had made Tilapia fish curry and coconut rice and Nita complained that on Maria's insistence she had put too much salt. "Maa, I've tried so many times, yet my fish breaks once it's cooked. You'll have to tell me what to do."

She kept staring straight up at the ceiling, barely awake, due to the medication and morphine for the pain. In the last week or so she had lost the use of her hands and one side of her face which had been part paralysed for a few months was worsening by the day.

Nita held her hand and narrated her telephone conversation that morning with Peter. "He's become a partner in a large law firm in Los Angeles. Maa, he was saying that his firm sends a car to pick him up from home to take him to his office; can you believe that? Mind you, he works almost twelve hours a day..."

Papa said he was tired and lay next to her while we continued talking for another hour or so, until Nita and I realised that they were both asleep.

I was awakened by acute silence. My eyelids flickered and opened wide. It was dark. There was no movement, no sound. I could not hear anything but I was wide awake. This night was different from others; everything was still, eerily quiet, as if the world had been forced into stillness. After a minute the silence became unbearable, almost stifling. It was as if a dream had been stilled in a picture-frame. Without intending to, without thinking about it, I got out of bed and tip-toed along the corridor. The floor should have felt hard, but it didn't. It was pitch-dark yet I could see clearly. I was being carried by unknown forces. The night air should have felt cold, but it didn't. I felt nothing, heard nothing and saw nothing until I reached my parent's room, and turned to look inside. I can't recall why I stopped under the doorframe and peered inside, I just did.

Maa was lying still, but not in bed! She was a few inches above it, horizontal, arms folded across her chest. There was a soft white light between her and the bed. I opened my mouth to call her but no sound came. I tried to move forward but my feet refused to budge. I stood still. The world stood still. Slowly, she turned her face without any effort to look at me momentarily and then resumed to look up at the ceiling with just a shadow of a smile. She was not in pain. Her face was calm. In the next few seconds the eyes closed and the light faded. She was back in the bed, lying still. She was gone.

I took a few steps towards the bed. At last, she was at peace. Papa was still asleep. My eyes focused on his and must have willed them to open. "What is it, Amar?" he asked softly.

I moved my gaze to Maa and back to him. "Maa's gone," I whispered, without moving my lips.

CHAPTER 37

"*Namaste Punditji*," I greeted the priest at the temple.

Pundit Ramsagar was a short, plump man with a long white beard and no more than a dozen strands of long silver hair on his head. He crossed the room, stooping prominently, hands clasped tightly in front of his face. His starched white *kurta* and *dhoti* rustled as he approached me. "*Namaste beta*, you are Dushant's son?" he enquired.

"Yes," I replied. "I rang earlier... about my mother—"

"Yesyesyes, so sad... I've known your parents for years... sit, please. Only yesterday, Mr. Bhatia, our temple secretary was telling me of your mother... sosadsosadsosad. I hope she went peacefully." He shook his head, sighing through his nose, "Sosadsosadsosad."

I nodded.

He peered at me through narrowed eyes, as if trying to remember where he had seen me before.

"Will you have tea?"

I shook my head. "*Punditji*, this is a shock for me. I don't know what we are supposed to do next—"

He interrupted me by holding up his hand. "You don't worry, son. Everything will be taken care of. That's what the *mandir* is for. We do God's work."

"Maa... my mother... she's still at home," I mumbled, not quite knowing what to say or ask.

He took a deep breath and got up. Stooping more than before he went to the door and shouted, "Kaka... Kaka... Oh, *Kaka!*" His voice got progressively louder each time he uttered Kaka by name.

Presently a youngish man, also in white *kurta* and *dhoti* appeared at the doorway, hands joined against his chest. "*Punditji?*"

Mr. Ramsagar introduced me to Kakaji. "This is Dushantji's son, Amar... I told you about his mother earlier—"

"Oh, yes, yes." Kakaji held my hands, smiling kindly. "So sorry, Amarji...so sorry. *Baghwan ki marzi. It's God's will*, nobody can fight His wish." Nodding gently, he continued, "He has his reasons."

"Thank you," I muttered. "What do we do now?"

He walked away, chin close to his chest, to a desk nearby and grabbed a notebook and pencil. "Give me the exact time of death and your address. We'll do the rest."

"Three O'clock this morning. When will the..."? My voice trailed down as he raised a hand to calm me.

"The cremation will be before sunset." He consulted a diary. "*Punditji*, four O' clock?"

Seeing *Punditji* nod, he continued, "We will send food for family and friends at one O' clock and do the *havan* ceremony straight after that to offer prayers for her body and soul. I will organise for an announcement on the radio... to follow the one O' clock news tomorrow. Is that okay?"

I nodded.

"Are you the eldest son?"

"I'm the only son," I replied.

"You will need to light the funeral pyre, with your father," He leaned across towards Mr Ramsagar and conversed in lower tones.

After a while Kakaji turned to me. "Where do you wish to disperse the ashes?"

I stared at him. The *ashes?* I hadn't thought that far.

"I...I don't know. I'll have to discuss with my father."

Mr Ramsagar clasped his hands together. Kakaji followed. "Now, you go home to your family. Kakaji will see you there."

"Thank you *Punditji*."

"Yesyesyes," he muttered, "go in peace."

Suddenly, I was reminded of the song that Paal Uncle had recited the night he died some years ago:

Ye zindagi ke mele
duniya main cam na honge
afsos hum na honge

The funfairs of life
will always remain
sadly, I won't

CHAPTER 38

Three days later, Nita left for Los Angles. Peter was quite happy for her to stay longer but the children needed more attention and support, particularly as Arun, their eldest was starting at a new school. Without her, the house grew quiet. I ached to go back to England- to my routine, friends and Paro Aunty, and above all, Azra. Sometimes, I felt stabs of guilt thinking of Azra when I had just lost Maa. Papa was all confused about how he was going to cope. On numerous occasions, I tried to persuade him to move to England with me but the more I tried, the more irritable he got. "What would I do there? I have businesses here to take care of. My friends and relatives are all *here*."

The house was everything to him- his adobe, his wife and children. There were too many memories and he could not leave it. It was his world.

To overcome the boredom, I took him for mid-morning walks around Parklands and sometimes to some restaurant in the shopping mall in Westlands, though after a while the persuasion time got longer and I gave up trying.

Maria was wonderful. She cleaned and cooked without complaint, humming for hours on end and scolding Papa whenever he came in her way. She felt that being the only female in the house, it now fell upon her to run the place.

On one occasion when Papa was in town, I went over to Uhuru Hotel just to talk openly to someone. Kip was genuinely sad to learn of Maa's death, sure that she had gone to heaven and that she was looking down at me right now. The piping hot chai and the boiled beans with a hint of salt and lemon juice were exceptionally good. It was there, under the eucalyptus and jacaranda trees, sitting in one of Kip's make-shift chairs, holding a mug of chai that I cried. He let me for a while then came over to sit close to me. "*Rafiki*, it is

Mungu's will. He calls those that He likes. There is only one thing certain in life, we all have to go up there." He kept looking at me until I smiled my appreciation. "You know, *rafiki*, in this world we are mere tourists. Sooner or later all have to go back."

The simplicity in his profound statement touched my heart. I smiled wryly, "Kip, you should be a priest."

He threw back his head and laughed. It suddenly struck me that I hadn't heard a laugh for weeks. I felt lighter. "What's funny?"

"A priest? *Me*? *Rafiki*, you don't know, but I've been in prison!"

I searched his face. "*You*? *Why*?"

"*Ayee*, it's a long story my friend. See this scar?" He pointed to the deep line running from his cheek bone to his jaw.

I raised my eyebrows. "How did you get that?"

His expression hardened. He grew silent and locked eyes with mine. I waited for his answer.

"My brother, my own *ndugu* did this! Yes, *ndugu yangu.*"

I said nothing for fear that if I did, he may not continue. His eyes were burning with hatred. "One day, I came home early from my *shamba* and I found my brother on top of my screaming daughter. Her clothes were torn and she was struggling wildly. She was only just fifteen at the time..."

"Oh my God, I'm sorry, Kip."

"We had a fight... both of us got hold of knives and he did this to me," he hissed, pointing to the scar.

Kip grimaced and shook his head. "*He* was a priest!"

I was visibly shocked.

"*Ndio*, a church in Ruiru."

After a long silence, he took a deep breath and stood up.

"*Chai mwingine, rafiki?*" More tea, friend?

I shook my head. "*Apana, santa*. I'd better head home."

I tapped him on the shoulder with a flat palm and handed him a hundred shilling note.

"Keep it, Kip."

As I passed him, I turned and asked, "Where is your brother now?"

He rolled his eyes towards his creased forehed and rised a finger above his head.

I smiled wryly and waved a hand, "*Kwaheri*, Kip."

"*Kwaheri rafiki, Good-bye friend.*"

Among the friends who came to pay their condolences were Mrs Webber and Ribena. She hugged me and Papa affectionately. "Your mother suffered so much in the last year or so. Poor dear, I shall pray for her soul."

Ribena was beginning to resemble what Mrs Webber looked like ten years ago- tall, slim, with a straight back. Mrs Webber had put on a bit of weight all over since I last saw her two years ago. There was a hint of a double chin but otherwise she still looked elegant. I thanked her for coming to comfort us but had I known then what I know now, I wouldn't have bothered. *May she rot in hell!*

Before I flew back to England, I arranged to meet Munir for lunch at *Curry Pot*, a stone throw from the Ismaili Mosque. The restaurant was known more for the quality of the dishes than its ambience. The place was crowded so we decided to go upstairs, which was equally crowded and we had to strain to hear each other.

"Sorry. I should have suggested some other restaurant, could have gone to *Supreme* restaurant."

"That's OK *yaar*," Munir said loudly," I like the food here, and I don't mind the noise, reminds me of Pakistan."

"You seem to go there quite often."

He shrugged his shoulders. "My roots. And I've relations there. What will you have?"

The menu was just two pages. I looked for some chicken dish- masala or curry. I chose masala chicken with tandoori rotis. Munir ordered lamb curry and pilau rice. As usual, he chose plain water with his food.

As we waited for our food, he waved to a few people around the room.

I enquired about his parents.

"They are fine, *yaar*. Did I tell you that Masood's gone to England? He's bought a warehouse for car spare parts."

"No, where?"

"Some place called Glasgow..."

"That's in Scotland, not England," I corrected him. "It's part of Britain though. Does he like it there?"

He shrugged his shoulders again. "I suppose so; he hasn't complained so far, except to say that he has problems understanding their English."

I laughed. "I can understand that."

Our dishes came. The aroma teased my senses and on tasting, the chicken was delicious.

"Why haven't you been to England as yet? Everyone else has."

"You know I don't like the *goras*. I was born and bred here, *yaar*. This is the only country I love."

I gave him a quizzical look. "But you've been to Pakistan a few times, so why not try England? I'll make sure you have a good time there."

He played with a piece of lamb, pushing it deep into the rice. "*Inshallah.*" God *willing.*

We ate in silence for a while. The waiter came and asked if everything was fine. We both nodded without saying a syllable.

"Munir," I muttered, "I've been told that Billie is seeing someone? Do you... know who?"

He stiffened and stared into my eyes. "I? No... no, I don't." Putting his fork and spoon down carefully, he added,

"I thought it was over between you guys? You yourself said that in one of your letters."

I nodded, studying his face carefully but his expression betrayed nothing.

Twenty minutes later, the waiter came with a menu for dessert.

Munir shook his head.

"Staying trim, eh?" I commented. "You look good."

"What *yaar*, all these sweets, nothing but sugar."

I studied his face again. It was expressive, especially his eyes - deep, very alert. Over the years, his jaw had firmed, giving him an almost menacing look. He insisted on paying. As we descended to the ground floor he asked, "Are you worried who Billie is seeing?"

"No, not really, I just wondered, that's all." At that moment, I suspected that he had been economical with the truth but what I didn't realise was that some years later I would be proved right.

PART 3

CHAPTER 39

2000

The millennium was about to come to a close with endless talk of computers going haywire, traffic lights getting stuck at red, alarms going off without warning and even operating theatres not functioning. Y2K was the new buzz-word. Amidst all this was incessant talk of the millennium celebrations.

The red and gold leaves had all gone, surrendering to the cold frost and mist of winter. Bare trees swayed in freezing winds gritting their teeth, waiting for the warm spring breeze. Their endurance was worthy of admiration, they had lost their leaves but not their will.

It was almost six years since I had lost Maa. Sometimes, I looked back at the events of those previous years and felt how slowly time had moved, chained to memories. For months after her cremation the melancholy had hung heavy within me, breathing lethargy into my body.

I worried about Papa after I left him at the airport in Nairobi. He seemed so helpless. But time heals, and as he gradually fell into his routine with his friends he became more self-reliant and happy. Sometimes Maria would pick up the telephone and give me news of how he was coping, "*Apana fikri ndugu, mimi iko hapa.*" *Don't worry brother, I'm here.* It was only when Bimla went to stay with him a year later and rang me to say that he was fine that I finally relaxed. She put my mind at ease, "He's got a good circle of friends and every Sunday they gather at a house in turn to play cards. Sometimes, they go to the club and have a game of snooker or watch cricket. His health is fine, so please do not worry unnecessarily. He's planning to visit his relations in India in March. He *may* visit you when it gets warmer over there. "

The surprise had come a fortnight ago. I received a call from Papa to say that he needed to move on and that he was desperate for companionship. I whole-heartedly agreed. A few days later, he asked me what I thought of Mrs. Webber. A fine lady, I had replied, intelligent and understanding. Suddenly, he blurted out that he was fond of her and that they had discussed living together, even marriage and would I come to Nairobi next month.

After the simple registry wedding but before I left for England, at the airport in Nairobi, I finally found the courage to ask him something that had been tugging my heart for some time. "Papa, how long have you and Mrs.Webber... I mean... have you been seeing her long?"

He stiffened. "Amar, there's no point in unearthing histories—"

"I just need to know the truth, Papa."

He exhaled loudly and his shoulders drooped further. I very nearly said that it didn't matter. But it did! I had to know!

I drew a long sigh, "Before Maa's death...or after?" I asked in a low voice, looking into his eyes.

He remained silent for for a good minute before nodding slightly, revealing a tinge of regret and guilt.

"Before?" I asked, not realising that my voice had raised.

He suddenly looked much older, the pain visible in his face, "Yes, Amar... yes." His face took a slightly contorted appearance.

"You had an affair *before*—"

My accusation was quickly interrupted. "It wasn't like that Amar. It *was* before, yes, but it was *after* she... your Maa was confined to bed with cancer—"

"Hell!" I hissed, looking into his eyes. "That's when she needed you most!"

319

For a few seconds, we looked at each other as strangers do. A few years ago we were the same height. Looking at him at that moment I realised that he had shrunk; my eyes levelled above his forehead. The lines running down the sides of his nose were deeper than ever and the corners of his mouth curled down. I wondered how much of it was due to Maa's illness.

He took my hand in his. "Amar, forgive me, but I swear, I did everything, *everything* possible for your mother. Anna meant nothing, just comfort and companionship. With all children away, life was unbearable without..." He paused for breath. "Anna's not a bad person; she gave me the strength to care for your mother." His eyes pleaded for understanding.

I didn't want to leave him feeling depressed. I was annoyed with Papa cheating on Maa, but perhaps I was being too harsh on an old man. *Anna gave him strength to look after Maa.* Perhaps he had done the wrong thing for the right reason or perhaps he had done the right thing for the wrong reason...who was I to judge him? I hugged him - lightly at first, then firmly. "I understand," I whispered in his ear.

Later, as I turned to wave from the passport control point, I saw in Papa an old man stooping and tired, clearly in need of companionship.

CHAPTER 40

Azra and I met at least twice a week. When I was with her, I felt that time was flying past, too quickly. I loved her more that anyone or anything I had known. After the awkwardness of the first few weeks, when communication between us seemed unnatural and confusing, we gradually began to read each other's mind, eyes, lips, the raising of an eyebrow, the movement of shoulders or hands.

After two months, her disability was forgotten. What we couldn't discuss naturally, she used her mobile text-screen to aid her. I remember the first time she used it. I had asked her who she lived with. She tapped a name on her mobile. Smiling, she added: *my aunt.*

"Is it a flat or a house?"

Azra brought her forefinger and thumb closer.

"A flat? How many rooms?"

Holding my stare, she showed me three fingers and mouthed the words.

"Why don't you move in with me? I don't work anymore and I've got a big empty house. Give up your job and flat and live with *me.* It would save me coming to Southall every-time." I was serious.

She studied my face and gently shook her head. The green eyes implored me never to ask her to do so, ever.

I held her hand. "Azra, it makes sense. This job of yours doesn't pay much. Why are you slogging there for seven hours a day, six days a week?"

Her eyes grew hard. Lowering her face she tapped on her mobile: *Pls don't ask me to leave my aunt or my job."*

I raised her face by her chin. "Okay, I understand, sorry." I knew that her aunt had helped her when she had arrived from Pakistan penniless. Furthermore, I realised that her job brought her respect and got her through the day. "I won't mention it again."

A few seconds later she tapped on her mobile: *Why don't you get a job?*

I thought about it. After the profit I had made from using Swenberg' funds, I had decided to leave. I had almost been caught once when in Sanjay's absence the bank had rung my Company to enquire why a payment had been made to AB Swenberg and not Swenberg AB. *A simple mistake by the bank I had said. I'm sure the bank will correct it.* There was another instance when Mr. Woolmer, the Production Director had refused to sign a cheque made payable to AB Swenberg and I had to go behind his back to the Sales Director who, just rushing-off to a meeting, signed without even glancing at the payee name. Being afraid that sooner or later my luck would run out, I decided that enough was enough and left my job as soon as the Swenberg balance was cleared.

"I get by with my writing. As you know, I'm currently working on a project about European cathedrals for the Readers' Digest. It's great fun researching different topics. Last month, I wrote an article for the Daily Mail on the Nomads of Africa, for which I was handsomely paid."

Azra didn't seem convinced.

"Look," I continued, "I also keep a look out for bargain properties. In the last few years properties have taken a hammering- some almost half of what they were a few years ago. I buy the odd one here and there because I'm convinced that house prices will rise sooner or later.

She brought her hands closer, palms almost touching.

"Yes, sooner, I hope," I grinned.

I loved being with her. Of course she was gentle and lovely but what I loved most about her was her positive attitude to life.

Once, after we'd been to see a film in London and were having a meal in an Italian restaurant, I asked her if she would like to meet some of my friends. I had on several occasions talked about them to Azra, though never mentioned her to any of them. She smiled and shook her head.

"Perhaps some time in the future?"

She nodded and pointed to my plate to say that my food was getting cold. Later, we walked along Regent Street, aimlessly, just looking at shops, hand in hand in the cold winter air. On an instinct, I side stepped and entered a shop selling cashmere sweaters. We approached the ladies' section with an endless colour range. She protested, pointing at herself and showing me seven fingers.

"You have seven?" I asked

She nodded.

"Cashmere?"

She shook her head.

"Well then, I insist."

We looked at various colours and she tried a couple for size. In the end I succeeded in buying her two, a cream polo-neck and a pink V-neck with a red diamond print on one shoulder. She looked beautiful in both and the casual jeans only highlighted her slim figure. The appreciative turn of heads from other customers in the shop filled me with pride. As we walked out of the shop, she punched me lightly on my shoulder and locked arms with me. She was happy and seeing her like that pleased me. After a few minutes, I stopped suddenly. Turning to face her, I asked, "What about your aunt? Shall we buy her one?"

She paused and shook her head, though her face told me that she would love to give her aunt a present.

I turned around, dragging her back to the shop with me and we bought a lime green cashmere V-neck sweater.

It was almost midnight when we approached her aunt's residence. She always insisted that I drop her a hundred yards or so away, lest her aunt saw us together. "She's bound to find out sometime," I protested once, "so why don't you introduce me to her now?"

She shook her head and joining her palms moved them apart, denoting that she would do so some time in the future.

She opened the car door and moved to leave. I was about to bid her good night when she turned and put her arms around my neck. As if it was the most natural action in the world, her body slid gracefully against mine and my hands held her by the waist. She was warm and her chest felt firm against mine. Her fingers caressed the back of my neck softly, teasing. A few strands of her fragrant hair brushed my face. I had never held her so close to me. The years of waiting, wanting, rolled forward into those few seconds as I felt her, smelt her and realised that we were one. The car door swung shut and the interior light dimmed, finally fading out. In the dark her lips found mine.

CHAPTER 41

"Why don't we go to Edinburgh?"

Paro Aunty raised her eyebrows quizzically, "Why Edinburgh?"

I shuffled the brochures spread haphazardly on the dining table. "Nobody," I replied, "celebrates the New Year like the Scottish do, and this is the Millennium we are talking about."

She pulled a face and lifted it away from her palm where it was resting in contemplation. Her elbow remained on the dining table. "It's too far, Amar; and what about Azra? Will she go all that way to see the new millennium?"

"She doesn't mind. Her Aunt's visiting relations in Leicester, so she can come with us without her aunt knowing."

"I'm... not sure," she mused. "London should be good this year. The fireworks at the London Eye should be spectacular, don't you think?"

I heaved myself from the chair, heading for the kitchen, "How about some masala tea?"

"How about London Eye?"

"OK," I shouted from the kitchen.

"OK," Paro shouted, half-laughing.

"OK, what?"

"OK, I'll have some masala tea."

"O...K, fine. There are some pakoras here. Would you like some?

"Yes, please. Warm them in the oven while the water boils."

Five minutes later, I was back with steaming masala tea and warm pakoras.

"Yum," she said sipping her drink and reaching for a potato and onion pakora, "the best thing for a cold winter day."

I agreed. Nothing seals an agreement like tea and pakoras. London Eye it is."

We fell silent for a while, concentrating on the food and drink.

Presently she peered at me over the rim of her nearly empty mug. "Have you heard from Inayat and Saira?"

I cleared some grains in my mouth with my tongue. "Yes," I replied, "he rang me a few days ago." I took two long gulps of tea, and sank further back in the setee. "He's happy to be back with his family though Saira's not sure and young Mahmoud hates it there- wants to come back."

"Hmm... takes time to un-root and live in a different country."

I sighed. "I miss them all and in a funny sort of way, Mahmoud most of all. He wants me to go over there and continue to teach him football."

"Why don't you?"

"What? Teach football in Iran?"

"You know what I mean, visit them; you are your own boss."

"Maybe...perhaps next year when Inayat is more settled." I made a mental note of visiting some travel agents for flights to Iran.

She stood up to clear the table. As she balanced the mugs and plate in her hands she asked, "How's Robin? What's he up to now-a-days?"

"Oh, he's doing fine," I replied, following her into the kitchen to avoid another loud conversation between the kitchen and the dining room. "He's been promoted to Marketing Director and flies around the world. I believe he's in Singapore at the moment. Cheryl's not coping with the recession and is planning to sell her health club. She'll still get a decent goodwill I think."

"So what will she do, with her husband away most times?"

"She's planning to take a part-time job to keep her brain ticking."

"And the rest of the time?"

I lifted my shoulders. "I don't know...she'll find something. I can't imagine Cheryl sitting still."

Paro Aunty placed the dishes carefully in the dishwasher and straightened herself with a sigh.Her back had been playing up lately but she insisted on doing everything herself, believing that stretching and moving around was the best cure for stiff backs.

"And Sanjay; still enjoying life?"

I laughed. "He'll never change. Carla knows he's cheating on her. The poor girl is trapped.With all that weight she's put on and Neel to look after, she has limited options. She told me some weeks ago that all she can do is grin and bear it. He makes sure she's never short of money...that buys her some happiness. Money *can* buy happiness you know."

"I wouldn't trust that man, he's so selfish. You be careful of him."

"I hope we are not going to discuss BMW friends again."

"Amar, you mark my words—"

"OK, OK, if and when the time comes, you can tell me: *I told you so.*"

She pouted, "And Neel?"

"What about him?"

"Does he get his father's love?"

I thought about it for a few seconds."God knows. All I know is that he deserves better. I take him to the park on Wednesday afternoons and we both enjoy that. *I* certainly look forward to that. The problem is that if I do more, Sanjay might think that I'm stepping in his shoes."

"He's so self-centred. I'm sure that one day he'll pay for his actions. There is a God you know."

"Well..." I mused. "I've known him since childhood and we've been through a lot. He's fine with me and I suppose I owe him a lot for what he's done for me over the years."

"Ah, yes, but did he have an ulterior motive? I think he's one of those who gives with the left hand and takes with the right hand."

"I suppose...yes, but people generally do, don't they?"

"No, not all; there are a lot of people who have benefited, financially or otherwise from society and have put something back."

I thought about that for a while. "O...K, but if they made their money fairly and squarely and paid their taxes, do they have to do anything more?"

She fidgeted with her ring for a few seconds. "Has he made his money fairly and squarely? I believe that the better off should always put something back into society, whether by physical actions or financially, like paying into some charity."

"Most charities end up just covering their financial costs. Very little reaches the intended destinations."

She gave me a sharp look. "Amar, I'm shocked by your view. If everyone thought like that—"

"Sorry Auntyji, what I mean to say is that we should be *selective* in who we give our funds to. And anyway, there's always someone better-off or worse-off than you. So, who gives who?"

She was losing her patience. "Does that mean that you don't—"

I was interrupted by the doorbell. Saved, I thought.

We looked at each other, both shrugging our shoulders.

"I'll go," she volunteered.

I heard excited voices in the hallway and after a minute or so she ushered Liz and her two beautiful little girls into the lounge.

I rose to greet the new arrivals.

Liz gave me a gentle hug. "I was just passing and saw your car outside. Thought I'd stop by and say hello."

"Always good to see you Liz." I meant it. Over the years, she had become a good friend and support to Paro Aunty. I bent to greet her daughters, Florence and Rimini. They were extremely well behaved and shy. "And how are my favourite young girls?"

Rimini stuck a thumb in her mouth and swayed sideways shyly. Florence, at eleven and two years older than her sister gave a slight smile. "Very well, thank you, Uncle Amar."

"Ahhh," Paro Aunty muttered delightedly. "Aren't they *sweeeet?*" Straightening herself she addressed Liz, "And how are you young lady?"

It's strange how people can change. Over the years, especially a few years after her marriage, Liz had let herself go. The smart clothes and the sexy body gradually faded and gave in to loose casuals to cover her chubbiness. The more weight she gained, the more casual her clothes got. And the more casual her clothes got, the more weight she gained. *It was Catch 22.* Lately, she had opted for spectacles instead of the contact lenses she had once worn; her only admission of femininity seemed to be a tired dab of lipstick. Even more surprising, she had turned very anti-smoking and had also given up red meat. Her main priority in life now was her daughters, with whom she spent a lot of time- drama classes, piano lessons, French tuition and anything the girls fancied. Her affection and offers of help towards Paro Aunty were genuine for which I was touched and thankful. A few years ago, she had moved to Gerrards Cross, a popular area for the rich where she ran a successful Pharmacy and John ran an equally successful consultancy firm.

Liz handed Paro Aunty a shopping bag.

"What's this?"

"They had nice fresh papayas from Brazil; I thought I'd get you a couple."

"Liz!" Paro Aunty exclaimed. "You must stop buying things for me. It's very kind of..."

Liz waved a hand. "It's nothing Paro, don't fuss. They had a special offer- buy one, get one free. I bought loads." She sat herself down on the settee and pushed her legs forward, "I'll have some tea, please, after which I must dash. Rimni's due for a piano class in an hour."

CHAPTER 42

2005

Munir is coming next month!

I stared at the words on the mobile. I had spoken to him on the 'phone only a week ago and he hadn't mentioned anything about coming.

With my eye still on the mobile I asked, "Who told you?"

Azra moved a hand about six inches above her head, a sign that I was by now well familiar.

"How does your Aunt know?"

She placed a thumb against her ear.

"He rang her?" I was thoughtful for a while. She was searching my face and I could tell she was worried.

"Is he planning to stay with her?" Although I appreciated Azra's predicament, I was excited about Munir coming after all those years that he had steadfastly refused to come.

She nodded and I immediately saw the problem.

"Oh *hell!* What about you? Unless you move out, he'll find out about you. Hasn't your Aunt suggested something?"

She was visibly worried. She shook her head and grasped my hand.

I knew she would never want Munir to know that she was in England. As far as he and his family were concerned, she was still in Pakistan.

"Let's go somewhere and have some nice hot tea."

We strolled along Southall Broadway and found a cosy corner in a small snack bar. I ordered tea and samosas.

Her palms, resting flat on the table were very white. I placed mine over hers. "It's okay," I said reassuringly. "Do you know how long he's coming for?"

She looked down and shook her head.

"Why don't you come and stay with me for a while? I'm sure he won't be staying too long."

She typed her mobile: *Can't, he'll probably visit you too.*

Damn I thought. Of course!

A waiter who appeared to be no more than fourteen brought two mugs of tea and a plate-full of three samosas with tamarind sauce on the side.

Azra quickly went for the tea but shook her head when I pushed the plate a few inches in her direction.

"They are good you know," I said biting into the crispy crust."

She pursed her lips, continuing to look worried.

"I know!" I said excitedly, slapping my thigh. "You could stay with Paro Aunty! You two get along so well together and she would welcome your company. Munir will certainly not be visiting Denham. "

Her lips betrayed a flicker of a smile.

"Azra, she is so fond of you, you know that. She even sometimes refers to you as her daughter-in-law."

That made her smile broadly though she still seemed unsure.

"Look, I'll ask her, okay? Now relax." We both knew the answer would be positive. She sighed hopefully and mouthed her thanks.

That night, unable to hide my excitement, I rang Sanjay and told him about Munir coming to England.

"Really?" he exclaimed, "after all this time? Hey, are you sure?"

"Sure, I'm sure," I replied.

"Who told you?"

Damn! I couldn't answer that. In recent years my friendship with Sanjay had tapered somewhat, especially after the Swenberg affair. He had no knowledge of Azra and because she was Munir's sister, I had always thought it safer not to mention her to him.

"Oh... he told me," I lied. "I was speaking to him on the phone a while ago."

"What! With the three hours difference, it must be past midnight over there."

"Sanjay, I've got to go, someone at the door. I'll give you the details tomorrow, okay?"

As I put down the phone, I could hear his crackling voice.

I cursed myself for my mistake and made a mental note to ring Munir first thing in the morning.

"*As-salaam alaikum* Uncleji," I greeted Maqbool Uncle when he answered the phone. "This is Amar, from England."

"*Wa alaikum us-salaam, beta.*" *Upon you be peace.* The voice was weak and faint. "It's so good to hear from you. Are you coming to Nairobi?"

"No, I just wanted to speak with Munir. But how are you? You sound very weak."

"It's nothing, *beta.* Your Aunt and I are both suffering from a bout of 'flu - nothing serious. You just missed him; he left for Egypt a little while ago."

The receiver nearly slipped from my hand. *Egypt!* I couldn't imagine why he was going there. "Uncleji... do you know when he's coming to England?"

"England? I don't know, *beta*...I don't know. These days Munir is hardly at home, and he is always entertaining strange visitors. I don't understand him anymore—"

"He must be very busy. You mustn't worry about him."

"No, *beta*, something is wrong. I can feel it in my old bones. If he comes to England, please have a word with him."

"I will, Uncleji. Meanwhile you and Auntyji, please take care of yourselves."

"Thank you, *beta*. Shamima sends her best wishes. God be with you."

I replaced the receiver, puzzled. Perhaps Maqbool Uncle was mistaken. I decided to liaise with Azra and take things as they came.

Paro Aunty was overjoyed, "Oh, Amar! She can live with me *forever*!" She searched my face, "When is she coming?"

"I don't know as yet. In a week or so- I'll let you know."

She lowered her voice. "Why don't you two get married?"

"Auntyji! We've been through that. I'd give my right arm for that but Azra's not ready for marriage. Religions come in the way—"

"What difference does that make nowadays?" she asked sharply.

"Give her time, Auntyji."

Munir arrived at his aunt's flat one late night and stayed with her for just three days before flying to Amsterdam for business. As I was not supposed to know of his arrival or of his aunt's existence, I did not call him. My one concern was that back in Nairobi, Maqbool Uncle would mention my call to Munir. I had already asked Sanjay to be surprised if and when Munir got in touch with him and not mention that I had let the cat out of the bag. However hard I tried, I could not figure out why he was not contacting me. Knowing him all these years, I would have expected him to announce his arrival well in advance.

Azra too couldn't figure it out. And according to her aunt, Munir hadn't even been in touch with his brother in

Glasgow. Perhaps he had come on a hectic business trip, I kept thinking. Although Azra and Paro Aunty got along well with each other, she longed to get back with her aunt. One week-end, we all went to Oxford and spent the day visiting colleges, shops and restaurants. Azra loved the place- the spires, the meadow and river, the college grounds and the long-horned deer in the grounds of Magdalen College. Later in the afternoon, she wanted me to take her punting. I had never tried it in all the years I had lived in Oxford and I certainly wasn't going to chance it then. We got an experienced punter to take us along the river Cherwell by Christ Church College for about forty minutes. Azra's eyes glowed. She clasped Paro Aunty by the elbow tightly and waved to the numerous tourists taking pictures of punters.

A month passed and Azra's aunt came to the conclusion that Munir would not be coming back to her place. Despite Paro Aunty's insistence that Azra should stay with her for a bit longer, she decided to take her aunt's advice and made preparations to return. They were both tearful at the separation. "Come back any time, Azra, you are like a daughter I never had. The house won't be the same without you." she said, solemnly.

Luck being what it is, it was while I was driving Azra to her aunt's place that Munir rang. He was the last person I was expecting to hear from as I answered the mobile in my car.

"Hello, Amar?" the voice crackled loudly.

"Yes."

"It's me, Munir! You know, from—"

"Munir!" I glanced at Azra. She sat upright, looking straight ahead, lips pressed against each other. "How are you?"

"I'm fine, Amar. Guess where I'm ringing from?"

I smiled to myself. "Some beach in Mombasa? Where—"

"No, *yaar*, I'm in *London*!"

I pretended to be surprised. "*London*! When did you come? Why didn't you let me know before? I'd have met you at the airport." Azra pulled a face.

"It was all very rush-rush, *yaar*. I just fancied a change."

"Where are you staying Munir? And how long are you going to be in England?"

"I'm staying with an aunt of mine in Ilford for a week or so, after which I shall be visiting some relations in Bradford for another week before heading home. When can we meet *yaar*?"

I was ready for that, "How about tomorrow?"

"To...morrow?" He hesitated for a second or two before replying, "OK, that's fine with me."

"Give me your address in Ilford; I'll collect you from there; how about eleven in the morning?"

"Eleven is fine, but not Ilford. Can we meet somewhere else, somewhere more central?"

"Where?"

"Oh, you tell me."

After a few seconds of silence, I suggested the entrance to Selfridges in Oxford Street.

"Sure."

"OK, Munir, see you at eleven tomorrow morning." I switched off the mobile.

Azra shook her head in a way to suggest that Munir was lying. I too, had got the same impression, but why? I could think of no logical reason why he would do so.

"Do you have an aunt in Ilford?"

She shook her head.

"I thought so. That's why he didn't want me to go over there. But why is he being like this?"

She shrugged and let her shoulders drop heavily, sighing at the same time.

CHAPTER 43

Munir was by the main door of Selfridges as I made my way through the crowds at a few minutes to eleven. He caught my eye, crushed his cigarette on the pavement and smilingly broadly took a few steps in my direction. We shook hands and embraced tightly as we've always done after a long absence.

"Welcome to England, Munir! You look good."

He laughed. Holding my shoulders he took a step back. "You don't look too bad yourself." Tapping my belly lightly he added, "What's this, *yaar?*"

I looked down at the slight protrusion above the belt-line. "Prosperity."

His shoulders seemed broader and his waist trimmer from what I could remember. The face was taut with a strong jaw-line and the eyes, still alert seemed a shade deeper. Whereas I had put weight in the wrong places, he had lost weight in the right places. I envied his lean, mean looks.

"I rang Sanjay, after I rang you yesterday, to see if he could meet us here, but he's got an important bank meeting all day today."

"Yes," he told me about it," I said. "He can meet us at the week-end though."

Munir shook his head. "No, I might not be here. Never mind, I see him regularly in Nairobi. I'm free all day today, what shall we do?"

I thought for a few seconds. "Depends...do you want to do some sight seeing? There's Buckingham Palace, Madame Tussauds, London Eye—"

"No, *yaar,*" he interrupted. "I went up London Eye yesterday." He glanced at his watch, "Let's go eat somewhere."

"Munir, it's only eleven!"

He grabbed my arm. "I haven't had breakfast, and by the time we find a good restaurant and get served, it will be time to eat. Come on *yaar*."

"Don't you want to see some famous landmarks here? For heaven's sake, Munir, you've come all this way from Nairobi...how about an open bus tour of London?"

"I'm starving," he said, weaving between the avalanche of shoppers. "Let's get away from this mad street first. Afterwards, we can have a tour of London."

"Fine," I was puzzled and at the same time hurt by Munir's abrasive manner. Perhaps he had been travelling a lot and was suffering from fatigue and jet-lag.

"How about Chinese? We could walk up to China Town – won't take more than fifteen minutes."

At Oxford Circus, we turned into Regent Street where the crowds were a bit lighter. Munir showed little interest in the stores we passed, even the seven floor Hamleys toy shop and when I commented on Veeraswamy being the oldest Indian restaurant in London, he merely nodded. His expression only softened and registered some interest as we approached Leicester Square, though not as much as I would have expected from someone who had never seen London before.

"By the way, it's such a shame about Rajesh; shocking!"

"Yes," I muttered casually. "I was shocked at first, but if that's what he wants—"

He clutched my elbow and stopped in the middle of the pavement, causing others to move around us. "What are you talking about?" he interrupted me.

I stared at him. "The Night Club, *Sili Sili*—."

Still not moving, he looked at me in amazement. "Don't you keep in touch, haven't you heard?"

I shrugged my shoulders, "Heard what?" I quivered.

"The fire!"

I looked him in the eye. "No! Where? The Night Club?"

"Yes! But that's not what I meant. Rajesh...he lost his sight!"

I froze! "Lost his...but he only *had* sight in one...I haven't heard. When did you—?"

"What's the matter with you guys? What planet are you on?"

"What the hell happened?" I demanded, feeling a twinge of guilt at not having been in touch with Rajesh for some time.

We started walking again, slowly. "Well, I rang him for a get together and some woman answered and told me about the accident."

I shot him a glance. "Yes, but, what the hell happened?" I asked again.

He shook his head. "From what I heard, there was a fight in the club over some girls and things got nasty. Rajesh's bouncers roughened some of the trouble-makers and threw them out. A couple of hours later they came back with half a dozen friends and torched the club. Rajesh wasted time trying to get his takings and got trapped in the fire and smoke. When he woke up in hospital he realised that his one remaining eye was—"

"Hell!" I swore. "I'm sorry...I didn't know."

For a while we walked in silence. I was deep in thought. I knew Rajesh was running a risky venture, but, no one deserves such bad luck!

"I'll look him up soon," I promised.

He shook his head. "I wanted to as well but this woman, she said that he's not seeing anyone as yet- too distraught!"

Perhaps in a few weeks, I thought to myself.

We fell silent again and turned into Wardour Street, towards China Town.

The moment we turned right into Gerrard Street his eyes lit up. "This is great, *yaar*. Let's go in here. He grabbed my arm and pulled me into the spacious *Jade Palace*, where we were greeted by two young lovely girls in Chinese tunics with slits up to the thighs. One of the girls led us to a table towards the middle of the restaurant.

Munir frowned. "Isn't there a table near the window?"

She looked around and we followed her to a table close to the window.

"Have you been here before?" he asked, seating himself.

"Yes, the food's very good, the place and service too. We are early, but in an hour or so, it will fill-up."

"You order *yaar.*"

Knowing that Munir didn't drink alcohol, I abstained and ordered Chinese jasmine tea for both. "Do you like dim-sum? And duck?"

"Sure, anything except pork."

"I know."

I ordered a platter of sea food, chicken with ginger and cashew nuts, and roast duck with egg fried rice.

As we waited we enquired into each other's families and mutual friends. I took the opportunity to ask about Azra, pretending that I couldn't remember her name. "Is she still in Pakistan?"

Munir's expression did not change and he preferred to scrutinise the decor before answering. "She's still there...I haven't seen her since she got married." He paused, "Between you and me, *yaar*, I have nothing to do with her now."

The food arrived. Wanting to hear more, I remained silent and raised an eyebrow quizzically.He took a mouthful and munched for a while. "Food is good." Rolling his tongue over his teeth he clucked his lips loudly. "Azra has brought shame on our family. Soon after her marriage, she left her husband. *Abbu* thinks she ran away with a younger man. Her husband's family thinks she ran away with some rich man. I

340

think she's run away from all men." He waved a hand in dismissal. "It's very messy, *yaar.*"

"I know what you mean." To change the topic I asked, "So, how do you like England?"

"It's fine," he said, without much enthusiasm and without looking up from his plate.

His indifference surprised me, "Just *fine?*"

He lifted his gaze and looked me in the eye. "Yes, fine, rich; advanced." He fell silent for a while, biting his lips with his teeth. "Amar, do you know that one third of the world's population live in slums?" He leaned back in his chair levelling eyes with mine. "You've never visited a slum, have you?"

I wondered what had prompted the change of conversation. "Let's just eat, eh? Enjoy yourself- you are on holiday."

"No I'm not," he said quickly, leaning forward. "Do you know that the West is responsible for a lot of the world's poverty, slums, diseases, pollution—?"

"Come on Munir, there isn't much you and I can do about it—"

He dropped his fork on the plate. "Come on *yaar?* A lot of the slums are a legacy of the colonial racial segregation. Have you forgotten Nairobi? Don't you remember, Europeans living in nice affluent areas, black Kenyans away from the town centre and Asians somewhere in-between? Almost *half* of Nairobi's population lives in slums. Can you believe that?"

"*Half?* No, I wasn't aware of that." I was genuinely surprised.

He leaned back, eyes blazing, "Yes, guess where Africa's, perhaps the world's, biggest slum is?"

I knew that and replied slowly, "Kibera, in Nairobi." I had seen it of course, but from a distance.

341

"That's right. But you've probably just *read* about it. Next time you're in Nairobi, I'll take you there. It's nauseating! The narrow alleys are perpetually wet with sludge and shit. You can't imagine the stench- it's everywhere, day and night. And people have to walk in those alleys - people who can't afford shoes or slippers! Imagine half a million people, perhaps more, living in shanty houses with no lavatories. I'm telling you *yaar*; it's only a matter of time before we have an epidemic of unimaginable proportion in Nairobi. Nobody knows what toxins and germs are breeding in slums all over the world. Some combination of typhoid, cholera, tuberculosis and God knows what, perhaps aids as well, just waiting to be unleashed on to this world."

It was a sobering thought which brought a lump in my throat but I had to interject to mollify him. "Until then, let's enjoy ourselves. I'm sure the scientists can take care of that."

His eyes flashed like burning coal and could have killed someone with a weaker heart than mine. "When the time comes, no one, and I mean it, no scientist will be able to do anything about it. It will be pandemic! Too late! Your country, together with other rich western countries is too busy selling arms and deadly weapons to anyone with money."

I remained silent hoping that it would take some of the steam from him, aware that some customers were passing uncomfortable glances our way.

His inscrutable eyes under dark bushy eyebrows glared at me. "Amar, do you have any idea, how the West is exploiting the poor in third world countries? Do you?"

"No, sorry," I answered simply. "Mind you, we give a lot in aid to—"

"What!" He snapped, his chiselled jaw jutting in my direction. Even above the cacophony in the crowding restaurant his voice was loud. "Aid? That is just a clever way of tying-up a poor country in knots."

I raised my hands in exasperation. "We are dammed if we give aid; we are dammed if we don't."

He frowned darkly and continued as if I hadn't uttered a word. "I'll tell you what aid and loans do. The ministers swallow the aid and my country has to pay back the loan with *interest*. And who gets the money? The ministers and the corrupt people at the top. The West has no bloody interest in where and in whose pocket the money goes. All they want is to sell arms and weapons. Believe me *yaar*, the man in the street doesn't see a cent of that money, but the West doesn't give a damn. And in return, the West, your country too, rapes us of our resources."

Although flushing at the rising tension, I spoke in a low tone, "That's a bit unfair—"

His voice took an exasperated tone. "Amar, you don't know how much the West and their multinational organisations are exploiting the third world countries. Take for example, toxic waste; Africa seems to have become the dumping ground for that, perhaps even nuclear waste. The West just bribes a few politicians at the top, and who doesn't have a price?" Shaking his head he continued, "God knows what chemicals are breeding in the oceans around Africa. Your country tells the world that it is reducing pollution. Wrong! They are *exporting* pollution to *us*."

We sat quietly for a minute or two poking at meat cubes. Suddenly he sat up straight and strained forward towards me. "You are probably aware how sensitive the people in *your* country are about animal testing."

I wasn't sure if that was a question or a statement. I nodded.

"So, what do the pharmaceutical companies do? They test products, including drugs on *humans!* Animals in *your* country hold more value than the poor humans in *my* country. And England holds big bold posters saying: '*Not tested on Animals*'." He paused then laughed in disgust.

I had vague recollections of an article that I had recently read where the writer had written something along those lines. Drugs and beauty products had been tested on humans in some poor areas in Bangladesh with devastating results, causing long term blindness and organ failure.

"You probably know this, *yaar*, for a radio or fresh clothing and a bit of pocket money even *you* could test on the starving people of this world. These people would sell a kidney for the bill of this meal. That's how the West spread Christianity all over Africa. Have you forgotten your history books? They came, a few handful first, bearing smiles and presents, only to be followed by business money-suckers and armies grabbing every inch of land. Have you forgotten what Mr Joshi, our History teacher taught us in school? White men came with bibles and no land. Within a few years the blacks were holding the bibles and the whites the land. And when the Kenyans, particularly the Mau Mau fought for their land, they were branded as terrorists! Later they forced the dumb sods in Africa and other under-developed countries to fight the World Wars. Did those innocent people fighting at the front line for *your* king and queen even have the faintest idea where Britain or Germany is?"

I looked down at my plate. He was right but I was not prepared for for a full scale outburst of this sort.

"Amar, in the second World War, over ninety thousand East Africans fought for the British, most died from enemy forces, others from disease or hunger. Does your Government ever pay tribute to them? Most of who didn't even want the British on their soil!"

He leaned further towards me with questioning eyes, arms crossed and elbows on the table, "Do you think we should just turn a blind eye and carry on living in our silken cocoons?"

Suddenly I lost my appetite and remained silent, aware that Munir's eyes were on mine. In order to rescue the day from turning sour I tried once again to change the topic, "At least God has blessed Africa with nice weather; we have to put up with rain and grey weather for half the year. I've been caught in hailstorms in *August*, can you believe that?"

His eyes, already hard, kept smouldering, piercing mine, "Nice weather, for how long?" he snarled. "You guys in the West are polluting the world to such an extent that Africa will turn unbearably hot and barren by the time my grandchildren are my age."

"Oh, come on Munir, that's a gross exaggeration." I spoke as calmly as I could; lowering my voice a bit, hoping that he would do the same.

He stared at me in utter disbelief and spoke without changing the tone, "Amar what planet do you live on? Countries like yours are responsible for the climate change. Per square mile or per person, Britain is probably the most polluting country in the world, but the sad thing is that we in Africa and parts of Asia will suffer the most. Vast lands will turn arid and too hot for crops, live stock will die, even wildlife. You will see, generation by generation the world will see millions of refugees trapped by poverty knocking at your doorstep. The West will be unable to turn them away; if they do, the poor will fall into the hands of terrorists who will exploit them for their own agendas. Ultimately the West will reap what it sows."

I heaved a huge sigh. When I spoke, my voice seemed alien to me, "What can the average person do? The West is too powerful, financially, politically and economically."

He replied quickly, so alert was his mind. "Unless you keep asking that question, you will never get to answer it, and you will never do anything about it. We can *all* do something, by talking, by writing and by actions." He stared into my eyes. "You are a writer, *yaar*; you can write about these exploitations- do some research, give real examples, speak to your local ministers, community leaders, newspaper editors, or just friends. Write about the Mau Mau movement. If you don't feel you can take physical action, take the verbal and written action. I tell you, *every* person on this planet can contribute."

Just listening to him, my chest felt tight. My hands on my thighs were moist and I wiped them with the napkin. Suddenly I felt very small against him. The thought of the easy money I had made pricked my conscience; I was having trouble meeting his eyes. Munir had grown into someone much bigger than me and although his outburst unsettled me, my respect for him remained undiminished.

"I'll do something about it," I said in a low hoarse voice, "I promise."

He looked into my eyes for a very long time and after almost a minute his long blink thanked me. When he spoke, his tone was less aggressive, "Amar, you should invest in Africa, you know."

"Are you serious? With all the problems they are having?"

"I know, I know, but the long term future is bright. Just look at countries like Thailand, Korea, and Taiwan – the Tiger economies. They are now the new 'Japan'. Tomorrow it will be India and China. And then?"

I raised an eyebrow and half shrugged.

He slapped the table. "Africa! It's a vast continent with untapped minerals and land." He shifted in his chair and clenched a fist. "The Africans are strong and hard working. In twenty years when the labour cost of the Asian workers becomes uneconomical, the world will be investing in Africa and pay the poor sods over there a pittance for a hard day's work. And as for land, any country that wishes to invest in an African country can obtain as much of it as they want, for a factory or whatever, for next to nothing."

"But the political situation—"

"Come on, *yaar*, its early days- independence and all. Things will settle down, and when Africa becomes stable..." He clenched his fist, "millions will become millionaires!"

Munir had changed. His compassion and love for the underdeveloped world was of course commendable but I found his anger towards the West unsettling. "I'm finished," I declared, carefully placing my cutlery together in my plate. "How was it?"

He smacked his lips and taking his time, lit a cigarette. "Delicious."

I settled the bill and pushing back our chairs we stood up. As we exited I asked, "How about the London tour?"

"Look, *yaar*, this was great fun. It's always good to meet you—"

"But?"

"But, I have to go to Bradford this evening... relations... you know how it is?"

"When will I see you again?"

"Soon, *Inshallah*." *God willing.*

I didn't know at that time of course, but that was the last time I was to see him.

CHAPTER 44

"Have some *nimbu-pani*," Carla was saying to Robin. "It's the best thing to quench the thirst. Sanjay showed me how to make it"

"And it's so refreshing," Sanjay added. He was lying on his back on a cotton sheet spread out on the lawn: face up partly covered by a base-ball cap. "We could do with some breeze."

It was early June and certainly hot. The leaves were still and the lawn was parched and hard. We were in my garden, enjoying late Sunday lunch. Carla had brought roast lamb and Cheryl had prepared tiramisu, a dish she had perfected to such a degree that none of us could remember where we had had better. I had made tuna salad with sweet-corn for starters but judging by how much was left over, it hadn't been a favourite with any of us.

"Is it any better than the bottle of Pimm's we've just finished?" Robin enquired.

"Try it. It's particularly good after a meal, and it won't dehydrate you," I added.

"So what is it, this nimb...?"

"*Nimbu-pani*," Carla corrected, "just water with lots of fresh lime juice, sugar, a pinch of salt and lots of ice. Perfect!"

"Okay, I'll have a glass."

She poured some into a tall glass and passed it to him, "Anyone else?"

We all waited for the verdict from Robin.

"Nice." Robin declared, smacking his lips. "Make everyone a glass."

"Not for me, thanks," Cheryl said. "I'm full-up, too much chicken." She leant back and cast an eye around the garden. "Amar, I can't help admiring your Wisteria. The colours are so intense."

Looking up at the deep mauve flowers dangling like bunches of grapes I thought of the cutting I had taken from the Woods' garden. "Yes," I agreed, "I'm very proud of its heritage. The flowers bloom later than most varieties, but I'm not complaining."

Everyone gazed at the Wisteria for a while in silent admiration. Somewhere a bee was moving from flower to flower infringing the peace. Seated under the large parasol, except for Sanjay, most of us were on the verge of dozing-off, content to remain quiet and recover from the heavy lunch. Presently, Sanjay stood up and grabbed a chair under the parasol.

"Hey it's bloody hot." He poured himself a glass of *nimbu-pani* and turned to Carla, "Is Neel okay?"

"I think so," she replied, "he's in the conservatory with Tom, watching some DVD."

"Who's Tom?" Cheryl enquired, still eyeing the Wisteria lazily.

"He lives a few houses away," I answered. "Nice boy, he's in Neel's class; I take them to the park once a week for footfall, kicks well."

"Bet Neel misses Mahmoud," Cheryl said, softly, as if half asleep.

"Tremendously! But luckily, he makes friends quickly and easily."

"Like his dad," Cheryl mumbled, still sounding half asleep.

"What's wrong with that?" Sanjay demanded, stirring himself in the chair.

"Nothing," Cheryl replied, glancing at Carla and giving her a quick wink.

Sanjay muttered something. No one understood what he said nor did they want to. Everyone fell silent for a while.

Music drifted onto the garden through the open French-doors.

"I just love Mozart," I remarked dreamily, almost to myself.

"He was brilliant, the greatest composer of classical music," Robin added, cocking his head to one side to savour the sound.

Cheryl cocked her ears and joined in. "That's the Requiem, isn't it?"

Robin and I nodded together.

Sanjay placed his glass on the table and came out of the shadow of the parasol. "Most people believe that when he wrote the Requiem, he was thinking of his own imminent death." He addressed Robin, "Do you agree with that?"

Robin shrugged. "Don't know. All I can say is that he popularised the piano concerto almost single-handedly." We all sat still in the warm air around us. After a few minutes or so he asked me, "Have you heard from Inayat and Saira?"

"Yes," I replied, "I got a long letter from him just last week. He's doing *really* well. He and Saira are planning to visit England in October, but just for a week. I rang him on Friday to say that they must stay with me."

"October! They'll miss the summer," Robin said.

"Ah, don't forget, living in Tehran, they are not too thrilled about hot weather."

"English summers are so heavenly, don't you think?" Carla commented. "Wish it could be like this *every* day of the year."

"That would be too perfect. One needs some imperfections in life to appreciate the good things," Robin said philosophically. "Anyway, if it remained like this every day, who would leave England to live in—?"

"Australia?" I interjected.

Cheryl: "Spain?"

"France?" Carla asked, joining in the fun.

Robin flushed to the roots of his hair. "You know what I mean; we'd have to live shoulder to shoulder."

"And swim shoulder to shoulder," Cheryl added.

"Sleep shoulder to shoulder," I added

"Hey, that could be fun," Sanjay said hastily.

"Yes, you *would* like that," Carla said, equally hastily.

Sanjay sat upright, facing her. "What's *that* supposed to mean?"

She gritted her teeth. "We can discuss that later," she hissed, avoiding his gaze.

He swallowed his pride and fell silent.

Cheryl gave me a *"he's guilty"* look.

There was a long awkward silence during which Carla's face grew red and I spotted her taking short bursts of air. Her hands were tightly clenched and her lips pursed. She was desperately trying to control herself from getting things off her chest.

And then she let a short but loud wail. "You think I don't know what's going on?" she burst out to everyone's amazement, though not to anyone's surprise. "The residential courses you claim you go to! And the so called business trips to Kenya and Tanzania! You think I'm *blind?*"

Sanjay was taken aback, "Carla! That's enough. We can talk later," he bellowed.

"Oh yes, that would suit you—"

"Carla!"

"Oh shut up," she sobbed and stood up as if to rush indoors.

"*Carla!*" he snarled sharply, the warning loud and clear, cutting the air like a knife.

Hearing the commotion, Neel came out to investigate, closely followed by Tom. Carla was beginning to sob softly in the tissue she had earlier used to dab her eyes.

Sanjay stood up and walked to her. "Carla, please, that's enough!"

She raised her head high and shouted vehemently, "Cheat!"

He swallowed hard and pursed his lips tightly.

We sat frozen in our seats and it was left to Cheryl to place a comforting arm around Carla's shoulder.

Nothing ruins a party more than a full blown quarrel between a husband and a wife!

CHAPTER 45

"Whatever did she mean?" Paro Aunty demanded when I met her a fortnight later.

We were in Jyoti's in Southall Broadway, waiting for Azra and trying to cool ourselves with cold *faludas.*

I shrugged my shoulders. "Perhaps he has a mistress in Kenya. Knowing Sanjay, that's possible. Carla is sure, that he's seeing someone."

"To put it bluntly, he's cheating on her. Who do you think he's seeing in Kenya?"

I shrugged my shoulders. "Search me."

She leaned over her *faluda* and peered directly into my eyes. "You don't think he's seeing Billie, do you?"

Startled, I shook my head. "No, I'm still married to her, remember? Sanjay might be a rascal but he wouldn't have an affair with a friend's wife...with his looks he can get so many others."

She leaned back. "You do have some odd friends. What about Munir?"

That question too surprised me. "What about him?"

"You said he's acting strangely."

"Auntyji, your imagination..."

"You yourself said how tense he got when you mentioned Billie to him in Kenya—"

"But that doesn't mean that—" I began.

"Amar, call it intuition or a feeling... in my bones, I can feel—"

"Auntyji, I can't accuse a friend on the evidence of some feeling in your bones."

She looked down and took a few sips. I watched the grey hair on one side partly covering her face. I had often suggested that she dye her hair. *Age gracefully,* she always replied.

I took a few more sips of my *faluda* and scooped some of the ice-cream at the base with the long spoon. The ice-cream was softening- just the way I liked it, neither too hard nor too soft.

"Divorce her."

The spoon slipped between my fingers and fell noisily against the base of the glass. "You can't be serious?"

"Divorce her," she repeated, "you've been separated for years. No children, therefore no complications. You are seeing Azra, remember?" She dropped her head forward and had a few mouthfuls of *faluda*. "I'm willing to bet that Billie is seeing Sanjay... or Munir—"

"Or someone else? Auntyji, you are getting carried away!" I took a deep breath, and exhaled. "Call me old fashioned or stubborn or whatever. If *she* asks for a divorce, I'll agree. But I don't want to take the first step and be damned for it. Remember, *she* walked out on me- if divorce is on the cards, *she's* got to ask for it. I'm quite happy as I am."

"But you can —"

I interrupted her quickly. "Anyway I can't marry because *Azra's* still married."

She placed both palms against her face. "God, what a mess!" she whispered through the gaps in her fingers.

I laughed.

She looked up. "What's funny?"

I shook my head, "Nothing."

"Something is, let's share it."

"It just struck me," I said trying to keep a straight face, "*you* are the only person who *can* marry."

She frowned and then seeing the funny side, threw her head back and echoed my laughter.

"Not in my menopause stage dear, too late now."

I raised my glass and chinked it against hers. "Here's to single- hood!"

As she lowered her glass, she looked beyond me. "Ah, here's Azra."

She breezed in and took a seat next to mine. Heads turned appreciatively in our direction for the first time. I faced her and squeezed her shoulder lightly. "Hi."

Paro Aunty observed us for a while, approvingly.

"What's the matter?" I asked.

"You two are like the sun and the sunlight," she commented.

Azra raised a smiling eyebrow.

"Inseparable," Paro Aunty explained, "and may God always keep you like that."

"Like the sun and the..." I mused, not finishing the sentence. "I like that Auntyji, very profound. Where did you hear that?"

She shook her head and placed a hand against her chest, "Straight from the heart."

Azra placed one hand on her heart and the other on mine, giggling. She pointed to my faluda and I ordered one for her. Grabbing the menu she started fanning herself. Paro Aunty followed suit. "God, it's hot," she muttered, puffing her cheeks and blowing out loudly. "I'll have another faluda."

"*Another* one?"

"This place needs air-conditioning," she remarked, fanning herself furiously with the menu.

I picked up a menu from the next table and did the same, also including Azra in the act. "Global warming is here to stay."

Shortly we all finished our *faludas*, Paro Aunty, her second.

"Excuse me," she said, getting up, "I'll just nip over to the Ladies."

"Must be those faludas," I laughed.

"A woman's got to do what a woman's got to do," she purred, turning over her shoulder.

Just as she left the table, Azra held my hand excitedly.

"Steady on, Azra, this is a public place," I joked.

Smiling, she tugged at my hand and placed it on her stomach.

"You are very warm. Did you have a curry for lunch or —?"

She shook her head, giggling and moved my hand on her stomach in a slow circular movement.

The penny dropped. "Azra!" I shouted, astonished, oblivious of others, "You are not... are you...?"

She nodded, eyes gleaming. Suddenly I realised how flushed her face was.

"Azra, this is so exciting, have you told anyone else?"

She shook her head and pointed at me.

"Just me? Oh, I'm in heaven! We must—"

"What's going on here?" Paro Aunty demanded, approaching the table. "You two seem so happy; have you won the lottery or something?"

"Yes, something like that," I replied excitedly. "Azra's —"

She placed a finger on my lips to quieten me.

I squeezed her hand. "You tell her, Azra."

Paro Aunty sat down. "Tell me what? What's going on?"

Azra moved to sit next to her. She held her hand and placed it on her stomach.

They faced each other. In one swift motion, Paro Aunty hugged her tightly. "Azra! I can't believe it!" Tears were streaming down her cheeks. "Amar, can you believe this?" Azra's cheeks were wet as well.

"Everyone's looking at us!" I whispered, leaning forward.

"As if I care," she retorted, snatching a tissue from the table and drying her face. "Buy everyone a faluda or something!"

"What! Why?"

"You heard me. It's our family tradition! You have to celebrate the good news with all present."

"All present! Good thing I'm not in the middle of Oxford Street!"

She raised a hand and shouted, "Waiter!"

The next day, I met Azra after she finished work. "What about your aunt? Have you told her?"

She nodded.

"Was she mad at you?"

She nodded.

"So?"

She hit the buttons on her mobile, her fingers flying quickly over them: *She was mad at me, called me all sorts of names, even threatened to send me back to Pakistan. But I told her that this was God's will. At my age, it was now or never. I told her that I already have one disability and that unless I have a child I shall remain unfulfilled. It was fate that my marriage was a sham, it was fate that you met me after all these years and it is fate that I can now have a child.*

"And then?"

Azra hugged herself tightly and drew tears running down from her eyes with a finger.

I took her trembling hands in mine. "That's great! So... does she know about me? Have you told her everything?"

She nodded, not meeting my eyes.

"Shouldn't I meet her?"

She shook her head and again hit her mobile: *Not ready to meet you as yet. I know her well. She'll come around to it soon.*

Let's go for some snacks. We can talk there. We strolled along the Broadway, taking in the music from the pavement-sellers and the numerous restaurants. Songs from the Hindi film, *Bunty aur Bubly* were playing at each corner. The evening air felt cool and refreshing after the day's heat and strands of sunlight from between the buildings streamed across the pavement.

Jyoti's was busier than usual and we had to wait ten minutes for a table for two. We ordered chilled *lassis*- plain for me, sweet for Azra and a plate of samosas.

She was looking radiant and happy but there was something that had been bothering me since her news.

"Azra, you must have some tests as soon as possible. It is not usual to have a baby at our age. We need to be sure that everything is fine- with you and the baby, and that everything continues to remain fine."

She pointed a finger to the heavens, her way of saying that God will take care of things.

"Yes, I know He will help but so can doctors."

The *lassis* and the samosas came. Azra quickly grabbed a samosa and took a few long gulps of *lassi*. She pointed towards her stomach with two fingers.

"Just because you are eating for two you don't have to gobble your food."

She took no notice and beckoning a waiter pointed to the plate of samosas.

The waiter rushed to our table, "Another plate madam?"

She nodded and he wobbled his head in acknowledgement.

"Azra, I know of a very good doctor in London. He's expensive but an expert in matters of mature births. I think we should go see him and have you checked up." I shrugged my shoulders, "just a precaution."

She met my gaze, nodded and smiled broadly.

"I'll ring him tomorrow and make an early appointment."

The second plate of samosas arrived. She grabbed one and held the other against my lips.

An hour later I dropped her near her flat. As I drove off happily, I could never have guessed that her death was imminent.

CHAPTER 46

I rang Doctor David Bell early next morning. A very efficient secretary answered my call. No she couldn't give me an appointment after ten in the morning for another month. It *is* the holiday season, sorry. I expressed disappointment and explained the case- Azra was a mature woman and I *had* met Doctor Bell at a Writers' reception a couple of times. She appeared to be sympathetic to my case. Perhaps there could be a cancellation and if I cared to leave my number...

I was getting flustered, "How about an early appointment?"

After a brief crackling I heard her say, "The only free slot is nine-fifteen next Thursday."

I checked my diary. Damn! I was meeting the Editor of the Mail on Sunday for a breakfast meeting on Thursday. Of all the days!

"Sir, the early morning after that slot is on the 22nd —"

"No, 22nd is too late," I interrupted. "Next Thursday at nine- fifteen will be fine." It wasn't ideal but it would have to do.

She took all details possible and promised to email me a map of the location with directions.

Later, I exchanged texts with Azra:

Dr. appointment nxt Thurs. 9.15A.M. OK?

Fine. Where?

Will send details shortly.

R U coming?

V.sorry.can't. Prior engagement.Can't cancel. Will meet U later- around10.30.U can take yur aunt or Paro Nty.

Don't worry, I can manage.C U there 10.30.

Bye.C U this Saturday, usual place. Luv Amar.

Look forward to it. LOL Azra.

On Saturday, I apologised about not being able to be with her until 10.30 A.M. for the checkup. The appointment with the newspaper editor had been arranged weeks ago. He had agreed to review some articles on slums in Africa and I was hoping that this would open doors with a few major publishers in the near future.

She hit her mobile: *Don't fuss, I'll be OK. Anyway, you'll be there by the time I finish.*

"I'll try to be with you earlier," I promised. "Take a taxi, it will be more comfortable."

She shook her head and placed a hand against my chest as if to say: *Leave it to me.*

"The alternative is to take the bus to Ealing Broadway-they are very regular. From there take the central line to Notting Hill Station and switch to—"

She smiled and put a finger on my lips to stop me fussing.

"Fine, so you know. Take this email and the map they sent me. I've highlighted Whitechapel Street." I squeezed her arm. "Sure you'll be alright?"

She turned to face me and exhaled loudly. *Don't fuss*, I read on her face.

"I'll see you there," I said, "no later than ten thirty."

Paro Aunty was annoyed that I was letting her go on her own and more annoyed that I was not going to be with her during the check-up. She brushed my explanations aside. "Supposing something is wrong?"

"Please don't say that. Anyway, I shall be there before they finish."

"*I'll* go with her, why *can't* I go?"

"Auntyji, I suggested that. But she doesn't even want *her* aunt to go with her. She has her reasons."

She gave me an icy stare. "Am I a dragon or something? Amar, please explain to her—"

I was beginning to lose patience. "Auntyji, *please* don't worry. Perhaps she wants to be alone with me afterwards..."

She pulled a face. "Ooooh... two's company, three's a crowd?"

"Please, you know what I mean, it's an intimate situation. We'll come back here in the evening for dinner, okay?"

She sat down and immediately stood up. Glaring at me she snapped, "I just can't understand how you can let her go on her own. What's so important that you can't be with her, are you seeing the Queen or something?"

"We've been through that a dozen times. I—"

"Okay, okay. Make sure you *both* come here for dinner. No further excuses." She sat down with a hump and an exaggerated sigh. "What shall I make?"

"Anything," I replied quickly, not wanting a discussion.

"What does *Azra* like most?" she asked sharply.

I thought for a few seconds. "You know that, chicken in thick curry sauce, red kidney beans —"

She interrupted me sharply. "Okayokay. I'll make both. Be here at seven, on the dot!"

I put an arm round her shoulders. "You are very understanding. And for dessert, can you—"

"I know what she likes!" Paro Aunty snapped. "*You* don't have to tell me everything!"

CHAPTER 47

THURSDAY

Azra died that morning.

An hour before that, I had met Thomas Whitmore, the editor of the Mail on Sunday at the Thistle Piccadilly in Coventry Street, London. It's a charming Victorian hotel near Piccadilly Circus not far from Trafalgar Square.

We were seated in the lounge near Cupid's bar discussing slums in Africa and the epidemic waiting to explode when his mobile rang. The hotel clock showed 09:02.

"Excuse me," he whispered apologetically, reaching for the mobile in the inner breast pocket of his jacket. "Nobody rings this mobile unless it's an emergency."

How many mobiles has he got? I asked myself.

I realised something was wrong when his face turned pale and the creases on his forehead darkened. He gave me a brief glance and turned his back to me. After listening for a full minute without interrupting he stood up and started pacing around.

Domestic Problems, I thought.

"Okay, Charles," I heard him say, "keep me informed." He slipped the mobile back into his jacket.

Within five seconds the mobile rang again. Displaying some irritation he answered without interrupting the caller, nodding constantly. Once again his face turned pale and the creases on his forehead darkened. Finally he spoke, "Yes, hold on... hold on..."

What the hell is going on? I thought.

He turned to me. "Mr. Dushant, we'll have to reschedule our meeting. I have to go. I'm so sorry... I'll call you. I have your card."

He snapped his brief-case shut, shook my hand quickly and hurried towards the exit. "Be careful," he shouted to me, holding the half-open door. "Stay in the hotel." And then he was gone.

Confused, I picked-up the documents spread on the coffee table and carefully shuffled them back into my case. Suddenly, I was aware of a tall, well dressed man standing beside me.

"Excuse me sir, I'm looking for Mr. Whitmore. I believe he—"

"I'm sorry; you've just missed him." Then observing his strained expression, I asked, "What's going on?"

"Sorry Sir, I'm not sure. But please don't leave the hotel."

"Why is everyone telling me not to leave—?"

He smiled stiffly, "For your own safety Sir...please."

"Why? Who are you? I have to meet someone in an hour's time."

"Where?"

"Not far, Whitechapel Street near Aldgate. A friend of mine is—"

"I'm afraid that won't be possible Sir. All roads are sealed. Please don't leave the hotel." He rushed past me and disappeared.

Gulping the last of my coffee I made my way to the reception. A few people were huddled in front of a television. I hurried out and hailed a taxi. "Whitechapel Street, please."

The Driver made an apologetic face. "Sorry, Sir, we've been advised not to go in that direction. If you've just come out from the hotel, my suggestion would be to go back and not leave the hotel."

"Not leave...Why? What's happened?"

"Apparently there's been a power surge and all tube stations are closed. I'm awaiting instructions."

My confusion turned to worry. I wondered if Azra had made it to the Doctor. Switching on my mobile, I texted her: *R U OK? Where are you?* I pressed 'Send'. I waited a couple of minutes for the reply. *Nothing! She always had the mobile switched on. What was happening?* I decided to ring her but obtained no tone.

Suddenly my mobile rang. It was Sanjay!

His voice sounded distant, echoing in my ear. "Hey Amar, are you alright?" I detected a hint of anxiety in his tone.

"Sure, but I can't understand what's happening here. I'm trapped in some hotel. The trains and taxis—"

"They are not running. Stay in the hotel. Did your newspaper chap come?"

Stay in the hotel! I was getting sick of the advice! The mobile felt moist in my hand.

I was developing a sense of foreboding. "I met the Editor for a few seconds and then he disappeared without giving me a proper explanation. Do *you* know what the hell's going on?"

There was a brief pause before he replied. "Looks like London's been hit by bombs - at least three tubes. You'd better stay—"

For the first time fear gripped me. "What! Which stations?" I was aware I was shouting.

"Hey, calm down, Amar. At least you are safe. Look, take my advice and stay —"

"No- I'm not going to hide in the hotel!" I cut him off. *Azra! Where was she?*

With trembling hands, I scrolled through the calls I had made in the previous week. *David Bell!*

I rang.

"Good morning, Doctor Bell's surgery. How may I help—"

I recognised the voice. "Good morning. I am a friend of Azra Khan, who had an appointment with you this morning. Could you please tell me if... if she is there, please."

"Are you her—?"

"Oh, for heavens sake! I'm Amar Dushant. I made the appointment for —"

"Mr Dushant, we were just about to ring you. Ms. Khan has not turned up as yet. Doctor Bell has another appointment soon—"

"Look, I'm sorry. The moment she arrives, tell her to text me and to stay there, please." I was aware that my voice was hoarse, my mouth dry.

Her voice crackled in my ear. "Okay, Mr.Dushant, understood. Bye for now."

Where could she be?

All of a sudden, sirens started sounding all around me. *I had to know! I had to find out!* I rang Azra's mobile every few minutes. *Nothing! Suddenly I feared the worst! Bombs! In London?* Standing in the middle of the pavement outside a hotel was no good. With no taxis, buses or tube, I decided to walk to the surgery. *Better than doing nothing.*

I half trotted in the direction of Leicester square, not quite knowing the right direction for Whitechapel Street. Nearing the square, I found the area cordoned off by the police and a large crowd looking confused and helpless. I asked someone for the general direction to my destination. He directed me to Saint Paul's Cathedral and suggested I walk east from there.

An hour and ten minutes later, I approached Aldgate station. It was completely cordoned off and the area around it clogged with ambulances, fire-engines and police cars. Crowds surged in from all directions, some screaming amidst the sirens and the police, who were shouting to control the situation. The acrid smell was everywhere. People around me were talking about terrorists and bombs. My heart sank. I rang the surgery several times; the line was always engaged. Helpless, I ran in the direction of Whitechapel Street and up the few stairs into the surgery. There was no one in the reception area except for a young woman behind the counter speaking hysterically on the phone. I interrupted her. "Excuse me; has Azra Khan been here as yet?"

She shook her head emphatically. "There have been several incidents in tube stations. I'm afraid—"

"What exactly—?"

"My husband rang me a minute ago. He told me that some suicide bombers had detonated bombs in a few stations. I'm not sure what's happening. None of the patients have —"

"What about Aldgate station? Was that... was that –?"

"I really don't know, Sir. I hope your friend is safe."

"Yes, I hope so too. Thanks." I ran out, down the steps and in the direction of Aldgate. *Azra would have to get off Aldgate station to make it to the surgery.*

Amidst the confused crowds and the increasing sirens, I tried to calm myself and visualise what she would have done to make her 9:15 appointment. She would have taken a bus to Ealing Broadway and then the Central line as I had suggested. She would then have switched from Central to the Circle line at Notting Hill Gate and got off at Aldgate, from where I had informed her that the surgery was about five minutes walk. Working backwards and allowing for some slack time, I reasoned that she would have aimed to be at Aldgate around nine. *It was hopeless.* My brain was exploding, the drill boring deeper into it. The tightness in my chest tore into the ribs, my heart pounding painfully. Azra might have wanted to be early...might have missed her train...might still be trapped underground...I felt helpless! She could be anywhere! *The one day in over two years that she had taken the tube! The one day! Why did this carnage have to happen today?*

Paro Aunty rang just before two in the afternoon complaining that my mobile was always engaged and wanting to know if Azra and I were alright. "Auntyji, I'm not sure about Azra, there is no news; she's not answering her mobile."

"Did she reach the surgery?"

"No."

I heard a sharp intake of breath. "God, let's hope she's just trapped somewhere and not—"

"Auntyji, do you know what's happened?"

"I've been watching TV all day. A little while ago there was confirmation that suicide bombers, possibly Al-Quaeda members detonated bombs during the rush-hour on the Circle line between Liverpool Street station and Aldgate station, the Circle line between Edgware Road and Paddington and Piccadilly line between Kings Cross, Saint Pancras and Russell Square. Oh, Amar, I'm so confused, it's horrible." Her voice sounded distant. I shook my mobile.

"Do they know how many people have been killed? And who?"

"No. Oh God, I should have gone with her. There isn't a lot of news as yet. There are a lot of people still trapped underground, let's hope Azra is among them. Amar, please pray."

Her voice was getting fainter. I suspected my mobile battery was running low. I asked quickly, "Is it only tubes that have been targeted?"

"Oh, about an hour after the tube bombings, a bus travelling from Marble Arch to Hackney Wick was blown-off at Tavistock Square. It's awful! The world's gone mad!"

CHAPTER 48

A part of me died with Azra that Thursday, 7th July, 2005. The seventh day of the seventh month, and the digits in the year added to seven. I often wonder at its significance. For four days I continued to visit Aldgate in the hope that by some miracle Azra would be found and brought up alive. The pungent smell and patches of grey dust still persisted. But like mortals, hopes die too.

On the fifth day, I got a call from the police on my mobile. They had traced part of a badly burnt note-book with my name and mobile number near a woman who fitted the description I had given them a few days ago.

I identified the body at a mortuary in London- badly burnt, with one arm missing, legs charred. A ring that Paro Aunty had once given Azra was confirmation of her demise.

I stayed with Paro Aunty for a fortnight after that, unable to be alone. We wondered what Azra's aunt was going through. I cursed myself for never finding out where she lived. We gave the police a photograph of Azra that I had taken at the deer-park in Magdalen College. Later I cried over the faces of the fifty-two innocent victims in the newspaper.

A month passed by –seemed like a year. I read about the 7/7 bombings in every newspaper. Each morning, I woke up listening to Radio Four about it and did not sleep without watching the news and Question Time on television.

Most of my spare time was spent in the company of Paro Aunty, other times with Sanjay and his family or Robin and Cheryl. The only thing I looked forward to, was taking Neel and Tom to the park for football each Wednesday, though when I was there, my mind was still elsewhere, nowhere.

Inayat rang twice to make sure I was not affected by the bombings. Each time I lied to him. He had no knowledge of Azra and I kept it like that.

Papa, Bimla and Nita rang many times asking me over for a holiday in Nairobi but I couldn't bring myself to be away from England under the circumstances.

Of all the people, Paro Aunty tried her best to get me back to normal life- asking me to take her shopping, Liz's house, for a cup of coffee somewhere, though even she didn't mention Southall.

Just as I was beginning to accept God's will, I got a call from Munir that was to change my life again, forever.

It was well past midnight and after a lot of tossing and turning I had eventually fallen asleep. *Azra and I were sitting on a fine sandy beach with swaying coconut trees admiring the sunset. She was pointing to a place where the sky and the sea met. We gazed at a spot far, far away. I followed the direction of her finger. True enough, there was a spot where they met. The sun was turning crimson and its rays flickered gently on the sea waves. It was going down fast. No! No! Please stop! Amar don't let it go. Azra was crying, clutching my arm. I stood up waving wildly at the sun. Don't go! I was shouting but my words carried no sound. Like Azra, I had lost speech. Now she was standing beside me waving even more frantically at the sinking sun. Only its tip remained. It was getting dark, and cold. Azra started crying, tears streaming down her cheeks. It pained me to see her so. In despair, I sank on my knees. Now I was crying too. Finally the top crescent of the orange ball disappeared, and with it, its light. Darkness enveloped me. Suddenly, I was alone! Azra! Where are you? Please don't leave me! Azra! I looked around me, but saw nothing, or was there nothing to see? The sun, the sunlight and Azra were no more!*

I was woken. It was dark. For a few seconds, I was unable to decipher the noise; the mobile was ringing and vibrating on my bedside cabinet. I managed to bring it against my ear.

"Amar? There was urgency in the voice.

"Yes, who—"

"Amar, it's me. Don't say my name—"

"Mu—"

There was a loud crackling sound against my ear. "No!" The voice interrupted me sharply. Don't say my name!"

I rubbed the sleep away from my eyes. "What is the matter? Are you okay?"

"Yes, do you know who I am?"

"Yes, of-course I do. God, it's... past midnight; are you alright? Where are you?"

He replied with undisguised annoyance. "Amar! Just listen. Please don't say a word."

My yawn died mid-way. "Okay."

The voice dropped, almost breaking. "Amar, Azra's dead."

I sat up straight, nearly saying that I knew. The phone was pressed hard against my ear.

"Mun—"

"Amar, don't speak!"

"She died in the London bombings a month ago, I saw her picture in the papers," he continued.

"I'm so sorry. I don't see—"

He cut me midway, speaking sharply, with restrained urgency, "I don't have much time. Just listen. Be careful of Sanjay, don't trust him."

I could have been knocked down by a feather. "What!"

"Just listen!" His voice was raised and sharp with annoyance, but controlled. "You asked me once, in Nairobi, if I knew who Billie was seeing."

I did remember, it was in that restaurant, over lunch. I remembered thinking at the time that he was being evasive. "I know."

"It's Sanjay. He's been seeing her for some years."

"*Sanjay?* Are you sure?" I was annoyed now. "Why didn't you tell me at the time?" I realised I was shouting. "Why tell me now?"

"He's my friend too, remember? I couldn't betray him. It was up to you to find out. I'm telling you now, because..." His voice choked and trailed off. I had a distinct impression that he was suppressing tears.

"Because what?" I shouted, aware that I was doing so and trying to control myself.

Munir was breathing hard. "Because, you'll probably never see me or hear from me again. She... Billie... she left you because she was pregnant."

He might as well have slapped me. "That's impossible!" The phone went dead. "Hello... hello..." He had gone.

I sat in the darkness for a while, cold, despite being covered in sweat. *Surely this was just a bad dream!* After a while I tried to digest what Munir had said about Billie and Sanjay. I decided to ring him on his phone. Nothing! The line was dead.

I guessed he must be in trouble. *But so much trouble that he said I would never see or speak to him again? What could be wrong? And Sanjay was seeing Billie? For how long? Why would Billie leave me because she was pregnant?* That didn't make sense. Nothing did. If Billie was pregnant, that would be the last thing she would have done. She always *wanted* a baby. Munir must have made a mistake. *Yes, I thought, Munir must be wrong. The way he talked about not seeing me again. He didn't seem right. He must be mistaken.*

My brain was exploding. I went down to the kitchen and gulped a glass of cold milk. The night was warm. Opening the French doors, I paced around in the garden.

Why would Billie leave me if she was pregnant? She had badly wanted a baby. She should have rejoiced and stayed with me, a loving wife and mother. I decided to wait till dawn and ring Munir. This time of the year, Nairobi was two hours ahead of England. Yes, I would ring at five in the morning and catch him before he left for work.

I also needed some answers from Sanjay.

CHAPTER 49

Maqbool Uncle was surprised that I was not aware of Munir's whereabouts. "I thought he was with *you*, *beta*. That's what he told us when he rang last week. We haven't seen him for over two months. I hope he isn't in any trouble. That boy has changed."

So as not to worry him, I said, "I'm sure he's alright. Probably busy with some business deal. I'll get him to ring you when I see him next."

"Thank you, do that *beta*. *Khuda hafiz*."

Where the hell was Munir? And what was he up to? However hard I tried I couldn't work it out.

I waited till seven before ringing Sanjay. After a dozen or so rings a sleepy Carla answered.

"Carla, I'm sorry to wake you. I was hoping to catch Sanjay before he goes off to work. It's rather—"

"That's alright, Amar. I would have got up in ten minutes anyway to get Neel ready for school. Didn't Sanjay tell you about his trip to Nairobi?"

"Nairobi? No. When did he go?"

"Last night. Some bloody bank business... at least that's what he told me."

"Oh," I tried to sound casual. "Don't you believe—"

She cut me short. "Amar, I've been married too long to care. If he wants his bit on the side he can have it. I'm past caring. Why should I ruin my health for someone who's never going to change?"

In two hours she was the second person I didn't want to worry. "I'm sure he has a good reason to go, please don't worry."

I pondered my next move over hot coffee and toast. There was no way I could find out where Munir was, but Sanjay... perhaps there was a way.

Two hours later, I rang his office. Paulette, his Secretary answered in her usual sing-song voice. I recognised her at once. She was an attractive brunette and on a few occasions Sanjay had brought her along to lunch.

"Hi Paulette, this is Amar Dushant," I said, trying to sound cheerful. "How's it going?"

She replied quickly, "Oh, good morning, Mr Dushant. I'm fine thanks. How can I help you?"

"Nothing really, just thought I'd have a quick word with your boss about something."

"Oh, he's not in this week, sorry."

I tried to speak casually, "Away on business?"

"No, he's on leave and will be back on Friday. Shall I tell him you called?"

"No, that's OK. I'll catch him at home. You have a good day and keep out of mischief."

"You too Mr Dushant, have a good day."

I slammed down the phone. *What the hell was Sanjay up to?*

Realisation took time but I accepted what I had half suspected for some time; Sanjay had been cheating on Carla. *Was he seeing someone in Nairobi? Billie?* I found that difficult to comprehend. Of all the women, Sanjay could have, why would he want to have an affair with *her*, thousands of miles away, especially when she had a child. *My child!*

One half of me wanted to catch the next flight to Nairobi and see Billie and my child while the other half exercised caution. Sanjay would be back in a few days and he might provide answers. I didn't particularly want to leave Paro Aunty under the circumstances. If he was seeing Billie behind my back, I needed some answers from him first.

I decided not to follow my heart and rush into things but to plan my actions and act in a measured way. It would have been easy to ring Sanjay on his mobile in Nairobi but a face-to-face confrontation would be in my favour. It would be better to see his reaction and observe his body language to determine whether he was lying or not... Four more days!

The house which had for years seemed too big for me suddenly felt small, claustrophobic. For hours on end I moved from room to room, switching the television on-off-on-off. The clock ticked slowly and I grew restless. If I sat down, a hundred questions flooded my mind, answers to which seemed illogical or unacceptable. I searched my mind for things to do, anything to occupy myself but when it came to actually doing something- arranging old photographs or buying fresh flowers the tasks seemed insignificant, irrelevant. They could be put-off for later. After a few spoonfuls, I would loose my appetite and the only thing that my body found acceptable was wine. I drowned two bottles by tea time and another with a Chinese take-away late evening. Whilst watching the News at Ten on television, I dozed off on the sofa. Sometime between midnight and dawn I woke up covered in sweat. Once, as I reached for the television remote, I felt sick and threw up. Trying to control myself, I cleaned up, had a hot-cold-hot-cold shower and went to bed, exhausted.

I was not aware of the early twittering of the birds at dawn or the milkman leaving the milk and juice on the doorstep, nor the postman's van on the gravel. What woke me up was the mobile vibrating on the bedside cabinet. My head felt as if it was about to explode and my mouth felt like leather. No sound came from my lips when I placed the phone against my ear.

"Amar!" Paro Aunty's voice pierced my ear like a missile.

"Yes."

"You sound... are you still in bed? It's eleven O'clock! Are you alright?"

"I'm okay; had a rough night. Too much—"

"Amar, your friend Munir, what's his full name?"

I couldn't see what she was driving at. "Why?"

"Because...never mind. What's his full name?" She seemed annoyed with me for being dozy late morning.

"Munir...Munir Ahmed Khan. Why?" I croaked with eyes shut, "Can't this wait?"

"He's in trouble!" she shouted sharply.

I nearly dropped the mobile. "What trouble?" I sat up straight in bed, almost knocking down the bed-side lamp.

There was a long silence, "Auntyji? Are you still there?"

"Amar," she replied in a calmer tone, "your friend's in big trouble. Why don't you come here, I'll tell you more?"

"Don't keep me in suspense. What's he done?"

"Amar, come here as soon as you can. That will give me time to buy a few more newspapers."

I wanted to know right there and then, but knowing Paro Aunty: I knew that arguing would be a waste of time. "Fine, I'll be there in an hour or so." I said curtly.

CHAPTER 50

I stared at Munir's and Masood's pictures in most of the national newspapers. Paro Aunty had never met them but knew Munir just by name and that he was my friend from Nairobi.

Brothers arrested over 7/7 bombings.
Munir Ahmed Khan, a resident of Kenya and his younger brother, Masood Ahmed Khan, a UK resident were last night arrested and questioned over the 7/7 carnage ...

I shook my head in disbelief. "There must be a mistake," I shouted.

Paro Aunty merely stared at me.

I slumped in the settee. She placed a hand on my shoulder and I leaned my face against it. Sitting down beside me she sighed audibly without uttering a word.

I took a deep breath and exhaled loudly. "There's no mention of the charges against them," I said finally, almost to myself. "They are merely being questioned, it could be *anything.*"

"Not yet," she said in a controlled tone, shaking her head in disbelief and unfolding another newspaper, "Their own sister!"

"What?"

"Their own sister!"

"What?" I repeated.

"They are responsible, albeit indirectly for Azra's death, together with a few others. I could never forgive them."

The thought drilled painfully through my mind, disarraying it for a while. I bit my lip, "Their beautiful sister...my Azra." I shook my head and looking for the invisible spider on the wall muttered softly, "they were not to know. He and Masood will have to live with this for the rest of their lives...especially if they find out about Azra. In a twisted way I feel sorry for Munir and Masood."

"Did he ever give any clues to this sort of activities, or—"

"No." I leaned forward and rested my head in my hands. "I must see Munir," I whispered against my palms.

Her voice was shrill. "Don't be silly. We don't even know where he is. The papers don't say, neither does the television. Amar, there are times in life when one has to accept the truth, however hard it may be to do so. In my bones I believe that... what do you feel?"

I turned to look at her. The pain of Azra's death was still evident in her eyes. "I don't know... perhaps... you're probably right."

We sat in silence for a long time, trying not to believe the believable.

"I feel so sorry for his family back home. Maqbool Uncle will be devastated. Why did Munir get involved in something like this? I despair."

"Innocent children can end up as wild adults," she said softly. "There's some poem... *sweetest things turn sourest by their deeds...*"

"And *Lillies that fester smell far worse than weeds...* Shakespeare," I added, sighing. "If only I could see him, speak to him, find out why..." I thumped the table and turned to face her. "If I ring the police—"

"Amar, there's no way the police will let you anywhere near him or Masood for that matter. They were only arrested last night and they'll be questioned in secrecy for days. As to the question of their innocence... my gut feeling is that —"

"Yes," I interrupted, "you are probably right." My mind went back to Munir's anger, even hatred for the West. He passionately believed that the rich nations were exploiting third world countries. And then there were all those secret foreign visits. Even Maqbool Uncle was concerned about the change in him. I felt a pang of guilt for seeing the signs and not doing anything about it.

"Look, Amar, you've lost a good friend and Azra. Unfortunately they will not come back to you, at least not Azra." She placed her hand on mine. "It's time to look to the future."

I shook my head in despair. *What future? What next? Sanjay? Billie?* "You are right," I said, almost to myself.

She cocked her head sideways and observed me. "You look awful; are you alright?"

"Just tired, I suppose all this is getting to me."

"Looks like you haven't even had breakfast. Let's have lunch. There's fish and roast potatoes in the oven. I boiled some broccoli earlier."

"No. I don't feel like eating, right now."

She spoke sharply, "Amar! You've got to eat. Just look at you—"

"Okay, I'll have some muesli with cold milk."

"Good, that's sorted. Have your cereal, then go upstairs and shower while I take care of lunch."

I shaved, showered and came down for lunch.

"Why don't you stay for a few days?" Paro Aunty suggested.

I thought about it. I had to see Sanjay on Friday, until then I had no plans. It would be better than moping around alone at my place.

"OK, thanks, but I'll have to leave Friday morning, got to see someone from the Oxford Gazette," I lied.

"How's Sanjay?" she asked out of the blue.

I was visibly startled. "Why?"

She laughed, "What's the matter? You seem on edge. This isn't the first time that I've asked you about him."

I shrugged. "OK, I suppose. I haven't seen him for a while, he's in Kenya."

"Again? Why does he keep going over there?"

"Why do you ask?"

She half laughed. "Amar! What's the matter with you? I'm only asking. You seem so tense."

I felt guilty about not sharing my thoughts with her as I had done for years.

She decided to change track. "Have you heard from Billie?"

I sat up straight. "Why?"

"Amar! *Relax!*" she shouted sharply.

"Sorry, no, I haven't," I replied curtly. Then, suddenly, I decided to get a few things off my chest. "There's something I found out recently... about her."

"About Billie?"

"Yes, she has a child, mine—"

"Impossible!" After that she lost her speech for a while. "I don't understand. Amar, If she was pregnant, why did she leave you?"

"Search me." I replied throwing my arms wide towards the ceiling.

She stared at me. "I still don't understand. She wanted a child so badly, why didn't she tell you about the pregnancy? Why go *away*? Why didn't she come back?"

"I can't work it out. I'll have to swallow my pride and get them back. Perhaps she only discovered she was pregnant *after* leaving me and by that time matters had gone downhill so much that she couldn't force herself to come back."

She fell silent for a long time, as if her mind was engrossed in a debate. "Yes, yes, that is probably what happened," She concluded. "And she hasn't informed you out of spite," she added.

The next few days dragged by. We bought and read as many newspapers as we could. The television was always on and we picked up some more information of the al-Quaeda plot. There was little coverage of Munir and Masood, except to say that although they were not directly involved with the 7/7 bombings, they had provided technical know-how and funds to the suicide bombers. I rang the Police Station several times but in vain.

Next day I booked a return flight to Nairobi, to leave London on Saturday 6 August.

I rang Sanjay's office at ten, Friday morning. Paulette, in her sing-song voice informed me that he was in a meeting and not likely to be out till lunch time. "Shall I let him know you called, Mr. Dushant?"

"Yes, please. He has my mobile number. Tell him it's urgent."

I went for a long walk in the park near Headington because I could not bear to be alone in the house. The air was fresh and the sky devoid of clouds but I still felt stifled, my heart heavy with apprehension. By eleven the place was crawling with schoolchildren and mothers with toddlers. A Labrador kept sniffing around me much to my liking but not to his pretty, size zero owner. I clucked my tongue and whistled slowly every-time he came near me which prompted the lady to shout, "Here, boy. Come on Stocky- that's a good boy."

At twelve, I had a large coffee and a cheese and pickle sandwich at the park café. The coffee was decent enough but the cheese was something that even the park mice wouldn't have touched. Perhaps they *had* touched it.

By two in the afternoon, I still hadn't heard from Sanjay. I keyed my last number on the mobile. Paulette greeted me again. "I am so sorry, Mr Dushant, but he's in a meeting right now. I *did* give him your message... I'll tell him you called again."

"Thanks Paulette, I'll text him on his mobile." And so I did:

Sanj – hope all OK. Wd like 2 C U ASAP. Pls call.

After an hour or so, I decided to go home, where I had a couple of beers and made myself a chicken sandwich. I watched *The Dirty Dozen* on Sky TV for the third time in my life and then spent twenty minutes switching channels for something interesting. It's amazing that with so many channels to choose from, it's still difficult to find something to hold one's attention. The emphasis on the news channels had shifted from the London bombings back to the Coalition's war on terror in Iraq. The American President's popularity was waning as the public gradually realised that winning the peace would prove more difficult than winning the war.

Around six in the evening I again tried Sanjay's mobile, it was switched off. I rang his home, hoping that Carla might throw some light as to his whereabouts. No answer. Perhaps they had gone out to dinner together. My anxiety grew, turning to anger. *Was he avoiding me, if so, why?* I was supposed to fly to Nairobi the next day and I had less than twenty-four hours to find out if he was seeing Billie or not. *I had to know! Was Munir right?*

Just as I had given up hope of hearing from Sanjay, he rang. It was just after ten at night. "Hi, Amar, sorry I couldn't get back to you earlier. You know how it is on the first day back from a business trip? How's life?"

I tried to remain calm. "I'm fine, flying out to Nairobi tomorrow. I wanted to see you before—"

"Sure, listen, it's terrible about Munir. I can't imagine him involved in terrorism. There must be some mistake."

"Sanjay, when can I see you?"

"How about tomorrow, over lunch?"

I thought about it for a few seconds. I couldn't go through another sleepless night. I had to find out the truth, as soon as possible.

"I know it's late, Sanjay, but can we meet now? It won't take long."

"Now?" I could almost see his concern. "It's pretty late, something bothering you, Amar?"

"I'll explain when I see you. Where are you?"

"I've just finished at the Gym. You know, in Abingdon—"

I knew the one. "By the White Horse pub?"

"Yes, meet me in the bar."

"I'll be there shortly," I said quickly.

CHAPTER 51

Sanjay was sipping Guinness when I entered the bar. He was in chino shorts and a pale blue polo shirt, collars turned up in James Dean style. Except for a middle aged couple in a corner, the place was empty. His recently showered hair was glistening with hair-gel. He rose to shake hands. "Hey, what's this all about?" He took a step back to examine me. "You look like hell. What's up?"

I didn't tell him about Azra. With a shrug of the shoulders, I mentioned Munir.

"Yes, it's terrible. I bet it's a mistake. What will you have, Guinness?"

I nodded. "I hate to say it but I think he *was* involved. He had changed a lot in the last few years."

He shook his head slowly in disbelief. "We don't even know our best friends. You know, I've known him since I was four."

"He was probably influenced by the company he kept. Who knows what he was up to in the last few years? Sooner or later we take different paths."

My drink came and I gulped half the glass without pausing. "It's hot tonight," I said, wiping a bit from my chin with the back of my hand.

"So, you're off to Nairobi tomorrow. Seeing the family?"

I nodded. "Sanjay, there's something I want to ask you—"

"Hey, shoot," he said bashfully.

I tried to stay calm and made a mental point to observe him carefully. "It's about Billie."

He stiffened and the stool he was sitting on screeched on the laminate floor. There was a small intake of breath. "What about her?" It was either my imagination or a trick of the light, but his eyes didn't smile like his mouth.

385

I locked eyes with his and made sure that they didn't stray. I blurted the words burning in my throat. "I've been told that she's been seeing someone for some time." I had to tread carefully. He held my gaze and took his time to construct his question. "Do you know who?"

His eyes hardened and he tried to give a weak smile. "I thought it was all over between you two," he said stonily.

I fixed him with a stern stare. "She's still my wife - legally," I hissed.

"Hey, she's an adult and a few thousand miles away. Let it be, Amar."

I bristled and cautiously put my glass on the counter, for fear that it might slip from my hand. "So you don't know if is she's having an affair?"

He was distinctly uncomfortable. He shrugged his shoulders and moved his eyes off me to look down at his moccasins. "What if she is?"

"*Is* she?"

He looked up, "You need to ask *her*." Beneath the mock calmness there was a volcanic irritation.

I lowered my voice. "Have you seen her lately?"

He gave me a surreptitious glance and fell silent for so long that I thought he wasn't going to answer. Just as I was about to repeat my question he replied, "I... I've bumped into her on my business trips to Nairobi. It's a small place and..." His voice trailed off.

The bar was very warm, even at that time of night. My shirt collar was sticking to me. I ran a finger between my neck and the collar. He was evading my questions. I decided to come straight to the point. "Are you having an affair with Billie?"

"*With who?*" Sanjay's voice started loudly and ended with a sharp hiss. His face had turned tense and he licked his lips for moisture.

"Billie," I replied with surprising calmness.

He fell silent for a while and then decided to turn on his charm. "Come on Amar," he said finally, smiling and gently patting me on the shoulder dismissively. His smile never quite made it to the eyes. "We've known each other for years. Yes, I've seen Billie on occasions, but that doesn't mean that I'm having an *affair* with her."

I shrugged my shoulder as if his hand had left a dirty mark on it. "Why didn't you tell me?" I demanded, with undisguised hostility.

He stared at me and said in a forced laugh, "For heaven's sake! I thought it was over between you two. I didn't want to open old wounds."

"These trips of yours to Nairobi, they are not business trips, are they? Tell me truthfully."

He shifted his gaze and when he spoke his voice was no more than a whisper, "I don't know what you mean"

I banged the counter, causing the glasses to wobble. "They are pleasure trips, nothing to do with your business."

He looked around the bar and took a deep breath. "We are all adults, so let's behave like—"

"We are adult *friends!*" I shouted leaning towards his face.

"Look, Amar," he said patting my hand, which I withdrew instinctively, "it's late and we are getting heated up. Why don't we talk tomorrow?"

"No," I replied, ignoring his suggestion. "I need to sort this out now Sanjay, for once, give me a straight answer. How long has this been going on?"

He sat back taking a deep breath and exhaled loudly through his nostrils. "What good would it do you to know?"

I swallowed hard. The room grew smaller. "Sanjay, I *need* to know. I need to know *everything*. Tomorrow, I'm going to Nairobi, to get her and my child back." I hadn't meant to bring the child into it but the words came out in a rush, unplanned.

His reaction couldn't have been more noticeable if a bolt of lightning had hit him. "You can't do that!" he snarled, and this time *he* banged the counter.

I was taken aback, "Why not?" I growled evenly. "She's still my wife and I want my child here."

"Damn you, Amar!" he snarled, "You don't know what you are saying or doing! I'm warning you, don't go *anywhere* near Rocky—"

I caught my breath. "Rocky? Rocky who? Who the hell is...?" Suddenly the penny dropped. The air was detonated! A rage developed within me, erupting in my head. "Is that his name, my son's name? Is it?" I was aware that my fists were clenched tightly and that my nails were digging into my palms. "Damn you, I deserve an answer!"

He stood up, clearly angry and confused. "Yes! No!" he answered.

I stood up facing him. My lips were dry. I tried to moisten them with my tongue but that too was dry. "Yes or no?" I demanded, enunciating every syllable with venom; my voice sounding alien to my ears. I had never spoken to Sanjay like this but I needed a straight answer.

He glared at me for a while, eyeball to eyeball before softening his tone. He exhaled audibly before speaking, "Yes, his name is Rocky, but no, he's... not yours."

This was the final insult. "What the hell do you mean, he's not mine?" I shouted.

He blew air out. "Hey, I didn't ever think it would come to this."

"So who is his father?" I waited anxiously for a reply. From the corner of my eye, I saw the middle-aged couple shuffle out of the bar.

Sanjay stared at the floor. "Don't make me say it."

My quota of patience for the day was fast eroding. "For God's sake, tell me the truth!" I realised my voice was choking with anger and my fists were still clenched; I could have hit him there and then.

He mumbled something.

I forced myself to take an even tone, "Pardon?"

A brief silence ensued. He looked away. "I am," he whispered with liturgical finality, almost to himself and slumped down again.

His answer exploded in my head and I froze, aghast, not trusting my voice. We stared at each other, openly hostile. Finally, I overcame the incredulity. "*You?* How can that be?"

He remained quiet and I dropped heavily on the bar-stool opposite him not comprehending.

"Look, Amar, that's why Billie left you. Not because she and you couldn't have children, but—"

My eyes held his, contempt for him clearly visible in them. "But because she was pregnant with *your* child." I completed his sentence. The artifice was now clear. "So the affair started *here?* Under my very nose? *That's the ultimate betrayal!*"

He licked his lips. His voice was dry and low. "I'm sorry. It just happened. Billie thought that you couldn't... you know, produce children, and when she got pregnant, she panicked. I tried to talk her into an abortion, but you know her, she was so desperate for a child, she wouldn't hear of it. I'm sorry Amar, really, really sorry, if only I could turn back the clock..."

My head was exploding and I was having trouble breathing. I half stood up but feeling dizzy took to my seat again. The room seemed to be closing in around me. I wanted to say something but words froze on my lips. I decided there and then that I was finished with him *and* Billie. Suddenly I felt tired, empty, beaten. Everything stood still. Suddenly a realisation dawned on me; I had been living in Sanjay's shadow ever since childhood- the Kilimanjaro trip, the Watford flats, Swenberg, my large house, the cheap loans from his bank. No wonder Billie had once screamed at me that I was his pawn. I shuddered. Heaving my chest I took a deep gulp of air and let it out slowly. Without a word, I stood up and brushed past him, toppling my glass off the connter.

"Hey, listen," he called after me. "Amar... we can work this out. Amar..."

In a daze I reached my car, not sure what to do next or where to go. All I wanted to do was to drive away. I sat numb for some time and somehow started the engine, reversed out of the parking space and drove forward.

Suddenly, against the car lights, I saw him waving frantically for me to stop. He was running towards me. I heard my name through the open window. The car kept going. My foot pressed hard against the accelerator, as if in a dream. I had no control of my senses. My mouth opened to warn him, but no sound came. My hands were gripped around the steering wheel unable to let go and my foot, which had turned into stone was glued to the pedal, also unable to let go. In those few seconds of madness and anger, rage and resentment, my life was to be ruined. Mesmerised, heart pounding, brain frozen I gazed into Sanjay's terror-stricken eyes, his hand failing to shield them against the glare of the car lights. The car continued to roar ahead.

Azra's face was right against mine, horrified. Her mouth was open and contorted as if she was trying to utter some words. *Amar! Stop the car! Please! You'll kill him!*

Amar! Stop! Billie screamed from somewhere in the car. Her voice was deafening, booming around the car. *He's my son's father! Please, Amar! Pleeease!* The echo reverberated painfully inside the car.

Out of nowhere, Paro Aunty's face was pinned against the windscreen, screaming, "*Amar stop the car, don't do this, it does't solve anything. Amar please. Stop, stop, stop, you'll kill him! Stop!*

I looked around- no one! The next thing I recall was a loud thud and Sanjay's face against the windscreen. I screamed but the sound never left my throat. My foot stayed on the pedal for another few seconds, paralysed, unable to retract, as if filled with lead.

The car surged ahead, windscreen smeared in blood. *Where was Sanjay? What happened?*

Somehow instinct took over and I managed to slam the brakes. The car screeched to a halt. Looking back over my shoulder, I could see Sanjay sprawled motionless a good thirty yards behind me.

The horror of the accident became clear and my heart froze. *Oh God! Sanjay!* I prayed that he was alive. Leaving the car, door open, I ran towards him, lying face down and even in the dark I could see a pool of blood by his face. My hands shook violently as I turned him over. His face was covered in blood, nose broken, lips cut. A stream of blood was trickling from one side of his gaping mouth. His eyes were wide open staring at nothing.

"*Sanjay! Sanjay!* Speak to me. Say something. It will be okay." I lifted his arm and let go. It slumped back with a thud, lifeless. There was no pulse.

A car zoomed past, picking us in its lights but did not stop.

For a while, I stood there just looking at him, dazed and unable to move or turn my gaze away from my dear friend. Deep inside the pit of my stomach an ache developed. Suddenly, my defences started working, I had to get away! I had to move him from here! I grabbed his hands and walking backwards dragged him towards the car. He was heavy and by the time I reached the car I was sweating and breathing hard. Fearing that someone would soon spot me, I heaved him into the car boot in two attempts. Just as I closed the boot, two cars came in my direction. The first kept going but the second slowed down and stopped about twenty yards ahead of me on the main road.

A tall, athletic-looking man in a track-suit and vest opened his door and walked in my direction. "Alright there?"

My hands were covered in blood. I quickly hid them behind me. "I'm fine,"I shouted, "Just finished changing a flat tyre. Thanks for stopping though."

"Sure you don't need help?" He continued walking towards me.

"Yes, very kind of you. I'd better get going, it's getting late. My wife will be wondering—"

He stood facing me. "Want to use my mobile?"

I was aware that my shirt was damp and clinging to me. Sweat was trickling down from my forehead towards my eyebrows. My tongue felt dry and heavy. "Thanks, but I've got one in the car. Now that I've finished changing the tyre, I'll ring her."

He stretched a hand forward. "Well, I'll be on my way."

I panicked for a second. My saliva felt thick, sticking to my mouth. It took an effort to part my lips. "Excuse me for not shaking your hand, mine are covered in grease."

His forehead furrowed for a few seconds as if wondering why my hands were behind me even though they were greased. I continued my posture ineptly. Suddenly, he relaxed. "Mind how you go." He smiled tightly and turned around.

"Thanks for stopping," I shouted at his back, breathing again.

For what seemed like ages, I stood by the car in the thin drizzle, seized with terror, contemplating what to do. A knot grew and tightened around my throat. A drill bore deep into my head. I argued against whatever course of action my brain came up with. The situation was hopeless, I was doomed.

I started the car and sped away with no destination in mind. I just had to get away from that dreaded place. Taking different turns I drove aimlessly, constantly looking in the mirror to see if I was being followed. There was a throbbing in my temples and a nerve was pulling in my back, probably from lifting Sanjay into the car.

An hour or so later, I stopped for a pee away from the residential areas. It was dark and warm and I felt better being outside. I took a long deep breath to calm the disarray in my mind, not able to think for fear. Spotting a patch of grass by the roadside I sat down and gazed as far as I could see. In the distance some lights flickered- probably some hotels near the Oxford town centre. For a few minutes, I imagined the peace in which people were sleeping comfortably in their beds. Later, I looked up at the sky, clear except for a few floating clouds. Watching the stars reminded me of the night on Kilimanjaro when I had gazed at the same stars with friends in amazement. But tonight they seemed different- mocking me, some pityng me, others indifferent. I wondered if they had witnessed worse acts than the one I had committed. A cloud drifted away to reveal the three stars in Orion's belt. I sat still, thinking about Kili with a sweet nostalgic pain.Time passed. Suddenly, the belt was around my neck, tightening and choking me violently. I screamed and shouted in panic but the belt kept digging into my neck. After what seemed like ages, I managed to release myself from it, gasping for breath. My neck twitched with pain and my chest felt hollow. The stars were no more in focus.

Progressively, reality got hold of me and the panic that had gripped me gently released its hold. I had to dispose off the body! It felt strange thinking of Sanjay as *a body* but I couldn't give his lifeless body a name. I had thoughts of just leaving the car there and catching a plane to Nairobi the next day, of burning the car, even burying it in the woods somewhere. For over an hour I sat there, helpless, my heart and mind debating acrimoniously against each other as to what to do next.

Finally, with no clear plan of action, tired and hungry, I decided to go home and think things over rationally. I started the engine and stepped on the accelerator. The countryside roads were narrow, and poorly lit. I meandered through the roads for what seemed like ages, not quite knowing where I was going. Houses, mostly grand, were few and far between. Very few had lights; it was quiet and very dark. My throat and lips were dry from the alcohol and strain and I was dying for a cold drink.

Suddenly a lorry appeared from nowhere towards my direction with full lights. I cursed it for almost blinding me, swerving to my left to make more room for it. I was aware of some bushes scratching the side of the car as I tried to avoid the lorry in the narrow countryside lane.

Amar! Stop! Brake! Sanjay was screaming around me. *Stop the car!* I saw the figure, but it was too late! The lorry's lights were in my eyes. I squinted and tried to focus. In the next few seconds, Paro Aunty, Billie and Azra were screaming around me: *Amar stop! Stop! I can't, I screamed just as loudly. It's too late! Oh God, is this some nightmare? Please let it be!* I heard a deafening thud all around me, almost as if it was in my head and the car swerved off the lane. The lorry roared past, oblivious of the accident.

The car rattled on the grass verge for a while before I slammed the brakes and brought it to a sudden stop with a loud bang against a tree. The engine shuddered and the bonnet flung open in front of me, shattering the windscreen. I looked over my shoulder at a young girl lying by the road side. With a sinking heart, I got out of the car, drained of energy and ran weakly towards the motionless body.

FINAL CHAPTER

Pain is a terrible sensation, tortuous and gnawing. It is embedded in my heart, mind and dreams. I go to bed with a heavy heart and wake up exhausted, with no purpose in life, nothing to look forward to. Whilst I have experienced little physical pain inside prison, the mental anguish has been difficult to bear and it escalates whenever I see the pain my deeds have caused others.

Alison's death was needless. She was a lovely girl with a lifetime of opportunities and rewards. It was such a grim death. We stared at each other, unable to move and she trying to move her lips into a question- Why? I could not reply. For a while I held her hand, which gradually turned cold. Her eyes pleaded me to save her. Finally my conscience overcame my selfish defences and I rang the police. It was five hours later that I was told of her death. She had fought hard at the hospital but sadly, due to internal injuries and the loss of blood she passed away.

From thereon, the nightmare has continued unabated. Paro Aunty was the first of friends and relatives to visit me. She was heart-broken and kept saying that she didn't believe what the papers said- I was innocent. She seemed to have aged years. Her hair seemed greyer, there were dark circles under her eyes and the stress had inflamed the arthritis in her knees causing her to limp in one leg. Over and over again, I went through that night's events with her, confirming my guilt and pleading with her not to visit me again for it only resulted in causing us both pain. She clasped her hands as if in prayer and convinced herself that the devil had taken control of me that fateful night.

If the pain was torturous, shame was worse; there are no words for that. When Papa, Bimla and Nita visited me I could not look them in the eye, whatever bad things they *may* have done, mine was unimaginably worse. I felt like a diseased insect to be trampled upon and thrown into some gutter. Supported by his daughters Papa dragged his feet as he came closer. He had become thinner; cheeks sunk inwards, thinned-hair all white. Watching him, a dagger cut into my heart and the drill bore deeper into my mind.

Robin and Cheryl visited me twice in the second month. They were more philosophical than the others, understanding the situation and hoping that my penance would help heal wounds. Cheryl was too kind. These things happen all the time, she had said. They were both accidents and just because the justice system failed to recognise that, in God's eyes I was not guilty. I wondered for a long time afterwards if 'not guilty' was the same as 'innocent'.

Inayat and Saira were expecting their third child. He was spending most of his time jetting around the world on business while she stayed home with her children. They were shocked by what I had done but understood the circumstances. I have kept their joint letter to me, they felt my anguish and reminded me of the happy times we had had together. Inayat repeatedly reminded me to pray daily and seek freedom and happiness in penance, relief in remorse. I felt a mixture of nostalgic euphoria and sadness in a quote he wrote from the German philosopher, Nietzsche:

> *"Did you ever say yes to pleasure?*
> *Oh my friends, then you also said yes to pain.*
> *All things are linked, entwined in love with one another."*

The first six months were the worst. I had constant nightmares about Sanjay and Alison and her parents' anguish in court. Not once did they curse or swear at me, not once did their eyes betray any hatred for me, they did not even cheer when the sentence was passed, although as far as they were concerned, I had a tomorrow, Alison didn't.

During the trial, their eyes never strayed from me. They just felt sorry for me and my heart went out to them. I prayed to God to somehow make-up for the loss that I had inflicted upon them.

I have received hate mail, death threats, beatings from fellow prisoners and wardens. I have not, so far, complained for I know that whatever punishment I get is not enough, it is the balm that brings solace to my wounds.

A few days after my second anniversary in Bullingdon prison, I received a letter from Mrs. Webber that was to close another chapter in my life.

Dear Amar

Please prepare yourself for bad news. Last night, your father passed away. He had a massive stroke just after dinner and had to be rushed to hospital. Sadly, by the time he reached hospital, he had taken his last breath. Since visiting you, he had been in a state of constant depression and had on numerous occasions blamed himself for your upbringing and in not naming you Sita Raam. Despite my attempts at convincing him that it would have made no difference, he remained unmoved. I have informed Bimla and Nita and they should be arriving in the next few hours. By the time you finish reading this letter, they will have performed the last rites. By Hindu custom, it should be you, but, well, that is not to be. People at the temple have been very kind and have made all the arrangements.

The news is sad of course, but we can't fight God's will. However, please remember that until the last few years he enjoyed life to the fullest and had a lot of pleasure from family and friends.

I know it's not easy for you over there, but what can be done? If there is anything I can help you with, please let me know.

Best Wishes

Anna

I read the letter many times. The grief was too deep for tears, guilt gnawed me; shame tortured my heart. I had dishonured the family and that had played a part in Papa's passing away.

A few months later, I received a letter from Bimla informing me that Papa had never made a will, or if he had, it could not be traced and therefore, the whole estate had passed to Mrs. Webber. She and Nita plan to challenge the court decision, but knowing how these things move in Nairobi, there is little hope. Bimla also wrote that the rumours in Nairobi's legal circle were that Mrs. Webber had quickly made a will in favour of her only child, Ribena.

There are worse prisons than Bullingdon in Bicester. Of course, I resent the officials, the constant thuds on metal stair cases, the clanging of doors, the beatings and cries of fellow prisoners, but the last two years or so, I have been busy writing and my mind has strayed from prison misery. My lack of complaints and my discretions have progressively earned respect from some of the fellow prisoners and officials. As a result I have kept out of trouble and my sentence has recently been bearable. Every morning my mental clock wakes me at four for my yoga exercises and meditation, without which I would have gone insane by now.

Paro Aunty is now my only regular visitor. It is strange that for years, I had regularly visited *her* at week-ends, especially after Paal Uncle's death, and now she visits me every Saturday. I have said to her on numerous occasions, but to no avail that if she is busy, she can skip a visit. I don't want her to feel that it's a compulsion.

"What compulsion? Amar, I look forward to these visits. What else have I got to do with my life? You and Liz are the only ones I regularly see and talk to. Don't even think of keeping me away."

I know she is right, but I feel that I should make it clear that if she is ever in a position that she can't come, she needn't.

"Liz came last month," I informed her when she last came. She brought photographs of Florence and Rimini. They are so beautiful, like Liz used to be years ago."

"Did she tell you that Florence won the Inter-schools Piano Competition?" Paro Aunty asked, wiping her glasses.

"No, I'd love to hear her; music is so soothing."

"I'll bring some more photographs of them next week." She balanced her glasses on the bridge of her nose and immediately took them off, wiping them again. We both plunged into silence while she continued looking down, holding her glasses in her hand, fidgeting with the nose-clip. Her shoulders were hunched forward and the upper back arched outwards almost in a semi circle. The hair which had been dark and shiny when I had first met her, were now grey and limp, with specks of silver, tied hurriedly in a pony-tail with some strands sticking out carelessly. Suddenly, without looking up she spoke hoarsely but softly. "Amar, I'm selling the house."

I knew something was bothering her. "Why?"

She continued looking down and fidgeting with the glasses and then spoke in a small tender voice, "It's too big."

"What, the glasses?" I teased.

She looked up, bearing a tired smile, her eyes twitching nervously. "When Paul... and even when you were around, I never thought about it, in fact I remember saying to Paul that we should extend it, but—"

I finished the sentence for her. "But you think that now it's too big for just you."

She stared at me for a long time, searching for the right words. "What do I need a three bedroom semi for? It is big and empty, and so quiet. Do you know something; a quiet house is so distracting; it's difficult to concentrate. People yearn for peace and quiet, but I've now realised that in my quiet house I don't feel peaceful."

"So what are you going to do?" I enquired out of concern.

"O-ho," she replied with mild irritation, "move to an apartment, perhaps two bedrooms, with concierge and amenities."

I raised my eyebrows, chuckling wryly, "Where?"

She looked directly at me and spoke slowly. "I was thinking of moving nearby, perhaps Bicester—"

"No!" I said sharply. I knew why she wanted to move nearby, so that she could visit me more often.

She gave me a searching, hurt look, "Why not?"

"You have friends there - Liz, the girls, the Sethis, the Mehtas. Please don't leave them just for me."

She looked down again, this time blinking to suppress tears. I placed a hand on hers.

She smiled through the tears. "We'll see."

"No! Auntyji, please promise me, you won't move from Denham, promise me, please. Promise me."

She looked up, startled. "Why? What's the matter?"

I looked down. "Nothing," I whispered.

She looked at me pensively and took my hand in hers. "Amar, look at you, your —"

I sighed heavily. "Don't start Auntyji..."

"Your eyes are sinking, your shoulders are drooping. And your weight... Amar you need to see a doctor."

I withdrew my hand. I wanted to tell her my planned and now imminent intention. I wanted to apologise for the future, for what she would think of me, my madness, and my guilt. Fleetingly, I wondered how she would remember me. Instead, not wanting to worry her, I replied simply, "There is a strong possibility that I... that I won't be here for long—"

She jumped in her chair. "What! Where are you going?"

I shrugged my shoulders and replied in a hushed tone, "I don't know."

"Don't know! What do you mean? Amar, I know you. You are hiding something from me, what is it? Look at me. What's happened?"

I bit my lip, feeling trapped. "I might be moved somewhere else," I lied.

Days pass somehow, nights painfully slowly. I bow to the cruelty of time and life. Even in sleep the horror and shame weigh heavily upon me for they replay my deeds on the back of my eyelids, forcing me to lie awake and count the seconds. Almost every night Orion's belt tightens around my throat and just as I will it to complete its job, it releases its grip. My days of atonement will never be over.

Now that I have finished writing, there is little to look forward to, certainly nothing to while away my days. I can not bear to stay in prison for the rest of my life, and fade away, fragile and helpless, chained to memories. There is no justification in reducing a candle's light merely to prolong its life. I often remember discussing with Paro Aunty of lilies that fester smelling far worse than weeds and I do not wish for that smell to linger for years while the boulder within me grows bigger and heavier. Somehow, the past seems more real than the present, a clear sign that I'm getting old, with little to look forward to. I pray to God to look after Paro Aunty and ease her impending pain. There is a letter which I have requested the warden to hand her at her next visit. I hope time will heal her pain and that she will understand and forgive me for my final action. I sincerely hope that the funfairs of life will always remain ... *Ye zindaigi ke mele duniya main kam na ho* ... especially for Paro Aunty.

Suddenly, the boulder is lifted! There is neither pain nor joy, neither anger nor calm. There is no hate or love, no anguish or peace. Nothing is important, yet everything is.

Harmony and discord are one; intellect and madness blend into one another. All things are entwined. I am free.

Azra comes to me most nights. She is lovelier than ever and I am eager to be with her. We have a beautiful daughter, Maya, who is saying her first few words and taking her first few steps. *Be patient,* I say to Azra, *not long to go.* My task is finished and soon we will be together again, forever; inseparable, like the sun and the sunlight. "*Tomorrow,*" I whisper to her, "*tomorrow I will be with you.*"

WRITER'S NOTE:

The novel is a piece of fiction, so are the characters. Even though some events are real, the characters involved, for example, Munir and Sanjay are made-up and no offence is meant to the readers. Amar and Azra only exist in my dreams.